THE CHRONICLES OF THE
IMAGINARIUM GEOGRAPHICA

THE
DRAGON'S
APPRENTICE

Written and illustrated by

James A. Owen

SIMON & SCHUSTER BOOKS FOR YOUNG READERS

NEW YORK LONDON TORONTO SYDNEY

For Jimmy

SIMON & SCHUSTER BFYR

An imprint of Simon & Schuster Children's Publishing Division
1230 Avenue of the Americas, New York, New York 10020

For information about special discounts for bulk purchases, please contact Simon & Schuster
Special Sales at 1-866-506-1949 or business@simonandschuster.com.
The Simon & Schuster Speakers Bureau can bring authors to your live event.
For more information or to book an event, contact the Simon & Schuster Speakers Bureau
at 1-866-248-3049 or visit our website at www.simonspeakers.com.

Book design by Tom Daly and James A. Owen
The text for this book is set in Adobe Jensen Pro.
Manufactured in the United States of America
2 4 6 8 10 9 7 5 3 1
Library of Congress Cataloging-in-Publication Data
Owen, James A.
The dragon's apprentice / written and illustrated by James A. Owen. — 1st ed.
p. cm. — (The Chronicles of the Imaginarium Geographica ; [5])
Summary: Seven years after facing the Dragon Shadows, John, Jack, and Charles
return to the Archipelago of Dreams but their reunion with old friends is spoiled by the threat
of primordial Shadow Echthroi and the apparent splintering of Time itself, and they set
out on a new quest in which success and failure each carry a high cost.
ISBN 978-1-4169-5897-0 (hardcover)
[1. Time travel—Fiction. 2. Characters in literature—Fiction. 3. Fantasy.] I. Title.
PZ7.O97124Dr 2010
[Fic]—dc22
2009038674
ISBN 978-1-4424-0964-4 (eBook)

FIRST
EDITION

Contents

❖

List of Illustrations

✦

Acknowledgments

In many ways, *The Dragon's Apprentice* was the most difficult book to write so far, for a lot of reasons. Complexities abound, as the story progressed and evolved, and it would have been impossible to finish sequestered in my garret, in solitude.

David Gale was, and continues to be, the first champion of these books. From the very beginning, he had a natural grasp of the kind of story I wanted to tell, and has allowed me to keep the accelerator floored ever since. Under another editor, I truly believe these would have been lesser books. And Navah Wolfe, whom I knew casually as an online friend before her employ at Simon & Schuster, is without a doubt my most exacting reader. The questions she poses, whether regarding subtle nuances of character, or overarching plot threads, are the ones that shape and reshape my stories into their final form. That she is so caring about the work, while at the same time looks after the well-being of her author is a combination for which I am most grateful. Jenica Nasworthy and Valerie Shea are my seasoned coveterans of the editorial battle, who pull everything together into a cohesive whole, invented words and all. Without these people this series would not work.

My stellar attorney Craig Emanuel, and especially my management team at The Gotham Group—including Julie, Ellen, and Lindsay—have done wonderful work with the contracts, and handling my business relationship with my publisher. And Gotham's Julie Nelson has made other weights I've had to shoulder far, far easier to bear this year, and deserves much gratitude.

The rest of the team at Simon & Schuster has been equally supportive, from my publisher, Justin Chanda, to our Executive Vice President Jon Anderson, and the most attentive CEO I've ever known, Carolyn Reidy. They make it clear that we are partners in this endeavor, and my work is easier because of their trust and support.

My art director, Laurent Linn, continues to do extraordinary work. My publicists, Paul Crichton and Andrea Kempfer, have taken excellent care of me during my signing tours, and have always encouraged me through a very demanding process. And I want to also thank the other staff at Simon & Schuster for doing so much good work to package, promote, and sell these books. It is genuinely a team effort.

Without my team at Coppervale Studio, Jeremy Owen and Mary McCray, I would not have time to write or draw, and the whole process would be much, much more difficult. And my new partners in Hollywood crime, Rick Porras and Travis Wright, have helped restore my faith in both creative collaboration and the magic of Tinseltown. I'm still not moving there, though.

My friends are my rock, without whom I would have floundered long before: Daanon DeCock, who not only handles my websites, but also looks after my general well-being; the collective Book Babes, especially Faith, who have been so wonderful to know; Bill and Peggy Wu, for reminding me that magic is real;

Brett and Shawn, who have believed in me from the beginning; and Shannon, who has helped me remember that I became just who I wanted to be.

And most of all, I want to thank my family: Cindy, Sophie, and Nathaniel, for being the reasons that I do what I do, better than I would have done it without them. You all have my profound thanks.

Prologue

✦

Until it has been mapped, no thing truly exists. Not even time. To create maps is to be a Namer, and Naming makes things that are real more themselves, and things that are imaginary, real.

But even as there are Namers, there are also Un-Namers in the world. And these seek to undo all that the Namers have mapped, in both time and space.

Safeguard the maps within this atlas from such Shadows. Give to it your Names. And believe.

This simple inscription, written on the first page of the Imaginarium Geographica, bore no signature. It was possibly written by its maker, the Cartographer of Lost Places, but no Caretaker had ever asked, nor was the information ever volunteered. But someone had written it, and someday, someone would ask, and perhaps be answered.

From the foredeck of the White Dragon, the Far Traveler watched as the three new young Caretakers of the Geographica disappeared down the cobblestone streets to resume their lives. Not all that long before on that very spot, they had boarded another ship, the Indigo Dragon, as they fled from a terrible horde of creatures and their dark master, the Winter King. The days that passed between that moment *and this, a scant few weeks, had changed the fates of two worlds and irrevocably altered their lives. He wondered if they knew how much. No matter—they would learn soon enough.*

"They are the three, aren't they?" said a voice from somewhere on the docks. "The three Caretakers of the Prophecy. You would not have succeeded otherwise."

With a lively step that belied his girth, the Frenchman stepped from the fog and shadows enclosing the pier and onto the Dragonship.

"Master Wells," he said with a smile and a bow.

The Far Traveler returned the bow, if not the smile. "Master Verne. Well met."

The two men stood for a long moment, looking not at each other but at the city where the three young men had been swallowed by the winding streets.

"It was a close call, Jules."

"It was, Bert." Verne nodded. "Too close. But they handled themselves well, especially that young Jack."

"Everyone thinks that John is the fulcrum," said Bert, "but he's not. He's just the most adept at fulfilling the duties of a Caretaker. Jack may yet prove to be his equal."

"Of that I have no doubt," Verne said in agreement, "but Charles may outshine them both. He has the potential—he just doesn't know it himself yet. Did you give them any inkling that this was only the first conflict of several to come with the Winter King?"

"Of course not!" Bert shot back. "We have disagreed on a number of things, Jules, but not that. They were unprepared enough as it was for the conflict with the Winter King. What would it do to them to know it isn't over?"

"Not much worse than being thrown in headfirst to what they've already come through," said Verne. "They are, after all, the Caretakers of the Prophecy."

"Set aside your condescension, Jules," Bert said, irritated. "I know you don't believe in prophecies. Especially that one."

"I believe enough to help you, Bert. And them. And they show great promise. That's why we must keep their path as clear as we can, using all the allies we can recruit who will join our cause."

Bert raised an eyebrow and leaned against the railing. "You're still moving forward with the splinter group, then? These 'Mystorians,' as you call them?"

"Pshaw." Verne snorted. "Hardly a splinter group—Poe himself endorsed it. Hell's bells, Bert—he suggested it!"

"Yes, I know," Bert replied evenly, "but still not Caretakers, or even really apprentices." He took a breath. "They think I'm retiring, you know. They don't realize the process has just begun, and they won't comprehend it until it's all over."

"I understand," Verne said with sincere sympathy. "I know you want to tell them how quickly all of this is going to happen."

"Quickly for us, you mean," said Bert, "but not for them. To us, events will transpire over less than a year. But to them, it will seem to be decades. How do you explain to someone that all the years of service, and learning, and effort are all to prepare them for their truly important work, which may not begin until after they are dead?"

"That's as it must be, Bert," Verne said, gently chiding his colleague. "If Stellan had not been killed by the Winter King, it would not be necessary. But he was, and there it is. They had to be recruited now. He'll tell you that himself tonight back at Tamerlane House."

"Stellan . . . ," Bert said sorrowfully, shaking his head. "What were the odds of that happening?"

The Frenchman shrugged and smiled. "The same as everything, my friend. Zero, until it actually happens. Then it's a hundred percent."

"Is this going to work, Jules?"

"Yes," Verne answered firmly. "As long as the will persists to change events, everything is possible. Everything."

PART ONE

Independence Day

. . . the light that emanated from the ghost filled the courtyard . . .

CHAPTER ONE
The Ghost of Magdalen College

❖

Twilight had just fallen across the sky when the ghost pirate appeared at the base of Magdalen Tower. At first it seemed as if the ghost was on fire, but that was only a trick of the light. It was already quite dark along the cobblestone walk that crossed beneath the tower, so the light that emanated from the ghost filled the courtyard with an unearthly brilliance.

Eleven people were passing the tower in the moment that the apparition appeared. Three were professors who had seen many ghosts in Oxford, and so gave it no notice. Two more, also faculty at Magdalen, felt similarly about pirate costumes, and merely sniffed their annoyance as they passed, assuming as they did that it was some sort of student mischief. Four more were actual students, who reacted with surprise, awe, and no small amount of fear, and they scattered into corridors adjacent to the tower.

The last two people who witnessed the ghost's appearance were Caretakers of the *Imaginarium Geographica*, and a ghost pirate was at least as interesting as some of the other fantastic things they had seen, so they moved closer to have a better look.

John had arranged to meet his friend Charles at the base of

Magdalen Tower so that they might walk together to their friend Jack's private rooms there at the college, and they met just as the sun was setting. It was in that moment that the apparition had appeared.

Even if they hadn't been Caretakers, a ghost would have been nothing to cause them alarm—Oxford had long had a reputation of being a haven to spectres and spirits of all kinds, and as long as they didn't disrupt the business of the university, no one made a fuss. Even in the midst of the Second World War, it was also good for tourism.

"I didn't think I'd ever actually see this fellow," John whispered to Charles. "I've heard about the Old Pirate for years but never had the pleasure of seeing him in person, uh, so to speak."

"How many other ghosts have you met here?" asked Charles.

"Ah, none, I'm afraid," John admitted, "although I haven't exactly sought them out, either."

"Well, why not?" Charles retorted as he approached the ghost, hand outstretched. "They could prove to be really helpful to my writing, you know. Worth asking, anyroad."

The ghost simply stood there, hunched over, staring into the darkness as the Caretaker introduced himself. "Well met, old fellow. My name is Charles."

Suddenly the ghost began to move, jerking about awkwardly, as if it were a puppet in a penny nickelodeon. It seemed as if speaking to it had engaged it in some way. Charles dropped his hand. "Are you in distress?" he asked the ghost. "Why are you here?"

The ghost stopped, then turned and focused its rheumy eyes on Charles, who took full stock of it for the first time. The spectre had presence and looked as if it stood in bright sunlight—but it was transparent, ethereal.

By appearance, it was certainly a pirate, no doubt, but an ancient one, many, many years old. His hair was long and straggly, and the clothes he wore, once fine, were tattered with age. His hands were shaking, and his head twitched nervously. But his eyes were piercing, intense—and, Charles thought with surprise, oddly familiar.

"Caretakers?" the ghost said with a trembling voice. "Be ye Caretakers, here, at Oxford?"

Charles and John exchanged surprised looks. This was no run-of-the-mill ghost. Not if he knew who they were. Then again, there had been stories of the Pirate Ghost appearing in this spot for two centuries, and no one had ever reported that he spoke at all, much less that he had mentioned anything about Caretakers.

"Who is asking?" said John, stepping forward. "Who are you looking for?"

"Jamie?" the ghost answered. "Jamie, is that you?"

John sighed. "The only one of us who ever quit," he said to Charles, "and he's the one everyone asks for in a crisis."

"No," the ghost said, shaking his head. "Ye be John, I think. Ron John Tollers, unless I miss my guess."

John stepped back in surprise at hearing a mishmash of his nicknames. "That—that's right," he said. "I'm he. Do I know you?"

The ghost spread its arms and smiled. "In another life, another time," he said, his voice weary, "I was your friend Hank Morgan."

"Good Lord," said John, glancing again at Charles, who was equally stunned. "We can't even walk across Oxford without stumbling into an adventure."

◆   ◆   ◆

The old saying about absence making the heart grow fonder is over-rated, John had thought to himself as he prepared to go out earlier that afternoon. *Absence doesn't do anything except create longing, and an ache that cannot be remedied until the waiting is through.*

He and the other Caretakers of the *Imaginarium Geographica,* Jack and Charles, had been waiting for seven years for a chance to return to the Archipelago of Dreams. In earlier times, they had gone for longer periods without visiting, but there had been less urgency in those days—and maybe that was what stirred John's unease. That, or the fact that they'd been forbidden to return. *We never truly know we want something,* he thought, *until we've been told we can't have it.* Or perhaps it was the dark days of war covering the earth that made him long for the escape of the magical lands in the Archipelago.

Whatever it was, the price they'd had to pay for a victory in the future was steep. They'd jumped forward in time and defeated a terrible enemy, before returning to the time where they were meant to be. But to ensure that the victory remained certain, they had to stay away from the Archipelago, so as not to risk changing the outcome that had already happened.

They hadn't realized how hard it would be to wait through most of the new Great War that had swept the Summer Country.

The Darkness of the shadows was hardest to bear. In those days when the shadows of the Dragons swept over all the Earth, John in particular struggled mightily against the impulse to act.

"We *are* acting," Charles and Jack would remind him, "and we have. By waiting. We know that this is a battle we have already won, John. We just need to do our duty—and do nothing. Nothing but wait."

Now, however, the waiting was almost over. The clock had caught up with the past, and the future was about to become the present again. And they could finally return and fully take up their mantle again as true Caretakers.

John had put on his jacket and looked at himself in the mirror. He was finally feeling the years of his life—and not just because of the Wars. He had now been a Caretaker for longer than he had not. It was one of the roles that defined him—and yet it was still one of the greatest secrets he kept from all but a few. *Until*, he thought with a smile, *the new calling of Jack's comes to fruition. If that works, well . . .*

Everything could change. Everything.

He had kissed his wife and children good-bye and stepped out the door.

It was less than an hour later that he and Charles began their conversation with the Pirate Ghost of Magdalen College.

"Hank!" John exclaimed. "What's happened to you? You look so . . . so . . ."

"Old?" Morgan replied with a cackle. "Two centuries of waiting will do that to a man."

"Waiting for what?" asked Charles.

"For you," the ghost replied simply. "I was waiting for you, Good Charlie, and Ron John, and Jack-Jack the Giant Killer. I was waiting for the three of you." He narrowed his eyes. "Where be Jack, anyroad?"

"He's finishing a discussion," said John. "We, ah, we weren't exactly expecting to see you, Hank."

"And why should ye?" Morgan retorted. "I've only been appearing in this same spot for two hundred years, give or take."

"No need to be snappish," said Charles, "but you never spoke to anyone before now."

"Because no one has ever spoken t' me!" said Morgan. "It only works if *you* speak first."

"What are you talking about?" John said, clearly puzzled. "You've lost me."

"No time, no time," said Morgan, waving his hands. Then, he laughed, wheezing. "Or just enough, I suppose. Yes—it was just enough.

"Listen to me," the ghost insisted with a new urgency in his voice. "You must build the bridge. Shakespeare's Bridge. You can't get back without it. But the bridge won't work without a trump."

He stopped and pulled one of the familiar silver watches from a broad pocket. He flipped it open and grimaced. "I've told them," he murmured to himself. "The loop should have closed."

Charles gripped John's shoulder, and looks of worry creased both men's faces. They were missing too many pieces of a far bigger picture here.

"Hank," John began, "perhaps if we—"

"You must build Shakespeare's Bridge," Morgan said again. "It's the only way! The only way for you to—"

He stopped and looked down at his watch, which had begun ticking. "Oh, thank God," he murmured as he adjusted the dials on the device. "You've finally managed to make a new—"

In midsentence, Hank Morgan vanished.

"Oh my stars," said John. "What just happened here, Charles? What did we just see?"

"Nothing we can sort out on our own," Charles replied as he looked around the courtyard. Morgan was indeed gone, and whatever his cryptic message had meant, it was apparently all they were getting. "Hank's supposed to be joining us at dinner later at Tamerlane House, anyway. We'll just take it up with him then. Maybe it's some sort of joke. To welcome us back?"

John shook his head. Whatever else the ghost was, it was no joke. The age, the hard years that weighed on their old friend, were real. And that meant the warning was too.

"Let's go," he said, spinning away on his heel. "Jack will be waiting for us."

"What is it?" Jack asked his friends as he ushered them into his rooms. "What's happened?"

He knew by their demeanors that something was amiss. John went straight to the cupboard to fetch glasses for a drink, while Charles wearily draped himself in one of the chairs. "I'm not sure how to begin," Charles said. "Let's just say we've been having a little chat with a ghost."

"Really?" said Jack, smirking, as John handed him a snifter of brandy. "Which one?"

"The Old Pirate," Charles replied. "You know, the one that appears at the base of the tower."

"Good Lord," said Jack after a moment. "You're serious, aren't you?"

"Quite," John said, sitting next to Charles, "but that's just the start of it."

Over the next several minutes, and a round of drinks, John and Charles related to Jack their experience with the ghostly Hank Morgan. When they had finished, he sat back and rubbed his forehead.

"Amazing," Jack said. "Two centuries is a long time to wait to deliver such a cryptic message."

"I got the impression that's all he could give us in the time he had," John noted, "relatively speaking, that is."

Charles rubbed his chin, deep in thought. "I think it's more than that," he mused. "He said it only works if we spoke to him first, remember? I think that ghost may not have actually been Hank, but some kind of avatar that could speak only when spoken to."

"A recorded message?" asked Jack. "And interactive, to boot? That's some trick."

"Exactly," said John. "Who else but Hank would have the skills to pull it off?"

"Manipulating space as well as time," Jack said, pacing the width of the room. "Not too many, I think. Alvin Ransom, probably. Rappaccini's daughter, maybe. Verne. Bert. Possibly Kipling. That's about it. There are others, associates of the Cartographer, who might have the skills, but they wouldn't have the need to send a message so indirectly. Not now."

"Associates?" Charles asked. "You mean apprentices, don't you?"

"Not necessarily," replied Jack. "Several of them were, but others ended up joining with Burton's Imperial Cartological Society."

"Ah," Charles said as he leaned back in his chair, crossing his legs. "I see."

The Imperial Cartological Society had operated as a sort of shadow organization to the Caretakers Emeritis. Comprised of rejected Caretakers, former Caretakers, and those men and women of history who might have been Caretakers in another time and place, the Society was dedicated to spreading knowledge of the Archipelago of Dreams and all its secrets—by any means possible.

It was only after the Society was subverted by the Shadow King that there was a split among its ranks, and the de facto leader, Sir Richard Burton, brokered a truce with the Caretakers.

The Society would not attempt to spread knowledge about the Archipelago without the involvement and approval of the Caretakers Emeritis. And in return the Caretakers, under Jack's supervision, agreed to start a formal educational program at Cambridge in order to begin creating a greater awareness of the Archipelago among those who proved worthy to know of it.

It was an imperfect alliance, and it was likely to go through a succession of growing pains. But a tentative peace was better than war—and they had all already had more than enough of war.

"I'll just say it, then," John said, rising to his feet. "Shouldn't we consider that this could be some sort of trick of Burton's? He's done it before."

Jack dismissed the question with a wave of his hands. "Not using Hank, no," he said. "And besides, he's sitting at the Caretakers' table, so to speak. There's nothing he can gain through deception that hasn't already been offered to him on a silver platter."

"We can just bring it up with Hank when we get to Tamerlane House," Charles said, stretching as he rose to stand with his friends. "After all, it can't be much of a crisis Hank was warning us about. Not if he had to go walking through two centuries just to deliver the message. Another day shouldn't matter that much."

"Speaking of walking," said Jack, "we should start heading for the Kilns. That's where Ransom is expecting to take us through, and besides, I want to check in with Warnie and see if Mrs. Morris has shredded Magwich yet."

"Mrs. Morris?" Charles asked. "I thought your cat was a he."

"Morris *was* a he," Jack replied, "right up until the point she had kittens. It's been Mrs. Morris ever since."

"You have kittens? Charles asked. "I hadn't seen any."

"Oh, we don't let them roam the house," said Jack. "We keep them in the storeroom with that stupid talking shrub."

"I really do appreciate you taking him on," Charles said apologetically. "He and Michal were getting on horribly, and I had enough trouble with her already after I explained about the map tattooed on my back. Apparently, wives like to be consulted about that sort of thing."

Jack shrugged. "Maybe I ought to put him at Cambridge," he mused, "make him the centerpiece of the new Imperial Cartological Society. Sort of a living cautionary tale about what happens when an evil henchman turned green knight mismanages his chance at redemption."

"Does it really count as a secret society if everyone knows it exists?" Charles asked.

"As I have begun to plan it," said Jack, "it is most definitely *not* going to be a secret society. It's more like an invisible college. Those who know about it don't talk, and those who don't know don't care."

"I think that's half the reason the Caretakers Emeritis worked out a truce with Burton and the others," said John. "The number of people on the planet who would even give a flying fig about the Society is going to be roughly the same as the number of people who can be trusted to know about it."

"I still think we should have drawn straws," Jack complained. "No one warned me that being the Caveo Secundus would mean going to Cambridge."

"That was Burton's call, not to base it here," said John, "and besides, once we get you into a proper appointment there, you'll have a good shot at redeeming the whole University."

"It's strange how far apart we once were with Burton," said Charles. "We got the jobs he wanted, and he went renegade because he thought he could do it better. And now we have nearly identical goals. A bit chilling, that."

"We've been very bad at the job, by my accounting," said John. "After more than two and a half decades, the separation between the Archipelago and our world is more pronounced than ever. Sometimes I feel as if all we are doing is treading water."

"Holding the line," Jack echoed.

Charles let out a heavy sigh. "Our victories do seem to be becoming hollower and hollower, don't they?" he mused. "Of course, it doesn't help that we've had to put down the Winter King—Shadow King—Mordred. . . ."

"Madoc," said Jack.

"Whatever his name is, three times," said Charles. "Hopefully now he's contented enough not to come back around looking to conquer or subvert or whatever it is that's the fashion for dictators these days."

"We've seen the last of him," said Jack. "And time will prove we've made the right choices all along."

"That's what worries me," Charles countered. "Whatever else we decide to do now, the possibility remains that everything we know—everything we have done—may be completely wrong."

The Caveo Principia inclined his head in acknowledgment. "It's possible," he said. "I just get the impression that we're still being trained, being tested. That we have not fully been given the mantles of Caretakers."

"Well," Jack said jovially, "if they haven't made up their minds about us after almost a quarter century, then either they're very indecisive, or they're very, very selective."

John shook his head. "I don't know which one of those would be worse."

"I'm sorry Hugo wasn't able to come," Jack's brother Warnie said with real regret when they arrived at the Kilns. "It's quite nice to have someone else around to chat with when you three are off on one of your, ah, jaunts. And besides," he added with less regret, "I have this nice bottle of Château Lafite I was hoping to share with him."

"You could save it for another time, or for our return," Jack suggested.

"That wouldn't do," Warnie replied. "I've already begun to let it breathe. To recork it or set it aside would be criminal. No, I suppose it's just going to be for myself and Magwich over there," he finished, tipping his chin at the shrub sulking in the corner.

"In case you hadn't noticed," Magwich grumbled, "I don't really have a mouth like I used to. I'm not exactly able to enjoy a fine wine anymore, thank you very much."

"Oh, I have no intention of wasting good wine," Warnie said, winking at the companions. "But I promised Jack I'd look after you while he was out—so I'm going to drink this wine myself, and then in an hour or so, I'm going to make sure you're good and watered."

"Eww," said Magwich. "I think I'd rather be back in the room with the cat."

"That can be arranged," said Warnie.

At that Magwich started up such a clamor of moaning and whining that the companions thought Warnie might just chuck the plant straightaway into the fire.

"I don't see why I can't come," Magwich sniffed. "I was a Caretaker's apprentice too, you know. And after that, I was the Green Knight. Is it my fault I'm a weak-willed traitor at heart?"

"Well, that's honest enough," Jack admitted.

"We're not taking him," said John flatly. "All he's ever done is cause trouble. Why take the risk?"

"Just as risky to leave him here," said Jack. "Maybe more so. At least here, one of us has always been around to keep an eye on him."

"Which Warnie is more than capable of doing," John pointed out, "especially if he needs any kindling."

"Murderers!" Magwich howled. "Cutthroats and murderers, the lot of you!"

"For heaven's sake," Charles said, exasperated. "All right, we'll take you with us, you sorry excuse for an overgrown radish! But you're going to ride in the burlap bag."

"You know, Warnie," John said as the others bundled up the still complaining Magwich, "you're more than welcome to come along. There are a number of people at Tamerlane who would enjoy your company."

Jack's brother held up his hands. "Thank you for the invitation, but the first time Hugo and I went into the Archipelago has more than sated my thirst for adventure. Although," he added with genuine regret, "I would not have minded a rematch with the centaur. That was an excellent game of chess."

"It's your right, as an honorary Caretaker," John said, "as it would be for any others who know about the *Geographica*. I'm looking forward to finally taking my boy Christopher over myself."

"And I Michal, now that we aren't using the boats," said Charles. "You know she hates the water."

"It is easier on all of you, isn't it?" Warnie asked. "Being allowed to share what you know with those closest to you, instead of keeping it all to yourselves."

"Much easier," Jack said, clapping his brother on the shoulder. "It halves the burdens and doubles the joys."

"And besides," added Charles, "if anyone slips up and mentions anything about the Archipelago, everyone just assumes we made it up anyway."

Suddenly there was a knock at the door.

"I'll get it," said John, "although if it's anyone who wants to give me a magical atlas, I'm going to flip a coin before I let him in."

He strode into the next room and opened the door, holding it firmly against the gust of wind that entered with the tall, familiar visitor in a trench coat.

"Alvin!" John exclaimed in delight. "Come in, come in! So good to see you, old fellow!"

Alvin Ransom shook his head, scattering raindrops everywhere. "Sorry about that, old friend," he said, accepting Jack's offer of a dry towel. "It's quite the night outside."

"The storm's just come up," said Charles, "but we'd have let you in anyway."

"Maybe you should stand guard at the door," Ransom suggested to Charles, "in case someone with two shadows tries to enter."

"Still smarting over that one, are we?" Charles asked with a barely suppressed grin. "If it helps, I was just having an exceptionally good day."

Ransom scowled, then grinned back at Charles and clapped him on the back. "It doesn't, but I'm not offended. I'm more embarrassed that I spent all that time trying to suss out the identity of the Chancellor, and you spend five minutes examining a few photos and nail it on the head."

"That's why we got the job," Jack said, grinning, "and you're still a messenger boy."

Ransom took a playful swing at his friend and pretended to be insulted. "Fred sends his regards," he said to Charles. "He can't wait to see you tonight."

"Twice," Charles lamented. "Twice in seven years. That's far too little time to spend with an apprentice—or a friend, for that matter."

"Fred knows all the reasons you had to remain here," said Ransom, "and he understands."

"Alvin," John said, his voice tentative. "Have you spoken to Hank Morgan recently?"

"Henry?" Ransom replied. "Why, yes, just yesterday, in fact. He'll be at the dinner, if you're wondering."

"Glad to hear it," John said, with a quick glance at Charles and Jack. "It'll be good to see him again."

Ransom rubbed his hands together. "Well, I'm all warmed up. Are we ready to go?"

"Ready enough," Jack said, handing a pack to John. "We ought to take this along, don't you think?"

"You have the *Geographica* there?" Ransom asked, pointing to the pack. "You haven't left it in the back of your car again, I hope."

John rolled his eyes and sighed. "That was twenty years ago!" he exclaimed. "Who told you about that?"

Ransom chuckled. "It's one of James Barrie's favorite after-dinner stories," he said. "That's not the worst of it, though. Laura Glue has told it too."

"Uh-oh," said John. "To whom?"

"Charys. And the centaurs. And the Elves. And the Dwarves. And—"

"Enough already!" John yelled as the others convulsed with laughter. "Let's get going!"

Still grinning, Ransom removed a small case from his coat. In it were the trumps—the magical cards that allowed him and a few other associates of the Caretakers to traverse great distances as easily as walking across a room.

He removed the trump that held the drawing of Tamerlane

House and held it out in front of him. Ransom concentrated on the card, and it began to grow.

The trump grew wider and wider, filling the anteroom. The smell of the sea swirled around them. In moments the passage was open, and they could see the towers and minarets of Tamerlane House.

Grimalkin was sitting at the front door, idly licking one of his two visible paws. "Hello there, Caretakers," he said lazily. "Welcome back."

. . . the moon wore a frock coat, fingerless gloves, and sensible shoes.

CHAPTER TWO
Ariadne's Thread

Rose was startled but not surprised when the crescent moon appeared at one end of her attic room in Tamerlane House. What was surprising to her was that the moon wore a frock coat, fingerless gloves, and sensible shoes.

She was already awake, having been woken by the thunderstorm that had descended on the islands that evening. The wind was howling, and rattled the shutters, and the frequent flashes of lightning and rolling thunder made sleep all but impossible, so she had been reading Lord Dunsany when the strange visitor appeared. There was a flash of lightning that illuminated everything in the attic in high relief, as if it had been carved in white marble, visible only in that instant—and when it flashed again, the moon was there, sitting in the chair across from Rose's bed.

On reflection, she decided that if a moon were to come a-calling, that would be precisely how it would dress, so she shouldn't be surprised at all.

She changed her mind again when the moon spoke, addressing her by name.

"Hello, Rose."

"Hello," Rose answered. "Would you like a sandwich?"

She wasn't certain this was the sort of thing a girl who was barely into her teens should offer a visiting moon, but Bert and Geoffrey Chaucer had been instructing her in the rules of etiquette, and she didn't want to be rude.

The apparition paused for a moment, then bent forward in acquiescence.

Rose clambered from her bed and walked across the attic to the small icebox she kept in an alcove. She hadn't expected to have guests, but she spent a lot of time in the attic, and keeping a store of food and drink handy was easier than having to make her way downstairs to the kitchen.

For one thing, many of the rooms seemed to rearrange themselves at will, following no particular pattern or schedule, which frequently meant that she would take a customary route only to find she'd ended up on the wrong side of the house. She sometimes suspected she could hear the house snickering at her when it creaked and groaned under a stiff wind.

Tamerlane House, as its owner, Edgar Allan Poe, explained to her, was a house with a mind of its own. Thus, as a sentient structure, it tended to change and evolve, as do all living things. This also meant it could get grouchy, or play practical jokes—although, to be fair, the house never really messed around with any of its occupants except for Will Shakespeare, but then everyone there teased him, so that was all right.

Deftly Rose threw together a liverwurst and cream cheese sandwich and cut it in two; then she poured two glasses of milk from a chilled pitcher. She put the sandwich halves on plates, set one along with a glass of milk in front of her strange visitor, and climbed back onto her bed.

She blushed slightly when her visitor made no move to touch the sandwich or milk, and she realized that her offer had been accepted, as it was itself made, out of courtesy. She also noted, again with slight embarrassment, that the moon had no visible mouth.

"We thank you for your hospitality," the moon said, "but it is not necessary. We have come to speak to you regarding matters of the greatest importance."

"Who are you?" asked Rose.

"We are Mother Night," the apparition said, as if that explained everything. Rose took a bite of her sandwich and chewed as she considered this interesting happening.

For someone who had just appeared out of thin air, Mother Night gave no indication that her intentions were not good. Even in the event that she was some sort of enemy, the sword Caliburn was just under Rose's bed and could be drawn out in a trice.

There was a lot of comfort to be taken in being the wielder of the sword of Aeneas and King Arthur, Rose had often thought. Even if she hoped never to have the need to use it again.

Rose was at Tamerlane House in part because it was impossible to break into. For one thing, it was located on the centermost island in a group called the Nameless Isles, and as far as she knew, only a small number of people even knew they existed, and an even smaller number could actually reach them.

The great stones that stood on the smaller islands acted as a Ring of Power and protected the house from supernatural threats; and downstairs, in the Pygmalion Gallery, were some of the most significant men and women from history, who could be summoned by ringing a small silver bell.

True, most would have to be called forth from their portraits, which would take time—but Jules Verne, who had invited her here, was always close at hand. And Nathaniel Hawthorne, who was the de facto head of security—based on his ability to out-wrestle every other occupant—had not re-entered his portrait since she arrived, just in case.

There were enemies searching for her through time and space, so she had been required to spend all her time within the walls of Tamerlane House. But in just one more day, she'd have the chance to return to another place she considered home. It was possible that Verne's caution had lessened, and this visitor had slipped through the cracks. It was also possible that this Mother Night was not the type of creature who would be hindered by any precaution.

"Are you one of the Morgaine?" Rose asked.

"The Three Who Are One are an aspect of ourselves," answered Mother Night, "but they are not all that we are.

"Your education is about to begin," Mother Night went on, "and your true destiny will at last be revealed."

"I've had quite an education already," said Rose politely. "I've been to boarding school in Reading, and was privately tutored in Oxford, and have spent the last while as a student of the Caretakers Emeritis of the *Imaginarium Geographica*. So there's very little I haven't had the chance to learn before now."

"Arrogant words," Mother Night replied, but in a gentle tone of voice. "Knowledge is not the same as wisdom. And you are still far from wise."

Rose blushed and took a large bite of her sandwich, so that'd she'd have to chew for a while before responding. She swallowed, then took a sip of milk. Lightning flashed in one of the windows, and in her head Rose counted silently *one, one thousand, two, one thousand, three, one thousand . . .* until the answering rumble. Three miles away. The storm was coming closer.

"I apologize," Rose said at last. "I know there is still a lot I need to learn. But it's also very frustrating," she added. "It seems as if my entire life is about going where others want me to go, and doing what others want me to do, and never being able to decide for myself."

Mother Night shimmered slightly, and Rose got the impression that the moon was somehow pleased by what she'd said. "This is a wise thing, Rose," said Mother Night. "This is what separates childhood from maturity—the decision to act, and to take responsibility for those actions."

"If that's the difference," said Rose, "then some people never really grow up."

Again, Mother Night shimmered and bowed slightly. "Indeed. To be given a choice and still refuse to choose is to volunteer, whether one realizes it or not."

Rose's eyes narrowed, and she leaned back on her pillows. Had she just been tricked into volunteering for something?

Mother Night reached into her frock coat and pulled out a luminescent ball of string, which she handed to Rose.

"What is this?" asked Rose.

"Ariadne's Thread," Mother Night replied, as if that answered everything. "The skein of eternity has come undone. History itself has unraveled, and none remain who may yet reweave it. None," she said, her voice rising with emphasis, "save for you."

There was another bright flash of lightning, followed by an

immediate crash of thunder. The storm was right above Tamerlane House now.

"You will be visited by two other aspects of myself," Mother Night went on, "at the points in your journey where you reach a crossroads. They will offer you counsel and answer any questions you choose to ask. But they will not compel you to action. That choice, as always, will be yours and yours alone."

Journey? Rose thought. Was Verne planning something he hadn't told her about? Or did Mother Night perhaps mean she'd be returning to Oxford at last? "Where will I meet them? The aspects of you?"

"You must seek out the Dragon," Mother Night said, ignoring her question. "Seek him out, and speak to him these words:

> To turn, from time to time
> To things both real and not,
> Give hints of world within a world,
> And creatures long forgot.
> With limelight turn to these, regard
> In all thy wisdom stressed;
> To save both time and space above—
> Forever, ere moons crest.

"When you have done this," she said, "you will be ready. Your true education may begin."

"My true education?" said Rose. "And . . . a Dragon? But . . . there aren't any more! Unless you mean Samaranth."

"No," said Mother Night. "There is another. He is an apprentice, who has not yet chosen to become a Dragon. If he chooses not to be, all will be lost. You must help him to choose."

"What happens if he chooses not to? Become a Dragon, I mean?"

"The Shadows will be coming for you, child," Mother Night said. "They are coming for you now. Be ready."

"I'm not afraid of shadows," Rose said with self-assurance. "I defeated the Shadow King with the sword Caliburn, and I used it to free the shadows of the Dragons. My teachers have told me about what shadows can do, and I've learned to never be afraid of them."

"Afraid you may not be now," said Mother Night ominously, "but you will be, child. You will be.

"The shadows you have fought were only the servants, not the masters. The Shadows we are speaking of are those of primordial darkness—the Echthroi. They have labored long to keep this world in darkness, and have tried again and again to create a champion. Again and again they have failed. But there are those more powerful, who may yet be Un-Named and come to serve the Echthroi, and help them destroy the world. *You* are one of these, Rose."

Rose blanched. "Me? But all our enemies have tried to kill me, not convert me, or steal my shadow."

"And they were defeated," said Mother Night. "Now the attention of the Echthroi will turn to you. You will either be named, or Un-Named. You will become either the Imago or the Archimago. But you are our daughter, and it will be yours to choose."

"Mine?"

"You are the Moonchild," said Mother Night, "and this is your destiny, to use the greatest ability given to the Sons of Adam and the Daughters of Eve: to choose."

Rose lowered her head and closed her eyes. "What if I don't choose?" she asked softly. "What if I see a better path to take, or what if I simply don't want to choose? What then?"

There was no answer. Rose opened her eyes and looked around. The attic was empty.

A rumble sounded in the distance. The wind had died down, and the storm was passing. All that was left of the strange encounter was half a sandwich and a glass of milk, the glowing ball of string Mother Night had called Ariadne's Thread, and about a thousand questions. What journey was she supposed to be taking? To seek out a Dragon's apprentice and tell him a riddle? And what was this about Echthroi . . . or Echthros . . . She couldn't quite remember. Whatever else Mother Night had said that was confusing, that part was clear. The Echthroi, the true Shadows, would be coming for her. And perhaps already were.

"Are you going to eat that sandwich?" a broad smile said from atop one of the curio cabinets. "The storm woke me, and I smelled liverwurst."

"Grimalkin!" Rose said, happy to see a familiar face—or a part of one, at least. The Cheshire cat's smile filled out with whiskers, then nose and eyes, and ears, by the time he climbed down to the floor. He had attached himself to her uncle John, who was the Principal Caretaker of the *Geographica* but spent most of his time at Tamerlane House.

"Were you expecting a guest?" said Grimalkin, noting the extra glass of milk.

"Not really," said Rose, "but it's yours if you want it. Saucer?"

"Please."

She poured the milk for the cat and scratched its neck under the thick leather collar. The runes on it glowed faintly as she touched it.

The cat finished the sandwich and milk in pretty short order. "Anything else?" he asked, licking his lips.

"Not up here," Rose replied. "It'll be breakfast soon, anyway. Join us?"

"Perhaps later," said the cat, who had started to disappear again. "I was just looking for some ways to kill time while the storm was doing its blustery thing. I think I'll go downstairs and scratch on Byron's portrait."

With that Grimalkin vanished, although she could never really be sure he wasn't still lurking about somewhere. That was the only problem with a Cheshire cat—even when they weren't there, they might be.

Rose pulled on a sweater and some slacks, then brushed a few tangles out of her hair before heading downstairs. Almost as an afterthought, she tied the loose end of the thread to her bedpost and set the faintly luminescent ball on the floor. She wasn't certain what she was meant to do with it, but at least, she decided as she closed the trapdoor to the stairs, if she tied it to something, it wouldn't get lost.

"That was no ordinary storm," Bert proclaimed as the Feast Beasts cleared away the platters of food from the breakfast table. Ever since Rose had arrived as a resident, it had become traditional for several of the Caretakers Emeritis to take breakfast together in the southern dayroom. Bert still needed to eat on a routine schedule, and while Verne didn't, not eating still made him vaguely uncomfortable.

The rest of the Caretakers, who resided within their portraits in the Pygmalion Gallery, did not require food or drink at all—but they missed the memory of dining, and so were more than happy to accept Bert's invitation to have breakfast together.

Mark Twain was almost always there, as were Charles Dickens, James Barrie, and Alexandre Dumas. Jonathan Swift would occasionally join them, as would Rudyard Kipling, who, like Verne, was not a resident of the gallery but a tulpa—a younger, virtually immortal version of himself.

More unusually, Franz Schubert had often joined them as well, although he never spoke. Schubert virtually never joined in any of the activities at Tamerlane House unless they were a matter of official Caretaker business, for which his attendance was compulsory.

"I agree," Charles Dickens said, picking at his teeth with a pewter toothpick. "Something has changed."

"What do you mean by that?" Rose asked as she came down the stairs to join them.

"Ah, Rose, my dear!" Bert proclaimed, jumping to his feet. "When you didn't come down at six, we assumed you wanted to sleep in, especially with such an eventful day ahead. I'll summon the Feast Beasts back," he finished as he started to reach for a silver bell.

"No need," she replied as she took a crust of bread and sat down next to Twain. "I ate a snack rather late, so I'm not all that hungry. What did you mean when you said that something had changed?" she asked, looking through Twain's smoke at Dickens.

"It's the storm last night," Dickens answered, with a surreptitious glance at Bert. "Storms are omens of change, especially in the Archipelago. And after all the Time Storms that had bat-tered the lands in recent years, we were keeping a close watch on this one."

"I thought the Time Storms had nearly stopped?"

"They had, young lady, indeed," said Twain. "That's part of the bother and the worry. Their absence meant that the energy was going elsewhere, not that it had disappeared altogether."

"Perhaps it was an Echthroi . . . or is it an Echthros? I can't remember." She looked at Bert. "Whatever it is that the primor-dial Shadows are called."

All the Caretakers sitting at the table, including the dead ones and the nearly immortal ones, had gone white.

"Where, pray tell, my dear Rose," Twain said, having regained his composure first, "did you hear those names?"

"I had a strange visitor in the night," Rose replied. "You'd be quite pleased, Bert. I was very hospitable, although I don't think she really liked the liverwurst and cream cheese sandwich I made for her."

"What did this visitor say to you, Rose?" asked Bert, still a bit shaken. "How did she come to mention the Echthroi?"

"She told me that history was broken, and that it would be up to me to fix it, otherwise the Echthroi would win, and the world would end," Rose said as she reached for the silver bell on the table. "Does anyone mind if I request something more to eat? It turns out I'm feeling hungrier than I thought."

The table was soon restocked with baked goods of all kinds and fresh fruit. The Caretakers waited patiently as Rose heaped a pile of crepes, strawberries, and whipped cream onto a plate—which she put on the floor for Grimalkin, who wandered in preening with his just-sharpened claws. For herself, she made a sandwich of lettuce, mayonnaise, and crunchy peanut butter.

"It's when I watch her eat," Dickens confided to Twain, "that I suspect Bert and Jules are teaching her all the wrong things."

"Never mind that," said Bert, more irritated at the pause in the discussion than the fact that he agreed with them about Rose's dining habits. "Tell us about your visitor, Rose."

As she ate, Rose recounted the discussion that had transpired in the attic, occasionally pausing to answer questions or clarify points she wanted to make. When she was done, she had some questions of her own.

"What is this about a Dragon's apprentice?" she asked. "I thought they were all gone. I would know—I freed most of them myself."

"All the Dragons in this world, save for Samaranth, were corrupted by the Shadow King," Bert said with a still tangible melancholy, "and any apprentices they might have had were lost long ago."

Rose waited patiently for Bert, or any of the others, to continue. Twain leaned over to Dickens and whispered something, which Dickens wrote on a piece of paper and passed to Grimalkin under the table. The Cheshire cat's eyes narrowed as it scanned the paper, and it seemed about to protest about being a mere messenger, but a sharp look from Twain silenced it, and the cat disappeared.

"It's possible," Twain said into the silence, "that there are still Dragons somewhere, somewhen, in the Summer Country. But as Samaranth said, they would likely never return to the Archipelago, even if they exist."

"Mother Night said he wasn't a Dragon yet," Rose reiterated. "That he was an apprentice, who still had to choose."

"There have been rumors of such men and women," said Verne, who was looking cautiously at Bert as he spoke, "but none since the Histories have been recorded, and none since the creation of the *Geographica*."

"That we know of," said Twain.

"That we know of," Verne confirmed. "Although there's one possibility, which would make a strange sort of symmetry if it were true—"

"I'm more concerned about what this moon told Rose about the Shadows," Bert said, interrupting. "For her to have even spoken the *name* of the primordial Shadows . . ."

"Echthroi," another voice said. "Echthroi. Echthros."

It was Schubert.

Up to now he had been silent as he usually was, and so everyone had ignored him as they usually did. The Feast Beasts had dutifully placed trays and platters of food in front of him, but most of it remained untouched, save for a few cherry tomatoes, which he ate when no one else was looking.

"The Shadow. The Darkness. The Many-Angled Ones," Schubert said dully. "The Lloigor. The Nameless. The Unwritten. The Anti-Erl Kings. The Un-Makers. The Un-Namers. By all these names and more are they known. Against these, by any name, we fight. But they are always the same. . . ." He stood, looming over the table.

"They are the *Enemy*. And we must be strong, for they will not relent."

For the first time since Mother Night's visit, Rose felt genuinely frightened. For the Caretakers Emeritis to be taking this discussion so seriously was alarming, but for Schubert to be so actively involved sent a thrill of fear up her spine. Bert had once explained to her that he was more attuned to the supernatural than any of the rest of them, with the exception of Poe himself. And for Schubert to speak meant that there was something dangerous brewing.

"The Echthroi," Twain said gravely, "are why there must always be Caretakers, my dear Rose. They are who we protect the world against."

"But the Winter King—," she began.

"Was merely their agent on this planet," Twain interrupted, "and he had a mere fraction of their power."

"Why are they worse than anything else the Caretakers have faced?" Rose asked. "We've defeated shadows before."

"We've defeated their agents," Dickens corrected. "We have not yet faced the true Shadows. But," he added with a tense expression on his face, "it seems that time is finally upon us."

"Rose, dear girl," said Twain as he laid a reassuring hand over hers, "don't worry. This is what we do, we Caretakers. And we are going to use all the powers at our disposal to protect you."

That may be part of the problem, Rose thought. *If I am able to choose, and I don't because I know you'll try to protect me, will that be a mistake? Will we all pay a price, just because I'll be afraid to act on my own?*

"At any rate," Bert said as they all stood, "we should be discussing this with your three uncles when they arrive for the party. They'll feel terribly left out if we don't."

"Agreed," said Barrie. "I'm looking forward to their return as well."

"The storm has passed," said Dickens. "Take some comfort in that, Rose."

"What do we need to do now?" asked Rose.

"We have to prepare the banquet hall," Verne said as he swept past her into the foyer. "Today Time finally catches up with itself, and we want to make the Caretakers' return to the Archipelago a day they won't forget for *centuries*."

. . . a massive clock of stone, wood, and silver . . .

CHAPTER THREE
Chronos & Kairos

✦

Celebrations, like many things, are happiest after a long separation, or a period of trials and tribulations—and the event at Tamerlane House came at the end of decades of fear, and conflict, and dark days. Several of the Caretakers Emeritis had come into the front reception hall to receive the new arrivals, and everyone was moving about in a swirl of hugs and handshakes, greetings and salutations.

"Rose!" Jack exclaimed as she hugged each of the companions in turn. "You've cut your hair!"

"It *has* been seven years, Jack," said Charles as he kissed the young woman on the top of her head. "I'm surprised we even recognize her."

"Seven years for you, you mean," Rose corrected as she hugged John a second time. "For me, just days."

"Hugo is sorry he couldn't come," said Jack. "Warnie, too. They've both missed you terribly. You should come to visit as soon as possible."

"Now, lads," Bert said, even though they were well into middle age, "we shouldn't go rushing to make plans so quickly. We've got time to do things now."

"We've waited a long time," Jack protested. "What's wrong with a short trip to Oxford?"

"We'll discuss it later, Jack," Bert said, trying to change the subject. "Let's just enjoy the celebration, shall we?"

"Fine," said Jack as he hugged her again. "But Rose will be coming to see us shortly, I think."

"I agree," said Charles.

Rose folded her arms, closed her eyes, and smiled. "That's what we're going to do, then."

Jack grinned at Charles. "That's it and done," he said. "There'll be no persuading her otherwise, not now."

"Well enough and good," Bert said, knowing he was beaten. "But we'll still be having a discussion before you leave."

"What's this?" a gruff voice said. "I smell Caretakers about."

"Hello, Burton," said John, reluctantly offering his hand. "It's, ah, good to see you again."

Behind the self-professed barbarian were his two colleagues, the former Caretakers Harry Houdini and Arthur Conan Doyle, who were arguing about something.

"Three is a good number," Burton had said when the Caretakers Emeritis had pressed him for the whereabouts of the other members of the Imperial Cartological Society. "Consider us the Society's version of your three Caretakers—emissaries to an unknown region."

"All secrets out, Sir Richard?" Twain had asked him. "All trust, in the open?"

"That's a journey, not a destination," Burton had replied. "We should just focus on the progress we're making, and not on what we expect of the future."

"Benevolent, malevolent, what does it matter?" Houdini was saying, making frustrated gestures with his hands. "I just want to know how it was done."

"How what was done?" asked Jack.

"We made the mistake of showing Harry the Serendipity Box," said Twain, "and of course, he opened it straightaway."

"What happened?"

"It vanished," said Doyle. "Disappeared into thin air. He's been trying to suss out what happened. I keep telling him it was the faeries who took it."

"Oh, spare me," said Houdini. "They'd have returned it by now if they had."

A deep compulsion for finding things out was a trait shared by the Caretakers and members of the Society, and it had served them all well in various circumstances—but in none of them was the compulsion as deeply rooted as it was in Harry Houdini. He simply could not tolerate not knowing how a trick was done— even a trick involving time and space.

"All tricks involve time and space," Houdini huffed. "Any decent illusion is nothing but the manipulation of the viewer's perceptions. That's it, and that's all."

"What do you think, Bert?" John asked as they moved from the reception hall into the banquet room, where the rest of the Caretakers and their guests were waiting.

"I think," said Bert as he and Verne opened the great double doors, "that it gave him exactly what he needed. It's just going to take him a while to realize it."

◆   ◆   ◆

Two of the special guests at Tamerlane House were among those the companions most wanted to see: Laura Glue, the Lost Girl who had grown up to become the leader of the flying Valkyries; and the badger Fred, who was Charles's apprentice Caretaker. Both completely ignored decorum and bounded across the table the minute they saw their friends.

"Hello there, Laura dear!" Jack exclaimed as the girl threw herself into his arms and hugged him tightly.

"That's Laura *Glue*," she chided gently. "I'm so happy to see you all!"

Fred was only slightly less reserved and couldn't stop himself from hugging Charles before he stepped back to offer a more dignified handshake.

"Good to see you, Scowler Charles," he said, still beaming. "I've kept my watch in good order."

"I have no doubt," Charles said, beaming. "And how are your father and grandfather?"

"Tummeler is well, but not fit to travel out of Paralon," replied Fred. "As for Uncas, he and Don Quixote are off on some secret mission for the Prime Caretaker, or else you know they wouldn't have missed you."

"I know it," Charles said as he led them to their seats. "You're a good fellow, Fred."

"Where's Archie?" John asked Rose as they sat at the table. "I would have expected he'd be here too."

"He usually is," Rose answered, "but he hates it when all the Caretakers are present for a big party, so he stays in my attic. He says the proportion of authors to scientists fills the room with the stench of arrogance."

"From which side?"

"He never really clarified that," said Rose, "but then again, I'm not sure it matters."

The celebration was in full swing. All of the Caretakers Emeritis had come out of their portraits for the party—including, John noted, one who had gone renegade while still a Caretaker.

"So," he said to Bert, "you decided to let Lord Byron out, did you?"

"Yes," Bert said, sighing. "After the truce with the Society, we couldn't exactly treat him like a traitor any longer, so we took a vote. He managed to squeak through, so he's here. But on probation," he added. "Mary and Percy keep threatening to set him on fire again."

True to form, the contentious friends were already bickering when John, Rose, and Bert sat down across from them. "We haven't met," he said, offering his hand. "I'm John."

"George Gordon, Lord Byron," the Caretaker-on-probation said amiably. "A pleasure, I'm sure."

"Your attire is atrocious, George," sniffed Percy Shelley. "Also, you smell of smoke."

"Brilliant deduction, Watson," Byron shot back.

"Manners," said Doyle, who had taken a seat next to Bert. "At least I'm still in print. No need to show your temper."

Byron scowled at the Detective. "But," he continued, undeterred, "might it not be because one of my closest friends, someone with whom I have shared—"

"Mind the young ladies," said Houdini. Rose giggled, and to everyone's surprise, Byron reddened.

"—practically everything," he ad libbed, "tried to murder me by burning my portrait? Isn't that a good reason to be a bit testy?"

"There'll be no arguments here today," Verne said, holding up a glass. "Today we mourn old friends who are lost and celebrate the victory that was won at dearest cost. But above all, we're here to celebrate the new freedom we have as Caretakers. . . ."

Burton cleared his throat loudly at this, which got a scowl from Twain.

"The freedom," Verne went on, "to begin the process we have hoped for, been divided over, and thought might never be a reality—the reunification of the Archipelago and the Summer Country. Today is, as Jack named it, truly our Day of Independence."

To this, all the celebrants raised their glasses and let out a resounding cheer.

"Independence Day?" Charles whispered to John.

"Jack's way of tweaking our American counterparts," John answered. "I don't think he intended for it to stick. Did you know he was going to say all that?" he whispered to Jack.

"Not exactly," said Jack. "It's certainly a long-term goal for the New Society."

"Which you are in charge of at Cambridge," Charles whispered. "No pressure, Jack."

During dessert, which Rose had designed herself with the aid of the Feast Beasts and Alexandre Dumas, who was a surprisingly good cook, another guest dropped in, much to the relief of John, Jack, and Charles.

"So sorry I'm late!" Hank Morgan exclaimed as he strolled

in and grabbed a sandwich from one of the trays. "It seems I've missed dinner, but the dessert looks exceptionally good."

"They're called beignets," Rose said proudly. "They're a sort of French doughnut, except for these, we've added a special touch— each one you eat will suddenly be filled with something you love. Something delicious. Alex and I made the beignets, and the Feast Beasts arranged the filling."

"Don't mind if I do," said Hank, taking one from the overflowing tray. He bit into it. "Mmm," he said with real admiration. "Hazelnut."

"Mine's chocolate cream," said Charles. "Well done, Rose!"

"Mine's plain," said Fred, "but I like 'em plain."

"Eww," said Byron. "Is this spinach?"

"You must have gotten a faulty one," Dumas said, winking at Mary. "Try another."

"This is . . . ," said Byron, making a face. "Is this wax?"

"A shame," said Dumas. "Ours are delicious."

"Jules," Morgan said, stepping to the door. "A word, if I may?"

"Of course," Verne said with a glance at Bert and Twain. "We'll be back shortly. Carry on with the party!"

When the dinner had concluded, the Caretakers and their guests retired to one of the great libraries of Tamerlane House to have a smoke, drink brandy, and generally catch up on the affairs of the two worlds. Fred, Rose, and Laura Glue decided to forgo the cigars, pipes, and brandy in favor of aged Vernor's Ginger Ale and some warm Mexican pastries.

The library was shaped like a star, with fireplaces at the center and at each point. This allowed for an expansive meeting space that at the same time offered the opportunity for smaller groups to congregate.

For the first time, John realized that one of the Caretakers had not been present, either to greet them at the door, or at the banquet. "Samuel," he said, pulling Twain aside, "Poe hasn't come down yet. I know he rarely does, but for today I thought . . . Is everything all right?"

"We're trying to discover that," Twain answered ominously. "At any rate, we'll discuss it with you when Jules returns."

"I don't remember being in this library before," said Jack as he scanned the walls. "Of course, the last time I was here, we were rather preoccupied."

"This is the Library of Lost Books," Twain said proudly. "I've assembled much of it myself."

"What kind of books are lost books?" asked Jack. "If they're lost, who would know about them at all?"

"Ah," said Twain, "so you understand the challenge I had. Originally this was a repository of our own lost or unfinished works. Charles finished *Edwin Drood*, and I wrote a sequel to *A Connecticut Yankee*, among others, but mostly it contains books that were mentioned only once, in some obscure text, and never again."

He pointed with his cane at a leather-bound book just above their heads. "That one, there? It's a defense of Christianity written by Origen, who wrote it as a rebuttal to an anti-Christian Platonist named Celsus."

"Ah," Jack said, looking at Origen's book. "A kindred spirit."

"Don't relate to him too closely," said Twain. "He also grossly misinterpreted a verse in the Gospel of Saint Matthew and castrated himself. It was a terrible way for him to learn about metaphor and allegory."

"I'll keep that in mind," said Jack.

After an hour had passed, Verne came into the library still deep in discussion with Morgan.

"It's nice to see Hank in the flesh," Charles whispered to John, "and still younger than us."

"That's not so hard to do these days," John whispered back as Verne and Morgan approached them.

"Sorry I was late," Morgan said again. "It couldn't be avoided, I'm afraid. There's been a lot to do to get ready for your return."

"If we hadn't had obligations and family to return to," said John, "we might just as well have stayed to help you out with things here, then gone back to our proper time later."

"No," said Verne. "You couldn't have."

"Why not?" asked John.

As he spoke, Hawthorne and Fred came back into the library with trays of fruit that they set on the table.

"Because you are still alive, in what we have come to call your, ah, 'Prime Time,'" said Verne. He took an apple from one of the trays and began to munch on it as he explained further.

"You have an allotted span within which you are meant to achieve certain things," he said, sitting. "An allotted lifetime, if you will. You've already experienced how dangerous and difficult it is to go skipping around in time—and those occasions have been of brief duration. If you were gone for a more extended time, it would be even more so."

"The difficult part probably has to do with explaining one's whereabouts to the wife," said Hawthorne.

"Actually, I was thinking that's the dangerous part," said John. "But why couldn't we have stayed, especially if we could return to whenever we wanted, ah, whenever we wanted?"

"Because," said Verne, "you'd have started to burn more quickly through the years of your own Prime Time. And you can't afford to spare even one."

"If we can't, how is it that you can?"

"Easy," Verne replied as he began to devour the apple's core. "We're already dead. We have no more obligations to our natural span, and can therefore operate outside the bounds of Prime Time.

"Come with me," he went on as he grabbed a pear from the tray. "I want to show you something."

"For a professed dead man," Charles said as the companions followed the Prime Caretaker out of the library, "he certainly can put away the fruit."

"You'd be surprised," said Burton, "how much sweeter it tastes when you're living on borrowed time."

Verne led them all into the center of Tamerlane House, to a room that stood under the tallest of the minarets. In the center of the room stood a massive clock of stone, wood, and silver. It reached high into the room, standing some four stories taller than the ground floor, and it fell away below their feet into a vastly deep subbasement.

"How far down does it go?" John asked, leaning over the balustrade. "I can't see the bottom."

"We don't keep the lower floors lit, unless the clock needs maintenance," said Verne, "but it goes down some dozen stories. The house was built around it, in fact."

"Poe calls it the Intuitive Clock," said Bert, "although Jules added his own unique touch to it." He pointed at a plate that had been mounted on the clock at eye level. It read:

> The Moving Finger writes; and, having writ,
> Moves on: nor all thy Piety nor Wit,
> Shall lure it back to cancel half a Line,
> Nor all thy Tears wash out a Word of it.
> —Omar Khayyám

"Ironic," said Charles. "I think."

The face of the clock was twenty feet across and bore two elaborate overlapping dials—the inner one of silver, and the outer one of gold. From somewhere inside the mechanism, they could hear a steady thrumming sound.

"The center dial represents Kairos—real time, of pure numbers with no measurement," Verne explained, "while the outer dial represents Chronos, which is ordinary wristwatch, alarm-clock time."

"One mechanical, one metaphysical," said Charles. "Fascinating."

"You all have similar mechanisms on your watches," said Bert, "the ones that have been activated as Anabasis Machines, at any rate."

"The Summer Country is on Chronos time," said Verne, "while the Archipelago is on Kairos time. Now at the moment, they should be in sync. But the longer you remained here, you'd see . . ." He stopped, puzzled. "Hank?" he asked. "What do you make of this?"

Morgan looked up at the clock, and his jaw fell open. He looked at his watch, then back at the clock, and shrugged. "I have no clue what this means, Jules. I've never seen this before."

"What is it?" asked John.

"The Kairos time should be behind Chronos time," said Verne, "but it's exactly the reverse. The Archipelago is moving faster." He looked at Hank. "That explains why you were late."

"Maybe so," said Hank. "But we should consult with Poe just the same."

"I agree," said Verne. He turned to the others. "I'm sorry, but we're going to have to cut our evening short," he said, suddenly somber.

As the group began to filter their way back to the main hall, John, Jack, and Charles pulled Verne, Twain, and Bert aside.

"There's something else we need to discuss with you," John said quietly. "We didn't want to discuss it openly in front of Burton, but it concerns Hank Morgan."

Briefly the companions explained John and Charles's encounter with the ghost pirate at Magdalen Tower. When they finished, Bert turned to Verne with a puzzled expression. "An anomaly?" he asked.

"It must be," Verne replied, looking just as baffled. "I did recently send Hank on a mission to the seventeeth century, but as you saw, he returned just as he left. There must be some other answer. And as far as I know, Shakespeare never built a bridge in his life—or after." He put a hand on John's shoulder. "You were right not to discuss it openly—or mention it to Hank. Anomalies are my responsibility. I'll look into it."

"We also have something we need to tell you," Twain said to the companions, "and in just as much secrecy, I'm afraid."

The three men listened as the older Caretakers told them about Rose's strange visitor.

"A Dragon's apprentice?" said John when Twain was done. "I didn't know there was such a thing."

"Never mind that," said Jack. "Why is this the first time we've heard about these . . . Echthroids?"

"Echthroi," Bert said, glancing at Verne, "and we have no good excuse, I'm afraid, Jack. We were waiting until you were ready, and—"

"If you'd waited any longer, we'd all be dead," said Charles, "but we know now. Do you think the Echthroi have anything to do with the ghost-Hank we saw?"

"I don't know," said Verne, "but we'll not get this figured out tonight. Come back tomorrow, and we'll have a proper council to discuss everything."

"Good enough," John said, yawning. "It's always easier to fight primordial evil after a few hours' sleep."

"Not for me, I'm afraid," said Jack. "I have several papers to grade and two lectures to prepare. But yes, I'll come back with John."

"Just the idea is going to be a weight off my shoulders," said Charles. "This whole matter of not being able to travel to the Archipelago has had my sense of obligation all in a twist. I kept worrying that there was going to be some crisis I wouldn't be able to help with—sort of like listening to a radio report about your brother's house burning down. You might be able to do something eventually, but there, in the moment that you're needed most, you can't really do anything. Terribly frustrating."

"I know," Bert said. "I know how hard it's been for all three of you. But that's all, erm, behind us now, so to speak. For now, let's get you home, hey?"

They rejoined the rest of the Caretakers and guests in the main hall, where final good-byes were said, hugs given, and hands shook, and at last the three companions were ready to return home.

"Remember," John said to Rose, "we want you to come back to Oxford as soon as you can arrange it. We've missed you terribly, and Warnie and Hugo would be terribly hurt if you couldn't spend time with them as well—although your uncle Hugo is going to be merciless about your hair."

Rose kissed him on the cheek, then Jack, then Charles. "I shall, I promise," she said. "That works both ways. If you find you have a free hour or two, you can always come here. This is home too."

"Indeed it is," said Charles, "and you have my word, dear girl— I'll be back here before you know it."

"All right, fellows," said Ransom. "Let's have a little walk-about." He pulled a small leather case out of his jacket and untied the binding. Removing the stack of trumps from the enclosure in the back of the case, he shuffled to the one he wanted and held it out in front of him, concentrating.

Nothing happened.

"Hmm," he said after a minute. "I must have had a bit too much to drink. I can't seem to focus."

Hank stepped forward and extended his hand. "I've just gotten back from a visit to the seventeenth century," he said with a half-concealed smile, "so I haven't yet had the chance to indulge in as much brandy as you. May I?"

Ransom scowled a bit but handed his colleague the card.

Hank held up the drawing of the cottage where Jack lived with his brother Warnie—who could even be seen through one of the windows, reading and smoking his pipe—and began to concentrate. Again, nothing happened.

"If this is all a trick," Houdini said at length, "the setup has been astonishing so far. I only hope the payoff is just as good."

"It isn't a trick," Ransom snapped testily. "The card just isn't working!"

"Something's wrong with the picture," said Rose, looking closely at the card in Ransom's hand. "With Uncle Warnie."

"Is he all right?" Jack asked, suddenly concerned. "What's happening? Is he in danger?"

"No," said Rose. "It's nothing like that. I'm looking at his pipe. The smoke isn't moving."

John arched an eyebrow as he and the others moved in to peer more closely at the card. Rose was correct—there was smoke coming from the pipe, but it was frozen. In fact, nothing in the picture was moving.

"How is that unusual?" asked Doyle, who had not seen the cards used very often. "It's just a drawing, isn't it?"

"The drawings change with the passage of time," Ransom explained. "It was Hank who first figured it out, after our escapade in 1936. They move along with us, and change as time advances. It isn't usually noticeable, except when we're using one. Then, the scene begins to move as we step through. But the card isn't even expanding, so I don't know what to think."

"So the one we used to get to the keep," said John, "the one that jumped us from 1936 to 1943. What is it like now?"

"It's blank, save for the frame of runes," Ransom said. "The last time I looked, where the Keep of Time had been drawn, there was only open, empty sky." He shuffled the cards again and pulled one out. "See? It's . . ." He paused, frowning.

"What's the matter?" asked Charles.

"Something's off with the trump," Ransom answered. "Here, look for yourself."

Charles took the card and whistled. Ransom was right. The card was not so much blank as overfull with static. A pulsating gray crackle swept back and forth over the surface of the card.

"Perhaps it looks like that because the keep is finally gone," offered Jack. "A temporal flux of some sort, like the Time Storms."

"No," Ransom replied. "I looked in on it just a few days ago, and it was fine. Water, sky, a few seagulls—but a normal trump, otherwise."

"It's not just that card," said John, pointing at the others on the table. Ransom spread them out and took a quick accounting. All the trumps that led to places in the Summer Country had the same problem as the one for the Kilns—they were frozen in time. But all the trumps that led to locations in the Archipelago were filled with gray static.

"That's really disturbing," Morgan said as he examined his own cards. "Mine are the same way. And I just used one earlier to get here from London."

"How did that work?" asked Verne.

Morgan shrugged. "It seemed to be fine, mostly. I didn't give it much thought at the time, but now that this is happening . . ." He frowned. "It was a bit difficult getting back. I thought I was just tired, but it took me more effort than usual, since I was also using my Anabasis Machine to travel through time. That's why I was late arriving here."

"So were we," said Ransom. "By several hours, in fact. I thought it was just a fluke, though. And the trump seemed to work fine—but now it won't work at all."

"Oh, dear," said Bert. "That's going to present a problem."

"How so?" asked John.

"There is currently no other way to cross the Frontier," Bert said, hands spread apologetically. "If the trumps don't work, there's no way for you to go home."

Rose caught him by the arm before he could disappear . . .

CHAPTER FOUR
The Bridge

"This is a fine how-do-you-do," said Jack. Traveling by trump was so convenient, and so easy, that it had never occurred to any of them what might transpire if the trumps suddenly stopped working properly.

"If only we still had a Dragonship," said Charles, "getting back would be a walk in the park."

Bert and Verne exchanged nervous glances. "Yes, if only," said Bert. "Don't worry, there has to be a reason this is happening. We'll get you home, never fear."

"How about one of the principles?" Jack suggested. "The Royal Animal Rescue Squad would be more than eager to come and bail us out with a ride to Oxford."

"The vehicles are also unable to cross the Frontier," said Bert. "The magic feathers that allowed them passage lost their power when the Dragons died."

"Samaranth has feathers," said John. "Perhaps we should ask him for a few?"

"You're forgetting the first thing he ever said to us," said Charles. "'Will you drink tea with me, or plunder and die?' Do you really want to go ask him if he's molted any feathers we could borrow? Especially after that last speech he gave about the race of men being on their own?"

"I agree," said Ransom. "There's our dignity to consider."

"I'm fine staying here, if it's all the same to you," said Magwich the shrub. "They really do treat me poorly in Oxford. Why, just watering time alone . . ."

"Oh, do shut up," said Charles, "or we'll give you to Grimalkin. And if you thought Mrs. Morris had large claws . . ."

"Sorry, sorry," said Magwich.

"All right," said Twain. "So far we've got a stack of malfunctioning playing cards and our dignity. What else do we have to work with?"

"Burton," said John, "the Society has ways of traveling around expeditiously. Can you do anything here?"

Burton's eyes grew wide—he'd been enjoying the predicament the Caretakers were in, but only as an observer. He didn't expect to be drawn in as a participant.

"In time, yes, but not in space, and not across the Frontier," he said in clipped tones. "That's why I stole the *Indigo Dragon*, remember?"

John could tell that Burton hated admitting he couldn't do something. "Fair enough," he said before anyone could probe any deeper. "It's seems our work is cut out for us, then."

As the other Caretakers Emeritis began to discuss a plan of action, Rose noticed that William Shakespeare had been present throughout the entire discussion.

He didn't often join in, and on the few occasions when he tried, he was either maligned by the others or just dismissed entirely. The most useful contribution Rose had ever heard him make was to suggest that someone be flogged—but then that was usually all he ever suggested.

"Lord," Shakespeare said under his breath as he quietly rose and moved into the adjacent corridor, "what fools these immortals be."

Rose caught him by the arm before he could disappear into the bowels of Tamerlane House. "I heard you," she said plainly. "You know what we need to do, don't you?"

Shakespeare looked uncomfortably flummoxed and tugged at his collar. "I, er, I don't know what you're talking about, child," he said, guiding her over to a more remote corner of the hallway. "After all, there's no one to flog."

Rose didn't reply to this but simply kept a steady gaze on the increasingly uncomfortable Caretaker until he finally sighed and shook his head.

"All right, I submit. You're more perceptive than I gave you credit for."

"Everyone here in Tamerlane House is more perceptive than anyone gives them credit for," said Rose. "You have an idea, don't you? Why don't you tell them?"

"Do you know," he said with a mingling of resignation and melancholy, "what they say about me? Out there, in the world?"

Rose was confused. "You're honored and adored," she finally answered. "Your work is held up as the greatest of achievements—greater than any produced before or since."

Shakespeare put his head in his hands. "That's exactly what I mean. Do you know what kind of a burden it is to have such a reputation? To be, as I am, revered? It is troublesome bad, and more than any man should be expected to bear. And it was worse when I was recruited to be a Caretaker. My fame had outstripped even my life, and always, those around me—even my elders and betters—looked to mine own words for counsel."

He sighed heavily and looked at Rose. "It is a great responsibility to make decisions, and more so to be trusted, and risk being wrong in the counsel given, the choices made. Much, much worse."

At last Rose understood. "But," she said gently, "if you could convince them it was all reputation and not reality, that you were not as well-suited to the task as they thought you to be, then no one would ever look to you for advice."

Shakespeare nodded once, then again. "It has been a difficult fiction to maintain, especially in those dark days when no one quite knew what path to take, save I—and I could not break my act, lest it give me away."

"Sometimes it's better to do the right thing than the comfortable thing," Rose said firmly. "Like right now. You know, and you won't help. How is that a good way to live?"

"It isn't," Shakespeare agreed, "but after so long, I don't know how the fellowship would countenance a newly confident Will."

"They'll accept you," Rose prompted, "if you'll just go tell them what to do."

For a moment his eyes brightened, as if his resolve had returned—but then he slumped back onto a couch in the corridor. "I—I can't," he admitted. "You just don't know how hard it is, being William Shakespeare."

Rose folded her arms and sat back. "Oh, you don't think so? Would you like to trade places with me?"

"What do you mean?"

"I mean, I'm the one they call the Grail Child, even though I'm no longer really a child, and I'm supposed to be the descendant of more gods than even exist anymore. Odysseus was my grandsire. Merlin was my uncle. And my entire childhood was about being ready to give up my life to save my cousin Arthur. Believe me, I understand what it is to live under the pressure of high expectations."

Shakespeare rubbed his chin, appraising her. Then he smiled. "I do believe you've cornered me, dear child," he said at last, still smiling. "If you'll be so good as to accompany me, we should go have a word with Jules."

Rose stood and offered him her arm. "My pleasure, Master Shakespeare."

He groaned and took her arm. "But please," he said as they left the room, "just call me Will."

"Pull the other one," Shelley said dismissively when Rose suggested to the assembled Caretakers that Will had a plan. "His wick isn't lit. How is he going to be of any help? All he ever wants to do is have people flogged."

Will reddened at this, but Rose shook her head. "He's brighter than you think," she said firmly, "and if you'll just give him a chance, maybe he'll surprise us all."

"I have not been myself," said Will, "not for a very long while. But circumstances dictate that I need cast away the mask of the fool, if we're to succeed."

"It was all a ruse, was it?" Twain said with a wan smile. "Well played, Master Shakespeare."

"I knew it all along," said Byron. "I was just playing along to be polite."

"Oh, do shut up, you nit," said Shelley. "All right, Master Wordsmith," he said to Will. "If you are indeed a closeted genius, what pray tell is your great plan to solve our dilemma?"

"We're going to build a bridge," Will declared firmly, and with as much courage as he could muster. "A bridge between the worlds."

John's mouth dropped open in a mix of amazement and shame, and he noted a similar expression on Charles's face. In the stress of the moment they'd forgotten the message from the ghostly Hank Morgan: *You must build the bridge. Shakespeare's Bridge. You can't get back without it.*

Charles began to say something about the ghost pirate, but Verne caught his eye and shook his head. The meaning was clear: not yet.

"If the trumps won't work, then why would a bridge?" Ransom was asking. "That's quite a conceptual leap."

"We don't even know *how* the trumps work," said Will, "just that they do. But I have another plan.

"It was the stones that gave me the initial idea," he explained, "after I'd read about them in your books, Bert."

"Mine?" Bert said in surprise. "What did my books have to do with your discovery?"

"The cavorite," Will answered. "The material in your stories that made space travel possible."

"It's also a major component in the watches," said Verne. "It's part of what allows them to function as time machines."

"That's what I'm driving at," said Will. "When you activate them, one doesn't simply view another time, one is transported to that time, whole and unharmed."

"Or whole and unclothed, in Morgan's case," Twain said with mock seriousness.

"Har har har," Morgan said drolly. "Only you would see traveling in time as an opportunity for a practical joke. But I think I see what Shakespeare's getting at. The Anabasis Machines do have an effect on the physical person, so it's as if there is an effect on space as well as time."

"Better," Will said, smiling. "I think it means space and time may be, in fact, the same thing."

"Pppthhbbbth." Burton blew a raspberry and folded his arms. "This is why we never tried to recruit him," he said dismissively. "He *is* a moron."

Will blushed slightly but refrained from responding to Burton's slur. Instead he continued. "We know there are cavorite mines where the material can be found in large quantities, which is where we've gotten it for use in various devices. But I've found another place where it resides, if in less abundance. It's laced throughout all the stones in the Ring of Power. And it's in the very foundations of the Nameless Isles."

That got the Caretakers' attention. There was a flurry of discussion, argument, and expressions ranging from intrigue to disbelief. It took several minutes before Verne was able to bring the room to order again.

"These are indeed astute observations, especially coming from . . . ah, one such as yourself, who is not trained in the sciences. But I fail to see the significance of your discovery."

"There's one other place where the cavorite is plentiful," Will went on, nonplussed by the resistance of his colleagues. "Avalon. The island that exists in two worlds at once."

"Half there, and half not," Grimalkin said, having suddenly appeared over Burton's shoulder. "Sounds implausible to me."

"Get away from me, cat," Burton exclaimed, swatting at Grimalkin with a fork as its midsection disappeared, leaving two thirds of a cat, which then walked away in opposite directions.

"What is it you're proposing, Will?" asked Verne, pulling them all back to the discussion at hand.

"Come with me," Will said, rising from the table. "I'll show you."

Shakespeare led them all out into the night air, to one of the large storage sheds at the back of the house. He walked inside and took a seat at a makeshift desk, amid the straw, and gardening tools, and odds and ends. Above the desk on a support beam were several drawings of a bridge, all drawn in Shakespeare's hand.

"I've done all my work out here," Will explained, "so no one would see. Nobody comes out here much anyway."

"Who helped you with these?" said Ransom, amazed. "No offense, but I didn't know you had engineering skills."

"None taken," Will said, hooking a thumb over his shoulder. "I did indeed have some help."

Standing at the rear of the shed was the giant Tin Man— formerly the Caretaker Roger Bacon, one of the great inventors of history. He moved forward and put a supportive hand on Will's shoulder.

"It appears," Verne said, putting his arm around Rose, "that you and Master Bacon have both been better judges of character than the rest of us."

Morgan and Ransom, who were both examining Will's drawings, looked at Verne and nodded. The bridge might work.

"All right," Verne said to a beaming Shakespeare. "Ask what you will of us, and then get to work. Time's a wasting."

Will chose several of the burlier Caretakers—Hawthorne, Dumas, and Irving among them—to help him and the Tin Man build the bridge. Bert, Rose, Laura Glue, and Fred decided to go into the kitchen and find something else to eat, while the others returned to the meeting hall. Before they got there, Charles had already started an argument with Ransom about Chronos time and Kairos time.

"You're far too concerned about reconciling your own experiences with everyone else's," said Ransom. "You need to understand: There is no such thing as past or future, not to the individual. To the individual, there is only the Now."

"It's one great advantage to being a tulpa," said Verne. "We get to live in Kairos time, because we've already done our years in Chronos time."

"That stands to reason when we're talking about you, and Burton, and the other members of the Society," said Charles, "but where does that leave Bert? H. G. Wells is still a contemporary, still in our, uh, 'Prime Time.' Yet he seems to travel as freely between worlds and times as you do."

"Bert is a dimensional anomaly," Verne explained. "The one I originally recruited is the one you know, the one you have met, Charles. In the beginning of his apprenticeship, they were one and the same, until his first trip through time.

"We were equally inexperienced with the intricacies of time travel, and the problem arose when he took his trip into the future."

"The one he wrote about in *The Time Machine*, yes," said John.

"Exactly," said Verne, "but unlike his unnamed time traveler, Bert did not safely return to the point at which he left, or moments after. He overshot the mark and arrived two full years before he ever left, and at a point when he was barely an initiate as a Caretaker. Bert, our Bert, was older, more experienced, and brought with him a three-year-old daughter."

"Aven," Jack said, exhaling. "That was Aven."

Verne nodded. "We didn't know how to send him back to try to fix the anomaly, and we weren't even sure what had gone wrong to begin with. Even Poe himself was at a loss as to what to do. Finally we realized that Bert could not leave, but also that the younger version of himself could no longer be a Caretaker."

"How did he—the young one—take the news that he was being displaced?" asked John.

"To the Devil with that," said Charles. "How did he react when he met himself?"

"The other Wells—let's call him Herb—and Bert have never met," Verne replied. "To have another version of himself walking around—and to be fully aware of him—would have interfered too much with Herb's Prime Time. Too many variables would come into play. So Dickens and I conferred with Bert, and we agreed that he should continue in his role as the third Caretaker. As for Herb, I realized I would have to not only cease instructing him in the disciplines needed to become a Caretaker, but I would also have to convince him that many of the secrets I had shared were fictions. Only one man was meant to live the lifetime that was already being lived."

Charles cleared his throat and raised his hand for attention. Jack slapped his forehead in resignation—he and John were comfortable mingling with the Caretakers Emeritis as equals, but Charles, for some reason, still felt like he was in grammar school among the greats.

"I don't mean to contradict you, Jules," Charles said, "but then how do you explain Chaz? I wasn't there myself during the Dyson affair, but he was essentially me from an alternate dimension. Yet he was able to come here to this one without changing my position with you at all." He paused and looked around nervously. "Or has he?"

Twain clapped him on the back and blew a puff of well-intentioned cigar smoke in his face. "Worry not, dear boy, worry not. For one thing, you were already far deeper into your course than young Wells was. Shades, you were already a full Caretaker! And for another, your friends didn't bring him back here—they dropped him off several centuries back. No fuss, no muss."

"Samuel's right," said Verne. "He fulfilled a purpose in this dimension, but in a different time. Think of the temporal plane as a great map." He pointed to a whorl of wood on the top of a table. "This is you, in this time. And this," he said, pointing at another pattern on the opposite side, "is where Chaz ended up living his life. One person, two temporal places. He never interfered with your Prime Time. But if we had kept Herb in the loop, so to speak, then both he and Bert would have been in one spot," he finished, tapping the first whorl. "Not good, temporally speaking."

"Also, Chaz wasn't precisely you, Charles," said John. "He was Charles-like, but he had lived in a different world there in the Winterland. He might have started taking on more of your attributes, but he was not you, and his thinking had become different enough that he certainly could not have taken your place."

"Bert and Herb also diverged in this same way," Verne said, vigorously nodding his approval. "You've no doubt noticed that Herb's viewpoints and my own were often at odds when it came to writing."

"And science, and politics, and social development," intoned John. "You were at opposite ends of the spectrum on just about everything, Jules."

"And so it is with Bert, also," Verne agreed, "but with the difference that he and I are colleagues, whereas to Herb, I was a potential mentor who abandoned him."

"Why abandon him if he was going to end up going into the future in two years anyway?" asked Jack. "What was the need?"

"That's just it," Dickens put in, as he went to refill his pipe. "He never went."

Verne coughed. "Yes. We made certain that his studies never reached the point that he really believed in time travel, not really, and we made equally certain that he would never lay eyes on the device, much less use it."

"How much did he know?" asked John.

"Enough to know that I was no longer being truthful," Verne said, casting a sorrowful glance at Dickens, who nodded. "That single rift widened into a chasm, and in only a few years, he was no longer the man who was once so suitable as an apprentice Caretaker. The imagination, and integrity, and ingenuity were still there, but the spark of belief was gone."

"But he still wrote *The Time Machine*, didn't he?" John asked. "Or was that our Bert?"

"They both did," said Twain, "only Bert's will never be published. Of all of us, only he has written the full and accurate version of his adventures into the Histories. He feels no need to express himself outside of our quorum because in a way, he's already out in the world doing it.

"Granted, he reads his counterpart's work—and, I daresay, improves upon it, especially in his nonfiction—but the paths of Bert the Caretaker and H. G. Wells the respected author diverged a long time ago."

Jack scratched his head and squinted at the others. "But without being involved in the Archipelago," he said wonderingly, "how was he able to create all those extraordinary stories?"

"Because he's a brilliant writer," said Dickens, who had just come back into the discussion. "A great many of us have been inspired by our adventures in the Archipelago and incorporated some of those tales into our stories. But not everything is borrowed—we are, after all, still writers of great ability."

This last comment brought up a round of grunted assent and table thumping, which, Jack figured, was probably why Dickens said it.

"Conversely," Dickens continued, "there have been many talented men and women who had the imagination to be Caretakers, and who believed in the Platonic idea of the Archipelago, even if subconsciously, but yet never had the chance to become Caretakers themselves."

There was more grunting and "hear, hear's" and table thumping, and several of the Caretakers recited names.

"Chesterton," said Barrie, "and he's still living, I should note."

"Charlotte Brontë," said Dumas. "And Jane Austen."

"Longfellow," said Barrie, "and John Ruskin."

"George Gordon," said Twain.

"I'm *right here*," Byron said, irritated.

"So you are," Twain said, winking at Jack.

"We could name a hundred, or a thousand like them," said Dickens, "all brilliant, and all completely ignorant of the affairs of the Archipelago of Dreams. Yet still, they created great works. As have those here. After all," he concluded, looking at Jack, "you don't base all of your own writing off of your experiences as a Caretaker, do you?"

"All of it?" Jack asked, fingering his collar. "Well, I mean . . . that is, of course not!"

"Right," said John.

"Uh-huh," said Charles.

"What?" said Jack.

"What are we discussing?" Bert said as he entered the room, pocketing a now empty vanilla bottle. "Sounds lively."

"Plagiarism," John replied, grinning.

"Swipes," said Charles.

"You can't plagiarize from history!" Jack exclaimed, giving both of his friends the stink-eye. "*Homages.*"

"Ah," Bert said, as if he completely understood. "Shakespeare and Kit Marlowe been at it again, have they?"

"Then our Bert, the one who's been in the kitchen sipping the cooking vanilla," said Jack, "shouldn't exist at all. If Jules stopped him from going to the future, then the Bert who returned shouldn't have existed to begin with!"

Twain thumped the younger Caretaker on the arm with his cane. "Boy," he said with equal parts exasperation and mirth, "just what part of the word 'anomaly' don't you understand?"

"They're telling you I'm an anomaly, eh?" asked Bert. "Well, in this crowd, I'd have to be."

"How's that?" asked John.

"Simple," said Verne. "He's the only time traveler who is still among the living."

The construction of Shakespeare's Bridge took more than three days, but before the rays of the morning sun broke over the Nameless Isles a fourth time, it was complete.

The bridge was made of cavorite-laced stone, and arched shallowly from a bend in the path behind the house to a spot in the sand about fifteen feet out. It was a fairly ordinary looking bridge, except for the two stones at the apogee of the arch.

"That's what should allow it to function," Will explained. "The capstones, into which we'll be placing these," he said, showing the others two small golden orbs. "They should allow the bridge to span the two worlds, and if we've designed it right, it should take you to somewhere in Oxford, if not directly home."

"What are they made of?" Jules asked, examining one of the orbs. "They look like . . ."

Will nodded. "We believed that the life force of the Dragons was not all that allowed them to cross," he said somberly.

"Their eyes," said Jack. "The golden eyes of the Dragons."

"Ordo Maas built them to cross over," Will said, "before they were living ships. I think we can still use the eyes and this bridge to breach the Frontier."

With no ceremony, Will stepped onto the bridge and placed one orb in each capstone. Nothing happened.

"Will?" Ransom asked. "Are you supposed to throw a switch or something?"

"I don't understand," Will murmured, more to himself than the others, as he examined the bridge. "It should have worked right away."

Verne looked at Charles and pursed his lips. "Now," he said softly. "Now is the time to share what you know."

Charles looked nervously from Verne to John, and then at Morgan. "I ah, er," he started, tugging at his collar. "That is, John and I, we know how to make the bridge work."

"How do you know that?" asked Will, surprised.

"We know," said Charles, "because Hank told us."

With all the Caretakers and their guests gathered about them, John and Charles related the details of their strange experience at Magdalen Tower.

"Interesting," Hank said when they were done, "but I'm afraid it wasn't me. I've never actually been a pirate, much less a ghost pirate."

"The timing is right, though," said Verne. "You were just there, two centuries back."

"The problem is with the trumps, not the Anabasis Machines," Morgan protested, "and I made it back just fine. Although . . ." He paused, finger aside his nose. "I have been working on a new device. Remember, Alvin?"

"Yes," said Ransom. "It's a modified version of the Lanterna Magica, but without the limitations of the slides—"

"Because we'd be using trumps," Morgan finished, snapping his fingers. "I'll go fetch it and we'll give it a try."

"So," Burton rumbled as Hank ran back into Tamerlane House, "you are keeping secrets, Caretaker?"

"Not just from you," Verne answered. "I didn't want Charles and John to tell what they knew. Not until now."

"Why?" asked Dickens. "Why not tell *us*?"

"Why not?" asked Hawthorne. "We might have believed in Shakespeare *more* if we'd heard Charles and John's story first."

"Maybe *you* would have," Verne said, looking over to where Will was adjusting stones on the bridge, "but he might not have believed in *himself*. It needed to be his choice to offer—not just because of a ghostly warning from an ally who is decidedly unghostlike."

"Whether or not he's an idiot has yet to be proven," said Burton. "The bridge doesn't work."

"Not yet," Morgan said as he hurried back to the group, "but this might do the trick."

He was carrying a strange contraption that resembled an electrified diorama box. "It's meant to be portable, usable anywhere," he explained as he set it up at the foot of the bridge, "and it operates using a trump."

He took the front off the box, revealing lenses and gears, and a slot where a card could be inserted. Carefully, he and Ransom removed one of the stones in the center of the bridge and placed the box inside the shallow hole. Morgan ran leads to both capstones, then turned to face the Caretakers.

"It's already functional," he said, nodding at Will. "You were right about the Dragon's eyes. But," he went on, "you gave it nothing to connect to on the other side." He leaned over and swiftly inserted a trump into the slot.

Instantly, half of the bridge vanished.

"Gentlebeings," said Morgan, "I give you Shakespeare's Bridge."

Will turned to the companions, beaming. "I think," he said, bowing, "you have a short walk to take, and you'll be home, safe and sound."

"I'm impressed," Ransom said, giving the functional bridge a once-over. He checked the time, then shook his watch, tapping it on his hand. "Dratted thing. I'm going to go in and check it against the Intuitive Clock. John, Jack, Charles," he called out as he left. "See you soon?"

"Of course," said Jack, who was hugging Rose one last time. "We'll get things caught up at home, then we'll be back."

"I'm going to have to explain we weren't out at the Bird and Baby," said John. "Again."

"Don't work too hard," said Fred, waving.

"I can't promise," Charles called back over his shoulder as he waved good-bye. "After all, some of us have less time than others— and we need to be making hay while the sun shines."

"Where in heaven's name did you get that expression?" John said in mock disgust. "You've been fraternizing with the American scholars again, haven't you?"

The three companions laughed as they stepped onto the bridge—and disappeared.

"Well done, Will," said Verne. "You've just changed the game."

Ransom was crossing through the dining hall when Grimalkin appeared. "So," said the cat. "Does it work?"

"Well enough to get them home," Ransom answered without looking down at the cat, which probably wasn't there anyway.

"Although I'm sure I can figure out what's wrong with the trumps, given enough time."

"The trumps?" asked Grimalkin's voice. "Like the one you just used?"

"Yes," Ransom said. "I—" He froze midstride. "It still shouldn't have worked," he murmured. "Not if it was a spatial problem . . ."

He looked down at his watch, and his eyes widened in horror. Quickly, he spun about and ran back toward the other end of the house.

"It's quite a relief, actually," Morgan was saying as he congratulated Will. "Your bridge will make traveling back and forth a lot easier."

The other Caretakers Emeritis voiced their agreement—this was a paradigm shift or a rare kind.

"Of course," said Burton, "you've also rendered your safe house functionally unsafe. As of now, all roads lead to Rome, as it were."

Suddenly a voice rife with terror rang out as Ransom burst out of Tamerlane House, waving his watch. "No!" he shouted. "Don't cross over! Don't cross the bridge!"

"You're a moment too late, I'm afraid," said Bert. "They've already gone through."

"It's a discontinuity!" Ransom exclaimed, panting. "A rift! A rift in time, between this world and the Summer Country! We've got to get them back!"

Without warning a terrible earthquake shook the island, throwing them all to the ground. A howling noise like a hurricane filled the air, and for a moment it seemed as if Tamerlane House was going to be shaken to pieces.

More ominously, the other half of the bridge had reappeared—and it brought something else with it.

"We aren't in Kansas anymore," said Twain, "or even in the Archipelago."

Through the bridge, they could see the ghost image of England, almost real enough to touch. Behind them, they could still see the Nameless Isles, but beyond that, gray mists.

"Oh my stars and garters," said Bert. "I think we've been ripped free of the Archipelago altogether."

"And what of the Caretakers?" asked Twain. "Where did they go?"

"Not where, when," said Ransom. "And there's only one way to find out. We've got to follow them across."

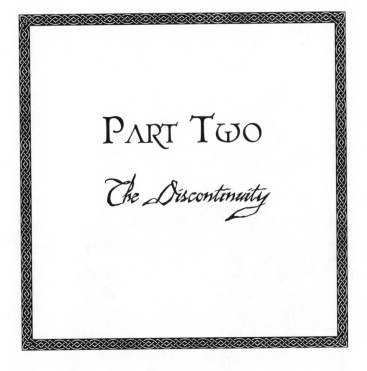

PART TWO

The Discontinuity

From the garden, all that could be seen was half of a stone bridge . . .

CHAPTER FIVE
The Pirate

✦

The man called Elijah McGee dipped his quill into the watery ink and continued to draw on the broad parchment on the desk before him. The map, which was the seventh he had created for the man who was not quite a friend, and yet was more than an acquaintance, was almost completed. It was the most unusual of the maps he had made, and the most complex. But it was correct in a way he could not explain—as if it had existed in the parchment already, and was only being pulled forth by his penstrokes, not drawn upon it by his hand.

Mapmaking was not his original calling; Elijah McGee was a silversmith of great renown in the Colonies, and particularly there in Charles Town. None had a greater reputation save for one or two in Boston. But for the finest detail work, every man in every trade knew to seek out Elijah McGee.

Even if such a man was a pirate.

The young man who had first come to him was barely thirty years old, if that, but his face bore the lines of a longer life, as if the years he lived had worn down his spirit before they showed on his flesh.

He had approached Elijah with a strange watch, which was made of a metal he had never seen before. It had been damaged in some way, or so the man had claimed. At the first meeting, he was strangely reluctant to describe to Elijah all the supposed workings of the device, but during subsequent encounters he shared more and more extraordinary tales of what it was capable of, and the adventures he had had through its use.

He had taken it to other silversmiths, some in London across the ocean, and some in the Colonies, but none could help him. One of them in Boston had agreed to allow him to try to repair it himself—but the young man had fired up the smelter when his master was at Sunday services, and had a terrible accident: He had tripped and burned his hand in molten silver. A surgeon later restored much of its usefulness, but the hand would never be the same.

Without the watch, he explained to Elijah, he could not communicate with his colleagues, and worse, he would be consigned to remain here in this *time*, rather than return to his own.

He had said "time" as if it were a place, Elijah remembered thinking. As if it were something to be traveled to. And he spoke of it reluctantly, as if a great confidence were being breached.

More was the pity then, Elijah mused, that he was unable to determine the reason for the device's malfunctioning. It operated as a watch, and nothing more, and that would have to be good enough.

He had always taken the story of the watch as he had taken the other tales—with a grain of salt. The stories were simply too outlandish to believe: accounts of a group of men and women called Caretakers, and an extraordinary place called the Archipelago, and of a singular personage the man had called the Cartographer, from whom the man had begun learning the art of mapmaking.

If even a few of the stories were true, it would be extraordinary enough, but they were generally too impossible to believe. Still, he seemed a decent enough sort, and he paid in gold (albeit coins of ancient origin), so Elijah had come to look forward to his visits.

When it was evident Elijah could not fix the watch, the young man disappeared for several months, then reappeared. He had become a pirate, which was not all that disreputable a profession— and quite a successful one at that. And he had a curious request: that Elijah draw for him a *map*.

With his ruined hand, he could no longer do it himself—but he could teach Elijah, and Elijah, with his skilled fingers, could create it. And Elijah agreed, in part out of sympathy, and in part because one does not argue with pirates.

That request was the first of several to come over the years, and in time, Elijah developed a reputation among the other pirates. Before he realized it, he had entered a new, secret profession. And it was all begun by the strange young man with the watch who had become a pirate.

I was a silversmith, Elijah thought, *before I became a mapmaker to pirates—so who am I to criticize a craftsman such as my young friend in his choice of careers?*

The visits from the young pirate became more sporadic, and Elijah wondered if some mischief had befallen the man. And then one day he returned, with the strangest request of all: He asked that Elijah try to create a map that would guide him not to a specific place . . .

. . . but to a specific *time*.

The years had taken their toll; both Elijah and his pirate

friend had aged and weathered. But as Elijah was about to protest that such a thing could not be done, he noticed the fellow fingering the silver watch—and for some reason, he heard himself agreeing to try.

It did not come easily. Many conversations were had about the nature of maps, and time, and the paths that men take in their lives. And Elijah realized that it might be possible that his whole purpose in life was to create this single drawing. It was, he thought with astonishment, going to *work*.

And besides, he thought as he dipped the quill again to finish the drawing, even a failure would bring him gratitude from someone who had become a very influential man. If one was to find oneself an ally and friend to a pirate, he could do worse than to have that pirate be the most successful, ambitious, and noble of them all. So if Captain Henry Morgan wanted a map of time, Elijah McGee would oblige him. After all, isn't that what friends are for?

It was decided that Verne, Bert, Ransom, and Morgan would cross the bridge to see what had happened to the companions. Twain and Dickens stayed behind to alert Poe, and to console an inconsolable Shakespeare.

"A bit risky, isn't it, Caretaker?" Burton said to Verne. "Crossing over with so many?"

"It's my responsibility, mine and Bert's," said Verne, "and if we get stuck ourselves, we'll need Ransom and Morgan to find a way back."

"Fair enough," Burton replied, sweeping his arm in a grand gesture. "Be my guest."

Bert stepped across first, then the others.

They were in the garden just outside the Kilns, and it was in full bloom. "Spring, not autumn," Bert said bleakly. "This bodes ill for us all."

Verne was looking at his watch and shaking his head in disbelief. "This can't be right," he murmured to himself. "It's not possible."

"It's all too possible, Jules," Ransom said grimly. "And all too real."

They moved around to the entrance that led to the large drawing room, where they hoped to find the three Caretakers. John appeared at the door, nearly trampling over Bert in the process.

He was dressed differently than he had been just minutes before in Tamerlane House, and he held a drink in his hand. After a few seconds of stunned disbelief, he set the drink aside and embraced his mentor.

"Knew you'd come," John said, his voice a mix of joy and barely-restrained sorrow. "I knew you'd find a way!"

Behind him they could see Jack, his brother Warnie, and Hugo Dyson. All were dressed very formally and were drinking strong liquor.

There was some confusion as the new arrivals entered and introductions were made. Warnie and Hugo had never met Verne or Bert, and Ransom and Morgan only briefly.

"We're so glad to see you're all right," said Bert. "When the earthquake happened, we worried something had gone terribly wrong."

"Earthquake?" Jack asked, looking at John, who shrugged. "Nothing like that happened. The bridge worked like a charm, but then it vanished. We've been terribly worried all this time about *you*. And when we didn't hear from anyone—"

"All what time?" said Bert. "You just left, not five minutes ago!"

"Bert," Jack said slowly, his voice trembling, "we came home two years ago. We've been trying to reach you the entire time."

Verne closed his eyes as he suddenly realized: They were having a wake. "Then Charles . . . ," he began.

"You've come too late," said Jack. "Charles is dead."

It took a few minutes to let the terrible news sink in before the Caretakers could even speak. Charles was dead—which meant that it was no longer 1943, but 1945. Somehow, the creation of the bridge between worlds had shifted Tamerlane House forward in time two full years.

"We have to speak to Poe," Bert said when he had regained his composure. "He may be able to help."

"What about Poe's portraitist, Basil?" John said, suddenly animated. "He was working on one of Charles. Can he still—"

"He never finished it," Bert interrupted. "Charles asked him not to."

"Oh," said John, suddenly crushed. "But he still has it, doesn't he? It can still be completed, correct?"

"Yes," Bert said, casting a hesitant look at Verne. "But . . ."

"There's something you need to know," Verne said, "but it may be best discussed when we get back to Poe's house. Please, John—trust us on this. Charles has not been abandoned."

"All right," said John, deflated. "I do trust you, Bert."

"We don't even know if we *can* get back," said Ransom, who

seemed to have taken the news of Charles's death worse than any of them. "Do we?"

"We do," said a voice from the door. It was Mark Twain. "We've crossed back and forth several times," he said as he entered the Kilns with Burton close behind. "Tamerlane House, in fact, all of the Nameless Isles, are now connected to Oxford."

It was true. From the garden, all that could be seen was half of a stone bridge, leading to nowhere. But looked at straight on, one could see the ghost images of the other Caretakers and Tamerlane House just beyond.

"Whatever it was that caused this particular problem seems to have ended when the Nameless Isles were wrenched away from the Archipelago," said Twain. "Tamerlane time and Oxford time are the same, now, so it's safe to cross."

"Maybe," said Verne, "but we still have no idea what's caused the discontinuity to begin with."

"That matters less to me," Jack said, wiping tears from his eyes, "than it would have just a week ago, when Charles was still alive."

Warnie and Hugo stayed behind while John and Jack returned across the bridge with the others to tell the bad news about Charles to the rest at Tamerlane House. One among them took the news worse than the rest. The sorrowful howling echoed throughout the isle.

It was Fred. "Awooo . . . ," he howled again, eyes filled with tears. "I—I should have crossed over with him!" the little mammal said, sobbing. "I'm his apprentice! I should have been there! He didn't have to die alone!"

John and Jack both knelt and grasped the small badger by the shoulders. "He didn't, he didn't, Fred," Jack said soothingly. "There were many people with him, all of whom loved and admired him. He wasn't alone."

"Take heart, little apprentice," said Burton in an almost sincere effort to seem supportive. "You'd have been broasted by the fellows at Magdalen the minute they caught sight of you. So really, you saved him a bit of grief already by not having to mourn you."

Strangely enough, Burton's poor attempt at a joke was more buoying to Fred than anything else anyone said, and after a few moments, he regained his composure.

"Does this mean I'm to take his place?" Fred asked Bert. "Not that I'm in a hurry to, or in any way as capable as Master Charles," he added quickly, glancing at John and Jack. "I'm just thinking that in a crisis I don't want the Caretakers to be left shorthanded."

It occurred to John that at that particular moment, between the Caretakers, past and present; the members of the Imperial Cartological Society; and the Messengers, Morgan and Ransom, they were anything but shorthanded when it came to bootstrap Caretaking. But he kept this to himself—Fred didn't need to hear something that made him think he wasn't essential.

Once more the Caretakers Emeritis gathered in the meeting hall, where, for most of them, they had dined just hours before. But for John and Jack, it had been two years.

"The war is all but won," said John. "There's a new American president, and the Germans surrendered only a week ago. It was terrible—especially the waiting, knowing it would have to eventually end. But we stuck it out, and I think Charles held on just long enough to know that we'd done what was needed. And then he let himself go."

"When we didn't hear from you," Jack said, "we feared the worst, especially as the war continued. But then suddenly things turned around—and we realized that our defeat of the Shadow King was finally being reflected in events in our world."

"We're very happy to see you," John said, "even as sad as we are to have lost . . . to have . . ." He stopped, groping for words, and wiped at his eyes. "Well, yes. I wish Charles were here. But tell us: What happened? Obviously the bridge works."

"Works now, you mean," said Shakespeare miserably. All of Rose's consoling words could not bring back his earlier confidence. From his point of view, he'd done worse than fail. He'd failed because he was too confident he'd succeeded.

"The best we have been able to figure," said Morgan, "is that Will's principle was sound, but he missed a few things in the execution."

"Indeed," said Ransom, who was still a bit ashen. "The orbs allowed the Dragonships to pass between worlds, but they were also moving. At some point, they would cross. The bridge didn't move—it was forming a fixed point in both worlds. And because of the discontinuity I discovered, we think that the Nameless Isles were pulled out of Kairos time and into Chronos time, and we lost two years in the process."

"But how is that possible?" asked Jack. "I thought time moved more slowly in the Archipelago."

"It did," said Verne, "but now it appears to be speeding up. We think that's why you couldn't use the trump—the time differential was too great. The cavorite in the bridge let it function enough for you to cross over, but we lost two years in the transition when the chronal stresses became too great, and now we've been completely cut off."

"Tamerlane House is now connected to Oxford," said Ransom, his voice shaky. "But that is nothing compared to what we fear is going on back in the Archipelago."

Before he could elaborate, Ransom's eyes widened, then rolled back in his head as he collapsed to the floor, unconscious.

"What's wrong with him?" Jack asked as they got Ransom to bed in one of the spare rooms. "He looks deathly ill."

"He may be," said Bert. "He's gone past his Prime Time in Chronos time now. We've never seen that happen before."

"His Prime Time?" asked John. "Then he was meant to . . ." He paused. "Like Charles," he said suddenly. "He's *exactly* like Charles."

"An aspect," said Verne. "Not so much a direct analogue of Charles, as your fellow Chaz was. But an aspect is enough. Think of him as a Charles from another dimension—somewhat like your H. G. Wells, Herb, is to our Bert."

"However you choose to think of him," said Bert, "Alvin Ransom is dying."

"It's time to call a full council of Caretakers," said Twain, "and you, as well," he added, waving at Burton. "We need all our friends now, and our old enemies, too."

The group waited to start the council until the elder members of the Caretakers Emeritis had joined them. Some, like Chaucer, had been at dinner the night before. Others, like Malory and Tycho Brahe, had been busy with other matters. But the one they were all waiting for was Edgar Allan Poe.

He was the master of Tamerlane House, and more of an anomaly than Bert was. John was the Principal Caretaker of the *Imaginarium Geographica*; Verne was something called the Prime Caretaker; but Poe stood above them all as an enigmatic adept in matters involving time and space. His abilities and counsel were oracular in nature—he was not always present, not always involved, and did not often offer advice unless Verne specifically requested that he do so. But when he did choose to involve himself in matters at hand, it was both a relief and an added fear. For despite all the good he could do, he only got involved when the situation was most dire.

The rest of the caretakers had been seated for several minutes when Poe finally took his place at the head of the long table. "This note," he said to Twain, "about Rose's visitor. Perhaps we should start there."

Rose recounted the details of her visit from Mother Night two evenings before. Following that, Verne, aided by Morgan and Bert, elaborated on the happenings after the celebration, when they discovered that the trumps weren't working. When they got to the part about the bridge, Shakespeare bravely took the stage himself to explain.

"Interesting," Poe said when he had finished. "You demonstrate the same sort of genius that Arthur Pym had."

"Thank you," said Will.

"You also made the same mistakes," added Poe.

"Oh," said Will.

"Do you think the events are related?" Verne asked. "Could the discontinuity be the fault of the Shadows?"

Poe pondered this. "The Echthroi," he said at last, "exploit weaknesses, but I don't think they are the cause of this. I think we are."

"How so?" asked Twain.

"Independence Day marked another event," said Poe. "The final destruction of the Keep of Time. I think this is what Mother Night was referring to when she said the threads of history had come undone. I think that caused the discontinuity."

"Great," said Burton. "You fools have broken history."

"I hate to admit it, but he's right," said Jack. "We have. And we've just assumed that it would take care of itself, but it hasn't."

"So how do we fix it?" asked John. "It isn't like the *Geographica*, where we can just replace the tower with a book of maps."

"Maybe we can, at that," said Verne. "Time *is* mappable, you know. It's difficult in the extreme, but not impossible."

"Only one among our number has ever had the facility to map time," said Chaucer, "and I know it pains you, Bert, to hear him referred to thusly, but it was our renegade, John Dee."

"Cambridge man," Fred said, before spitting over his left shoulder and winking twice.

"Hey now," said Jack. "Enough of that. Or have you forgotten I'm a Cambridge man too? Or about to be one, anyway."

"Big diff'rence between being drafted an' enlisting," said Fred. "We know your heart will stay pure, Scowler Jack."

"Actually, that's exactly what we were using Morgan, Ransom, and the other adepts to do," said Verne. "We had begun by mapping the Keep of Time itself. The Messengers were our primary exploration force, venturing through each doorway and then reporting on what they found there."

"Ransom was one of the latecomers," Twain added, "though

he certainly made up for his relative inexperience with a marked ability to report on unorthodox environs."

"With their experiences in time travel," John said looking at Burton, Houdini, and Doyle, "it had to be helpful to draw on the Society's collective knowledge. Was that part of the reason you agreed to the truce?"

"It was a bit of a Hail Mary pass on their part," Verne said with a barely concealed smirk. "There was practically nothing left of the original Imperial Cartological Society after the split in the ranks, and other than Burton's core group, all of the members were either missing, dead, or permanently indisposed."

"Permanently indisposed?" asked John.

"Kit Marlowe was stranded on a fictional island, which is entirely different from being stranded on an imaginary one," Chaucer said, his face an impassive mask of memory. "De Bergerac is on a comet, I believe. Or the moon. I forget. Anyway, he's no longer of this physical world. Defoe you know about, and also Coleridge, who still sits in despair on that island past the Edge of the World.

"Wilhelm Grimm was killed by the Shadow King," he continued, "and Byron is on probation, so he will remain out of circulation as either a Caretaker or a member of the Society."

"We can still make that a more permanent state," Percy Shelley grumbled.

"Christina Rossetti is in Fairy Land," Dickens said, consulting a notebook, "and Milton was last said to be in the Underworld somewhere."

"Which underworld?" asked John.

"Does it matter?" said Dickens.

"So," Chaucer concluded, taking a tally on his fingers, "that's six we know of then. Burton, Houdini, Conan Doyle, Byron, and Magwich here—and Dumas *fils* and William Blake unaccounted for."

"Does Magwich really count?" said Jack.

"I heard that," came a whining voice from the next room. "Just because I'm a tree doesn't mean I can't hear you. Trees have feelings too, you know."

"Here," John said as he handed his jacket to Fred. "Cover up the shrub, will you?"

"My pleasure," said Fred as he covered up the vehemently protesting plant. "Time for a nap, Maggot."

"Blake was never one of us," Burton said. "We had . . . diverging opinions about the direction of the Society. One day he simply left. I've not seen him since."

"We can discuss Blake another time," Verne said with a mysterious expression on his face. "For now, the one I'm concerned about, who may be the most significant player on the other side, is still unaccounted for."

"Who was that?" said Dickens, consulting his notes. "I don't—"

"Dee," Poe said. "Dr. John Dee. The renegade."

All eyes turned to Burton, who scowled.

"No one really knows what happened to him," Burton said. "He was the originator of the Society, but he operated more as a mythic archetype than a colleague. I've never met him myself—not face-to-face."

"We'll take your word on that," said Twain, "for now."

"If it's just one man," said Jack, "then why would he be of any concern? Can't we just put him in the 'missing' column next to Blake and young Dumas and focus on other matters that are in the here and now?"

"Not like Blake," Verne said brusquely, "and perhaps not missing. Just because we can't find him doesn't mean he hasn't already found us."

"And he's not likely alone, either," added Burton. "There were always other recruits to the ICS, but Dee was never forthcoming about who they were, or in what numbers he'd recruited them."

"So what *do* we know?" John said, exasperated.

"Only this," said Verne. "Our enemy is more skilled than any here in mapping time, and he may already know everything he needs to know about *us*—while we know almost *nothing* about him."

"I'd like to ask something," said Rose. The Caretakers fell silent, in deference to Poe, who immediately turned to her. "The keep has fallen—that was going to happen regardless. But how does that affect your ability to move through time?"

"That's a good question," said Bert, "which I can't begin to answer."

"I was just thinking," Rose continued, "that if I'm supposed to restore the threads of history, then maybe I'm meant to go back in time and fix the keep before it can be damaged?"

"That's a tall order," said Verne. "Too much of that can just make things worse. And besides, we don't even know if we still *can* travel in time."

"We can certainly find out," Morgan said as he whipped out his watch and twirled one of the dials. "We *are* a part of the Summer Country now, right? So why not have a look? Back in just a bit," he added with a wink. "Don't let the badger steal my chair."

"I would never . . . !" Fred huffed before Laura Glue elbowed him in the ribs. "Uh, I mean, not again, anyway."

Morgan disappeared. There was a soft popping sound as the displaced air rushed in to fill the Messenger-shaped void where he had been standing.

A few moments later, the air pressure of the room increased ever so slightly as he reappeared—but it was not the Hank Morgan who had just left. Or rather, it was, but he was not in the same state. This Hank Morgan was old—impossibly, inconceivably old—and he was dressed as a pirate, exactly like the apparition Charles and John had seen at Magdalen Tower.

"Zero point!" Hank said as his eyes rolled back in his head.

John, Jack, and Twain rushed forward to grasp hold of the old man as he collapsed in front of them. He was sobbing, not from pain, but from relief.

"Oh, mercy," he cried. "I'm back! I'm finally back!"

"You weren't gone but thirty seconds!" Jack said as they lowered the fragile Messenger into a chair.

"Fifteen," Fred said as he offered some silver to boost Morgan's strength. "Twenty, tops."

Morgan's eyes widened in alarm, and he pushed aside the silver and mug of ale proffered by the badger. "Twenty seconds?" he wheezed. "I've been leaping through time trying to return here for over two hundred years!"

"I was going to say he looked pretty decrepit," Houdini said to Doyle behind his hand, "but for two hundred and forty-odd years old, he actually looks pretty champion."

"At least we know when he was," Verne said, "or at least, when he was *last*."

"Tried to send you a message, yes I did," said Morgan.

"We got it," John said, leaning close. "Charles and I—we got your message. How did you do it?"

Morgan closed his eyes. "Chronal stereopticon," he murmured weakly. "Like I made for Shakespeare's Bridge, only better. Projected a message through time, to tell you how to make it work."

"But why did you project it at Magdalen Tower?" John asked. "Why not the Kilns, or our offices?"

Morgan cackled. "Weren't built yet," he said, "not in the seventeenth century. But the tower was. Had to make a trump of what was there then, to reach you here now."

"I wonder how his watch malfunctioned," said John. "Will ours do the same?"

"Yes!" Morgan said as he staggered to his feet and clutched at John's lapels. "But it wasn't a malfunction! There are no zero points! Don't you understand? There was nothing for the Anabasis Machine to cling on to. Nothing to show where, or when, I was. I have spent three lifetimes leaping blindly from instant to instant trying to find my way back to now."

"No zero points?" asked Jack. "What does he mean?"

"A zero point is created by events of great significance," said Bert. "The watches are attuned to all of them through history. He should have been able to leap straight back. And for some reason, he didn't."

"But here you are at last, my dear young lad," Twain said gently, taking Morgan's hands in his own, "and here you'll stay. The watch finally brought you home."

Jack found it a bit disconcerting to hear Twain refer to the more elderly-appearing Morgan as young, but not as disconcerting as he would have when he himself was younger. Still, neither the gesture nor Twain's soothing words seemed to help—Morgan was still frantic.

"That's just it!" he said as he loosed Twain's hands and rummaged around in his pocket. "The watch still doesn't work!"

This, at last, seemed to get Poe's attention, and he leaned farther over the table. "That isn't possible," he said softly. "The cavorite in the watches never loses its energy. They will function indefinitely."

"To keep time, yes," Morgan shot back, clearly incensed by the fact that no one was really paying attention to his protestations, "but not to traverse time. It took me out, then stopped functioning as it's supposed to." He pulled out a rumpled parchment from his pocket and flattened it out on the table. "This is the only reason I'm here now."

It was a map. Slightly charred around the edges, and shot through with a few holes, but a map nonetheless.

The drawing on the parchment was almost holographic in nature and gave the impression of being a palimpsest, as if several drawings had been created, then erased, leaving a faint impression of what had been drawn before under what was now there.

The locus for Tamerlane House and the Nameless Isles was clearly visible in the center, and other markings indicated the placement within the Archipelago of Dreams, but there were additional lines that were almost mathematical in nature, and calculations that involved symbols, pictograms, and runes, all wedded to the location of the islands. It was at once simple and complex, and unlike any map any of the Caretakers had ever seen—the images drawn upon it almost . . . *moved*.

"Is that one of the trumps?" asked John. "It looks too large."

"It *is* too large," countered Jack. "It's one of Merlin's spares, isn't it, Bert? One of the extra sheets he pulled out of the *Geographica*."

Bert moved around the table and peered more closely at the sheet, then at Morgan's harried expression, before turning to the others and nodding. "It is. I didn't know Hank had it, but I'm glad he did."

"He needed a new map, because the old one, the one that catalogued all the zero points, is gone."

"What map?" asked John.

"The keep," said Bert. "The Keep of Time was how we mapped zero points."

"Take this," Hank said to Twain, pressing the parchment into his hand. "Take what I've done and learn from it. You can still find a way. I know you can, Samuel."

"We will, we will," Twain assured him as he leaned him back in a soft chair. "You've done a marvelous job for us, Hank. We're very grateful."

Morgan didn't respond, but instead closed his eyes and took a deep breath. A moment later his watch fell out of his hand and to the floor.

"Ah, me," Twain said heavily. "Good-bye, my noble friend. Sail well into that good night."

The others stared at one another in disbelief. Hank Morgan was dead.

All the various time travel devices . . . were stored in the repository . . .

CHAPTER SIX
Strange Devices

◈

Morgan's body was put into his room to lie in state until the Caretakers could get a better grasp on the escalating crisis. In just one day a Caretaker and a Messenger had died, and another Messenger lay on the edge of death. They returned to the meeting hall, frustrated, saddened, and subdued—most of them, anyway.

"I'm thinking we chose a terrible time to ally ourselves with this lot," Burton said to his two colleagues. "The Caretakers are dropping like flies."

With a sudden explosion of energy that none of them had expected, Mark Twain burst out of his chair and struck Burton full in the jaw with a brutal right cross. Burton flew backward and fell flat on his back, cracking his head against a cabinet.

"What the hell . . . ?" Burton sputtered as Doyle and Houdini helped him to his feet. "I should kill you for that!" he spat at Twain as he glowered, held back only by Doyle's good sense and strong arms.

"Better men have tried," Twain answered as he straightened his cuffs and sat down, "and anyway, I'm already dead, so you'd be trying to harvest when the cows already ate the cabbage. You can be angry at me if you like, but we will have respect in this house, especially for our own fallen."

Burton didn't reply, but relaxed his stance and shrugged off Doyle's grasp. "It's a strange business," he murmured gruffly, "when dead men such as we must mourn another dead man."

"Does he have to stay that way?" Jack asked with a burst of excited insight. "This *is* Tamerlane House! Can't you bring him back with one of the portraits?" He started for the stairs to the upper rooms. "Where's Basil? We need to fetch him, quickly!"

Several of the other Caretakers reached out to Jack to stop him, offering gestures of comfort for the words they knew he was about to hear.

"It's not possible, young Jack," Chaucer said as they moved him back to the table and his seat. "Not for one such as Henry Morgan. I'm sorry."

"How about you?" Jack said to Verne. "And you?" he said to Burton. "Can you make him a tulpa?"

"It doesn't work that way," Burton said dismissively. "For one, it's the same problem—it wouldn't work for Morgan. And anyway, our methods take longer—at least a year would be necessary."

Bert took his protégé by the arms and looked into his eyes. "Jack," he said, "the reason that we cannot create a portrait for Hank Morgan is because he is a Fiction."

Jack blinked and narrowed his eyes. "You mean, as in Samuel's book? But all of us have fictionalized things we have seen and people we've met."

"I don't mean to say he is a fictional *character*," Bert said with emphasis, "but that he is unique—what we refer to as Fictions. Unique works in creation."

Verne stepped in to elaborate. "You know that there are analogues of us all in other times, other worlds, other dimensions. You've even met some of them."

"Like Chaz," Jack said.

"Precisely," said Verne, "but Hank was not like that. He was unique in all the worlds. There was one of him, and one only. There have been others like him, but very, very few."

"Herman Melville," said Chaucer. "Prime Caretaker material, just prime. A brilliant creator, with marvelous insights."

"We considered him before Jules," said Dickens. "No offense, Jules."

"None taken," said Verne.

"He would have been a Caretaker," Dickens continued, "but there were . . . ah, complications. And we moved on."

"Complications?" asked John.

"Crazy as a bedbug," said Hawthorne.

"Nathaniel!" Dickens exclaimed. "Bad form."

Hawthorne sighed. "His creative genius was coupled with madness," he explained to the others. "We could never be certain which of the traits would become dominant, and we couldn't take the risk that the insanity would prevail."

"We still wanted him," Twain interjected, glancing sternly at Hawthorne, "if only to have him as an apprentice to our group. That was when we discovered he was, in fact, a Fiction. Unique."

"We tried to get him ourselves, for the Society," said Burton, "but we noted the Caretakers' apparent disinterest and withdrew. If we had only known . . ."

"It would have done you little good, Richard," Twain said in as stern a voice as they had ever heard. "He would not have become a tulpa, and as we discovered, painting a portrait does not work on Fictions. It drove Basil nearly insane, mixing and remixing the resins to try to fix what he saw as his own mistake. But it had nothing to do with the resins, or the quality of the painting. It was because Melville could not be duplicated. And Hank Morgan was unique in exactly the same way."

"Despite Morgan's rashness in testing the theory," said Poe, "Rose's suggestion still has merit. There may be a point in time where something may be fixed. And as he demonstrated, zero points may still be created—and mapped."

"We can't stop the fall of the keep," said John. "That risks sacrificing our victory over the Winter King."

"I wasn't even thinking that far back," said Rose. "What if we just went back far enough to avoid the discontinuity?"

"To keep Tamerlane House from being separated from the Archipelago?" asked Chaucer.

"No," Rose said. "I was thinking that we'd start by saving Charles and Mr. Morgan."

"You're a sweet girl," said Bert. "Your heart is in the right place. But before we could even try, we'd have to find a way to do it. And we already discovered that the watches will not work."

"Let's try the repository then," Verne said, rising, "before anyone else tries something rash."

The repository was by far the largest room the companions had seen within Tamerlane House, with the sole exception of the Trophy Hall that Poe kept in the basement. It contained, among other things, a stuffed tyrannosaurus rex, a giant American penny, and both halves of the Titanic—from which, Poe had claimed, they had gotten all the dinnerware used at Tamerlane

House. John kept meaning to turn one of the plates over to check for the maker's insignia, but always forgot until after the tables had been cleared.

All the various time travel devices used by Verne and Bert were stored in the repository, Poe explained, including the ones that had never quite worked as they were meant to. There was one that resembled a blue police box from London—"Stolen by a doctor with delusions of grandeur," said Poe—one that was simply a large, transparent sphere—"Created by a scientist with green skin and too much ego," said Verne—and one that was rather ordinary by comparison.

"This one looks like an automobile," John said admiringly, "with wings."

"The doors open that way for a reason," Verne explained, "we just never figured out what it was. The inventor of this particular model tried integrating his designs into a car, an airplane, and even a steam engine train. He was running a crackpot laboratory in the Arizona desert, and he never realized that it was not his inventions themselves, but his proximity to some sort of temporal fluctuation in the local topography, that allowed them to work."

"What happened to him?" asked Jack.

"He'd get the machines up to one hundred and six miles per hour," said Bert, "and then he'd run out of fuel and promptly get arrested by whatever constabulary had been chasing him. The sad part was that Jules figured out if he'd just gone two miles an hour faster, he'd likely have been successful in his attempt."

"And this one?" asked John. "It looks like a treadmill."

"The Cosmic Treadmill, if you please," sniffed da Vinci. "It may have never operated as I planned it to, but the theory behind it is sound."

"Only if you can find someone who is capable of running one hundred eight miles per hour," said Bert.

"It's hardly my fault that human potential has not yet risen to match my invention," da Vinci replied. "At any rate, I'm not going to stand around here just to be insulted. I'm going back to my portrait."

He stormed off in a huff, and Bert flipped open a book to make a note. "Insult the treadmill, da Vinci leaves the room," he murmured, clicking his tongue as he finished and snapped the book shut. "Good to remember. He's going to drive me up a wall someday."

John and Jack moved away from the mobile devices toward one far more elaborate. It resembled a theater balcony, with a low banister across the front and a wide, red velvet seat in the center. In front of the seat was an instrument panel filled with switches and dials, and behind was a large metallic disk.

"This is the one you traveled in, isn't it, Bert?" John asked, circling the machine with unabashed admiration. "It looks brilliant."

Bert folded his hands behind his back and blushed. "Well, yes. Thank you, John. It's the only machine here created entirely from my own design."

"After all the grief you fellows gave Arthur and me," Houdini complained, "it's a bit insulting to find you sharing Archipelago secrets in your books."

"Technically speaking, the machine and my accounting of the journey were not of the Archipelago," said Bert. "The trip was done entirely in London."

"Also, it wasn't so much that you broke the rules," Verne chided, "but that you were so noisy about doing so."

"The man has a point," Burton agreed, glaring at Houdini and Doyle. "Now will you please be quiet?"

"You have a lot of machines here," said John. "Will any of them work better than the watches do?"

"That's a difficult question to answer," said Bert.

"Here's the main problem we have encountered," said Verne. "While it's true that we have discovered many ways to travel through time, each way works only once for each traveler. Once, and never again."

"The main reason we turned almost entirely to the watches— the Anabasis Machines," said Bert, "is because they *could* be used over and over again. What they didn't have is range—to be able to go more than a millennium required either a Lanterna Magica, which was limited in use too, or one of these devices."

Chewing on his lip, John turned to Bert as another piece fell into place. "So your first journey out, when you traveled eight hundred thousand years in the future . . . ," he began.

Bert took a deep breath, then nodded. The sorrow was undisguised, and it occurred to John that perhaps the old man wanted them to realize the depth of his feeling on the matter.

"Once, and never again," Bert said, echoing Verne. "I took one of our earliest devices, a contraption designed by Leonardo da Vinci and assembled by Nemo, Bacon, and the animals, and a few minutes into the trip, I made a terrible miscalculation. I tried to correct it, but the knob broke off in my hand. By the time I was able to replace it, I had traveled more than eight thousand centuries."

"With such an accident," said Verne, "there was no way to track or follow him. He was utterly on his own."

"As you found out, I discovered I could be happy there," said Bert, "but I also thought I could leave again and return at will—that the accident was only that. Not that I couldn't go back."

"So when you returned here . . . ," Jack began.

"We didn't know," Bert said with painful bluntness. "We were monkeys playing with . . . well, with a time machine. I believed that I could easily move back and forth as I liked, and so when Aven was only a few years old, I offered to take her on a short trip to the Archipelago, to visit, only to discover I'd abandoned her mother in the far future. I can only imagine," he said tearfully, "how lonely she must have gotten."

"Well, from a certain point of view," offered John, "she hardly knows you've left. That is one of the advantages to traveling in time, isn't it? That you can go back almost to the moment that you left, with no one the wiser?

"After all," he added conclusively, "isn't that what you did with us when you returned us to the Inn of the Flying Dragon shortly after we'd left?"

"Not quite," said Verne. "Always moving forward, remember? You still aged the days you were in the future—you didn't shed those years when you came back."

Jack nodded in understanding. True, Bert and Aven could possibly return to almost the same point they'd left, if a means for returning could be finely tuned enough to do so. But they would be the age they were now—an elderly Herbert George Wells instead of a young adventurer, and a pirate queen named Aven, a mature, fully grown woman, rather than a child bubbling with laughter on her father's lap as they vanished into time.

Like Morgan, they could go back, but they would not be the

same two people who had left. It was possible that Weena, Aven's mother, would not miss them at all, but it would become immediately apparent to all three of them that something had been lost—three lifetimes together, never to be recaptured.

"Why do you think he gave up being a full-time Caretaker?" Verne murmured. "Stellan was killed, true, but Bert had become semiretired already—although he never took it to the extent that Jamie did in refusing to be involved at all."

"So all those occasions, all these years," John said, "all the moments when you were unavailable to us as a mentor . . ."

Bert choked back a sob and gave one short, sharp nod of his head.

Verne put a steadying hand on his friend's shoulder. "Yes," he said gently. "He was here, in the repository, trying device after device in hopes he might finally be able to return to Weena."

"The most ironic thing about mourning her?" Bert said as he wiped a sleeve across his eyes. "She won't even be born for more centuries than I can count."

"Can you leave her a message somehow?" John asked. "Like Hugo did when he went back to Arthur's time, with the message he wrote in the Booke of Dayes?"

Bert shook his head. "I was there, remember, lad? In that much time, cultures fade and vanish. To be sure, it's not geologic time, or even Deep Time—but eight thousand centuries is too long to expect anything familiar to persist. No Caretakers, no Archipelago to speak of—at least in the form we know it today, or whatever day this is. The libraries were gone, the buildings, the—" He stopped and stared curiously into space.

"No, wait," he continued after a moment. "There *was* one

artifact that did survive, although I seldom spoke to her myself. She was a frosty one."

"The Sphinx!" Fred exclaimed. "That's who you mean, isn't it? My father and Quixote told me about her."

"Yes," said Bert, "but other than her, I saw almost nothing—*nothing*—in the future that had survived from our time, or any other. Nothing that she would be able to recognize, at any rate."

"Hmm," said John. "I wonder why they only work once? There has to be a physical principle at the heart of the dilemma somewhere."

"There's a rule of conservation of energy of travel in time," said Poe, who hadn't spoken since they'd entered the repository. "A journey into the past must be balanced by one into the future."

"This is one of the reasons we know as much as we thought we did about the near future," Verne put in. "All the voyaging Hank and Alvin were doing into the near past had to be counterbalanced with similar trips into the near future."

"What we didn't understand at the time," said Bert, "is that in time, distance equals energy. Thus, a trip into the deeper past had to be counterbalanced by one into the far-flung future."

"What happened when you didn't balance the energies?" asked Jack.

"It wasn't an academic question," said Verne. "The energies did just fine at balancing themselves—sometimes in a catastrophic fashion."

"We lost Pym that way," Bert said with a reproachful glance at Poe, who remained impassive. "Arthur took an ordinary trip out into what should have been the fourth century. Instead, as far as we have been able to determine, he was ripped from his planned pathway and flung into Deep Time. To where—ah, when, we have no idea."

"Hank didn't have to come back, but he did anyway," Jack said in awe. "He spent two centuries trying to get back just to tell us what he'd learned."

"Small acts of conscience are what make the world, and eternity," said Poe. "Those little choices, those moments, when everything diverges. Those are what we are trying to preserve."

"We didn't change the past, we changed our own future," said Jack. "You said that it was necessary that we do so, and jump forward, because according to a 'possible' future history, we already had."

Poe inclined his head. "That is so."

"But," Jack went on, not giving ground, "it seems to me all we've done for decades now is meddle in time trying to make up for mistakes we'd already made! Instead of trying to patch up the mistakes, and fight the Winter King over and over again—"

"He's dead now," Fred offered. "The bad part, anyway."

"I know that, Fred," said Jack. "But that's my point. No disrespect to our own dead friend, but if all this grief and suffering is because of the accident that destroyed the Keep of Time, why *don't* we go back and try to stop ourselves from doing it? Or better yet, find a way to go and defeat the Winter King in the first place, so that all the rest never needed to have happened at all?"

"It didn't have to happen, although it did," said Poe. "Master Wells, do you have the book?"

Bert's eyes widened in surprise, and he looked not at Poe, but at Verne. He paused a moment, as if considering a response; then, without answering, he stepped out of the room, only to return a moment later carrying one of the Histories.

Bert handed the book to Verne, who skimmed through the pages to the one he expected Poe was seeking. He tapped the page and handed it to Jack.

"This was, at one point in time, another future history," Poe said, looking Jack directly in the eye. "It was what we call a 'might-have-been.' That's a history that has not happened, but is likely to. In some cases, a might-have-been can even be viewed, as this one once was, by Masters Wells, Verne, and Sigurdsson. They recorded what they witnessed here and shared it with only one of their successors."

"Charles," Jack murmured as he scanned the page. "Charles knew about this?"

Poe didn't reply. Jack continued reading, and suddenly the blood drained from his face. "Dear god in heaven," he breathed. "I—I never realized . . ."

"What is it?" asked John, a look of concern etched on his face. "What does it say?"

Jack looked up, his face still ashen. "The destruction of the keep wasn't supposed to happen," he said slowly, as if he could not quite accept the words he was speaking. "In fact, according to this, we weren't supposed to reach the keep at all."

"Then what did happen?'

"You were the three Caretakers of prophecy," said Verne, "who were meant to defeat the Winter King. And you did, during your *first* encounter."

"We did?" John said, astonished. "What went wrong?"

"Indeed," said Bert, "but nothing went wrong, practically speaking. What happened is that something went *right*."

"Our first meeting," Jack said to John, pointing with a shaking finger at the pages, "when the *Black Dragon* overtook the *Indigo Dragon*. The Winter King offered me a choice, remember? To join him?"

"And you declined," John said, meeting his friend's eyes, "as you knew you must."

"But that's just it," said Jack. "I almost didn't decline. I nearly chose to go with him! And according to this book, that's exactly what I did!"

John looked at Bert and Verne, who didn't reply. Their silence was confirmation enough.

"A man's greatest enemy is himself," Twain said as he lit his pipe, "and that day, in that might-have-been, Jack was defeated, and he sided with Mordred. You—and he—never went to the keep, but back toward Paralon, where Nemo was already prepared to engage in a battle. The *Black Dragon* attacked, and this time, was defeated. The *Imaginarium Geographica* was recovered, and Mordred was bound, and imprisoned in the keep along with his brother, and," he added, eyes glittering, "you."

Twain was pointing his pipe at Jack, who lowered the book to the table and gently closed it. "After that, Artus still became king. Nemo never died. E.R. Eddison becomes the new third Caretaker. . . ."

"The Great War ended a year later," said Poe, "and this new conflict, which some call the Second Great War, never began—but not because Mordred's shadow, as the Chancellor, wasn't there. It never started because the Archipelago was in harmony with the Summer Country. The entire world moved forward into an idealized society, much like the kind Master Wells espouses in his writings. And all because, in that moment, you succumbed to Mordred."

"I—I wish I didn't know about this," Jack said wearily. "It's too great a burden to bear. That all the grief of two worlds is my fault..."

"You misunderstand," Verne said gently. "We don't tell you this so you'll be burdened. We're telling you so you'll understand how great, how important it is to be able to choose."

"And was my choice good or bad?" Jack asked. "I'm not sure I know."

"Yes, you do," answered Bert. "You always have, Jack. You chose according to the dictates of your heart. And you chose wisely and well. It was in that choice that you set the course of the future, and we have rallied all the powers at our disposal to see that it was not a choice made in vain."

"My heart was tempted," said Jack. "I really was considering his offer. I didn't really know John or Charles. I didn't know you. And..." He paused. "I was probably just trying to impress Aven, if you want to know the whole truth. It wasn't an epic choice of good versus evil. It was just a choice. I'm going to have to grapple with that, Bert."

"We all do," Verne put in, "every day. We all grapple with the two sides of ourselves—but it's not what you consider that matters, Jack. It's what you do. And when it did matter, you chose not to betray the trust of your friends."

"Small moments of conscience," Poe repeated. "Those are worth the world, and more. So to answer your question, yes— there are zero points in time wherein we could have changed a might-have-been to an is. But in doing so, we would have lost you, and lost the man you have become. We would have Un-Named your choice. And that is the one thing we could not countenance."

"I'm glad I never knew," said Jack. "It would have been harder, not easier, to choose."

"The future Histories are guides," said Verne, "not instruction manuals. But they should never replace free agency. That's why we didn't tell you what we knew before—we needed you to choose, freely and unafraid."

"I don't see how we can risk trying any of these machines," said John. "If they only work once for each of us, then there's no point in risking another accident. We'd just be losing someone every time we tried to find a zero point that can be changed. We simply don't know enough about what's happened."

"We need someone who knows a lot more about time travel," said Jack, "and if that isn't any of you, then I'm out of options. We'd be better off sending Hugo again."

"That would at least be interesting," a voice said from the ceiling, "considering the mess he made the last time."

"Cats should be eaten, not heard," Burton said, irritated. "What are you doing down here, anyway?"

"He's a Cheshire cat," said Bert. "He goes pretty much wherever he wants to go."

"Uh-huh," said Burton. "Poe doesn't strike me as an animal lover."

"You'd be surprised," Bert replied. "He keeps an orangutan in the larder—mostly to guard the pistachio nuts. But the cat belongs to John—or more properly, John belongs to it."

"It sort of adopted me," John said as Grimalkin's torso disappeared, leaving a head and tail floating in midair. "It used to be Jacob's cat, I think."

"And Edmund Spenser's before that," added Bert, "and . . ."

He stopped and scratched his head. "Who had him before that?"

"Dante, I think," said Verne, "but I think Roger Bacon had him first."

"He's sort of the animal familiar for Tamerlane House," Bert said. "It's hard to remember a time when he wasn't there."

"He wasn't there five minutes ago," said Jack. "And then suddenly, he was."

"That's a Cheshire cat for you," said Bert.

"Grimalkin," John said as a tail appeared above his head. "What *are* you doing down here?"

"Offering advice," the Cheshire cat said as its head appeared, sans body. "There is an expert in time who is here and not in the Archipelago."

"I hadn't actually considered him," Verne said thoughtfully, "but if all the Nameless Isles are here, the chances are good he is too."

"What are you suggesting, cat?" asked Twain.

"You already know what to do," Grimalkin said. "You need to seek the counsel of the Watchmaker."

CHAPTER SEVEN
The Watchmaker

✦

Having made this pronouncement, the Cheshire cat promptly began ignoring everyone in the room. Verne stroked his beard in thought, considering the idea. John and Jack had no idea what to think. Houdini was intrigued, as were Doyle and Burton. Having been separated from the Caretaker culture for so long, they knew very little if anything about the being who made the watches.

"If that's such a wise course of action to take," Burton said to the cat, "perhaps you would like to go along and make introductions."

"For one thing, I'm not allowed there," Grimalkin said as he licked one of his paws in apparent disinterest. "He is a Maker, one of only seven in all of creation, and as such, creatures like myself are not welcomed. Also, there are dogs."

"What do you mean creatures like yourself?" asked John. "You're a cat."

"So you understand," Grimalkin replied. His lines were beginning to fade, and his tail had already disappeared. "Cats and Makers should not mix, especially this cat, and this Maker. It was bad enough when we saw each other socially, but this is business, so it's best for all that I stay behind."

The Watchmaker . . . had a prominent nose . . . and small, close-set eyes.

"I'll go," said Verne. "He knows me well enough, and Bert will be needed to explain what's happened. John and Jack as well."

"I insist—," Burton began.

"No," Verne said, cutting him off. "Principal Caretakers only." His expression said that he would countenance no argument on this point, and Burton withdrew.

"What about me?" asked Fred. "Shouldn't I go along as well?"

"In other circumstances, yes," Verne said, patting the badger supportively, "but not here. The Cheshire cat is correct—the Watchmaker does not socialize well with your kind."

"With animals, you mean?" said Fred, chagrined.

"No," Verne answered. "With intelligent animals."

"Mmm," Fred mused. "That's a little better, I guess."

"I thought we were cut off from the Archipelago," said Jack. "How are we to get to him?"

"He's not in the Archipelago," Verne said with a sly grin. "In fact, he's much closer than you realize."

Within a hour the tides were low enough that the companions were able to cross to the small island in the northeastern corner of the Nameless Isles, where Verne said the Watchmaker could most likely be found. "He's often here, working," the Frenchman explained as they waded through the shallow water. "He isn't confined, as Merlin was."

"Is he like the Cartographer, then?" John asked.

"In some ways yes, in others, no," Verne replied. "We don't know much about him, to be honest. We know he's old, very, very old, but doesn't look it. He's a friend of Samaranth but seldom speaks of him and how they met. And once, when I came to see him with no advance notice, I saw him—only it was not him. He appeared to be a twelve-foot-tall mantis. I blinked, and an instant later he was just a man again."

"Did you ask him about that?" asked Jack.

Verne laughed under his breath. "I did. He apologized for being dressed too formally and said he had not yet had time to change after another meeting."

"Intriguing," said John. "So he isn't human, then?"

"Oh, he's human," said Bert, "or at least, he started as one. Whatever else he became, who can say?"

The companions traversed the next hollow, where Verne signaled for them to stop. Up above them were three massive dogs standing guard at the crest of the hill.

One was the size of a normal, large dog. The next was the size of a small pony. And the third was the size of an ox. All three had massive round eyes the size of dinner plates—and those eyes were fixed intently on these possible trespassers.

"Ho, Fios," Verne said as he raised a hand in greeting.

"Well met, Master Verne," the smallest of the dogs replied. "Is your hunting good?"

"It is," Verne replied. "Ho, Luaths."

"Well met, Master Verne," the second dog said, sniffing. "One of your friends—he smells of cat."

John frowned. "Uh, sorry about that."

Verne looked slightly alarmed but continued to smile. "Ho, Tron," he said to the largest dog. "May we pass?"

"Well met, Master Verne," the dog replied, stepping aside to make an opening between himself and the other dogs. "You may pass."

The four companions walked between the huge animals and down the other side of the hill, where there was a small structure made of stone and marble. It resembled a crypt, or an elaborate barrow, and it had a broad door that opened onto steps that led to a shallow chamber.

"That was a bit chilling," Jack said as he and Bert removed four torches from a niche in the wall. "I suppose if you're being guarded by fellows like that you don't need fancy locks or a riddle in code."

"Exactly," Verne said as he lit the torches. "The dogs, whose names mean Knowledge, Swiftness, and Heaviness, incidentally, are good judges of character. They go by scent alone—anyone who doesn't pass is ripped to pieces."

"So the cat thing . . . ," John began.

"Oh, I'm sure it would have been nothing," said Verne as he stepped down into the darkness, "although for a moment there, I did think it was a shame we hadn't had Basil start a portrait for you yet."

Inside the chamber a great stone tablet was set into the earth and ringed about with smaller stones, all covered with runes.

Jack touched some of the stones, which were worn smooth with age. He looked questioningly at John, who shook his head. "They're beyond my skill," he said. "They may be some sort of proto-Aramaic, or Akkadian. The forms are vaguely familiar, but I can't suss out the structure."

"Not Akkadian," said Verne. "Think older."

"Cuneiform? Sanskrit?"

"Older," said Verne. "Poe thinks they may be prehuman."

"What can possibly be prehuman?" said Jack. "Except . . ."

"Angelic," said Bert. "There's no way to know for sure, but that's our belief. We haven't dared ask the Watchmaker."

"For fear he won't tell you?" asked John.

"No," said Verne. "For fear he *might*."

Bert placed his watch into an indentation in one of the stones. Suddenly the great stone slab began to slide back into the hill, revealing a narrow set of steps that dropped away into the darkness.

Bert nodded in satisfaction as he pocketed the watch and lit up the torch he was carrying. "It's always a comfort to do that," he said, grinning. "It's like a ritual of acceptance, to ask for entry and be approved."

"I'm all for security," said Jack, "but really, after the dogs, this might be overkill."

"Oh, we only just put the dogs here seven years ago," said Bert as he stepped down onto the stone stairway. "Verne thought it was time to start considering some extra security, just in case."

"How long had he gone without the extra security?" John asked as he followed Bert.

Bert shrugged. "How old are the runes? Those were the first safeguards set up. I really can't tell you when."

John looked back at Jack, and they traded an expression of wonderment. The runes were deep, and carved in granite. To have been worn smooth by the wind and rain would take hundreds, if not thousands, of years. Their suspicion that the runes were Angelic in nature might not be so wild an idea after all.

Wordlessly they followed their mentor into the earth as the tablet slid closed above them.

✦   ✦   ✦

The passageway was neither steep nor narrow, and the torches they carried provided more than enough light for the companions to clearly see the steps above and below. The descent to the Watchmaker's cavern did not take long—less than twenty minutes passed from the time they entered until they reached a place that was well-lit enough for them to extinguish their torches.

The enormous room looked to John as if someone had filtered a cave from one of Jacob Grimm's stories through a London clockmaker's shop, and then sprinkled in some Greek myths for good measure.

There were mirrors of all shapes and sizes spread throughout the space, mingled with crystal formations and stalagmites. Each one reflected not just the observers, but also some additional form—some were human; some, like the giant mantis Verne had mentioned, were not. They appeared as ghost images laid over the real reflection.

John found himself in front of a tall mirror that showed a rough-looking woman, dressed in skins and carrying a Bronze Age hammer. For a moment John thought she was real enough to touch, and he reached out with his hand.

"I wouldn't if I were you," Bert murmured, grabbing his hand, "unless you fancy living out your years in a form very different than you'd imagined."

Verne moved around the others and walked to the Watchmaker, who had been too absorbed in his work to notice he had company.

Predictably, he was sitting at a broad workbench amidst a scattering of tools, wires, cogs, and other sundry items that had no apparent purpose. Some of the objects were made of gleaming metal, while others were obviously stone. At the moment he seemed to be trying to coax a miniature sun into a porcelain clock.

The Watchmaker himself was shorter than the companions, but not noticeably older. He had a prominent nose that curved up and into his brow, and small, close-set eyes. His hair was black and slicked back over his head out of the way of his face, so as not to obscure his vision as he worked.

He was dressed simply in a tunic and breeches, and he wore a thick leather apron covered with pockets that were all laden with tools. On the companions' approach, he stood and greeted each of them, shaking their hands and repeating John's and Jack's names.

"I've met so many people over the centuries, you see," he said in explanation, "that I find repeating the names helps me to recall them. Of course, the fact that you are Caretakers who bear examples of my handiwork will help to narrow it down a bit," he added, winking conspiratorially.

On his prompting, both John and Jack pulled out their watches for him to examine. "Nice, very nice," the Watchmaker proclaimed on seeing Jack's, which was all silver, with a silver bas-relief dragon on the cover. "Egyptian. Or maybe Chinese. I forget. I can never keep track of these young cultures and the things they do—but I know when they've done something worth incorporating into my own work."

He moved on to John's watch. "Ah, the classic," he murmured approvingly. "Silver case, silver chain, glazed ceramic disk with the Red Dragon on it." He turned the case over and noted the engraving: CAVEO PRINCIPIA.

The Watchmaker looked up at John appraisingly. "You're the

Principal Caretaker, then?" He looked at Verne. "Well, French-man? Is he worthy?"

Verne nodded. "Eminently so."

"Good enough," said the Watchmaker as he handed the watch back to John. "Not that my opinion should matter, overmuch. You have a harder row to hoe than I."

"For a Watchmaker, you don't seem to have many actual, uh, watches hanging around," Jack said to their host. "No offense."

"Why would I want to surround myself with watches?" said the old man matter-of-factly. "I spend a great deal of time making them, but they aren't an all-encompassing obsession."

"How many have you made?" asked John.

"Several hundred for the Caretakers, of course," the Watchmaker replied, "and perhaps fewer for others."

"You make watches for people other than Caretakers?" John replied before Verne could caution him not to ask. "Isn't that dangerous?"

The Watchmaker fixed John with a gaze that was so intense it was almost a physical blow, and his smile belied the gravity of his words. "I am not the judge of all the Earth," he said, unblinking, "nor do I wish to be."

"These are very interesting mirrors," Jack said, trying to steer the conversation in a less tense direction. He was peering at an oblong one that reflected some sort of multi-tentacled creature. "They don't actually reflect very well."

"They reflect well enough for me," said the Watchmaker, "as they should, since they are my mirrors. What good would my mirrors do to me if they reflected someone else better than I?"

"I guess you have a point," Jack admitted. "Is that a winged centaur?" He pointed to a large rectangular mirror above a worktable.

"It is," replied the Watchmaker, "when that's what I want to be."

John threw a surreptitious glance at Jack, who widened his eyes in response. Whatever this Watchmaker was, he was not a kind of creature they had met before. It was no wonder he was friends with Samaranth—they were similar in both mystery and temperament.

"You all have watches," said the Watchmaker, "so I expect you have come for some other reason."

"We've come," Verne began, "because they don't seem to be working properly. In fact, one of the Messengers has died because he could not return to us in, ah, time."

"Not working?" the Watchmaker exclaimed. "Improbable. Let me take a look."

Verne handed over his watch, and the Maker looked at it for barely a moment before he handed it back. "The watch is fine," he proclaimed. "Something else must be broken."

"History," said Bert. "History has come undone."

"History?" the Watchmaker repeated. "History is a self-defining term. By necessity, it is an accounting of the past—and that past is not real, not solid. At least, not as much as we'd like to believe.

"The present is real. The future is malleable. And the past is both, because although all stories are *true*, some of them never *happened*.

"Events and accountings may become undisputed components of history not merely because of the truth they hold, but because of their perpetuity: The stories we believe are the stories we know."

"He talks just like Merlin used to," Jack said to John. "I never thought I'd miss it so."

"Merlin?" the Watchmaker asked. "I know that name, don't I?"

"The Cartographer of Lost Places," said Verne.

"Oh, yes," said the Watchmaker. "I remember him now. The young stallion with fire in his belly."

"Young?" Jack exclaimed. "Merlin is one of the oldest people I ever met."

"Youth is a relative term," the Watchmaker replied. "I prefer to think of it as a state of mind."

"I know a lot of youthful students who might argue that point," said Jack.

"I've no doubt you do," the Watchmaker replied. "That's what gives my point of view credibility. Everyone argues against it at first, but eventually they all come around. So," he said to Verne, "how is young Merlin?"

"Gone," Verne said simply. "Freed from Solitude, just before the Keep of Time fell."

"Ah," the Watchmaker said, leaning back in his chair. "I suspected that might be why you've come. Sit, and tell me what's been occurring."

As quickly as they were able, the four Caretakers related all the events that had happened, including the mystery of the discontinuity.

"It's not a mystery," the Watchmaker said when they had finished. "Without the Keep of Time, there is nothing to connect Chronos and Kairos, and Kairos itself is loosed.

"Chronos time is merely a record of the passage of objects

through physical space," he explained, "but Kairos time is what gives those events meaning. This is why your watches cannot find any zero points. The meaning has been lost. The connection is gone."

"Is that why there were doors in the keep?" asked Jack. "To connect to zero points in time?"

"The doors merely acted as focal points for the energies within the keep," the Watchmaker said. "Once attuned to a specific time, they would continue to work, as you noted with the false tower the Barbarian—Burton—built for the Shadow King."

"And the door that Hugo Dyson stepped through in Oxford," added John. "That makes sense to me."

The Watchmaker nodded approvingly. "The Barbarian's design was faulty to begin with—the doors opened to the same energies, and had you not dispatched it, it would have no doubt eventually fallen on its own accord. But it was in his original premise that he made his most grievous error. The doors were not the aspect of the keep that made it function—that was something integral to the keep itself. Something about the construction design, and the stones used, and perhaps even the runes carved into the stones. The doors focused the energies to allow passage, but the Keep of Time served a larger function: It anchored Chronos and Kairos. And now that the anchor has been lost, time is flowing freely in the Archipelago, and there is no way to harness it again."

"How can we repair it?" John asked. "We've gone back in time before and managed to not do so badly. We believe we can do so again—we just don't know where to start, or how to get there without the watches."

"So, you need the watches to fix time, but you cannot use the watches until you already have."

"A paradox?" asked Jack.

"A pickle," said the Watchmaker.

"I wish we were able to consult Samaranth on this," John said miserably. "I think he'd have an idea or three as to what to do."

"I spoke with him before the fall of the keep," the Watchmaker said. "He anticipated that this might happen—but he is also reluctant to participate in the matter."

"You've spoken to Samaranth?" John exclaimed. "Did he say anything else?"

"All that he would volunteer was to say that as he has already given you the means to solve this problem, he is not obligated to do anything further. A Son of Adam put these events into motion, and only a Son of Adam should put them right."

"He isn't going to help us, then," said John.

The only response the Watchmaker gave was a steady, almost sorrowful gaze, and silence.

Jack's shoulders slumped. "What are we to do now?"

"Find a way to create zero points," the Watchmaker said. "Find a way to give meaning to Chronos again. And then you will be able to use the watches."

"We *have* traveled through time without the watches before," said John, "when we used a trump from the future, remember?"

"Except that didn't really work out so well the last time," said Bert. "Needed a bit of a push to get through. And you lost seven years of Chronos time. We can't risk another loss like Hank—not when the trumps aren't working properly anyway."

"We never discovered who your mysterious benefactor was

either," said Verne. "The old man in the white room."

"People have a way of becoming their own benefactors," said the Watchmaker. "That may be the case here."

"Not the future," Jack said, thinking about the trumps. "That won't help. We need to go into the past."

"The Histories?" asked John. "Can we use those?"

"They're just books," said Bert, thinking. "No spatial or temporal properties to them."

"But," said Jack, snapping his fingers, "we do have something with those properties. Remember the map that Hank brought with him? He said it was what brought him to Tamerlane House. He used a map to go through space and time. And he made it using one of the spare pages from the *Geographica*."

"I'd almost forgotten!" Bert exclaimed. "I have the rest of those extra pages, back at Tamerlane House."

"If we can use those to create zero points," said Jack, "then we'll have something to attune the watches to. We can create a sort of chronal *Geographica*."

"A sort of Archipelago of Lost Years," the Watchmaker said as a thoughtful expression flashed across his face. "It could be done in such a way. Yes, exactly so. In fact, one of your own tried such a thing many years ago. He even came to be called by a name that reflected this: the Chronographer of Lost Times."

"He went renegade," Verne said with a careful look at Bert. "We haven't seen him since, and have no idea how to find him."

"Ah, that's right," the Watchmaker said. "I did hear about that. There's no way to contact him, then?"

Verne shook his head. "Not that we know of."

The Watchmaker spread his hands and tipped his head. "It

seems simple then," he said. "You need to find *another* Cartographer. Another Cartographer of Lost Places. You have apprentice Caretakers," he added, gesturing at John and Jack. "Surely there were also apprentice Cartographers?"

Bert sighed heavily and traded resigned glances with Verne. "There were, in fact, a number of individuals who trained with Merlin, but replacing him isn't going to be anywhere near that easy," he said wearily. "To do what the Cartographer did, to attain his skill and intuition, would take generations. Centuries, perhaps. And no one I know who studied with him possesses either. Not to the degree we would need."

Verne pursed his lips and nodded tersely at John and Jack in answer to their unspoken question. There had been one apprentice and one only who might have taken the Cartographer's place: Hank Morgan. But he had been drawn away by his escapades through time with Verne. Ironically, his experiences with time travel would have made him an even more ideal choice to do what the Watchmaker said was necessary. And now, just when they discovered he might be the one man they needed most, it was too late.

"Remember what Samaranth said," the Watchmaker reminded them. "You have the tools you need to fix this. All you need to do is believe that you can, and then do it." He turned back to his workbench. The audience with the Caretakers was over.

"Thank you for all you've told us," Verne said, bowing. "Hopefully, much good will come of it."

"All good things happen in time," the Watchmaker said. "Trust in that wisdom, as I have."

"A chronal *Geographica?*" John murmured to Jack. "Do you really think we can create one?"

"Someone already has," the Watchmaker cautioned without pausing in his work or glancing up. "The watches still work, so time is flowing. Someone's found a way to begin mapping time, and unless you discover who is doing so and why, your race may already be lost."

It occurred to John that the Watchmaker's last remark may have referred to the human race, and not the ensuing conflict to somehow fix the flow of time in the Archipelago, but by the time he had the presence of mind to ask, the old Maker was already engrossed in his work, and Verne was closing the door, a finger to his lips.

CHAPTER EIGHT
The Black Dragon

✦

The march back to Tamerlane House was largely silent, as each of the Caretakers pondered what they had learned from the Watchmaker. The visit had birthed almost as many questions as it answered, but still, it seemed there was no way out of their dilemma. If there was no way to traverse time, then there would be no way to fix it. And worse, it seemed that far from reuniting the two worlds, they had lost the Archipelago of Dreams completely.

"We move into the future one second at a time," John murmured to no one in particular. "It seems it would be an easy enough thing to move a few days into the past."

"I know what you wished to ask him, John," said Verne as they began their crossing to the central island. "It would not have aided you to know."

"Sometimes information is a comfort," John countered. "I'd like to have known if it was possible."

"To make Charles's death into a zero point?" Verne answered. "I don't know that he could answer that. Or would."

"It would have been a start," said John glumly. " Can you tell

The second enclosure . . . housed the Black Dragon.

me," he went on, suddenly switching direction, "why Charles chose not to have Basil finish his portrait?"

Bert inhaled deeply. "He didn't want to have the limitations that the others did," he said consolingly. "After what happened to Stellan, Charles saw that as more of a living death than a chance to carry on as a Caretaker. I disagreed with him, but it was his own choice."

"I only wish," John said to Verne, "that he had chosen your path. That you had been able to be with him before his death and create a tulpa. I keep feeling that if he were only with us, he'd know exactly what must be done—and it would be a plan too outrageous for any of the rest of us to think of."

Jack quickened his pace and put his arm around his friend, whispering words of comfort to him as they walked.

Bert started to approach them both to say something, but Verne held him back, shaking his head sternly. "Not yet," he said softly. "We can't say yet. Later, when it's sure, we'll tell them. But not now."

Bert stared at his mentor, struggling to form a response, but finally nodded in agreement and turned away.

"We have to return to the Archipelago," John declared firmly. "That's the only way to discover what's caused all this."

The report of the meeting with the Watchmaker had not gone over well at Tamerlane House. The Caretakers split into factions, all arguing over what they thought should be done, and why everyone else's plans were impossible. Fred, Laura Glue, and Rose did their best to mediate, while it was all Burton and his colleagues could do not to make things worse by venturing any opinion at all. Only John's pronouncement ended the arguments. The room went silent so they could hear what he had to say.

"We have to recreate a map of the zero points in Chronos time," he said calmly, "but time travel here is impossible at the moment. So we must go to the source of the problem. This all began when the keep fell. We caused that to happen. Samaranth said we have the means to repair what is broken, and I don't think that can be done here, in this world.

"There's another reason to restore the zero points. I don't think Rose being visited by the Morgaine—or one of them, anyway—was a coincidence. I think she was giving us a warning. 'The threads of history are undone,'" he quoted. "That's exactly what has happened.

"And Mother Night said to seek out the apprentice of the Dragon," he reminded them. "Samaranth is the last Dragon. Where else should we seek his apprentice if not in the Archipelago?"

"Well reasoned, young John," said Twain.

"But how will you cross?" asked Chaucer. "The Nameless Isles are connected to the Summer Country now."

"We might try modifying the bridge," Dumas suggested. "It did shift us forward in time."

"But at what cost?" asked Twain. "What happens to Tamerlane House if the bridge is severed, or reset?"

"He's right," said Verne. "We can't risk that. It's the only stability we have."

"Where did the orbs come from?" John asked Will Shakespeare. "The Dragon's eyes you used in the bridge?"

"The *Indigo Dragon*," Will answered. "In the south boathouse."

"Could we use another Dragonship?" asked Fred. "I'd be willing to risk it."

"There aren't any more. When the Shadow King corrupted all the Dragon shadows, we also lost the use of the Dragonships," lamented Jack. "As living ships, anyway."

"And when we were ripped out of the Archipelago," said John, "you left all the other Dragonships there, so we don't even have any extra eyes to experiment with."

"Ah," said Verne, rising. "But we just might have an extra Dragonship."

"What?" John exclaimed. "Even with the golden eyes, they're still just ships, and may not be able to cross."

"Not all of them," Bert said with an unusual twinkling in his eyes. "There's one left that is still a true Dragonship."

"I'm sure the Shadow King made particularly certain to get the Dragons who became our ships," said Jack, "just to keep us from being able to voyage back and forth across the Frontier."

"A plan that worked, for the most part," said Bert, "but recall, he was going by the History of Dragons in the Last Book, using their true names to seize their shadows. That's where he missed one—a Dragon who was never named, because he was never known. A cipher, a mystery . . ."

"An enigma, a conundrum, yes, yes, yes," Houdini said in exasperation. "How is that possible? Whose Dragonship did he overlook?"

Bert smiled. "His *own*."

The south boathouse was large enough to hold several ships within two enclosures. One contained the *Indigo Dragon* and several smaller boats. The second enclosure, which was double-locked and safeguarded with runes, spells, and the seal of both the house of Arthur and the Caretakers, housed the *Black Dragon*.

During the companions' first encounter with the Winter King, he attacked them and the much smaller *Indigo Dragon* with this dark, foreboding warship. It was only in the heat of battle, when the *Black Dragon* shifted course of its own accord, that they had realized it was a Dragonship in more than name alone. It was a true Dragonship—one that had melded the heart and living soul of a flesh-and-blood Dragon with the hull of a ship.

Ordo Maas, the great shipbuilder of ancient days gone by, knew of it, but not who built it. The Winter King claimed to have done so, but only Ordo Maas and the Dragons themselves ever knew the secrets of passage between the worlds—or so they had believed.

The ship was sleek and undamaged, and the chest of the great Dragon on its prow heaved with restrained energy and life.

When it was first captured, Ordo Maas had taken possession of it, but because of its mysterious origins, he relinquished it to the Caretakers' stewardship. It had been locked in the boathouse ever since.

"We can only assume that the Shadow King thought we had destroyed his ship, Dragon and all," said Bert, "or else why wouldn't he have sought her out?"

"It makes sense," said Burton. "Destroy what you do not use. It's standard tactics. It's what I would have done."

"Lucky that it wasn't you, then," said John, "or we'd be out a resource now."

"Even a stopped Caretaker is right twice a day," said Burton. "If he wins the coin tosses."

"Can it be controlled, is what I want to know," asked Jack. "Not to sound too prejudiced against Dragons, but I was scared enough of the ones I knew of, and even more of the ones who actively liked me. I'm not sure I want to trust my life to one who has tried to actually kill me."

"I think it can," said Bert. "The Winter King was its master, but I don't think it was a willing servant. Not completely."

"All right," Jack said. "I think we have the means. Now we just need to decide on a plan of action."

The Caretakers reconvened in the great meeting hall to call for a consensus. The vote was unanimous, even including Byron and the Society members. Only Magwich and Grimalkin weren't permitted a vote, and likely wouldn't have voted if they had been. Or at least not quietly, in Magwich's case.

"It's decided then," Chaucer said, thumping on the table for order. "We must discover what has happened in the Archipelago. The Dragon Samaranth must be sought, so his apprentice may be named. And somehow the zero points must be mapped so that time itself can be repaired."

He turned to John. "Caveo Principia," he said with respect and reverence, "this is under your purview."

"We'll sort it out," John said, glancing quickly at Jack, who winked in agreement. "We may not be the young Turks we once were, but we're still the Caretakers. It shouldn't be anyone else's responsibility."

"And risk," Jack added. "The two of us—"

"Ahem-hem," Fred interrupted, clearing his throat. "That would be three of us."

"My apologies, Caretaker," said Jack. "Three of us."

"As you wish," said Chaucer, to a round of table thumping by the others.

"Hold on," Burton said suddenly. "I see three—make that two and a half—Caretakers planning to go, but no representatives of the Imperial Cartological Society?"

"Pardon me?" said Jack, who was slightly offended. "I can represent both."

"I'll keep my pardons for myself," Burton replied. "You may represent the ICS to the outside world, but in matters of the Archipelago, we all know what the reality is. I'm going along as well."

"The Caretakers and Sir Richard—," Chaucer began.

"Three and three," Burton interrupted, gesturing to Houdini and Doyle. "They come with me. More witnesses, better reportage."

"He has a point there, Geoff," Twain said, tapping out his pipe. "And Richard is the most experienced among us for reporting on odd cultures and unusual scenarios."

"It will be dangerous . . . ," Dickens began.

"If anyone else has the scars to match mine," said Burton, stroking his cheek, "I'll listen to their arguments. But I think I'm beyond contestation in this."

"I have some bad scorch marks," said Byron, raising his hand.

"Oh, do shut up," Shakespeare said, "or I'll ask the faeries to give you the head of a donkey."

"Can he do that?" a horrified Byron whispered to Twain.

"Probably," Twain said, winking at Shakespeare, who returned a halfhearted smile. Will was still stuck in a mood that was half elation and half misery. The first, because his bridge had worked—and the second, because the rest of the Caretakers, with a few exceptions, still wondered if his cleverness was just another mask he wore to conceal the idiot underneath.

"Burton does address a valid point," said Chaucer. "This could be dangerous in the extreme. We should send someone else to help safeguard the Caretakers."

"Whom did you have in mind, Geoff?" asked Twain. "Hawthorne, maybe?"

Nathaniel Hawthorne was, among the Caretakers Emeritis, the most able-bodied and skilled scrapper. He was precisely the sort of man one would want to have in a fight. There was only one problem.

"He can't," said Chaucer. "This is a matter of time, and we have no way of knowing how that would affect a Caretaker who has already passed and is now a resident of Tamerlane House and the Pygmalion Gallery. We can't risk a loss like . . ."

His voice trailed off, but everyone at the table knew he was thinking of John's old professor Stellan Sigurdsson. He had traveled with Rose, Quixote, and Archie beyond the Edge of the World, but he'd exceeded the one-week time limit imposed on all Caretakers who resided inside the portraits. One week away from Tamerlane, and no more. And to take such a risk so close on the heels of the loss of Charles would be too much to countenance.

"Burton, Harry, and Sir Arthur are tulpas," Chaucer said, hardly masking the distaste in his voice, "and so are not at risk with another time displacement. John, Jack, and Fred are still living in their Prime Times, and so are also at less of a risk. So there's only one other among us we can send."

"Of course!" Bert exclaimed. "Roger!"

"You do know he hates that name, right?" Twain said bluntly. "He prefers to be called the Tin Man now."

John and Jack looked at each other in surprise. They hadn't considered him as an option. Roger Bacon, one of the great Caretakers of antiquity, had never died—he had manufactured for himself the massive mechanical body that kept his brain, his soul, and his intellect intact. All within a form that could shatter boulders and wade through doors as if they were tissue.

"I'll go fetch him," said Hawthorne, rising from his seat. "I think he's still in the workshed he shares with Shakespeare."

"I'm going too," said someone from the back of the room.

Jack started to shake his head in protest. It was Laura Glue who had spoken, and she was already glaring at him defiantly.

"Laura Glue, you can't think—," John began.

"You really expect to go?" said Dickens. "It could be very dangerous, child."

"Of course I'm going!" Laura Glue exclaimed indignantly. "I was *born* in the Archipelago, and I've spent my entire life there, remember? Can anyone else here say the same?"

"Ahem-hem." Fred cleared his throat.

"Except for Fred," she added, winking at him.

Burton chuckled. "She has a point, I think."

"That's where home is for me," she continued, walking the perimeter of the table so that she could look at each Caretaker. "You may think it's safer to be here in Tamerlane House, but I'll remind you, I am the head of the Valkyries. I can take care of myself. And no one here is going to stop me."

Bert and Verne both looked askance at Jack, who shrugged his shoulders and raised his hands. "Don't look at me," he said sheepishly. "I couldn't win an argument with her when she was eight."

"I want to go too," Rose suddenly said, realizing that her request sounded more like an afterthought once they'd given in to Laura Glue. "I think I could be helpful to you, Uncle John. And Mother Night did say that I was the only one who could reweave the threads that had come loose from history. Isn't that just what the Watchmaker said we needed to do? To find those special points in time, to make them significant again? For that reason alone, I don't think you can do this without me."

As if her argument had been decisive enough to end the discussion, she folded her arms, closed her eyes, and smiled.

"She must," Poe's quiet voice spoke from somewhere above them. "Rose must go."

"I disagree," said John. "We've already lost Charles and Morgan—and that's without the threat of these Shadows, these Echthroi, that Mother Night said were coming for Rose. I think she'll be much safer here in Tamerlane House."

"Not anymore," said Burton. "The door has been opened for good, by way of Shakespeare's Bridge." He looked up into the shadows. "The islands are still Nameless, but they're no longer lost, are they?"

Poe didn't answer, but simply stood there, watching.

"This is going to be dangerous, Bert," John reiterated, folding his arms. "She should stay behind, with the rest of the Caretakers."

"I don't think anywhere is going to be safe," Rose said mildly. "Is it, Bert?"

The Far Traveler shook his head. "The girl is right, John," he said with obvious resignation. John realized in that moment that

Bert didn't want her to accompany them any more than they did. But for some reason, she was meant to go. He looked at Rose and realized that she had not offered just to have a chance at an adventure. She really believed she was meant to do this. And he had no good argument why she shouldn't go.

"She may not be safe anywhere," said Poe, "least of all with you, in the Archipelago. But the fact remains that this may be what she is meant to do—even if it costs her everything else."

John stepped into the center of the foyer underneath the railings where Poe stood. He looked up at the shadowed face of the great Caretaker. "Tell us why," he said, not bothering to keep the anger out of his voice. "We have done many, many things on faith, Edgar. Sometimes things work out, but sometimes they don't. And we have never defied you or the Caretakers Emeritis.

"I don't believe you're all-knowing," John continued, his voice still sharp with fury. " I think you're making this up as you go along, the same as the rest of us. So I think we deserve to know why we should have to do as you say."

Burton chuckled under his breath. "So, the little scholar has some dung up his neck after all."

"That was, ah, brave," Houdini whispered to Doyle. "I don't think anyone, even Chaucer, calls him Edgar."

"You don't," said Poe simply. "You have always had your free agency to choose—as does Rose.

"There are threads that are lost, and must be found again," he continued, echoing Rose and Mother Night's words. "She is the only one who can find them."

"What else haven't you told us?" asked John. "What else is happening here?"

"The Darkness is coming," Poe said somberly. "Perhaps not now, this instant, but soon. Some of its agents already work against us. Some of them have been here, in this house. But make no mistake—the Darkness *will* come. And all of our work over the centuries has been to find the one light that will be able to stand against our enemy."

"Echthroi," Schubert said from the far side of the stairway. "Our enemy."

"And you believe that Rose is that light?" John demanded. "Do you?"

Again Poe was silent. And John realized why. He didn't need to answer a question John had known the answer to all along. Rose *was* the light. She was the one they had protected, who had come out of history to save them once before—as she might do again.

"All right, so the Grail Child has to go," Burton said, "but with the addition of the mechanical man and the birdy-girl, you've got two more representatives of the Caretakers. I demand equal representation for the ICS."

"As the Valkyrie noted," said Poe, "she is simply returning home. She represents only herself."

"Fine," Burton acceded, "but you're still up one with the Tin Man."

"I had already planned on sending someone else along with you," Poe said as a door to his right opened slowly. "I trust you'll approve."

From behind Poe, a tall, muscular, dark-skinned man stepped onto the landing and descended the stairs. He was dressed in the manner of an Arab, with a linen robe and head wrapping and broad leather belts. He was barefoot, and his skin was so black it was almost purple-hued in the light of the meeting hall.

He moved through the Caretakers and went straight to Burton—who, to the shock and amazement of everyone there, embraced the tall man.

"The End of Time," Burton exclaimed. "I did not know you were still alive, but I'm not surprised!"

"Master Burton," the man said in a deep baritone voice that was flecked with a French accent. "It gladdens me to see you again."

"What are you doing here?" said Burton as he clapped the man on the shoulders. "When did you get here?"

"I have been here, in these islands, for a very long time," he replied. "I have been waiting for you, in fact."

Burton wheeled around and pointed at Poe. "What kind of game are you playing, Poe? You had my friend here, with you, all this time?"

Poe didn't answer.

"The End of Time?" Jack said. "I'm sorry, but I don't understand the reference."

"It isn't a reference, it's his name," said Burton, still eyeing Poe above. "He was my guide across Somaliland in the 1850s. I would not have survived if not for him. We called him Theo for short, and . . .

"Wait a minute," he exclaimed suddenly. Burton looked over the man he called the End of Time from head to toe, then took a step back. "How is it that you're here now? That was nearly a century ago."

"He's one of the Messengers," Verne said, trying without success to conceal the smugness he felt at disorienting Burton so. "An adept, like Ransom and Morgan. Or didn't you know that?"

"I . . . did not," Burton said frankly. Doyle and Houdini looked at each other in surprise. This was a rare admission for Sir Richard, to not have known something about his own man.

At that moment Hawthorne reappeared with the Tin Man, who agreed to go. "And I'm taking Archie," said Rose, as if defying Burton to argue with her—but he was too stunned by the appearance of the End of Time to care.

"Then we have our fellowship," Chaucer declared. "Luck be with you all."

The travelers left Tamerlane House to go prepare the *Black Dragon*, just as another argument broke out among the Caretakers Emeritis. "We've already shared so much," Bert was saying, pleading with the others. "Why couldn't we have told them this, too? Why not put all the cards on the table, so they can be fully informed about their choices?"

"It isn't a matter of being fully informed, Bert," said Twain, "but about how much they can bear."

"It would have only added to their burdens," Verne said wearily, "to reveal that according to the future Histories, today, Jack's 'Independence Day,' also marks the first day in the War of the Caretakers."

PART THREE

The Shadowed World

There, on a protrusion of rock, stood a man.

CHAPTER NINE
The Waste Land

✧

In a world where the power of a nation was determined by the power of its naval forces, a skilled mapmaker was as valuable as the most ruthless of privateers. The ability to see what others could not see, and know what they could not know, was embodied in the accuracy of the maps made for the various principalities, and the brotherhood of mapmakers skilled enough to have come to the notice of the kings and admirals was small and select. But even among these there was a hierarchy, and the best, most elite of their number was a man who had never drawn a map for a king or country.

In mapmaking circles, no one was better than Eliot McGee, and he only made maps for pirates.

It was the family trade, begun by his father Elijah, who was recruited by the pirate governor, Henry Morgan, to make maps to his own hidden treasures. In time, word of both Elijah's skill and his ability to keep tightly bound the most fragile of secrets brought all the pirates of the age to the McGees' door.

Eliot's childhood, once meant for his apprenticeship as a silversmith, became an endless game of art and imagination, of hidden lands and lost treasures, as his father taught him the art of mapmaking.

Once, during one of Morgan's late-night meetings with Elijah, Eliot thought he overheard something about a Cartographer, and Caretakers of a place called the Archipelago of Dreams. He had assumed it was just another discussion about the Caribbean. Almost all the maps that Elijah made were for islands in that part of the world—in part because that was where all the pirates were.

Then, when he was old enough to have passed from apprenticeship to mastery, he met another man who spoke of the same things, in the same way. They spent many long nights talking of imaginary lands, and in the process became the best of friends. And in due time, his friend introduced Eliot to his own master—a man who referred to himself as a Caretaker. And this Caretaker had also taken on another apprentice, who was destined to have a great impact on the life and career of Eliot McGee.

And thus did Eliot Mcgee, Charles Johnson, and Daniel Defoe become apprentice Caretakers to Cyrano de Bergerac.

Burton argued with Jack about which of them was to captain the *Black Dragon*, until Fred pointed out that John was actually the Caveo Principia, and he should choose. John, for his part, didn't want to embarrass Fred by ignoring his obvious show of loyalty, but he also didn't want to overrule Burton in so blatant a manner. So, he asked one of the others to flip a coin, and Burton was to call it.

It turned out the only one of them who actually had a coin was Houdini. "All right," he said, readying a quarter on his thumb and finger, "I'll flip it. But how do you know I won't cheat? I can make the quarter do anything I want, as you probably know."

"If you do it fairly," John said, "I'll tell you the secret of how the Serendipity Box works—uh, worked."

Houdini's face lit up. "Deal!" He flipped the coin expertly into the air. "Call it, Richard."

"Tails," said Burton.

Houdini caught the spinning coin and slapped it on his wrist.

"It's heads," Fred said as Houdini showed him the coin. "Scowler John chooses."

Burton started to protest, until John interrupted him. "Burton should captain the ship," he said. "Any objections?"

"Not really," said Jack.

"I don't understand," said Burton. "Why put us through this little game if you were going to let me do it anyway?"

"Because," said John, "I wasn't going to 'let' you do anything. I was going to choose you, because you've had more experience, and more recent experience, than any of us. And I made us flip the coin to point out who's in charge here."

Burton's eyes narrowed, then he grinned and moved to the foredeck to loosen the moorings, while instructing the Tin Man to loosen those in the aft.

"How did you know you'd win the toss?" asked Doyle. "Not much of a way to establish yourself as leader if you'd lost."

"Oh, Harry made sure I won, didn't you, Harry?" John said with a wink at the magician.

"Well, er . . . that is," Harry stammered, glancing over his shoulder to make sure Burton wasn't in earshot. "You did win, and that's what counts. So," he added, rubbing his hands together in anticipation of an earned reward, "how does the Serendipity Box work?"

John clapped him on the back and leaned close. "Magic," he whispered before striding to the cabin with Jack and Fred. "It's *magic*."

"That was dirty pool," Houdini fumed as Doyle laughed. "Completely dirty pool."

The *Black Dragon* seemed almost grateful to be free of the boathouse, giving Burton only a little bit of resistance as he steered her out to sea. The water that had come with the Nameless Isles extended only a few miles from the shoreline, where it vanished under the gray mists that now surrounded the islands.

"If this works," John said to the others, "we should know right away. And if it doesn't, we'll just take a little jaunt around the islands."

"It will work," said Rose. "I can feel it."

As if she had predicted it, in short order the Frontier loomed up before them, replacing the gray haze with a stark blackness and Jack was suddenly glad and relieved that Burton was in command of the ship instead of him.

The barrier between worlds usually manifested itself as a line of thunderheads, electric storm clouds roiling with wind and rain and crackling with lightning. The Dragonships were designed by Ordo Maas to withstand the crossing, but most ordinary ships— those that would dare approach such a fearsome storm—would be driven back. Even the occasional few that made it past the Frontier were usually battered into uselessness and had to be abandoned soon after.

The ruins of Atlantis, the drowned lands past Avalon, were littered with the wrecks of vessels that had crossed the Frontier but were unable to continue.

The mermaids usually took care of whoever survived of the crews that sailed them. Mer-people were not ones to waste food, whatever its source.

This time the situation was different. The storm clouds reached to—past?—the surface of the torrential seas and formed a distinct, almost solid wall of darkness. Even Burton, who was usually in complete control of his reactions, was showing trepidation, if not fear. He was a cunning and bold captain—but the *Black Dragon* had not been built by Ordo Maas. There was proof in the Histories that it had gained passage through the old Frontier more than once, but there was no way of telling how it would fare against the nightmare that lay ahead.

Archimedes, Rose, and Laura Glue were already strapped to mainbeams inside the cabin, and John and Jack were considering joining them. There was little else they could do on deck that Houdini and Doyle were not already doing—and the two tulpas were both younger and more physically fit than they. Even Theo was more actively involved, as he seemed to be helping Burton choose a path to take through the blackness ahead.

It was all Jack could do to resist offering unsolicited advice, which Burton would probably throw back in his face anyway. He had a terrible urge to grab the ties to the sail and leap on top of the cabin, steering the ship into the storm like a bullrider.

A spar broke on one side of the deck and spun crazily across the planks before spinning off into the night.

"I had the thought that this might have been better if we'd converted the old girl to an airship," John shouted to Jack over the roar of the wind. "Fly over the clouds, you know? But I'm reconsidering."

The hull shuddered and groaned with the strain as the sails whipped about in the wind, tearing, pulling. . . . And then, without warning, the center mast snapped and fell directly toward Burton.

In a trice, before any of the others could react, the Tin Man leaped in between the massive wooden beam and the wheel and caught it before Burton could be crushed.

With an immense effort, the Tin Man slowly pushed the mast back into position and over, snapping it off completely.

"What have you done?" Burton screamed over his shoulder. "You fool! You've killed us all!"

But Jack realized that the Tin Man had in fact done just the opposite—the main mast, which was taller than the others, was catching more wind in its sails and making it harder to maneuver the ship. Broken, it was even more of a danger to them. But gone completely, there was more leverage for the rudder, and more control for Burton.

"I should have let you drive," John said, seeing the familiar look on his colleague's face. "Sorry, Jack."

The darkness of the storm seemed to be reaching for the ship itself, as if the very storm had will, and intent.

"It is an Echthros," Theo said, his voice strangely clear in the din. "It is trying to prevent us from passing through."

"You mean the Echthroi," Jack called back. "Our enemies."

Theo shook his head. "Not many. Only one."

"Oh, for cat's sake," John complained, looking at the breadth and intensity of the storm surrounding them. "If this is just a single one of our enemies, we're going to be in a lot of trouble."

"Hold on," said John, lowering his head. "We're about to go into the worst of it now."

With a barbaric yawp, Burton spun the wheel and steered the *Black Dragon* into the heart of the darkness.

✦ ✦ ✦

The ship crossed the Frontier.

There was a great deal of damage, but no cracks in the hull. And none of the companions had been injured or swept overboard. The Frontier disappeared behind them as quickly as it had arisen, and the dark storm clouds gave way to gray fog and endless open seas.

"I can't believe we've come through alive," John said, brushing off his jacket and checking his pack to make sure the *Imaginarium Geographica* was safe. "Well done, Sir Richard."

Burton acknowledged the compliment with a shrug and continued to examine the boat to better appraise the extent of the damage, but everyone who'd been on deck knew what had happened, and who was deserving of the credit. The Tin Man was the only reason the secondary masts were intact, and after saving Burton's life he had ridden out the passage holding fast to the rudder, which was nearly ripped free from its bracings.

Houdini seemed unperturbed, as did Doyle. Both men were in remarkable shape, particularly Houdini. It probably didn't hurt, John thought, that they were both tulpas—they had already gone through death itself. So what was a little hurricane to them?

Fred was the only member of their company who seemed distressed, and John knew that was probably just because he was wet. Badger fur did not take well to water and smelled horribly even in damp weather, never mind after being drenched in a thunderstorm at sea.

Fred noticed John looking at him and gave a cheerful salute to show he was all right—but conscientiously kept to the far side of the deck, downwind, just to be safe.

"Theo," Jack said, putting his hand on the tall man's shoulder and speaking quietly, so the others would not overhear. "The Echthros—is it gone?"

The End of Time didn't answer immediately, but stood on the deck, looking into the wind. He turned and looked back at the imposing blackness of the Frontier, then back at Jack. "I cannot tell, " he replied at length. "It may still be with us, or waiting somewhere nearby."

Jack folded his arms and bowed his head. "Is there any possibility that the Frontier kept it out of the Archipelago? That it didn't cross over with us?"

Theo looked at Jack, then, oddly, at Burton, who was still at the wheel, shouting curses and orders in equal measure. "All of this is being caused by the Echthroi," he said finally. "If one of our enemy chose to follow us through the barrier, there is nothing to prevent it from doing so. It could be with us even now, just biding its time, waiting."

"Waiting for what?"

"To do whatever it has been sent to do," Theo replied, "to prevent us from reaching our goals."

"I see," said Jack, looking up. "And if that's the case, is there any way to stop it?"

Theo never answered, instead moving to help the Tin Man clear debris off the decks. After a moment, pondering, Jack went to help.

After the ship was secured, and food and drink had been passed around, John and Burton huddled close over the *Geographica* to determine where in the Archipelago they were. "I can't quite figure it out," said John. "We didn't start at a normal place, and I haven't seen any landmarks yet."

"Technically, we sailed from Oxford," said Jack, "so we ought to be close to Avalon."

"If we're lost," Houdini suggested, "then perhaps we ought to just ask that fellow over there for directions."

The surprised companions looked in the direction Houdini was pointing. There, on a protrusion of rock, stood a man. He was nattily dressed in a waistcoat and tails, with a boutonniere and spats on his shoes. He was slightly stout at the middle, and his reddish brown hair was beginning to thin.

To one side, on a smaller protrusion of rock, was a table set for tea; on the opposite side, a large steamer trunk rested on another rock just above the waterline.

The man waited, arms folded behind him, as they approached, then lifted a hand in greeting as the *Black Dragon* bumped up against the rocks.

"Greetings, travelers," he called out with restrained cheer. "From whence do you travel, and to what destination?" If he was in any way taken aback by the strange assortment of characters aboard the ship, it didn't show.

John stood at the railing and quietly gestured for the others to hang back until he could better assess who and what they were dealing with.

"I'm the Caretaker Principia of the *Imaginarium Geographica*," he announced to the man. "Whom do I have the pleasure of addressing?"

"Oh, my stars and garters!" the man exclaimed. "I never believed I would be so lucky as to see you myself! All of us have imagined that we might be the one, but after so many generations, a hope unrealized becomes a dream and only a dream."

The man bowed deeply. "I am George Chanticleer, descended of the Chanticleers of Dorimare, and it is my honor to be of service to the Caretakers."

"I've read of a Chanticleer of Dorimare," said Jack. "Nathaniel, wasn't it?"

George bowed again. "My eldest forebear. You honor me by invoking his name."

"Eldest forebear?" Jack asked, a puzzled expression on his face. "Begging your pardon, but you and I seem of an age, and from what I knew of Nathaniel, he wasn't much older than I am. So at most, he'd be your father, wouldn't he?"

George stuck his finger in his ear and wiggled it about, as if Jack's words had gotten stuck there and not quite penetrated to his brain. "Father? Well, I suppose after a manner of speaking, that's true. To be precise, however, he would be my great-great-great-great . . ."

"Uh-oh," said Fred. "A genealogist."

". . . great-great-great-great . . . ," George continued, counting off the "greats" on his fingers as he went. ". . . great-great-great, uh . . ." He paused. "Maybe if I named them instead. I'm the son of Diggory the fifth, who was the son of Orson the ninth—"

"I'm starting to get the picture," John said interrupting him. "How long have you and your family been waiting for us here?"

"From the Day of Sorrows to this," replied George, his eyes welling up with tears, "it has been two thousand sixty-three years and a number of days. If you desire it, I can calculate the days."

"What deception is this?" Burton fumed as he grabbed John roughly by the shoulder. "Are you trying to deceive us, Caretaker?"

"You're seeing everything I am, Sir Richard," John shot back. "You're experiencing this in exactly the same way I am, so do all of us a favor and shut up!"

Theo stepped between the men and put his hand on Burton's shoulder. "Chanticleer speaks the truth," he said, his voice soft but clear in its conviction. "Twenty centuries have come and gone since any of you were last in this place."

Burton started to retort, then thought better of it and nodded. "All right," he said, turning to look at John. His temper had been cooled by the dark-skinned guide.

"I'm guessing that's why *he* needed to come along," Houdini whispered to Jack. "No one else I've ever seen has had that effect on Burton. No one."

"What happened, George?" John asked.

"There was a ferocious storm on the Day of Sorrows," said George, "and Avalon was caught up in it in a terrible way. The ocean heaved, and the black clouds descended from the sky and ripped the island into pieces. What you see," he finished, gesturing around him sadly, "is all that remains."

Instinctively, John and Jack both looked at Rose. Avalon was where she had been born and raised by her mother Gwynhfar and grandfather Odysseus. Once before they had come here, and they had not realized how strongly she identified with it as her home.

On that voyage, they had found the island to be much as they had known it—a ruined echo of what it once had been. But Rose had only ever known it as a pristine, gleaming jewel that could have been lifted out of mythic Greece, and in fact, all but was.

To see it in its dilapidated state had been a shock then—so how much worse would it be to find it utterly destroyed?

Rose saw their looks of concern and took them both by the hand. "It's all right," she assured them. "I had prepared myself to see . . . well, something worse than before. I knew it was not going to look like I remember it."

"It must have happened when the last of the tower fell," said John. "After the rift started to widen, Avalon couldn't stand the strain of the difference in time flows, and it was destroyed."

"That could have happened to Tamerlane House, too, then," Jack said with a shudder. "I think I need to sit down."

"I wonder what made the difference," Burton wondered aloud. "Your reasoning is sound, young Caretaker," he said to John, "but your conclusion isn't. The same thing absolutely should have happened to the Nameless Isles. Absolutely. So why didn't it?"

"Shakespeare's Bridge and the golden eyes of the Dragon," said Jack. "I think that made all the difference. John and I lost two years, but Tamerlane House was spared the fate of the rest of the Archipelago."

"So," John murmured to Rose, "the *Indigo Dragon* saved us yet again."

"So what now?" Burton asked. "What are we supposed to do?"

"Go on to Paralon," said George. "You're expected. Or at least, you were, long ago." He straightened. "No matter. You've come at last. In the end, nothing else will be important. Do you know how to get there?"

"Finding our way from Avalon, uh, rock, to Paralon shouldn't be a problem," said Jack. "We've done that voyage a hundred times.

It would be pretty hard for us to lose our way and end up at the wrong island."

"It's harder than you think," said George, "being as Paralon is the only island left."

"What?" Jack, John, and Fred said in unison.

"What are you talking about?" asked John. "What do you mean it's the only island?"

"That's all I know, all I can tell you," George said in apology. "The rest you will discover on Paralon."

"How can all the islands just disappear?" said Burton. "There's no sense to it. There must be an explanation."

"They were left on their own," George replied softly, his face reddening. "Not to put too fine a point on it, no one was here to, ah . . . take care of them."

John and Jack exchanged a rueful look. This was one of their worst fears—that in the time of greatest need, they would not measure up to the task. Or apparently, be there at all.

"You've done your duty," John said with a wave. "Do you wish to come with us?"

"Thank you no," said George. "I'm going to write this up—so exciting! And then, I think I'll have tea, and watch the sun set. Now that you've come, there won't be any need for a Chanticleer to wait. And there's no greater honor I can think of . . .

". . . than to have been the last, very last, Green Knight in the Archipelago."

John was able to give Burton an exact heading to take them to Paralon, and he and the Tin Man put the remaining sails to use to gather as much speed as possible. He even suspected that the ship itself was adding to their momentum, as if it had understood the urgency of their mission and had chosen to help them, rather than hinder them.

"I have to say," Jack remarked to John and Theo, "that I'm starting to gain a new respect for the Winter King. If he did build the *Black Dragon*, he did a bang-up job. I don't know how he persuaded the Dragon to go along, but it's an impressive combination."

"It is at that," John agreed as Rose, carrying Archie, came to stand with him at the railing. "She'll have us in Paralon in no time at all. So to speak."

Only Fred noticed that Laura Glue had withdrawn from the others to stand alone at the aft of the ship. He made his way back to where she was watching the wake in the water and sidled up next to her.

"A muffin for your thoughts," he offered meekly.

"Isn't the expression 'a penny for your thoughts'?" she said without turning or looking away from the water.

"Maybe for human beans," Fred replied, "but badgers seldom have pennies. However, we almost always have a muffin or two." As proof, he rooted around in his pocket and produced a small chocolate-banana muffin.

Laura Glue dipped her head and laughed, then turned to look down at the grinning mammal. "What did you bring that for?"

"First rule of being a Caretaker," he said nonchalantly. "Never go anywhere unarmed if you can help it."

"Wouldn't a dagger, or a slingshot, or something like that be more handy?"

"Maybe," Fred admitted, "but if you find yourself feeling peckish, you can't nibble on a slingshot."

"True enough," she said as she turned to look at the water again.

"Why are you looking at where we've been?" Fred asked. "Home is in the other direction."

"Is it still going to be home when we get there?" she asked somberly. "After so many years, will we recognize anything?"

"One thing I've learned," Fred said with as much authority as he could muster, "is that you must trust in the Caretakers. Not me, I mean—but Scowler John and Scowler Jack. They will do everything they need to do until things are set aright. I didn't doubt them before, and I don't doubt them now."

Impulsively, Laura Glue leaned over and hugged her furry companion. "Thank you, Fred," she said. "That helps. A lot."

Yes, Jack thought from the port side of the cabin, where he'd inadvertently been listening in on their conversation, *thank you. I only hope that we can live up to your expectations. And our own.*

It was an immense statue, half broken . . . it was a centaur.

CHAPTER TEN
Fallen Idols

After an uneventful night of sailing through the gray, starless gloom, the *Black Dragon* glided through the shallows and onto the beach at Paralon—or what was a pale, nightmare reflection of the Paralon they all remembered.

The island had changed.

The docks and the bustling business quarter were gone as if they had never been. Most of the buildings that lined the paved streets were gone. In fact, the only thing that resembled the old Paralon was the citadel that was carved into the mountain ahead. Everything else was gone.

"I was here just yesterday," Laura Glue said dully. "How can it have changed so completely, so quickly? How is that possible?"

"Two millennia makes a difference," said Jack. "Everything changes in that much time."

"I don't care about the island!" she said angrily. "I care about all my friends. What's become of them?"

Fred swallowed hard and hugged her tightly. She was right—his father, Uncas, and grandfather, Tummeler, had been here on Paralon. If what they saw around them was true, then Fred would have lost his family just as Laura Glue had lost all her friends. It was a prospect that became even more chilling the longer the companions thought about it, as the understanding of the magnitude of their predicament became ever more manifest.

Everyone was gone. Everyone they had ever known in the Archipelago.

"Surely there might still be someone left?" Jack stated as bravely as he could manage. "Samaranth, almost certainly, and perhaps Ordo Maas. Didn't they call him the Ancient of Days? Surely two thousand years would be nothing to him."

"It's not just the passage of time that worries me," said John, "it's that the worlds have been severed. The Summer Country, our world, is the living twin to the Archipelago."

"A Siamese twin," Burton said. "And what happens if the blood flow from one is disconnected from the other?"

John didn't reply, but merely frowned and turned away. Jack knew what his friend was thinking. John's son Christopher was still in the RAF, and the war, while winding down, was not yet won. What if, because of this crisis in the Archipelago, the war would not end? What then?

"Look!" Archimedes called out. "Over here!"

He'd been flying above the companions, looping in wider and wider circles, searching for someone or something they might recognize—and it appeared he'd found both.

It was an immense statue, half broken, as if it from the impact of something equally large. Still, the form was unmistakable: It was a centaur.

"Charys?" Jack asked Fred, who had scampered over to read the inscription at the base.

"Same vineyard, different vintage," Fred replied. "This is a statue of his great-grandson, Kobol, who was killed while defending Paralon in the Second Great War of the Races." He turned to Jack. "I don't remember there being a First Great War of the Races."

"You can miss a lot of wars in two millennia, little Caretaker," said Burton.

Fred's whiskers twitched. "He was my teacher, you know. Charys."

"Do you suppose this is the Winterland?" John suggested to Jack. "Could we have crossed back into that place?"

"I doubt it," Jack answered. "For one thing, the Winterland was back in our world, not here. And for another, that entire scenario was caused by a specific bit of chronal sabotage."

"What was that?" asked Burton.

"You," John said pointedly.

"Oh, yes," Burton said. "The Dyson incident. Verne told me about your end of that tale. I have to admit, I was rather impressed by the accounting of Bert."

"How so?"

"The fact that he was willing to sell out his colleagues to Mordred to save his own skin," said Burton. "It sounds like something I would do."

"Yes," John said drolly. "It does. And it was barbaric. I'd rather you not bring it up again."

"Not to defend Burton," said Jack, "but Jules *does* keep his own skull on his desk. If anyone has reason to be tweaked by the whole thing, I'd guess it was him."

"It may have seemed like a disaster to you," said Burton, "but this 'Winterland' you experienced managed to do one thing right that not a thousand years of Caretakers have succeeded in doing."

"What was that, Burton?"

"Unite the worlds," Burton replied. "In the Winterland, the Archipelago and the Summer Country were one again."

"Under the tyrant's rule, you mean."

Burton shrugged. "I didn't say it was perfect. But just so you know—it is possible."

"That's almost reassuring," said Rose. "If you ever try to do it again, I hope you choose a better ruler."

"Your own father ruled the Winterland," said Burton, "did he not?"

"No," said Rose. "*Mordred* ruled the Winterland. My father is Madoc."

"From the position of the city gates," Laura Glue said, shading her eyes to peer into the distance, "I'd say that we're standing where the royal docks used to be."

"Either they don't use boats very often anymore," said Jack, "or they haven't needed to in a very, very long time."

"Archimedes," John called out to the bird, "go do another aerial reconnaissance and see if there's anyone else about."

In only a few minutes, Archimedes swooped low over the companions and gave his report. Farther up the beach, he had found someone, the first living being they'd seen since Avalon—a single man, sitting close to a cold fire.

They approached him cautiously, but he barely gave any notice that he knew they were there until they were directly opposite the fire. The robes he wore were of a fine, rich material; ebony-hued, sleeker than silk. They dropped over one shoulder and wrapped around his midsection before falling almost to his shoeless feet.

"He has the features of an elf," John whispered to Jack. "But . . ."

"I know," Jack answered. "I've never seen an elf who actually looked . . . *old.*"

The man stood and looked at the companions oddly, as if he knew there should be some sort of decorum involved when greeting newcomers and simply couldn't remember what it was.

He moved his mouth in fits and starts, clearly wanting to speak—but he said nothing. His eyes were not quite vacant, but both John and Jack had seen the expression he wore all too often.

Shell shock. Battle fatigue. A war, perhaps many wars, had taken their toll, and destroyed whatever there had been in him that had made him walk tall and strong and confidently in another life that was long past.

Strangely, it was Houdini who first decided to approach this strange, emaciated figure. "Hello," he said tentatively. "My name is Ehrich."

Doyle reacted visibly to this—Houdini hated being called by his real name and rarely used it.

The man tilted his head, examining the magician as if assessing his intent. Then, without warning, he stepped forward and collapsed into Houdini's arms, sobbing.

"Are you really here?" he asked between long, choking gasps. "Are you real, or fantasy?"

"I sometimes wonder that myself," Houdini murmured as he held the man closer. "I'm here. We've come to help."

"You're too late!" the man said, still crying. "You're just too late."

◆   ◆   ◆

The others moved closer, and John and Laura Glue brought out some of the stores of food and water that had survived the passage of the Frontier. Burton, Doyle, and Theo gathered together more driftwood to add to the fire.

"This was all within reach," Burton grumbled as they added more sticks to the pile. "Why didn't he build it up? Why was he just sitting here, shivering and suffering?"

"I don't think he could build the fire," John said quietly, glancing over at the emaciated man. "I don't think he had the strength—or the will."

"If I have the will, I'll find the strength," Burton answered, scoffing.

After half an hour, the man seemed to have gotten enough of his strength back to converse with the companions.

"How do you come here?" he asked Houdini.

"In a ship," the Magician replied. "The *Black Dragon*."

"You have a Dragonship?" the man said. There was more interest in that single question than anything else he'd said to them.

"We do," said Jack, pointing down the beach to the faintly visible silhouette of the *Black Dragon* and the Tin Man. "We've only just arrived in it, though it's seen better days, I'm afraid."

"I have a Dragonship too," the man replied, weakly lifting his arm to point in the other direction. "It's there, on the sand. I hope to see it sail again someday, but sometimes . . ." He paused, and his eyes welled up with tears. "Sometimes I have had to use the wood for my fire, when there is no skrika, and the rain is coldest."

John cupped his eyes with his hands and peered in the direction the man was pointing. He'd seen a shape in the distance but thought it was simply an outcropping of rock; now he could make out the contours of a ship.

"Archimedes," he began.

"Wait," said Laura Glue. "I'll go take a look. I've been needing to stretch my wings."

"All right," John said, "but not alone. No," he added as she started to protest, "it's not because you're young, or because you're a girl. We don't know anything about this place. This is not the Paralon you know. None of us are going anywhere alone."

"I'll go with her," offered Doyle. "Won't be but a few minutes."

The bird, the Valkyrie, and the Detective disappeared into the mists along the beach, and were gone for only a short while before they returned. Doyle was nonplussed by their find, but Archie was excited and Laura Glue was visibly upset—enough so that she walked back alongside Doyle instead of flying.

"Laura Glue?" Rose asked, taking her friend's hands. "What was it? Is it really a Dragonship?"

Laura Glue wore the stunned expression of someone who had seen an impossible thing—and perhaps she had.

"It *is* a Dragonship," she said, incredulous. "It's the *Blue Dragon!*"

The companions all ran down the beach together to take a closer look at the legendary ship. It was the most elusive of the Dragonships, and the most powerful, because it belonged to one of the Elder Races in the Archipelago: the Elves.

It had been John's experience that when one spoke of Elves, people tended to think about sprites, and gossamer-winged fairies, and gentle, folklore magic. These were not those kind of Elves.

Bert had explained to him early in his apprenticeship about the Elves—that they had not come to maturity during the time of the Archipelago, as had many of the other races, but had in fact come from a far older culture, from when there was no separation between the Summer Country and the Archipelago.

Their land was contemporary with Atlantis and Mu. Some heard it was called Númenor; some Ys; others still Melniboné. But whatever it had been called was lost to all but the Elven race itself, and they had had enough of dealings with men.

When the Frontier was erected, Arthur himself went as an emissary to the Elf King, Eledir, who reestablished trade with the rest of the Archipelago, and by extension, the rest of the world. As a gift of good faith, Arthur allowed Ordo Maas to build the Blue Dragon, which he presented to the Elf King. In subsequent years the Elven craftsmen improved on the old shipmaster's design, turning an already formidable craft into a truly impressive instrument of war.

A remarkable history, John thought, that comes to its conclusion here, half-buried in the dust of Paralon.

Several dozen feet above their heads, the masthead of the great Dragon stretched high into the dusky air. Reaching away behind it were the spars and boards that had once formed a tight hull, now spread wide with age and disuse. The sides of the ship looked like a moth-eaten blanket, shot through with holes. The frame spread out on both sides like a skeleton, ribs pulling away from the spine—proof, stark and cold, that the living heart that it had once housed was long dead. Even the golden eyes of the Dragon were gray and cold—or at least one of them was, John noted. The other had been pried out of its socket, leaving a gaping hole in the noble face.

"Were you a sailor aboard the ship?" Rose asked gently, "or its captain, perhaps?"

"Not captain," the man said. "My ship. I built her. I and the Ancient of Days."

"Eledir?" John gasped. "Are you Eledir?"

The fragile face changed into a mask of hope. "Do you know me? You know my name?"

"Yes, yes I do!" John exclaimed. He wasn't certain what to think about this incredible and disturbing new discovery, but for the moment, he was happy enough just to find someone—anyone—he knew.

"Oh, thank you," Eledir said. "Do you have any skrika?"

John's face fell. He looked at Jack, who was similarly confused. Only Houdini and Theo seemed to understand what had happened.

This was indeed Eledir, the great Elf King of legend, who had fought beside Arthur in his youth, and with John and Jack in his golden years. But time, and whatever dreadful events had befallen the Archipelago, had taken their toll. His mind was gone—and with it the noble, majestic warrior who had led the Elven race for millennia.

"There must be a way to aid him," John said as he led the companions a few feet away to confer. "Fred? Is there anything in the Little Whatsit that might help?"

The little badger looked through page after page of ailments and maladies and remedies, only to come up regrettably short. "I'm sorry, Scowler John," he said sadly. "There's nothing here that really addresses this sort of thing. The only references that even come close say to consult the Elves—and he's the only one we know of here."

There was nothing the companions could do except leave the Elf King where they had found him, next to his fire. Doyle, Houdini, and Theo gathered up more wood for him, and Laura Glue and Fred gave him more rations of food and water. After a moment, Fred even went back and placed a packet of his beloved Leprechaun crackers in Eledir's hand.

"Tell the Tin Man," John instructed Archimedes, "that we're going to go into the city, but we're leaving Ele—we're leaving this fellow here. He doesn't need to do anything, just watch from a distance, but I'll just feel better if we're not leaving him completely alone."

"I don't think it matters, little Caretaker," Burton said as he shouldered his pack. "He's not in there."

"It matters to me," said John, turning away, his fists clenched in helplessness. "It matters."

CHAPTER ELEVEN
The Little Prince

Silence ruled in the streets of the city on Paralon. The broad, stone-lined thoroughfares were still there, but empty save for weeds and dust. The canals had gone dry, and most of the lower structures were too crumbled and broken down to even safely explore. The only structure that bore a resemblance to what had stood there before was the great citadel—the seat of the Silver Throne.

"I'll say this for him," John said, whistling in admiration. "Artigel built things to last."

Laura Glue was taking the destruction in stride. After the discovery of Eledir and the *Blue Dragon*, everything else seemed to be revealing itself in a natural, terrible progression. Still, John noted that she remained aloft on her wings as much as possible, and she spoke only to Archimedes. She might be feeling the impact of all this more than she was revealing.

As for Fred, he was putting up a brave front. John could tell by the nervous twitching of his whiskers that the badger was highly agitated—but he kept his composure, mostly by stroking his watch.

Ah, Charles, John thought. *You chose better than you knew, when you picked this little fellow to be your apprentice. He knows*

There, peeking from behind the timeworn throne, was a child.

*instinctively that bravery is not the absence of fear, but the willingness
to act in spite of it.*

There were high walls erected in concentric circles all around
the main towers of the citadel. They were massively solid but
seemed also to have been hastily constructed, with some of them
built over, on top of, and through the surrounding structures. The
patchwork construction of some of them attested to the fact that
they were built while Paralon was under siege—they were made
of the materials that were readily at hand. That meant roads,
castles, hovels—whatever could be broken down and used again
to reinforce the battlements.

"Those wars George mentioned," Jack said, drawing his finger
through the dust on a rampart. "I think I believe him now."

"They were trying to protect something," said Burton. "These
are battlements, and well-built ones."

"Something, or someone?" asked John. "And the more important question: Were they successful?"

"I don't think the citadel would still be standing if they
weren't," offered Doyle.

"I can't believe we haven't found anyone else here," said Laura
Glue. "There were thousands of people living on Paralon."

"There is probably no one left around except for the animals,"
Burton said as he pushed aside a fallen pillar. "They're usually
what remain when the people have gone."

"Talking, or the other kind?" asked Houdini. "I wouldn't
really mind meeting more animals that can talk."

"What does it matter?" answered Burton. "If they talk, they're
just servants and chattel. If they don't, they're dinner tonight and
food storage for tomorrow."

"Ahem-hem," Fred interrupted as politely as he could manage. "I know some animals who would say exactly the same things about *you*."

"That matters less to me," said Burton. "I don't believe in making friends with something I ought to be eating."

"Don't take that personally, Fred," said Jack. "He's eaten a lot of his friends, too."

"If there is anyone still left here," Fred went on, undeterred by Burton's disdain, "it's sure t' be the animals, precisely *because* we're a servant class race."

"So you admit you're inferior?" asked Burton.

"I said nothing of the kind," Fred retorted. "We do it because it's a calling humans can only aspire to."

"Hah!" Burton barked. "How do you figure that?"

"Animal logic," answered Fred. "We figure we're here in this life to help others, to be happy, and to try not to eat our neighbors. And not necessarily in that order," he added.

"Those are three qualities that Burton will never understand," said John, "including the part about eating his neighbors."

"Only when it was necessary," said Burton.

The last of the great walls was the stoutest, and tallest, and least damaged.

"I don't even think it's just a wall," Jack said, shading his eyes to look skyward. "It looks like they were trying to enclose the palace completely and never finished the job."

The massive doors resembled those that guarded the ancient library known as the Great Whatsit, or those of Samaranth's own cavern. There were Elven runes carved throughout the metalwork and stone.

"That may have been why Eledir was here," Jack suggested. "He closed them in and sealed the door."

"Possibly," said John, "but someone was expecting us to open them again." He pointed to the locks. "See here? *Alpha*, the mark of the House of Arthur. And here," he indicated the other side. "*Pi*. The Caretaker's mark. We were meant to come here together, Rose, to find this place."

John and Rose each placed their hands over their respective marks, and there was a faint glow and warmth as the magic engaged. But the doors did not open.

"Come here, Burton, Theo," said Jack. "Let's give it a push."

"Rusted shut," Jack declared after a minute of straining at the doors. He wiped his hands on his trousers and looked at the Magician. "I don't suppose you can do anything about this?"

"Me?" said Houdini. "Locks aren't a problem. Rusted twenty-foot-high doors . . . that's a different kettle of fish."

"Archimedes . . . ," John began.

"I know, I know," the bird grumbled. "You want me to go fetch Bacon. Your wish is my command, O master."

Archie wheeled around and flew toward the beach, grumbling as he went. "Servant class my feathered rear," he muttered. "I'm a teacher."

"Sorry to burst your bubble," Jack called out, "but in my experience, that's about the same thing."

"We're not going to wait," Laura Glue declared suddenly, as she caught up Rose under the arms and soared up the face of the wall.

"Laura Glue!" John shouted. "Oh, for cat's sake," he grumbled. "There's not much we can do, I suppose, if she won't listen to us."

"And why should she, Caretaker?" asked Burton. "In her world she's a trusted soldier. But you still see a frightened child. Is it her obedience or your vision that is too small?"

Archie arrived with the Tin Man in tow, and once more they put their shoulders to the doors. But again, even with the Tin Man's amazing strength, they could not move the doors an inch.

"Now what?" Jack panted. "We can't exactly have Laura Glue fly all of us over the top, can we?"

"You don't need to," Rose said as the mighty doors swung open—*toward* the companions. "All the pushing in the world won't do you any good if you're pushing in the wrong direction."

All the men looked around sheepishly at one another as the young women and the animals laughed and trooped inside. "Did you even try pulling on them?" John asked.

"Didn't even occur to me," said Jack. "If it was up to us, we'd have ended up sitting on the beach with Eledir."

"I was going to mention the huge silver rings on the outside," said Houdini.

"Oh, shut up," said Burton.

Inside the great wall, which they could now see was really a half dome, stood the palace of Paralon. Its defenders had been trying to erect a great protective shell around it, to better preserve whatever it was that remained inside. But of everything the companions had witnessed, the castle was the one thing that resembled their memories, and Laura Glue teared up at the sight of it.

"Now we're getting somewhere," said Fred, thumping a fist into his paw. "As long as there sits a descendant of Arthur on the Silver Throne, then the Archipelago is not alone."

John looked askance at Jack, who remained placid. After all these years, any mention of the Silver Throne pushed Jack into an emotional reserve of coolness. The last King they knew, Stephen, was the son of Jack's first great love—and he had never truly gotten over that feeling.

"Let's go see what there is to see," Jack said brusquely, pushing ahead of the others. He strode through the familiar corridors as quickly as he could until he finally reached the great hall where the Silver Throne of Arthur had stood.

Jack pulled open the doors—pulled, not pushed, John noted with amusement—and entered the hall.

Immediately he was surrounded by dozens of animals bearing a strange assortment of weapons. They were all chittering and howling and creating a terrible racket. Some were foxes, and others were smaller creatures he couldn't identify in all the melee.

They were pointing crude spears and long knives at Jack and the others who had come up quickly behind him—but some among the animals had weapons that resembled those of Nemo's time. That meant they were deadly, if not accurate.

"Stop!" Fred shouted, throwing himself in front of the companions. "We mean you no harm!"

At the appearance of another animal, all the rest stopped and grew silent. They seemed slightly confused, as if they'd been ready to go to war, and the appearance of this little badger had changed their minds.

"Who be you?" one of the foxes asked. "Be you friend, or be you foe?"

"I be . . . I mean, I am Fred, son of Uncas, son of Tummeler," said the little Caretaker, "and we mean you no harm."

"Caretaker?" the fox exclaimed. "Are the rest of you also Caretakers?"

"Some of us," said Jack. "I'm Jack, and this is John."

At this, all the animals, which they now saw were foxes and hedgehogs, dropped their weapons and sank to their knees. "Scowler John and Scowler Jack," the fox said reverently, "I am Myrret, and I am your humble servant. We have cared for him the best we could until you could arrive."

"Him?" asked Jack. "Him who?"

"The prince," Myrret replied with some surprise. "The last prince of the Silver Throne."

The animals led the companions through the great hall, and for the first time, they could see how it had been transformed. Far from being a place of government, it had been made over to resemble a giant nursery. There was a theater to one side, with half-completed sets from what appeared to be a Brothers Grimm story. There were books scattered everywhere, and stained-glass friezes that depicted a plethora of fables and fairy tales. There was even a miniature planet, large enough to climb on, that hovered above a silver base. It was every child's dream—or would have been, had it not been locked inside a fortress.

"Where is he?" John asked Myrret. "Is he here?"

In reply, the fox pointed to the fore of the room, to the Silver Throne itself.

There, peeking from behind the timeworn throne, was a child. A boy, dark-haired, bright-eyed, and all of six years old, if that, thought Jack—although the curious expression on his face and the absence of fear made him appear to be older.

He hesitated—these strangers were the first people he might have seen in a long time, if ever. Rose read his fear and approached the throne slowly.

"Hello," she said softly. "I'm your cousin Rose. Who are you?"

"I am the son of Radamand, who was the son of Homer, who was the son of Karal," he said, "who was the son of . . ." He paused and scratched his head. "I forget who else. But I am the last king of the Silver Throne."

Burton laughed, a short, sharp bark. "Hah! King? You're barely old enough to dress yourself."

"Richard, shut up," Jack hissed.

"You are a prince, and may be king someday," said Rose. "When you are older."

"I read about the king in the stories," said the boy. "The king of rocks. You know—Old King Coal was a merry old soul."

"You can read?" asked Rose.

"The animals tell me stories," he said. "They've also taught me how to read, so that if they are busy, I can read them myself," he said with no small pride.

"C-O-L-E, not C-O-A-L," Fred corrected, trying to be helpful.

"The animals call me Coal," the boy said. "I never got a real name. When I was born, there was no one left to name me. So I decided I came from a story instead."

No one left? John thought. Had they come too late? Just in time to witness the end of the Silver Throne?

"Knew you'd come," said Coal. "The stories all said you would. And now we can listen to the last story together!"

"What is the last story?" asked Rose. "Is it a book?"

"No," Myrret answered. "It's in the Whatsit."

"The Great Whatsit!" Jack exclaimed. "It still exists?"

"Not the Great Whatsit," Myrret corrected, "just the Whatsit. The Great Whatsit was destroyed by the Trolls in the Second War of the Races, and the last of the crows and the hedgehogs moved what they could save here, to the new Whatsit that a badger built underneath the palace."

"Badger?" said Fred, perking up. "What badger?"

"Charles Montgolfier something something," said Myrret. "I could look it up if you like."

"No need," Fred said as Jack squeezed his shoulder. "Attaboy, Pop."

"The prince's own ancestress left the last story for you," said a small hedgehog, "and she has guarded it herself all these centuries."

"She's still alive?" asked Rose.

"She sleeps forever in the crystal," the hedgehog said reverently, "never to be awakened. Come with me, and I'll take you to her."

CHAPTER TWELVE
The Regency

❖

Myrret and the other animals led the companions and the little prince to a spiral flight of stairs that was secreted behind the throne itself. It dropped away almost straight down, farther than the light from the torches showed. One by one they climbed down into the stairway, first the animals, then the Caretakers, with Burton and his colleagues bringing up the rear. The Tin Man stayed behind to make sure they weren't followed.

Shadows danced along the walls of the tunnels as the companions passed down into the new Whatsit. Jack occasionally looked back at Theo, who had taken up the rearmost position, and who was pausing every now and again to peer back into the darkness behind them. Each time, Theo would return Jack's unspoken question with a short shake of the head. No enemy was following them—not that they knew of. Or could see.

The stairway ended in a tall cavern filled with crystalline structures. All along the walls were tubes full of crystal shards, some of different colors, and they seemed to be organized by size.

"We started keeping all our records on the crystals," Myrret explained, "when the parchment and books became too unwieldy. Far more expedient this way, don't you think?" The fox was twisting

There on a pedestal . . . stood a very familiar-looking device.

his paws together, and it was obvious he was seeking some sign of approval from his esteemed guests.

"It's remarkable," said John. "Very good work, Myrret."

The fox beamed and scampered across the room to fetch one of the librarians. He returned with a ferret who was dressed in several weathered robes, all of which had been meant for larger animals.

"Glory be," the little tatterdemalion whispered as he pulled up his trousers. "The Caretakers! I never thought I would live to see them myself!"

The ferret was thrilled to be able to show them the pride and joy of the Whatsit—what they called the Last Story.

"Good heavens," Jack said, whistling. "It's a projector."

There on a pedestal in the center of the room, facing a tall structure of giant crystals, stood a very familiar-looking device. It was a reel-to-reel film projector, much like they had in the cinemas back at Oxford, but with a double set of lenses.

"It's definitely Hank's design," John said admiringly. "I think this is what he intended his chronal stereopticon to eventually become."

"Is it like the Lanterna Magica?" asked Jack, as his face lit up with the possibility. "Can we use it to leave the Archipelago?"

Myrret shook his furred head. "The ancestors had access to neither the Prime Caretaker nor the Tin Man, and the great Captain Nemo was long dead. Without their knowledge, we had no way to build such a device. All we could do was use what we had to keep a memory alive. And keep it we have, for many, many centuries."

"I've tried to turn it on," said Coal, "but it never would work. Not for me, even though I can work other things by touching them."

"The seal bears the Caretaker's mark, not the king's mark," Jack explained to Coal. "That's why you were never able to turn it on."

"Archie," John began.

"I'm way ahead of you," the bird replied. "I'll go get him."

With some difficulty, the Tin Man made his way down the stairs to the Whatsit, where he examined the device briefly, then shook his head. Whatever he might have been able to contribute to its construction was not possible now. It would do what it would do.

"We've replaced all the parts many times to keep it in order," Myrret said proudly, "but it is the selfsame generator that the great Hank Morgan built in the time of Arthur, lo these many centuries ago."

"How would you know about that?" asked Houdini. "That was in another world, wasn't it?"

The small animal brandished a familiar-looking if ageworn book. "The Little Whatsit," he said proudly. "The Histories are complete, at least in regard to the important things. And there was none more important than the story of the Great King and the Silver Throne."

"It isn't the same machine, you know," Burton said as he peered at the projector. "If you've replaced all the components, then the original doesn't exist anymore. It would be like taking your grandfather's ax and replacing the handle, then replacing the blade, then replacing the handle again, and then still insisting that it was your grandfather's ax."

The little animal was crestfallen. "I meant no offense, great Lord," he said meekly.

"Never mind him," said Jack, frowning at Burton. "He's only a barbarian."

Myrret opened a velvet-lined box and removed a large reel, which he carefully placed on the empty arm, then threaded into the projector. "Legend says the ancestor made this for her own son, who was king," he explained, "but that was many years ago. I don't think she expected it to be so long before you returned."

"Neither did we," said John.

"Great Caretakers," the ferret said, "would you do us the honor of turning on the device?"

"Be my guest," John said to Jack.

"How about our third?" Jack replied, smiling at Fred. "Will you?"

Fred swallowed hard and reached his paw up to the seal, which melted away at his touch. There was an awed hush among the other animals—to see one of their own as a Caretaker would create a new legend in the Archipelago. Or whatever was left of it.

The projector sputtered to life, and a broad rectangle of light appeared on the glassine wall of the crystal across the chamber. A logo appeared, bearing the insignia of Mr. Tummeler's production company, followed by an ad for the twenty-eighth expanded edition of the *Imaginarium Geographica*.

"Good old granddad," Fred said, wiping a tear from his furry cheek. "Never missed a trick."

"Now I'm getting hungry for blueberry muffins," said John.

"Same here," said Jack.

"What in Hades does that mean?" asked Burton.

"Never mind," Jack said, winking at Fred. "Inside joke."

A moment later a fox appeared on the wall and introduced himself as Reynard. He bowed, then stepped offscreen.

"Reynard, of course!" John said to Jack. "Just like back at Sanctuary."

"Yes," said Jack warily, "but didn't Verne set that up?"

"For all we know, he set this up too."

"Hush," Jack replied. "Someone's coming into view."

The image on the crystalline wall was of a woman, mature but not yet elderly, who was dressed in simple clothes, save for the elegant silk robe draped across her shoulders. Her hair was auburn shot through with silver, and it seemed to Jack for a moment that he recognized her.

"Hello, my young firebrand," the image said as she appeared to look fondly at Jack. "I'm not surprised to see you, although I wish it had been far, far sooner."

Jack and the others gasped—he had recognized her after all. It was Aven.

"Did she record this for me, then?" Jack whispered to Myrret. "I thought she meant this for Stephen."

"I did," the image replied, to the consternation and surprise of everyone in the chamber, "but I do not believe it is a coincidence that you should be the one to open the seal, dear Jack. You saved me once," she added with a wry smile. "Perhaps it is now written in your destiny to save us all."

"How is this possible?" Jack exclaimed, hardly daring to move closer. "Is it really you?"

The image of Aven laughed. "It is, Jack. It is the Aven you knew. But I'm not here—or 'there,' I suppose—in the flesh. I am just an image, but still, I have been waiting for a very long time, and I'm very glad to see you again."

"Actually, I opened it," Fred said, meekly raising his paw.

"Ah," said Aven. "So you've become a Caretaker too, Fred. Your family would be very proud of you."

John realized that just like the ghost of Hank Morgan, she couldn't see or hear the viewers until they had engaged the projection first. "I'm here as well," John said. "Hello, Aven."

"John," she said. "You haven't lost the *Geographica* again, have you?"

"Not so far," said John. "But I seem to have misplaced the Archipelago."

"Yes," she said, head bowed. "I imagine it would seem that way."

"What happened, Aven?" asked Jack.

"When it seemed that the Caretakers abandoned the Archipelago," she began, "we had no way of knowing what had happened to you—only that you didn't return, and there was no way to contact you.

"The Frontier had become impassable, as if the storm clouds had been replaced by stone walls," Aven went on, "and nothing we built could breach it. Stephen and the animals built machine after machine, but nothing worked. After almost a decade of trying, he abandoned his efforts and turned his attention to guiding the future of the Archipelago."

She paused, and bowed her head. "It did not go well."

"In the twenty-second year of the new republic, several of the races rebelled, and there was a violent split in the Senate. Several lands withdrew their support, and war was declared."

"War?" John sputtered. "There was a war in the Archipelago?"

Aven nodded. "Four wars, to be exact. The severing of the bonds between the races was all it took to divide the republic, and all the lands took to looking after their own interests.

"It was after the battle with the Shadow King that I stepped down as queen, and Stephen took over the affairs of the Archipelago," she continued. "I had lost my husband, but he left me with one final gift. I was with child."

"You and Artus had a child?" John exclaimed.

"Yes," said Aven. "I named him Charles. It was Tummeler's suggestion."

"Of course it was," Jack said, noting that Fred was practically beaming at the mention of his grandfather. "And what of Stephen?"

At the mention of her elder son, Aven's countenance darkened. "He went on a quest," she said after a pause. "The last great quest of the Archipelago. It remains to be seen whether or not his sacrifice will have been worth all we lost.

"There was one final message from him, before he . . . ," she said, her voice breaking. "He said that the sacrifices he made were not just for the Archipelago, or the Summer Country, but for the love he had for one girl, which he never got to share."

Laura Glue's face reddened. "I knew," she said.

Aven looked at her with gentle eyes. "He did love you, you know, even if you didn't feel it as strongly as he did. He spoke of you often, and regretted not having gone with you to Tamerlane House."

The Valkyrie's eyes began to well with tears, and Fred reached over to take her hand in support.

"So Arthur's own line did continue," said John. "That means the child had the same lineage as Rose."

"It became stranger than that," said Aven, "when Charles married Tiger Lily. It turned out to be a very successful union despite the matter of Lily's parentage."

Burton cleared his throat. "I'm right here, in the room," he said a bit brusquely, "but I forgive the slight breach of etiquette, as you have given me news of my daughter." He bowed slightly—not deeply enough to be subservient, but just enough that the gesture was sincere.

"Burton?" Aven asked, startled.

"Yes," said Jack, in a tone that was almost embarrassed. "You remember, Aven—the Caretakers Emeritis brokered a truce with the Imperial Cartological Society. We're all operating cooperatively now. And the ICS is being developed as an official organization at Cambridge by, uh"—he swallowed hard—"me."

"So he's your ally now," Aven said, her voice subdued. "Not enough time has passed, it seems, for that not to be a surprise. And you, Jack," she finished, looking up again and meeting his eyes, "you've become a true pirate at last."

Jack winced slightly. He couldn't tell if she was teasing or not.

The projection laughed. "Of course I'm teasing you, Jack. I know full well that appearances are fleeting, and you did what was necessary."

"What happened to the Archipelago, Aven?" asked Jack. "Where *did* all the lands go?"

"Samaranth took them," Aven said simply. "He took them all, to a place that cannot be reached in space or time."

"Where is that?" asked Burton. "Nether Land?"

"Farther still," Aven replied. "He took them beyond the great wall."

"Why would he do such a thing?" John asked. "How is that even possible?"

"The Shadows came to claim them," Aven said with deep sorrow. "The true Shadows, the Darkness that cannot be broken. Our great enemy."

"The Echthroi," said Theo.

"Yes," said Aven. "The Echthroi. That is the name of the Shadows. They have another name for those shadows they claim from the living: Lloigor. When a good creature, a servant of the Light, is turned, its shadow disappears—but not completely. It becomes a servant of the Echthroi. A Lloigor."

Jack exhaled hard and looked away. "Then that's what was happening to me when I started to follow Mordred's path," he said somberly. "My shadow was becoming a Lloigor."

Aven nodded. "But you chose to take it back, Jack. You chose to return to the Light. As long as there is life, there is always a choice. No matter what else has gone before, no matter how terrible the crimes or how strong the temptation, one may still choose to turn away from the pit of darkness, away from the lure of shadow. This is how the Echthroi are defeated."

"And what about after life?" Burton asked abruptly. "What about those living a second go-round?"

"Life," Aven said evenly, "is intelligence, and the ability to choose. Death is rejecting all choices."

"I don't think that quite answered the question," he murmured under his breath.

"I think it did," said Theo.

"If my shadow was becoming a Lloigor," said Jack, "what happened to Mordred's shadow?"

"He was to become their greatest champion," said Aven. "A Lloigor who goes willingly is nearly unstoppable. That's why it was able to return so often, first as the King of Crickets, and then as the Shadow King."

"If such a creature is so powerful," said Jack, "then how was it Rose was able to defeat it with Caliburn?"

"Because Madoc chose," said Aven. "He chose to turn his back on the Echthroi and what they represented. And in that hour the Shadow King lost much of his power, and the Echthroi lost their great champion."

"But it isn't always those who choose the darkness, as I nearly did, who become servants of the shadows," said Jack. "What about those peoples of the Archipelago who were made into Shadow-Born by Pandora's Box?"

"Or the Dragons themselves, who were touched by the Spear of Destiny?" added John. "None of them were willing, but they became servants of the Echthroi nonetheless."

"Their minds were clouded," said Aven. "Samaranth told me that the Echthroi could compel obedience through magic, or lies, or betrayal. But that is only a last resort—they prefer to convert, not compel. And sometimes they appeal to the darkness in all men's souls, and can confuse good men into service. Surely you can understand this?"

"Yes," Burton answered, as if she'd been speaking to him. "Yes, I can."

"A century after the Day of Sorrow," she continued, "we discovered that lands along the western edge were vanishing—being covered in Shadow. At first we feared that the Winter King had in some way returned. But we knew his Shadow had been destroyed, as much by his own choice to aid you when he repaired the sword, as by the sword itself. There have been other agents throughout history, others who served the Echthroi, but Samaranth came to us here and said that it was far worse. The Shadow covering the lands was the Echthroi *themselves*.

"That was when Samaranth opened up his own archives to

us and shared all the knowledge he could. And I realized that I would never be seeing him again."

"What did he do?" asked Jack. "Is that when he left?"

Aven nodded. "It was. He invoked the Old Magic, and as the first Caretaker of the Archipelago of Dreams, he took up all the lands and bore them away so they would not fall victim to the Echthroi."

"It seems that I've outlived my usefulness," John said ruefully, looking at the atlas in Fred's pack. "If there's no Archipelago of Dreams, then of what importance is the *Imaginarium Geographica*, or a Caretaker who can translate it?"

"Of great importance, John," Aven answered with a tone of reproach. "The greatest. Without the *Geographica*, it will be impossible to put them all back."

"What?" asked Jack. "The islands of the Archipelago? They can still be restored?"

"Yes," Aven said. "But not until you repair what was broken, and connect our worlds once more. Until then, only shadows remain."

"If all that remains of the Archipelago is shadows," Jack asked, "then will the images in the *Geographica* vanish?'

John understood the concern behind his friend's question. During their first conflict with the Winter King, they discovered that whenever a land was conquered, the corresponding map faded and vanished. The longer the Winter King was loosed in the world, the more likely he was to have control of all of the lands. Only restoring the shadows to the people of the lands brought the drawings back.

"Never fear, Jack," Aven answered. "The lands have not been taken by force, not even those of our enemies. They went willingly and unafraid, because they knew that taking them from these waters was Samaranth's responsibility, and his stewardship, as it has always been."

"What if Rose called him?" asked Jack. "Samaranth *would* come, wouldn't he?"

At once her expression grew dark and stern. "That you must never do," she cautioned. "You must never summon the Dragons again." This last she directed at Rose. "Even if Samaranth is the only one left, should he be summoned by one of noble intent, he would come and restore the Archipelago. And until time is properly restored, that cannot happen. Must not happen."

Jack was taken aback by the tone and fervor with which Aven spoke. Nothing else she had said had carried this degree of firmness. "We'll listen, Aven, and the Summoning will not be spoken. But why is it so important? Wouldn't Samaranth be a help to us?"

"It's too late for Samaranth to help you, even if he chose to," said Aven. "But there is still time to seek out his heir."

Rose looked sharply at John. Samaranth's heir? Could she mean the Dragon's apprentice?

"The two worlds were once one," the projection continued, "connected. And even when the connections were severed, and the worlds separated by the Frontier, there remained resonances . . . reflections. What happens in the one is mirrored in the other. What happens in one can impact the other. And with the flow of time set loose here in the Archipelago, the effects were mirrored a thousandfold."

"There's a lot you need to know about what's happened," John began, but Aven cut him off.

"The film isn't an endless loop," she chided, "nor is it infinitely expandable. It was shot using Verne's processes, so that a time loop could be instilled within the frames—but once it has been exposed to the projector light, the frames are set. This film can never again be replayed as it is being played now. When our time has run out, you'll have a recorded copy of this discussion, but nothing more. I'll be gone, forever."

Suddenly the images on the wall began to flicker, and chemical burns began to strobe along the edges of the frames.

"Wait!" Jack shouted. "We aren't done yet! Wait!"

"We don't know what to do!" John exclaimed. "There's no way to repair the Archipelago!"

"But there is," Aven said, her voice strained and growing weaker. "I would not have charged you with such a task without giving you the means to carry it out."

Without any further warning, the projection went blank, then the end of the strip started flapping noisily through the reel until Jack reached over and shut it off.

"That wasn't really a very good story," said Coal. "Do we have any more?"

"She couldn't tell us," Jack lamented. "She said she left us the means, but we don't know what that is!"

"I know, Master Caretaker," said Myrret. "It is one of the greatest stories we have after the Day of Sorrows. The great quest of King Stephen. It cost him his life, but he was successful. And it will perhaps give you the opportunity you seek."

He motioned to the other foxes, who guided the companions into a second chamber in the Whatsit. This one was broader, and covered in sand and stone rather than crystal. But something stunningly familiar sat in the center of the chamber.

It was a door. One of the doors from the Keep of Time.

PART FOUR

The Family Trade

In another chamber . . . lay a deep cradle of crystal and silk . . .

CHAPTER THIRTEEN
The Passage

❖

Cursing under his breath, Ernest McGee swept his arm across the table, scattering parchments and spilling ink. His family trade was mapmaking, and as far as Ernest could tell, it had brought both wealth and fame, and grief and misery in equal amounts.

His father's best friend, Captain Charles Johnson, had disappeared years earlier, and the subsequent deception that was put forth was an insult and a travesty.

True, the *History* was published, and it bore Johnson's name, but for Ernest's father Eliot to deny all knowledge of the man was not right.

It didn't bother Ernest that his father's collaborator claimed credit for work that was not his—it bothered him that they had created the fiction that Johnson never existed at all.

It had taken Ernest most of his adult life to properly assemble the two books that his father had worked so hard to complete: One described the wealth of the world, hidden in strange and curious places by terrible men who no longer sailed the oceans; and the other described entire worlds that might or might not even exist.

He might not have inherited the desire, or even the skill—but he was loath to deny the family a legacy. He only hoped that it would end with him, that perhaps his own son might choose to return to silversmithing, rather than follow the family heritage of making maps for pirates and madmen.

Even as he wished it, he knew it wasn't to be. Some things in life run too deep.

Some things are just in the blood.

Picking up the quill and a fresh parchment, he dipped the point into the ink and started to draw again.

"Oh my stars and garters," Fred whispered. "Is that what I think it is?"

"It's a door from the keep, you idiot," Burton said gruffly.

Rose laid a comforting hand on the badger's arm before he could draw a sword and defend his honor by having the stuffing beaten out of him by Burton. "He knows what it is," she said placidly, "because he's seen it before. We all have. That's the door we dropped over the waterfall.

"That's the door we gave to my father—to Madoc."

"So we may have a way out after all," said Burton. "Excellent."

"Is this what we want to do?" John asked the others. "We might be saving ourselves, but would we be giving up on the Archipelago?"

"Pardon my saying so," said Fred, "but what would we be giving up? Other than Paralon, there's nothing here. And the queen said that Stephen gave his life to give us this opening, so we could fix things. What else do you need to know?"

John scratched the badger on the head. "You may be the wisest of us all, Fred. We'll go through the door."

"Myrret," Jack said suddenly, "may I take the reel from the projector with me? Please?"

The little animal sniffed loudly and nodded its assent through a curtain of tears. "It was f'r you that we preserved it all these years, so it's well and just that you should have it. Besides, it can't be used again, so there's no point, is there? No point in us keeping our stewardship any longer."

"There's always a point, little fellow," Jack said, "and stewardships kept are among the noblest of causes."

"All we have to do now," said Myrret, "is say good-bye to her."

Jack's brow furrowed. "What do you mean?"

"The queen," Myrret said, confused. "We promised that when you came, we would wake her. She sleeps in crystal, here in the Whatsit."

"I thought you were talking about the projection," said John. "A metaphor."

"Take us to her, Myrret," Jack said. "Take us to her now."

In another chamber adjacent to the projection room lay a deep cradle of crystal and silk, and in it, covered by a sheath of the clear stone, lay Aven.

"She's still here," Jack breathed. "She's alive."

Aven was ancient, impossibly old. Her face and hands were pale, and her hair, which was draped behind her as if it were floating, was pure, colorless white.

"I'll wake her now," said Myrret. He touched a contact at the base of the cradle, and the crystal sheath slid back. Exposed to the open air, Aven suddenly took a deep breath, then another, and another. Then, slowly, she opened her eyes.

"Ah, my young corsair," she said when she saw Jack. "You came back. You came back to me."

"Of course," Jack said, his voice choked with emotion. "Of course I did."

He leaned in close as his ancient friend slowly closed her eyes, then opened them again. They still sparkled, but the light in them was fading.

"We should ask her to answer more of our questions," Burton began, but Theo pulled him back, and both Houdini and Doyle stepped in front of him. The purpose of waking Aven was not to ask questions. It was to allow her, finally, to rest.

"You saw the message?" she asked weakly. "You understood?"

"We did," said Jack. "We'll use the door, never fear. We'll right this, Ave. And we'll look after the prince."

Her expression darkened. "What prince?"

"Coal," he said. "The little prince. Your heir."

"He mustn't leave," she said. "It isn't safe." She drew a shallow breath. "Look after Charles, will you, Jack? Take care of him. He needs you. He can help you."

"Of course," Jack said, looking over at John. She was obviously fading—her son was long gone.

"Ah, Artus . . . ," Aven breathed. "You don't need to wait for me any longer. . . ." As the companions watched, the strength left her arms, and her eyes fluttered closed. Slowly she took a breath, her chest rising faintly with the effort. Then another. Then, nothing. She was gone.

Jack squeezed his eyes shut as the tears flowed down his cheeks, and he murmured a quiet prayer as he placed Aven's hands on her chest and stepped back from the cradle.

* * *

"It's decided," John said flatly. "We can't take the boy with us."

The companions had retreated to the projection room to decide what to do. They had already planned to go through the door—but there was some dissent about whether all of them should go.

"That isn't your decision to make, Caretaker," Burton said with obvious anger. "Not alone."

"I have to say that I agree with him," said Doyle, "and not just because we're both members of the Society."

"I agree with them," said Houdini. "After all we've been told, how can we consider leaving him here? There's nothing left, John. The Archipelago is a wasteland. There's no future for him here."

"That's part of the problem," said John. "It's *all* future here. We've already had too much experience with dropping people in the past, where they didn't belong. What kind of chaos will we cause if we bring back someone from the future?"

"That's not quite it," said Jack. "Remember what Ransom said? This isn't the future, not to us. It's our present. It's also," he added, jerking a thumb over his shoulder at where the boy was chatting with Fred and Laura Glue, "his present. It all moves forward."

"You're wiser than I gave you credit for," Burton said to Jack. "You're outvoted, Caretaker."

"I didn't say I was siding with you," said Jack. "I have reservations of my own. And Aven herself said he shouldn't leave."

"She's been sleeping in a crystal for two thousand years," said Burton. "She didn't know what she was saying."

"I still say we vote," said John.

"And of course the rodent will be voting with you," said Burton.

"Fred," Jack said pointedly, "qualified to be something you flunked, Burton. So try to have a little respect, if only for the office he holds."

"I have some respect for the badger," Burton shot back. "It's the office I think is weak."

The End of Time looked at Burton. "The child must stay," he said impassively. "He must."

Burton's jaw dropped open in amazement. Of all of them, the End of Time was the one man he had expected to back him in his arguments.

"Why?"

Theo refused to answer, and merely stared at Burton, who dropped his eyes.

"All right," Burton finally agreed, still reluctant. "The boy stays here, God curse you all."

It took some intense discussions and the direct involvement of both Fred and Archimedes to convince Myrret and the other animals that it would be best for Coal to remain on Paralon. By that point, even John was wavering—but Jack took both Aven's request and Theo's warning very seriously and persuaded the others that it really was for the best.

As Myrret distracted Coal up in the Great Hall, the companions began to examine the door. It was framed in stone, and despite all its travels, looked none the worse for wear.

"I'll give this to the Dragons," said Burton. "They could build a door."

Jack reached out and touched the door. It swung open slightly and vibrated. Peering through the crack, he could see some kind of street, and the sounds of horses and street vendors wafted through, along with an assortment of odors. There was no question—the door still worked.

Suddenly a stone fell from the arch and landed with a dull thump in the sand. "Uh-oh," said Houdini. "That's not a good sign."

"It's thousands of years old," said Fred, "and it's no longer being supported by the energies of the keep."

"We'd better go through quickly," said John. "It may not last for another trip."

But before the companions could open the door farther, an earth-rattling tremor threw them to the floor.

"What the hell?" said Burton. "Is it another discontinuity?"

"No," Theo said, looking up the stairwell. "That was something else. Something living."

There was another tremor, and then a deep, malevolent voice rang through the entire palace. "Little things," the reverberating voice said, "why have you come here?"

Rose's eyes widened in recognition. She had heard that voice before, not all that long ago. "It's the star!" she exclaimed. "The star, Rao, from one of the islands past the Edge of the World!"

"It is a dark star," the ferret said. "It is a creature of Shadow now."

"A Lloigor," said Theo, "with the power of a living star. We must go. We must go now."

Somewhere up above the palace, the star called Rao roared, and the earth shook. Two more stones fell from the frame around the door.

"It's not going to hold!" Fred cried as he pushed open the door. "The frame is breaking up!"

A huge figure lumbered around behind the door and grasped the stones, and Fred pushed it open all the way.

The Tin Man braced himself around the crumbling archway and held the stones together as, one by one, the companions passed through the vortex of energies that was the doorway into time.

Rao continued to rage, and now the roaring was closer—the star had entered the palace itself.

"Good-bye, Great Caretakers," the ferret said sadly. "Remember us."

"Ah, me," said John, closing his eyes. "How can I leave them like this?"

Suddenly a cry rang out—a plea. It was a child's voice, calling to them from the far chamber, and he was begging not to be left behind.

Coal.

"We can't!" John shouted, steeling his resolve. "I'm sorry, we can't!"

"We understand," Myrret called out as he barred Coal from entering the chamber. "Go! Go!"

"How stony is your heart, Caretaker?" Burton argued from the world beyond the door. "You'll leave him here, to face this, alone?"

John looked back and forth between Burton and the terrified boy, then dropped his head in resignation. Jack knew the expression on his old friend's face. He was thinking about his own son, Christopher, who was in the Royal Air Force back in England. One young man against a war was too much for a father to carry— and it was too much here, in the face of the dark star, the Lloigor

Rao. "All right!" John said to Burton. "Go! Grab him! We'll keep the door open!"

Burton dashed back through the door and took the terrified boy from the fox just as a dark, living mist began to descend the staircase. "Little things," the booming voice called out, "come to me. Come to Rao."

"Scowler John," Fred said, trying to keep the pleading out of his own voice, "what would Charles do?"

"All for one and one for all, then," John said under his breath. "Myrret!" He shouted. "Come on through! Bring everyone!"

Burton, carrying the little prince, passed through the door just before a rush of animals nearly bowled him off his feet. A dozen foxes, as many hedgehogs, and the ferret raced though between John's legs.

The outer chamber of the Whatsit was full of the black mist now, and the entire palace seemed to be falling to pieces. The rumbling was constant now, and the angry voice of Rao filled the room.

"What about Aven?" Jack shouted over the rumbling. "And Eledir?"

"Aven's already gone," John shouted back, "and Eledir's too far away to help. We're done here, Jack."

John was the last to pass through, and for a brief instant he considered suggesting that the Tin Man try to step around and through the door—but the great behemoth saw the thought pass fleetingly over John's face, and shook its head no.

There was no time left. The Tin Man was here, now, for this purpose—to ensure that the last efforts of Aven and Stephen had not been in vain.

"Little things," Rao boomed, "I see you!"

A great tendril of darkness shot out from the formless Lloigor, past John and through the open door, where it wrapped itself around Rose and began pulling her back.

"No!" John shouted, clutching at the darkness. "Burton! Jack! Hold on to her!"

The men grabbed Rose by the arms, and she screamed. For a moment it seemed as if Rao was going to pull her apart—then suddenly the tendril loosed and pulled away. It had gotten what it wanted.

"My shadow!" Rose exclaimed in horrified wonder. "It's taking my shadow!"

"Close the door!" John yelled up at the Tin Man. "Do it now, before it's too late!"

Something shoved John hard in the chest, and he fell backward through the door. The tendril had released Rose's shadow, which followed him through the door, writhing on the ground at his feet as Rao rose up to confront the Tin Man.

The companions despaired. The machine man was powerful and had a great will—but he would not last long against the power of the dark star.

As the door closed behind him, John heard the voice of the Tin Man speaking to him through the din. "Fix this," it said, in the softly accented continental English of Roger Bacon. "Fix this, Caveo Principia."

Then the door slammed shut and exploded with a violent burst of light and splinters and the shards of time.

CHAPTER FOURTEEN

Craven Street

❖

The companions found themselves standing in an alley off a busy street in London. It was dark, and narrow, and smelly, but it was concealed enough that they weren't going to immediately attract too much attention for the fact that they were accompanied by dozens of animals that walked on their hind legs, were dressed in human clothes, and spoke in accented English.

It took several minutes for the companions to gather their wits about them after the narrow escape from the dark star Rao. John's last act of compassion had brought them not only the little prince, but also an entourage. It also cost them precious seconds during which they'd nearly lost Rose to the Lloigor.

"She'd never have been at risk if you'd just allowed the boy to come with us from the start," Burton said to John, glowering. "You are a stupid man, Caretaker."

"It's all right," said Rose soothingly, her voice still a bit shaky from the fear and the adrenaline. "Because of the Tin Man, we all came through fine, with no harm done. That's all that matters."

"Not completely," Jack said, pointing at the ground. "Something's come loose, Rose."

One . . . was having a lot of difficulty getting his kite out of an elm.

He was right. Her shadow lay on the ground at their feet, completely disconnected from her—and pointing *toward* the light from the street.

Rose's eyes widened, and she leaned down to touch it, but it darted away and up a nearby wall.

"What does this mean?" she asked the Caretakers. "How can my shadow move on its own?"

"People have lost their shadows before," said John, "but usually they have to be given up willingly, or in the cases of the Shadow-Born, taken. But this is an entirely new dilemma."

"Does that make her a Shadow-Born, then?" asked Fred. "That would be terrible for you, Rose."

"She didn't lose her shadow," said Jack. "It's right up there. It just isn't attached to her anymore."

"To give up a shadow means choosing a dark path," said Burton. "Be wary, girl."

"I don't want to give it up!" Rose exclaimed, almost petulantly. "I haven't chosen a dark path! I'm the Grail Child."

"Well, it doesn't appear to be leaving you," John remarked, noting that the shadow was now dancing among the shadows cast by the other companions. "I don't think you have to worry about becoming a Shadow-Born, Rose."

"Not permanently, anyway," Jack said with a grin. "But if you wanted, you could get up to all sorts of mischief now, and just blame it on your shadow."

Rose's eyes widened. "Really?"

"Shame on you!" Archie squawked. "You of all people should know better than to joke about that, Caretaker."

"He isn't too bright either," said Burton.

"I'm sorry," Jack said, chagrined. "Forgive me, Rose. We'll figure out how to reattach it somehow."

"There's nothing to forgive," Rose answered. "We have bigger things to worry about."

"First things first," said John. "We've definitely returned to the Summer Country—but when?"

Burton checked his watch. "Hmm," he mused. "1768. That's not too shabby. And at least we're in the right hemisphere."

"1768?" Houdini repeated. "Are you certain?"

Burton simply scowled in response.

"Drat," said Houdini. "I've missed him by more than a dozen years."

"Missed who?" asked Doyle.

"Katterfelto," the magician replied. "The Prince of Puff, one of the great performers of the age. He doesn't arrive in London until 1782, blast it." He paused and rubbed at his chin in thought. "Then again," he said, his countenance brightening, "there was an influenza epidemic that year too, so I suppose it's not all bad."

"Not all bad!" John exclaimed. "We're in the eighteenth century! And worse, the entire Archipelago is all but destroyed! Are you out of your bloody minds?"

"Calm down, little Caretaker," said Burton. "They've traveled in time more often than you have and adjust more quickly to the novelty of it."

"If we're home," said Rose, "shouldn't there be someone who can help us? Another Caretaker, maybe?"

"Who is the Caretaker in this time?" Jack asked. "I can't recall offhand."

John removed the *Imaginarium Geographica* from Fred's pack

and unwrapped it. He turned to the endpapers, where all the Caretakers had inscribed their names, and ran his finger down the list. "It was after the point when they chose to enlist three Caretakers at a time," he said as he read the names, "so it's possible we could meet up with more than one."

He frowned. "Goethe, from what I can tell. But he may still be too young to have been recruited, and he'll be in Germany, not London. And Swift, although he would be at Tamerlane House by this point, having died already."

"William Blake?" Jack suggested, peering over John's shoulder. "I know he later went renegade with some of the others, but he was a Caretaker around this time."

"Not yet," Burton said, ignoring the remark about renegade Caretakers. "He's only about ten years old here. He won't be approached by the Caretakers for another decade, and he won't start painting the portraits for years after that, so Swift is right out too."

"Then who?" asked Jack.

"I can't tell," said John. "There's a gap here. No one is minding the store, so to speak, until Blake comes of age, and then Schubert after him."

At this Houdini, Doyle, and Burton exchanged surreptitious glances, but said nothing.

"Then we're on our own," Burton said as he snapped shut his watch. "Brilliant, young Caretaker."

"You have one of the watches?" Fred exclaimed, as his face wrinkled up in an expression that was a mix of both shock and distaste. "Aren't they s'pposed t' vanish when you become a traitor?"

Jack tried to hush the little badger, but Burton brushed off the implied insult. "It depends on what you've become a traitor to," he said, fingering the watch. "I've always remained true to my own code, and I'm guessing the watch would recognize that—if," he added with a dark smile, "it was one of your cheap Caretaker watches."

"It's not?" Jack said in surprise.

"Of course not," said Burton. "I gave that one back to Dickens ages ago. I got mine from Blake—and it doesn't have any image of a false god on the cover to slow it down."

"Samaranth isn't a god," Jack countered, "and you're still as misguided as ever, Burton. You scorn the wrong things, you're slow to learn, and you see yourself as infallible, even in the face of evidence that proves you aren't."

"You know what they call a person like that?" said Burton. "Caveo Principia."

"I'm nothing like you, Burton," John shot back. "Nothing."

"I'd be disappointed if you were," said Burton.

"Pardon me, gentlemen," Houdini interrupted, "but is this really the best time? People are starting to stare."

"We're just having an argument," Jack retorted. "Why would that be anyone else's business?'

"I'm not saying it is," Houdini said mildly, "but if none of us being dressed like the locals doesn't eventually get someone's attention, the two dozen talking animals and girl with wings will."

"You're right," said John, slapping his forehead. "Of course you're right. We've got to find someplace where we can regroup and get our bearings. It won't do the timeline any good if we end up in jail in eighteenth-century London."

"Speak for yourselves," said Houdini. "At worst, I'll start an entirely new career by escaping."

"What do you want to do, John?" Jack asked.

John pointed to a sign that was attached to the wall above their heads. "The door from the Keep of Time brought us here," he said, drawing a deep breath. "Let's have a look around and see why the Dragons thought this was an important time and place to visit."

The Caretakers explained to the animals of Paralon that they would have to remain in the back of the alley while the humans found a place for them to stay. The animals, being well-educated and mostly librarians at that, readily agreed.

"We lived in secret on Paralon for all these years," Myrret said with understanding. "We can certainly manage to stay hidden in an alley for a few hours."

"Maybe," Jack said, looking around nervously, "but there you were locked in, and almost everyone else was gone."

"Point," said Myrret.

"I can help with this," Houdini said, stepping forward. He licked his thumbs and peered up at the walls that framed the alleyway. Reaching up, he touched his thumbs to points just above his head on both walls, and then repeated the motions on several points farther down. All the while, he was murmuring words in some strange tongue.

"There," he said, straightening his vest. "As long as they stay behind this spot, no one on the street will be inclined to look inside the alley."

Doyle and Jack tested Houdini's claim by stepping out into

the street and turning around. The illusionist was correct—from without, none of the animals or companions were visible.

"That's not an illusion," Burton murmured to Houdini. "That's something real—someone else's magic. And knowledge like that comes with a price."

"I paid it," said Houdini primly. "It's *my* magic."

"That's them taken care of," said John. "What of the rest of us?"

Houdini excused himself for a moment, then disappeared around one of the corners before John could protest. He reappeared only a minute later carrying period clothes for all the men, the two young women, and the little prince.

"We'll be able to move more freely if we look the part," he explained. "Everyone, strip."

The men hung a sheet in the alley so the girls would have a place to change in semiprivacy, while they dressed on the outside.

"Where did you get these, Harry?" John asked as he pulled on a pair of breeches. "More magic?"

"Mmm, probably best not to ask," said Doyle. "Harry has a bit of a 'don't ask, don't tell' policy when it comes to this sort of thing."

"Wonderful," Jack grumbled. "Stolen. What happens if we end up in jail?"

"As I mentioned, I'd be fine," said Houdini as he pulled on a nicely appointed topcoat, "but the rest of you would probably be hard-pressed to find a way out."

"You wouldn't leave us there?" Laura Glue exclaimed from behind the sheet.

"Of course not!" Houdini called back. "I'm sure I'd break you all out—eventually." He smirked at the Caretakers.

"Rose? Laura Glue?" John called out as he and Burton helped

the prince with his shirt. "Are you ready yet, or do you need a few more minutes?"

"They're both dressed," said Fred.

"How did you know?" Laura Glue asked as she pulled back the sheet. "Were you peeking, Fred?"

"Not intentionally," Fred answered, "but you did hang the sheet kind of high, and I'm pretty short."

"So you watched us dress?" Rose asked. "Fred. For shame."

The badger rolled his eyes and made gestures with his hands that said he was embarrassed, but the broad smile on his badger face said otherwise.

"Fred, you scamp," said John. "If you were my son I'd take a switch to you."

"Oh, leave him alone," said Burton. "That's the first thing he's done since I met him that's made me not want to eat him."

"Uh, thanks," said Fred. "I think."

The clothing Houdini had gotten for the young women was innocuous enough and fit them well, but not even the hooded cloak he gave to Rose could cover the fact that she was shadowless. Occasionally her shadow came close enough to look normal, but then it would swing around in the wrong direction, or jump underneath a crate or passing carriage.

"I know it's making you crazy," Jack told her. "Best if you try to ignore it for now. It probably won't go too far, and most people won't notice that it's not playing by Hoyle."

"All right," Rose said, not entirely convinced. "I just hope it doesn't cause any trouble."

"It won't," Jack assured her. "It's still you, Rose. It's only your shadow—it can't do anything real, or harmful, while it's still yours. It's only when you give it up that it starts to stir things up on its own."

"So it's your shadow that makes people do terrible things?" she asked.

"It's more like your conscience," Jack replied. "There's no shadow if there's no light. As long as you are the light, you'll have a shadow. That's why giving it up willingly, as your father, Mordred, did, or"—he swallowed hard—"as I myself once did, is so terrible. You aren't giving up your shadow—you're giving up your light. Do you understand?"

"I think so," she answered, still pensive.

"Good," Jack said as he stepped over to the other Caretakers. "Don't worry, Rose. It's usually the grown-ups who make all the stupid choices, not children. So you ought to be just fine."

Rose didn't respond to his last remark, but instead looked down at her shadow, which was floating underneath her, almost touching her.

Almost.

Archimedes became a one-bird reconnaissance squad, being the only one of the group who could observe and report on where they were without drawing any undue attention.

"I was here once, you know," he said as he landed next to Rose to give his report. "The air was cleaner, but because of the horses, the streets were filled with more—"

"And that's enough of that," said John, clearing his throat. "Decorum, Archie."

"What?" said the bird. "Rose was raised by an old fisherman, and the Valkyrie didn't bathe until she was twelve."

"I'm not worried about them—I'm talking about the boy," said John.

"What boy?"

"Oh, no," John said, looking around. "I thought you were watching him, Burton."

"He was here just a moment ago," Burton snapped. "He can't be far."

They started out into the street, when a tall, finely dressed man with an imposing manner and a cane stepped into their path. His dress and markings said that he was the local magistrate— and his cane and tilt of his head said that he was blind.

"If it's a young lad you're looking for," the magistrate said, "you might follow the laughter and the running children." He lifted his walking stick and pointed to the far end of the street, where several boys were indeed streaming past, whooping and hollering.

"You could tell that just by listening?" Houdini asked, honestly curious.

"These old ears still hear very well," the magistrate replied. "I can distinguish among all the children in London, in point of fact."

"Can you now?" John said. He smiled and glanced at Jack, who seemed to be having the same thought. This was a preposterous claim on the magistrate's part, but a harmless one. No point in antagonizing the old fellow.

"I can hear well enough to catch that thought," he said to John, much to the Caretaker's surprise and chagrin, "and to know you are a stranger to London."

"Not a stranger, exactly," John stammered, "but yes, I'm not from around here."

"Hmm," the magistrate sniffed. "Oxford. And . . . a little Yorkshire."

"Impressive," said Jack.

"Hah," replied the magistrate. "You're perceptive, for an Irish."

At this Fred let out a short, sharp laugh—and was immediately silenced by a look from Burton. Rose put her finger to her lips and quietly shook her head, just for good measure.

At the sound of the badger's laugh, the blind magistrate stopped and lifted his head. "What was that?" he asked, turning his head from side to side. "There are no dogs on Craven Street."

Craven Street, John thought. *I thought some of these buildings looked familiar.* "The boy found it over near Trafalgar Square," he said quickly, gesturing apologetically to Fred. "He chased it here, and then we lost him."

"I see," the magistrate said, not sounding wholly convinced. "In any regard, follow the children, and you should find your boy."

"Thank you," said John, as he and the others turned to head down the street. "Good day to you."

"And to you," the magistrate replied.

"That was close," Jack said when they were a safe distance away. "We're going to have to wrap Fred in a scarf or something."

"Why is it always a dog?" Fred complained. "I never have this problem in the Archipelago."

"Just try to keep your head down and don't talk," Jack advised. "It'll be fine."

"He should have stayed with the other animals," said Burton.

"We're taking an unnecessary risk bringing him along."

"He's a Caretaker," Jack responded, half-ashamed that he did, in fact, agree with Burton. "He goes with us."

"There," said Doyle, pointing. "The boys are all congregating there."

At the end of the street that ran perpendicular to Craven Street was an open plaza. It was not quite a park, and not quite a broad intersection. There were trees and grass, and a bustling market at which vendors sold geese, and vegetables, and even hot cakes.

In the center, near the trees, a dozen or so boys were flying kites and cheering.

The kites were made in several different styles and were painted in a rainbow of colors. Some of the tails were too long and kept getting caught up in the trees, but others were flying free and high above the rooftops.

One of the boys in particular was having a lot of difficulty getting his kite out of an elm. He pulled at the string as if he'd never held a kite before—which, in point of fact, he hadn't.

"There he is," Jack said, exhaling in relief. "That was a bit of a scare. Let's go get him."

But at that exact moment, a constable appeared on the far side of the park, and he shouted at the boys with the kites.

"Oi! You lot!" he called out harshly. "No kites here! Stop where you are, in the name of the magistrate!"

John thought it was strangely funny that the magistrate knew all about the boys and their kites and didn't seem to care less. But this constable was certainly stirring things up. The boys were scattering in all directions—but several were coming straight toward the companions, with the constable in hot pursuit.

"Quick!" John yelled. "Grab Coal!"

Burton dodged between the fleeing boys and caught the little prince, who was clutching a green kite for all he was worth. "I have him!"

Two more boys plowed into Fred, knocking him sprawling. Rose and Laura Glue immediately jumped in to pull him up.

The constable stopped. "Is this your boy?" he asked Burton sharply. "You ought to know better, my lords."

Jack suddenly forgave Houdini for stealing the clothes. His good taste might have just saved them from a lot of trouble.

"I'll mind the boy's business," Burton said haughtily, "and I'll expect you to mind yours."

The constable flushed, then tipped his hat and ran on after another of the boys.

"Good enough," Jack said. "No harm done."

"Uh-oh," said Fred, who was frantically searching around in his pack. "We've got a problem."

"What's that?" asked John, kneeling. "Are you all right, Fred?"

"I'm fine, but it's gone!" Fred exclaimed, his whiskers atremble with anxiety. "I think one of those boys took it!"

John had a sudden sinking feeling. "Took what, Fred?"

"The *Imaginarium Geographica*!" the little badger cried. "It's gone!"

Magistrate Hawkins made his way down to the other end of Craven Street and found a familiar door. He knocked twice, then again, until a voice from the inside yelled out, "Come in!"

He entered and closed the door behind him, sniffing at the air inside the house as he did so. "Sulfur," he said, more of a statement than a question. "Calling up an evil spirit, or constructing some kind of infernal device?"

"What's the difference?" the occupant replied, his voice cheerful. "Either way, I'm likely to learn something new. What can I do for you, Magistrate?"

"I just thought you ought to know," the magistrate said as he settled into a chair with the familiarity of a frequent guest, "that some very unusual people have just come to Craven Street."

"I know many unusual people," came the reply, "including several on Craven Street. So you are bringing this to my attention, why?"

"Several of them are men who speak with strange accents," the magistrate replied, "and there are two young women, who speak the same. But what makes them really intriguing is the talking dog."

"A talking dog?" came the reply. "Do tell, Magistrate. Do tell."

The room resembled an Aladdin's cave . . .

CHAPTER FIFTEEN
The Reluctant Mapmaker

❖

"Which boy was it?" Jack asked. "Could you tell?"

"I think it was the taller one," Fred replied. "He had copper-colored hair and a brown vest."

"Almost all of them wore brown vests, you idiot," said Burton.

"Oh," said Fred, crestfallen. "Then I'm not sure."

"I remember him," said Laura Glue. "I'll get the book back, never fear." With that, she turned and took off at a dead run in the direction the constable had gone.

"This is getting out of control," John said miserably. "Archie, follow her and try to keep track of where we are. We'll stay on Craven Street until we hear from you."

"Not a problem," Archimedes said as he launched into the air after the Valkyrie.

"Hey," Jack said, looking around. "Where did Houdini and Doyle go?"

"I'm not their nursemaid," said Burton. "I was watching the boy. Besides, they're grown men. They can look after themselves."

"That's exactly what worries me," said John. "We're about one public disaster away from destroying the entire timeline."

✦　✦　✦

There were many reasons why Laura Glue had become the captain of the Valkyries at such a young age. For one, she was raised among the Lost Boys, and thus was a world-class authority at hide-and-seek. She was also the best flyer of her generation and could maneuver herself in ways that other flyers couldn't even fathom doing. But above all, she was captain because she never lost her quarry once she started tracking it. And a thieving boy in eighteenth-century London was not going to be any challenge at all—or was he?

She found him in short order, running about two blocks ahead of her, but when he realized he was being followed, he disappeared.

Twice more she found him, and twice more he lost her—until finally she took to the air and tracked him from above, finally dropping down and cornering him in an alley. It didn't hurt that she had Archie flying above to help her narrow down his possible paths.

"How did you find me?" he gasped, less startled by a flying girl than by the fact that he couldn't lose her. "No man is able to track me when I don't want to be tracked!"

"In case you hadn't noticed," Laura Glue said primly, "I am no man. And I've played hide-and-seek with boys a lot smarter and more skillful than you, so no matter where you went, I'd have found you eventually."

"But it took you no time at all!" he exclaimed. "How is that possible?"

"I have a secret weapon," she said, holding out her arm. There was a flapping of wings, and to the boy's utter astonishment an immense owl landed on her arm and fixed him with an intense glare. If he hadn't known better, he'd have thought the bird was preening at having tracked him so easily.

Laura Glue held out her other hand. "The book, if you please," she said sternly, "or you'll find out what else Archimedes is able to do."

He reluctantly handed over the atlas as Rose, Fred, and the men came running up behind her, having followed Archimedes.

"Bloody hell, girl," Burton huffed as the men caught up to the Valkyrie and her quarry. "You can run, can't you?"

"It helps that she's a tenth of your age, Sir Richard," said John, who was breathing hard himself. "I thought your type didn't get tired."

"We're hardy, healthy, and younger than you," Burton countered, "but we can still get winded."

"You wouldn't be," said Jack, "if you kept yourself in the same kind of shape as your colleagues."

"What are you doing stealing from people anyway?" Laura Glue asked the boy. "It's not polite to steal."

"I didn't damage it at all," said the boy. "I only wanted to look at the maps."

"Argh," John growled. This whole escapade was coming apart at the seams. "How did you know there were maps?"

"When I knocked over the little fellow, it spilled out of his pack, and I saw what it was. I only wanted a look."

"He's damaged it, Scowler Jack," said Fred. "Look, some of the pages have come loose."

"Come loose?" John said. "That's impossible."

Fred handed him several maps, all drawn on thick parchment. They bore a superficial resemblance to those in the *Geographica*, but on touch, John could tell they were different.

"These aren't from the *Geographica*," he said in astonishment.

"These are entirely new maps. I've never seen them before in my life!"

"Where did you get these, boy?" Burton exclaimed as he grabbed the youth by the lapels and lifted him off the ground. "Tell us, and tell us truthfully, or I'll cut your tongue from your head."

"I didn't steal them!" the boy exclaimed. "I didn't! I swear by King George I didn't! I just stuck them in the book when you started chasing me!"

"Oh for heaven's sake," said Jack as he pushed Burton aside and smoothed out the boy's collar. "There are better ways to persuade people, Burton."

He held up one of the maps with one hand and grasped the boy's shoulder with the other. He didn't approve of Burton's manner, but he knew a street-sharp boy when he saw one, and he didn't want to go through another chase-and-evade if he could help it.

"These maps you had," Jack said. "We just want to know where you got them." The boy didn't answer, just stared sullenly at Jack and the others.

"If you won't report me to the magistrate," he said finally, "I won't tell anyone about your talking dog."

"I'm not a dog, I'm a badger!" Fred retorted.

"Right," said the boy. "Pull the other one."

"Really," Jack went on. "We're not going to report you for stealing the maps. And no one will believe you about the badger, anyway."

"My master would, and for the last time I *didn't* steal the maps!" the boy retorted. "I *made* them."

◆　　◆　　◆

"What's your name, boy?" asked John.

"Edmund," he replied. "Edmund McGee."

"Who taught you how to make maps like these?"

"My father, but he hates making maps," Edmund explained, "even though that's what our family has done for three generations. When we lived on St. Lucia, in the Caribbee Sea, I was never allowed to touch his maps. I only made these because I'm apprenticed to someone here in London, who teaches me other things in exchange for the maps I make for him."

"But these maps," John said, "don't depict any lands I know, and I know all of them. Where did these come from?"

"I made them up," said Edmund, as if it were the most obvious fact in the world. "In the Old Way."

"Hah," said John. "I haven't heard that in a while."

"What does it mean, the 'Old Way'?" asked Fred.

"It's something the old explorers used to do many ages ago," John explained, kneeling to draw in the dust with his finger. "They'd start out on an expedition with only a vague notion of where they were going. They might have been spurred by some fragment of a myth, or a legend passed village to village, about some enchanted land just beyond the bounds they knew."

He traced a jagged outline of an island in the dust, then added a rough compass, and almost as an afterthought, a sea monster. "You see, they'd make the maps first—then sail out to prove that they existed. And more often than you'd believe, they found something at the end of their journey. Sometimes it was an island in the Archipelago, and sometimes it was Greenland, or Australia."

"So did wishing make it so?" asked Fred.

"Not wishing," John replied. "Believing. They believed, and they found what they were looking for."

"Namers," Rose said suddenly. "Like Mother Night and Mr. Poe mentioned. They were Namers, and they found the places they named."

"That's a remarkable insight," said Jack. "I suspect you're very close to the mark."

"Here," John said as he leaned over again. "Let's see if we can't make this one happen." He wrote "Fred's Isle" under the drawing and stood up. "Perhaps we'll run across it one day."

"Don't forget this," Edmund said as he crouched and added a notation in the dust. "You don't want anyone going there unawares."

John whistled. The boy had added the words *Hunt sic Dracones*—"Here Be Dragons."

Edmund shrugged. "I know that Dragons aren't real," he said matter-of-factly, "but it's bad form not to give people the warning."

"What does your master teach you in exchange for these imaginary maps you make?" asked Jack.

"Lots of things," Edmund said brightly. "Chemistry, and geology, and philosophy. He also invents things like kites, and, well, a lot of other things."

"He sounds like quite a fellow," said John.

"You probably know him," Edmund said, shoulders slumping as he realized he might be getting into trouble after all. "He wears a pocket watch just as you all do."

The Caretakers and Burton all glanced at one another. This might be exactly the stroke of good luck they needed. A watch meant a Caretaker—or did it?

"He can't be," John whispered to the others, "or we'd already know who it is."

"Maybe he's an apprentice we don't have a record of," offered Jack.

"Don't look at me," said Burton. "I haven't a clue who the boy is talking about."

"We'd like to meet your master," John said to Edmund. "Right now."

"He's a scientist, except for when he's a publisher," Edmund said as he led them back toward Craven Street. "Or a historian. Actually, I suppose he's a lot of different things rolled into one."

"And he makes kites," said Jack.

"That too," said Edmund. "Most of the children just call him the Doctor."

He marched the companions to a broad, well-appointed house that was several stories tall. It was in the nicer part of Craven Street, more sparsely populated than where they'd just come from.

"Privacy is good," Jack murmured.

"Doctor Franklin?" Edmund called out at the door. "May I come in?"

"Enter freely, and unafraid," came the response from somewhere in the bowels of the building. "Unless you owe me money— then I hope you'll pardon me while I locate my pistols."

"He's just joking," said Edmund, waving the others inside. "I think."

The companions followed the boy down a narrow corridor and past a staircase to a large room in the back, which was sunlit through an expanse of windows that ran almost floor to ceiling on the north wall. Every other wall was covered edge to edge with art, and newspapers, and maps, and all manner of bric-a-brac.

The room resembled an Aladdin's cave, if the genie had been some combination of Copernicus, Aristotle, Newton, and Hadrian. An immense round table sat in the center of the room. It was claw-footed and was covered with all manner of books and pamphlets in every conceivable language. On one side of the table and spilling onto the floor were small models in clay and metal, the use for which the companions couldn't even begin to guess.

Across the floor and piled on numerous bookshelves were volumes on the sciences, the supernatural, diplomacy, agriculture, history, and several other topics that John thought might get their owner either arrested or burned at the stake were the public aware of them.

Another worktable on the east wall was laden with more papers and scrolls, and several scientific instruments, only a few of which were readily identifiable. But of all the extraordinary paraphernalia that filled the room, those that were most intriguing were the expansive maps tacked along the west wall down to the floor. They were covered with notations that were more metaphysical in appearance than cartological, and seemed to include several hand-drawn corrections. Many were of European regions, based on the topography, but several others were completely unfamiliar to John, the Principal Caretaker of the greatest atlas in the world.

That alone, if for no other reason, made the stout occupant of the room compelling to John—and there were many other reasons to find him compelling. He wore a black skullcap that seemed barely able to contain the explosion of hair that sprouted underneath. He had on a silk dressing gown that was embroidered with numerical symbols and equations, as if he were an alchemist who was unwilling to walk the length of the room without his formulas at his side. The house was old and crumbling at the seams, but this room alone justified its existence—and the owner himself seemed as if he could justify anything by sheer charisma alone. His bearing was one of gravity and sage wisdom; but his face, dusty with plaster and drying powder, bore the liveliness and delighted curiosity of a child.

It's no wonder, John thought as he moved forward and offered his hand in greeting, *that the local children are drawn to this man. I've only just seen him, and already I find myself hoping to talk to him about anything and everything.*

"Greetings, gentle sentients," he said, rising from his chair. "I'm Benjamin Franklin."

One by one, the companions introduced themselves to the Doctor, leaving out the fact that they already knew exactly who he was and what role he'd played in history. John and Jack introduced themselves as Caretakers, although they didn't say what for, and Burton said he was a traveling historian, and Theo his aide-de-camp.

Oddly enough, of all of them, Burton seemed the most impressed on meeting the Doctor, although Franklin paused and blanched when he shook Theo's hand.

He greeted the young women more formally, and looked with rapt interest at Archimedes.

"And you, my fine young fellow," Doctor Franklin said,

scratching Fred's head. "You must be the third Caretaker, eh?"

"He's a talking badger," said Edmund, "but I promised not to tell the magistrate."

"You weren't supposed to tell *anyone*," John reminded him, rubbing his temples. "You're a bit of a trial, Edmund."

"I don't mind," said Franklin. "I'm rather fond of talking animals."

"How many do you know?" asked Fred.

"You're the first one," Franklin admitted, "but I'm a good judge of character."

While Edmund showed Burton, Rose, Theo, and Laura Glue around Franklin's study, Jack and John withdrew to a corner to converse privately.

"What do you think?" asked Jack.

John's voice dropped to a conspiratorial whisper. "I'm as impressed as you are, Jack. That's not my concern."

"It's Fred, isn't it?" asked Jack. "Franklin didn't so much as blink that a talking badger showed up in his parlor."

"If that was all it was, I'd be more relieved. What worries me is what he said to Fred about being the third Caretaker. We introduced ourselves as Caretakers—but we never said anything about whether the others may or may not be. So why assume there would be a third at all? And why go right to Fred?"

Jack pursed his lips and frowned. "Those are really good questions."

"Here's something else," John said, handing Jack one of Edmund's maps. "I recognize these."

Jack reacted with surprise. "You've seen them before?"

"Not these exact maps, but this kind of parchment, and the hand in which the map was drawn," John whispered. "It matches the map that Hank Morgan had made to return to Tamerlane House."

"Remarkable," said Jack. "We need to meet Edmund's father, I think."

"Why so reserved?" Franklin said, interrupting. "So many wonderful things to see here, and you're whispering in a corner."

"Forgive our rudeness," said John. "We didn't mean any—"

"Nonsense," Franklin said, waving his hands. "I've been talking to Burton, and he's told me you have no place to stay. Is that correct?"

"It is," said John. "We've only just arrived in London."

"As it turns out," said Franklin, "I have an entire upper floor that is completely unoccupied. I never use it—I prefer to stay down here, working. If you would consider staying as my guests, I'd be happy to have you."

It didn't take any discussion to decide to accept. "We will," said John. "Thank you, Doctor Franklin."

"Pish-tosh," he replied. "It's my pleasure."

"There's one other thing," said Fred. "How would you like to meet a few more talking animals?"

"Do tell?" said Franklin. "Another badger?"

"Not quite," Fred replied, "but the hedgehogs are pleasant enough."

Franklin laughed. "Really?" he said. "Bring them on, Caretaker Fred."

It took another two hours to move all the animals that had been at Paralon from the alley over to Franklin's house without being seen. But once they were there, John realized that they had found in Benjamin Franklin the ideal host. He was fascinated enough by the creatures to be preoccupied with them for days; and he was an unusual enough character that they believed him when he agreed to keep their confidences.

It was growing dark by the time Jack and John could persuade Edmund to take them to his father's house. As reluctant as he was to take them there, he insisted his father would be even more reluctant to discuss the family trade.

The house of Ernest McGee was at the far end of Craven Street, closer to the tumbledown homes of the ne'er-do-wells and rabble of London. It was probably significant in some way, Jack thought, that there was very little difference between the children at the poorer end of the street and those from the more well-heeled households.

Edmund seemed to be walking slower and slower the closer they got to their destination, and John realized he really was dreading this visit.

They were greeted at the door by the McGees' servant girl, a slim, clean-faced young woman named Lauren, who was not much older than Rose or Laura Glue. It was obvious she was responsible for maintaining the entire household. Ernest greeted them in the drawing room, flashing a brief smile when he saw his son, which was replaced with a scowl when Edmund explained why they wanted to speak with him. It didn't take very long at all for the discussion to turn rancorous and short.

"I don't have the skill my father had, and not even he could keep up with old Elijah," Ernest spat, making no effort to conceal the bitterness in his voice. "What does it matter, anyway? The age of piracy is over. Not even the privateers are called upon any longer, so of what use is a mapmaker to pirates?"

"There are other uses for a mapmaker," Jack said softly, "than to work as an errand boy for pirates."

Ernest wheeled about in a fury, ready to unleash venom in response to the insult—but when he saw Jack's face, he understood. It was not an insult. It was a respectful call to action.

Ernest set his jaw and considered whether to say anything, then turned away. He used a bell to summon Lauren, and when she appeared he murmured a few words to her, then dismissed her. She returned a few minutes later with a tray of tea and cakes. Ernest McGee might not have liked the reason his guests were there, but he was still going to treat them as guests.

"It's been more than two decades since my father died," he said at last when they'd drunk the tea and eaten the cakes, "and almost ten years since I compiled that cursed atlas." He gestured at the workbench near the corner. "The *Pyratlas*, they called it. It was to be a complete assemblage of three generations of McGee family maps, bearing all the secrets of the pirates."

"And yet you forbade your own son from following in your footsteps," said John. "Why is that?"

"I forbade it," Ernest continued, drawing resolve from well-worn arguments, "because mapmaking has already consumed too many decades of my life, and I'll not see it destroy his."

"It didn't destroy your father, or his," Jack replied. "They were the best in the world, according to Edmund."

Ernest responded to the compliment with a half smile, appreciating the effort, even if Jack was exaggerating the truth. "We were silversmiths," he said, shaking his head as if he were recalling another life, or a half-remembered dream. "My grandfather was one of the most renowned in the world in his trade, before he became a mapmaker to pirates. He passed along the craft of silverwork to my father out of a sense of tradition more than anything else, which ended up being arbitrary anyway. My father was the one who fully embraced the family calling, as he referred to it, and we have been nothing but mapmakers ever since. At times I've thought we ought to just throw in entirely and become pirates. It would not have changed our lives overmuch had we done so."

"Forgive my noticing," Jack said, looking around at the well-appointed room, which would have been more in place in a house at the other end of the street, "but being mapmakers to pirates seems to have benefited you rather handsomely."

"You think I'm ungrateful, don't you?" Ernest retorted. "Well, perhaps I am. There has always been enough—more than enough—money for my family to do as we pleased. But I think that would have also been the case had we remained silversmiths. . . ." His voice trailed off as he stood at the window, staring out into the street.

"If only Elijah had never started," Ernest said at last, "if only that pirate, Morgan, had never taught him the craft, our lives might have been very different."

"Morgan?" John and Jack exclaimed together.

"Which Morgan?" asked Jack.

Ernest turned to them in surprise. "I thought you would have known," he said. "The pirate governor, Henry Morgan, was the man who first recruited Elijah to be a mapmaker, and he taught him how to do it besides. Everything that's happened to my family started with him."

CHAPTER SIXTEEN
The Pirate's Biographer

❖

The best thing about being a magician, Houdini had decided long ago, was that people believed that magicians could do *anything*. Which, in point of fact, was not too far removed from the truth where he was concerned. No cell could hold him, no locks could bind him. He could not be drowned, or burned, or sliced in two.

He could make anything disappear, given proper preparation, from a mouse to a freight train. And he could dazzle a crowd with nothing but a handful of ordinary household items and his rolled-up shirtsleeves.

He was a showman, no doubt. And his life was the stage. But when he met and befriended Arthur Conan Doyle, another aspect took hold and soon became the force that motivated everything he did.

Sir Arthur believed in an ethereal world of spirit, where magic was commonplace and the dead communicated with the living. Harry believed that magic was the result of skill and hard labor, and that the world of spirit was the realm of tricksters and charlatans. And he never believed in the ability to communicate with the dead until he became dead himself.

"What do you think, Arthur? Is this a rational plan of action . . . ?"

Harry had often promised his wife that if there was some means of communicating with her from the great beyond, he would. What she didn't expect was for him to actually turn up at her door, flowers in hand, still young and in his prime, in the company of his dead friend, the writer of detective stories, Sir Arthur Conan Doyle.

She declared him a fake and a fraud and threw him out. For years after, she still dutifully held a séance on his birthday, in the belief that the real Harry would somehow contact her.

Since then, he had thrown himself into his new calling: going about the business of the world, trying to save all of history, partnered with his friend who had embraced this new life to become that which he admired most—a Detective. But as for Harry, dead or alive, he remained what he always had been, a showman.

"What do you think, Arthur?" Houdini asked as they passed Trafalgar Square. "Is this a rational plan of action, or sheer madness?"

"All the best plans are always slightly mad," Doyle replied, "but I think the only way the Caretakers are going to sort this out is if we give them a hand."

Houdini chuckled. "They always underestimated us as Caretakers, and Burton wasn't much better," he said, nicking a couple of apricots from a nearly stand, then paying the vendor with a penny from his own till. "They're good about practical matters, but they just don't have any sense of style. Except maybe for the badger. He shows promise."

"Rose, too," Doyle said, taking one of the apricots, "as long as she is allowed to have her own head about things. She's growing up faster than any of them realize."

"If we don't figure out how to reattach her shadow soon, she may grow up faster than anyone is ready for," Houdini replied.

"Don't I know it," said Doyle.

"Over here, this way," Houdini said, pointing. "There's a street where there are horses and carriages, and it's smoky and noisy. That means blacksmith shops."

"It's as I've always said, Harry," Doyle mused. "These Caretakers lack focus. Always, they lack focus. Oh, a few of them have vision—but they're never going to be able to see anything through while they're stuck in that gallery, or arguing all the time."

"I completely agree," Houdini answered as he finished the apricot. He dropped the pit into the tin cup of a match girl and waved his hand over the cup. A shoot of green sprouted up from the pit, and in a few moments it was a miniature tree, full of leaves and bearing fruit of its own.

"They're so preoccupied with having come through the doorway," he continued, "that they've completely forgotten the most important thing . . .

". . . who it was who came through the door *last*."

The visit with Ernest McGee ended cordially enough, with John and Jack thanking him graciously for his time and trouble, and Ernest agreeing, somewhat reluctantly, to meet with them again. The revelation that Hank Morgan had been Elijah McGee's teacher was too significant not to share with the others—but they did not yet know enough about this family of mapmakers to speak of it openly in front of them.

Lauren saw them to the door, pausing a moment longer than

was needed to say good-bye to Edmund, who was returning with them to Franklin's house.

"I still have some work to do," he explained. "I was supposed to finish earlier, but it was too good a day to waste being indoors, and not flying kites."

At Franklin's door, they found Theo waiting for them outside. He asked to speak with Jack privately, and so John and Edmund went inside, leaving the others to talk.

"I have felt our enemy," Theo said quietly. "The Echthros followed us through the door. It's here, with us, now."

Jack looked around, his hackles rising with panic. "Here? On Craven Street?"

Theo nodded. "I have felt its presence at the edges of my mind since we arrived, but I have only just decided that it was a certainty."

"Is it going to attack us like it did the ship?" Jack asked, scanning the sky above, which was sparsely dotted with clouds. "Or will it attack us more directly?"

"The Echthroi corrupt and subvert," he replied. "This one's goal was to stop us, and at the Frontier that meant stopping the ship. At Paralon it tried to summon its allies. Here I do not yet know what it intends—but we must be alert."

"Could it be the star?" Jack suggested. "Rao? The animals said it had become a Lloigor."

"No," Theo said. "Not the Lloigor from the Archipelago. The Echthros—the same that has followed us all along."

"Should we discuss it with the others?" asked Jack. "Warn them?"

"No, not yet," Theo replied. "The Echthros can take any

shape, appear to be anyone. It may have already done so."

"Great," Jack groaned. "So how do I know *you* aren't the Echthroi—Echthros?"

"If I were, you would already be dead."

"If we do discover our enemy, what then?"

"I have a way to control it," Theo replied, "so that we may escape."

"Escape to where? We've been in the Archipelago, and we've gone back in time. Where else can we go?"

The End of Time pondered this. "You are right," he admitted. "We can't hide. So we must be successful, or perish."

The night passed uneventfully, which was a blessing to the companions, who had had more than enough of commotion and chaos in the last few days. Better than just settling in, the animals had proved to be amazingly compatible with Doctor Franklin and had, in a single evening, reorganized his entire library.

"I can't find a single thing!" Franklin said, beaming. "It's glorious."

He was a gracious host and had asked Edmund for the loan of the McGee's maid to help prepare breakfast. The flapjacks went over extremely well with everyone, as did the fresh bread and fruit, but there was a minor diplomatic incident when Lauren lifted the cover on a platter of sliced ham.

The foxes were all for it, but the hedgehogs threw a fit and threatened to have a public protest. It didn't help matters when the ferret started quoting a book on cross-species ethics that had been written by Fred's grandfather.

Eventually everything settled back to a dull roar, and the animals went back to work while the others set about planning their day.

"I'm concerned," John began. "We haven't heard anything from Houdini and Doyle. Perhaps we should have Laura Glue out looking for them."

"Oh, please," said Burton. "You're worried about them, but not the effect that might be caused by a flying girl being spotted in London?"

"What else can we do?" asked John.

"Wait," Burton said firmly. "Simply wait. They'll find their way to us."

Jack's eyes narrowed. That was too pat an answer, too assured. "Sir Richard," he said casually, "is there something you're planning that we should know about? After all, they are *your* acolytes."

"I'm here as your ally, Caretaker," Burton replied. "Don't question my motives or take me for a fool."

"All right, enough," John said, standing. "We don't need to be arguing. Houdini and Doyle will just have to look after themselves."

Theo had basically taken up the post of watchman at Franklin's house, which was serving as their de facto headquarters on Craven Street, and Laura Glue was helping him. Fred had been conversing with Franklin on a number of topics and chose to stay. So John, Jack, Burton, Rose, and Archie followed Edmund and Lauren back to Ernest McGee's.

The Caretakers' second reception at the house of Ernest McGee was much warmer than the first. He had been poring over his father's journals and seemed to have found something that changed his outlook on the strange visitors his son had brought to his house. Ernest set Edmund and Lauren to doing other tasks in the house while he opened one diary for his guests.

"Here," he said, showing them a particular passage he'd underlined, "in one of his diaries, from when he was very young. He had been working closely with his two best friends on their *History*, and on the Pyratlas, and he mentions that they were doing it in hopes to become apprentices to someone called a Caretaker."

John and Jack didn't respond to this, but Burton let out a short, sharp bark of a laugh. Rose scowled at him, and Archie simply looked on.

"That's, ah, very interesting," said John. "Why are you showing this to us?"

"Because," Ernest said as he led them upstairs, "I remember once, when I was very young, sneaking into my father's study and seeing the Caretaker. He was a Frenchman with a high-born manner and a very prominent nose. I remember little of what they discussed, but I will never forget," he added as he opened the door to a large room, "that he wore a silver pocket watch, with the picture of a dragon on the case."

"Centuries," John whispered as they followed McGee into the room. "We spend *centuries* trying to keep the secrets of the Archipelago, and when we drop, unannounced, into eighteenth-century London, everyone we meet seems to know about the Caretakers."

"A validation of my arguments," Burton said with a wry smile, "and a preview of your life to come, eh, Jack?"

"I don't even want to think about it," said Jack.

"Excuse me," said a voice from somewhere in the back of the cluttered workshop, "but if you're burglars, as I suspect you must be, then I'd ask that you take me along with you. It's dreadfully boring being in here all the time, and I'd do just about anything for a change of scenery."

"I'm sorry," Ernest said as he cleared away some of the debris that blocked the space between the shelves. "I didn't mean to leave you here so long, Charles."

"I know that voice!" Rose exclaimed. "Archie, don't you? Do you remember?"

Ernest pulled aside a tarpaulin and uncovered a large oil portrait inside an elaborate oval frame.

It was Captain Charles Johnson.

"Hello," Rose said. "It's nice to see you again, Captain Johnson."

"How is it that you know me?" Johnson said, the suspicion in his voice quite clear. "To the best of my recollection, we haven't met."

"We have," said Rose, "or rather, we will. In your future. You may not remember, but I do."

"Ah, the future," said Johnson. "That would explain it. You aren't old enough to have met me in the past, when I was still among the living. Not that I'd remember you anyway, young lady. I was quite the rake, you know. I do like your bird, though."

"Pardon me for saying this," offered Archimedes, "You may not be among the living, but you aren't exactly dead, either."

"I might as well be," Johnson retorted. "I'm stuck in this stupid painting, and even my best friend's son manages to forget I'm here."

"I did say I was sorry," said Ernest.

"What are you doing in here?" asked John.

"I'm a spy, don't you know," said Johnson. "I'm spying on the family McGee for Daniel Defoe."

"Pardon my asking," Jack said, looking at Ernest then back at the portrait, "but isn't part of the point of being a spy that you try to keep it a secret from the people you're spying *on*?"

"Yes," said Johnson, "except that I really, really hate Daniel Defoe."

"That would do it," said Burton.

"The last thing I remember before waking up in this portrait," said Johnson, "was one of my best friends, Daniel Defoe, pointing to something interesting over the side of a ship. One good shove later and I'm condemned to a glorious second life in oil paint."

"He murdered you?" asked John. "Not really a very good best friend."

"Don't I know that," Johnson said glumly. "Anyroad, he told me that if I spied on the McGees for him and tried to discover where the treasures were hidden by watching the maps they made, then he'd make sure I got credit for my book."

"You're speaking of *A General History of the Robberies and Murders of the Most Notorious Pyrates*, aren't you?" said Jack. "Well, I've got some good news and some bad news for you."

"I don't care what the bad news is as long as my name's on it," retorted Johnson. "It's practically the only thing that proves I ever existed."

"Uh-oh," said John.

"Never mind that," Rose said, steering them to another topic. "Can you tell us anything about Henry Morgan?"

"Ah, Morgan," said Johnson. "A gentleman and a pirate, in that order. He was the one who taught Elijah McGee how to make maps, and started this whole family down the pirate road. He never made much noise about his own skills, although he certainly could teach. It's funny." He paused, thinking. "He's the one who pressed Elijah to teach Eliot, and young Ernest here. He said it would take generations for them to be 'good enough,' although I never got to ask him what they needed to be good enough *for*."

"Why not?" asked Rose.

"Because," said Johnson, "after old Elijah gave him the last map he requested, Morgan up and vanished."

"You mean he died?" Burton asked.

"No," said Johnson. "I mean he disappeared, right in front of Elijah. All he left behind were the treasure maps and a note I stuck in my other book, *The Maps of Elijah McGee*. He said that the note was to be given to anyone who came looking for him who wore a silver pocket watch."

"Do you still have the note?" John said excitedly. "Is it still in your book?"

"I haven't the faintest idea," replied Johnson. "I'm afraid I lost it. I haven't seen it, page or cover, in over fifty years."

It took the Magician and the Detective the better part of a day and a night to deduce the answer they were seeking. They bribed, cajoled, and otherwise sweet-talked half of lower London into giving them clues, and finally they found the shop they were looking for—although it was not the one they had expected to find.

A young man, not quite a master, but obviously not merely an apprentice, was sitting in the open door. He was working over a piece of leather on a stool that seemed designed for the purpose.

His tongue stuck out from his mouth as he concentrated on the leather.

"Pardon me," Doyle said to the man, "but we're looking for your master."

"He isn't here," the man said without looking up. "Come back tomorrow. It'll be done then."

"What will be done then?" asked Houdini.

"Whatever book it was you ordered," said the man. "It'll be done tomorrow, I swear."

"We're not looking for a book," said Doyle, "just your master. Is he"—he leaned back and looked over the shop—"is he really a bookbinder?"

"My master?" the young man asked, surprised. "Of course he is—the only one-armed bookbinder in London, as a matter of fact."

"A one-armed bookbinder," Houdini said, scowling at Doyle. "Who would have thought?"

"It's not my fault," said Doyle. "The last I knew of him, he was a blacksmith."

"I wouldn't know about that," the man said as he resumed his work, "but if you want to see him, he's in the back room."

Houdini and Doyle walked through the small but clean shop, which was filled with decoratively bound books, sheaves of paper and parchment, and new leather, waiting to be tooled. Toward the rear, with his back to the door, a large, stout man was working with a brush and paint on a large illuminated manuscript.

"He's a good boy, is Roger," the man said without turning around. "Mark me—in a few years Roger Pryce will be known as the greatest bookbinder in Europe."

He turned around on his stool, and Houdini couldn't help but gasp as he saw the arm that ended in a bright, curved hook.

"What can I do for you?" Madoc asked.

Doyle swallowed hard and looked at his friend, who took another step forward.

"Not to put too fine a point on it," said Houdini, "but we've come seeking a Dragon."

"More specifically," Doyle added, "a Dragon's apprentice. And we were hoping you might be able to tell us where we might find him."

Madoc's self-control was such that he didn't immediately react to their question. Instead he silently regarded them for a moment, then turned and strode to the door. He said something to his apprentice, who rose and left. He closed the door, then lifted the heavy crossbar that was leaning next to the frame and dropped it into the brackets.

"Uh, begging your pardon," Doyle asked, tugging at his collar, "but are you hoping to keep someone out, or keep someone in?"

Madoc ignored the question and walked to the cupboard in the corner, where he retrieved a small stoppered bottle. He pondered the bottle for a few minutes, turning it over and over in his hand before finally opening it and shaking a few drops of the liquid inside it onto his other arm, just above his scars.

"I was never much for scented oils," he said slowly, "but my brother favored them in our youth, and he once concocted a mix that was mostly cinnamon. I could always tell when he had been in a room by the lingering scent it left behind."

He turned and looked at them. "It smells of Greece to me, and of happier days."

Houdini and Doyle said nothing. Both were experienced enough showmen to know when someone was speaking in preamble. They waited, and Madoc continued to speak.

"The Dragon's apprentice," he said, voicing the words as if he were rolling them around in his mouth, tasting them. "That's something I never expected to hear spoken of again, not in this lifetime or any other. Especially now that the Dragons are all gone."

"We were told that Samaranth took on an apprentice once, long ago," said Doyle, "and as you are the only person we know in London who was there at the time, we were hoping you might be able to tell us who the apprentice is."

Madoc puffed on the pipe for a while, appraising them.

"Your watches give you away as Caretakers or their ilk," he said finally, "so I'm guessing that they are whom you represent."

"They are," Houdini said with a straight face, only slightly hesitant about the white lie. "*Did* Samaranth have an apprentice?"

"He did," Madoc confirmed. "He had exactly *one* apprentice . . . "me.""

PART FIVE

The Dragon's Apprentice

"Hello, Moonchild," the old woman said.

CHAPTER SEVENTEEN
Namers and Un-Namers

❖

The Bard wiped his brow and set his quill aside. It was done—or at least, as done as it was likely to be. Tycho Brahe had been of more help than he'd anticipated, but then, he was the only one among the Caretakers Emeritis who had been personally acquainted with Dee while they were still living, and before they had become Caretakers.

The fact that Brahe was looked down upon by some of the other Caretakers made his contributions especially sweet. Hierarchies were troublesome, especially among equals. And if they were not truly equal, being dead, then what was the use in trying to be accepted at all?

He shook his head to ward off the thought. That was past, when his facade was up. Now all the ruses had fled him, and he was being looked to for a glimmer of hope—even by those who had mocked him for a simpleton.

But, he reminded himself, that was yesterday. Today the name of Will Shakespeare might mean something different.

At least, he hoped it would.

"All right," he called out to the others. "I think I've gotten it. Let's see what we may see."

✦   ✦   ✦

Several of the other Caretakers who had chosen to remain out of their portraits for the vigil clustered around the Bard to view his handiwork. "I've adapted the trump so that we might be able to see what's happening in the Archipelago," Will explained. "I used some of Tycho's calculations and a few of Jules's notes from the Watchmaker to give us a clearer image."

"Will we be able to use it to go through?" Kipling asked. "If so, I'd like to mount a rescue for our friends."

Shakespeare shook his head. "I don't think so. The time differential is too great—that's why we can't see anything through the trump. The passage of night and day is creating a strobing effect that renders the card gray to us. Our side of the card simply can't keep up.

"What I hope I've managed to do is to convert the card to resemble a one-way mirror," Will continued, noting the new symbols he'd etched onto the card. "Instead of a portal that must take both sides into account, it will simply function as a window we can look through."

"Will you be able to convert it back?" Chaucer said with concern in his voice. "These cards are willing scarce."

Will shrugged. "Who's to say? But we can't use it now, so there's no harm in trying."

"Go ahead," said Chaucer, nodding approval to open the card. "Let us see what we can."

Tycho Brahe swallowed hard and gave Shakespeare a thumbs-up. Will rolled his eyes and inhaled deeply, then activated the trump.

The card shuddered slightly; then, to everyone's surprise, the image came into focus.

"Paralon," Verne said. "Well done, Will."

Shakespeare blushed at the compliment but kept his focus on the card. "It seems to be fuzzy at the edges," he said, puzzled. "The structures on the island don't seem quite right."

Verne's shoulders fell as he realized what they were seeing. "The picture's fine," he said tersely. "It's the island itself that is fading."

He was right. The castle, which lay in fractured pieces, the great statues, even the island itself were being eaten away by the passage of time. The edges were indistinct because they were crumbling into dust.

"It's speeding up," Will said. "I'll try to expand it so we can see better."

He touched two of the symbols at diagonal points of the card, and it trembled, then expanded to the size of a large atlas. The detail made the process of decay even more difficult to witness— the principal isle, the seat of the Silver Throne, was falling apart as they watched.

"Look, there!" Chaucer said, pointing to the rear of the island. "What is that shape?"

A dark, shapeless mass was beginning to cover what remained of Paralon. In seconds—centuries in the Archipelago—it had overwhelmed the island and begun spreading across the ocean itself.

Suddenly the card went black. Shakespeare tapped it once, then again. "What's happened?" asked Brahe. "What's wrong? Is it broken?"

"No," Verne said heavily. "I think something just covered the sun."

"The Lloigor," said a voice from up above. Poe was watching from somewhere in the upper hallways. "The enemy has taken over the Archipelago of Dreams."

"I can't believe he lost it," Jack said as they returned to Franklin's house. "A message from Morgan! It could be invaluable!"

"It could be nothing," Burton said dismissively. "For all we know, it could just be his last will and testament."

"Or instructions on how to make another map, like the one he used to return to Tamerlane House. That could be really useful."

"Because the other one worked so well," Burton sneered. "Thanks, but no. I'd prefer to get back while I'm still in my first century."

"Says the tulpa," Jack retorted. "You'd probably do fine, as would your fellows. It's those of us who are still in our Prime Time that I worry about."

A small figure appeared in the doorway and tugged hesitantly on John's coat. "Master John?" he said quietly. "Master Jack? Do you need any help?"

"Oh, Coal," John said, barely glancing up. "No, we're fine, thanks. Why don't you go play with Myrret?"

"He's busy," Coal answered, "and he didn't need any help either."

"Well, I'm sure there's plenty to read, isn't there, Coal?"

"I suppose so."

"I'm sorry, Coal," Jack said, hustling the boy out of the room. "We have some important grown-up business to conduct."

"So you still think he shouldn't have come?" Burton asked. "Or do you just tend to dismiss children out of hand?"

"There'll be time to deal with Coal later," said John. "For now, we need to speak with Franklin."

"A book by Captain Charles Johnson?" Franklin said in bemusement. "He didn't really exist, you know. He was an invention of Edmund's grandfather, Eliot, and his writer friend Crusoe."

"Defoe," Jack corrected. "Have you ever seen such a book? We thought that if anyone would know the whereabouts of such an esoteric book of maps, it would be you."

"You flatter me," said Franklin. "I have one of the finest libraries in London and the best collection of books of maps. You're welcome to avail yourself of it, if it will help."

"Thank you, Doctor," John said. He turned to Rose. "When Edmund gets back from doing his chores at his father's house, will you tell him I'd like to see him? He may be able to help us."

"Can't I help you look for the book?" Rose replied. "I might be able to see something you'd miss."

"We're scholars," said John. "Books are our business. We'll have a better idea of what we're looking for, Rose. But thank you for the offer." He glanced at the door. "Edmund?"

"Of course." Rose nodded. "I'll watch for him outside."

"While you're chasing paper," said Burton, "I'm going to go look for Theo. I haven't seen him today."

"Fine," Jack said as he and John entered the library. "We'll let you know if we discover anything."

John thumbed through a stack of books on Franklin's desk, then handed several to Jack. "Has it ever occurred to you," he said, pondering, "that our presence here, at this particular time, and the disaster in the Archipelago, might be part of the impetus for the Revolutionary War? You know, the way the Winter King spurred the Great War?"

"I can't tell if you think we should get credit or blame if we were responsible," Jack said as he emerged from underneath the desk and took the musty books. "It might have been nice to retain control of the Colonies for a while longer, but then again, without the Americans we wouldn't be winning World War Two either."

"Just think it through," John continued. "Events in the Archipelago mirror those in this world and vice versa. Do you think something is about to happen there that results in the conflict here, or is it the crisis in time that's somehow reverberating backward?"

"If it's going backward, then I'm worried it might reverberate forward, too," said Jack. "Like the ripples in a pond. Anyroad, I don't think the Revolutionary War has as much to do with us as it does a bunch of plantation owners getting their knickers in a twist."

"Probably," said John. "But it can't be coincidence that we're here, with other Caretakers, and in the same basic era that Morgan had jumped to."

"Not coincidence," Jack stated flatly. "We're here because that's where the door opened."

"Yes," John agreed, "but the builders of the keep chose to place the door here for a reason, and I think it's because our coming here has made it one of Verne's zero points."

Jack stopped, mouth agape. "That's a really good argument," he finally said. "I can't believe I hadn't thought of that."

"Funny," said John. "That's just what Charles would—" He swallowed hard. "Sorry. I didn't think."

"I miss him too."

John looked down at the sheaf of maps in his hand, then shoved them back into a drawer. "I think we're done. If the book is here, I can't find it. I'm awful at espionage anyway. We should have asked Fred to do this."

"He wouldn't have fared any better," Jack replied. "And is it really espionage when you have permission?"

"I don't think we really know what we're looking for anyway," said John as he opened the door. "And I don't think we should underestimate Fred."

"Point taken," said Jack. "Shall we go find some dinner?"

"Sounds good to me," said John as the door closed behind them. "Lay on, Macduff."

Rose went to wait for Edmund, but she couldn't shake the feeling that that was all she was able to do—wait. She hadn't slept well, having nightmares about the dark thing on Paralon, and she felt that she was of little help with the Caretakers' efforts here in London. So far, the most important thing she had done was not make things worse—which wasn't really helping at all.

Then again, she thought as she absentmindedly played foot tag with her shadow, *the Caretakers never really ask for my help, or my opinion. Not really. To them I still seem to be a child.*

Without Rose, the Shadow King would not have been defeated. Without Rose, Arthur would not have been saved. When there was a crisis, and she was the solution, they listened, because they had no choice—and that felt really good to her. To be the hero who saved the day. Perhaps it was selfish, but in a small way, she understood that was why she was frustrated—she wanted them to listen to her, to help, so that she could save them all again. *Maybe*, she thought, *that's why heroes do the things they do, anyway.*

She had been out on the street for only a little while when she saw Edmund coming across the cobblestones. She started to raise her hand in greeting when he suddenly turned left into an alley at the end of the block.

She started walking in that direction when she saw Lauren, who had been following Edmund from some distance behind him. Rose crossed the street behind a wagon, so as not to be seen, and then moved to the opposite corner where the alley was in full view.

Edmund was at the far end of the alley . . .

. . . with Laura Glue.

They were simply talking, nothing more. But it was obvious by the efforts they'd made to meet in private that they wanted to keep their meeting a secret. They were partially successful.

Closer to the street, Lauren was also watching, and it was obvious that she was feeling heartache over Edmund's interest in Laura Glue. Rose decided she should speak to the girl, but she didn't want the others to know they'd been seen. She moved farther down the street before crossing, so that she could approach Lauren quietly.

At that moment several horsemen rode by, stirring up dirt and muck, and when they had passed, Lauren was nowhere to be seen. The girl had vanished.

"Lose someone, dearie?" a voice croaked from behind her. "Or something?"

It was an old beggar woman. She smiled at Rose with a faintly frightening snaggletoothed grin.

"Hello, Moonchild," the old woman said. "You have come to another crossroads, I think—else I would not have been drawn to you here."

Rose looked the woman up and down and only barely concealed the expression of distaste that was rising on her face. The woman was a beggar, or possible an escapee from a sanitarium, or both. She was humpbacked and seemed to be missing several teeth. She smelled awful, and her clothing was an assorted mishmash of rags, discarded blouses, and skirts, which she had layered with no particular finesse, and a collection of belts and necklaces that would have outfitted the entire British navy. She wore boots and carried a tattered umbrella.

"Been having bad dreams, have we, dearie?" the old woman asked. "Would you like to tell Auntie Dawn about them? You might feel better if you do."

"Did Mother Night send you?" Rose asked, looking around warily. Her shadow was nowhere to be seen, and she wished she had thought to bring Archimedes with her.

She needn't have worried—no one else on the street seemed to take any notice of her and the old woman at all. "I'm here for you and you alone, dearie," she said, almost as if she were confirming what Rose had been wondering. "No one else will give us a come hither or go thither. I've come to speak to you about your gift."

Suddenly Rose was overcome with feelings of shame and guilt. She had left the glowing ball of string in her room at Tamerlane House. With everything else that had happened after Mother Night's visitation, she had completely forgotten about it.

"No, dearie," Auntie Dawn replied, answering her thoughts, "you didn't forget it."

On impulse, Rose stuck her hand in her pocket and pulled out Ariadne's Thread.

"We gave it to you," Auntie Dawn said, "and you accepted it. That can't be taken back, and it can't be left behind. It's yours now."

The way she said it was meant to be reassuring, Rose thought, but then why was the strange woman's face so sad when she said it?

"If I'm at a crossroads," Rose said, "what direction am I supposed to take?"

"You're about to discover the reason you are here," said Auntie Dawn. "To move forward, you must look behind. To gain something, you must sacrifice it. Nothing worth having comes without a price. And you needn't have nightmares, not if you don't want to."

Her head spun. What did all this mean? "I have nightmares," she said, addressing the last point honestly, "because the dark thing terrifies me."

"The only reason it's in your nightmares," Auntie Dawn said with a wink, "is because *it* is more terrified of *you*. Remember that, Rose. You have more power than you believe. You simply have to make the decision to act—and then see what follows."

"Rose?" said Laura Glue, hastily dropping Edmund's hand from her own. "Who are you talking to?"

"Who?" Rose answered. "I'm just . . ." She turned, but no one was there. Auntie Dawn had vanished. "No one, I guess. You're needed back at the Doctor's," she said to Edmund.

"We're heading over there now," he said. "We'll walk with you."

✦   ✦   ✦

When the trio arrived at the house, they found there were other guests who had just come in the door—Harry Houdini and Arthur Conan Doyle. The two men were alternately greeting and being grilled by the rest of the companions.

"How did you know we were at Franklin's?" asked Jack. "We had no way to communicate with you after you went on your little stroll."

"It wasn't hard to deduce," Doyle said with the pride of a Detective who'd detected well. "You couldn't go far with all the animals in tow, which limited you to Craven Street or the surrounding neighborhoods. On Craven Street, there are two notorious residents—one an eminent scientist and philosopher, and the other a reclusive mapmaker. The odds were you'd be at one of those two homes, and Doctor Franklin is the one who's better positioned to help you as a resource of knowledge and connections, while still being in close proximity to the mapmaker's house."

"Good Lord!" John exclaimed. "That's brilliant!"

"Elementary, my dear Caretaker," said Doyle with a slight bow.

"Oh for heaven's sake," Houdini said. "We came back here because this is where we started, and then we just followed the trail of Leprechaun cracker crumbs between the two houses. The blind magistrate told us who lived in them."

"Ulp. Sorry about the mess," Fred said, pocketing the bag of crackers he was munching from.

"The magistrate would be Sir John," Franklin said. "Very little of what happens on Craven Street escapes his ears."

Houdini leaned close to Jack. "Should we be talking in front of him? Oath of secrecy and all that?"

"For one thing, to hear you asking about the Caretaker's oath of secrecy is the funniest thing I've heard all day," said Jack, "and for another, there are two dozen talking animals in his library right now, arranging his books according to smell. So we're a bit past worrying about whether he can keep a secret."

"I can," Franklin assured them. "Make yourselves at home," he told the two newcomers as he disappeared into his study. "Everyone else has."

John poked a finger into Doyle's chest. "Where did you go?" he demanded. "We were very concerned."

"That's good to hear," said Doyle.

"He means, we were worried about the kind of trouble you might cause," said Jack.

"Oh," said Houdini. "Honestly, I can't say I blame you. But we didn't get into any trouble—we may have just saved the day, so to speak. You need to come with us. There's someone you need to meet."

"Can I come?" Coal said, running into the room. "Please?"

John started to answer, but Burton walked through the door and interrupted him. "Yes," he replied, looking at John. "You can come. Where are these two idiots taking us, anyway?"

"You'll see," Houdini said, scowling. "We've been working to all our good, Sir Richard. What have you been doing?"

"Looking for the End of Time," he said, "but I haven't found him yet. So we may as well go for a walk." He put his hand on Coal's shoulder.

"The others, too," said Doyle. "Laura Glue, and Rose, and Archie, and Fred. We should all go. Except the animals," he added. "We are going to be walking a fair distance and don't want to attract too much attention."

"Can Edmund go too?" Laura Glue asked, blushing slightly.

"Edmund?" asked Doyle, looking at the young man who was standing between Rose and the Valkyrie. "Have we picked up a stray?"

"He's the mapmaker's son," Jack said, "and a better than fair mapmaker himself. We'll tell you about it on the way."

"Where are we going, anyway?" said John warily. "Who are you taking us to meet?"

"The person we came here to find in the first place," Houdini said as the group marched out the door. "We're taking you to meet the Dragon's apprentice."

"I'm sorry," Lauren said . . . "but Master McGee isn't in right now."

CHAPTER EIGHTEEN
The Heir

✦

The meeting at the bookbinder's shop was full of old history. Almost everyone in the room had been connected to Madoc in one way or another, for good and for ill. Of them all, only Edmund and Coal saw nothing but a one-armed bookbinder, who was large and still in the prime of his life, and who simply wished to be left alone to do his work.

To Fred and Laura Glue, he was the man out of legend, the mythical Winter King, whose Shadow had returned again and again to wreak havoc on their world.

To Burton, Houdini, and Doyle, he was the martyred brother of Merlin, the betrayer, who prevented Madoc from becoming the ruler of two worlds, united in peace.

The last time John and Jack had seen him, he was plummeting over the edge of a waterfall, having tried his level best to kill them.

And the last time Rose and Archie had met him, which was the first time she had ever seen her father in the flesh, he helped them repair the sword of Aeneas, so they could defeat his own Shadow-self and save the Archipelago and the Summer Country from a devastating war.

The Caretakers and their motley entourage filled the small

shop, where they sat with Madoc, who kept his distance from all of them except for one.

"Rose," he said quietly, extending his good arm. "Come to me."

She walked to her father and wrapped her arms around him. He embraced her, then stood back, indicating that she should sit on the stool next to him.

He looked her up and down, appraising her, and then his eyes narrowed and his expression grew dark. "Rose," he said slowly. "Where is your shadow?"

Rose blushed furiously, embarrassed. "It—it's outside, under a bench, I think. It should be coming in soon."

He leaned back, looking from her to the Caretakers. "So. You didn't give it up, then? It's still yours?"

"Oh no!" Rose exclaimed. "I mean, yes. It's still mine. There was an accident, and it came loose. But it's still mine."

Madoc nodded, and his expression softened. "I was not chastising you, daughter," he said. "It's not my place, not after all that I have done. But I was just . . . I was . . ."

"I understand," Rose said, laying her hand on his.

Madoc looked up at the others. "I agreed to this meeting in order to see my daughter again," he said brusquely. "She kept her word to me, and because of her, I have a new life. But I don't see any reason why I should speak to the rest of you."

Burton's face colored, and he turned away, chagrined.

"We are here because we were told to seek your help, Madoc." Jack spoke the last word with deliberate emphasis. He had once been swayed by this man's magnetism, and the promises he offered for power and influence in the world. He was wary about speaking with him again, however good the reason.

Madoc turned his eyes to Jack, and they glittered as he spoke. "Yes, Jack, so I'm told. You need the help of a Dragon. But as I told your two associates, there simply aren't any left."

"No Dragons, perhaps," said John, "but you were Samaranth's apprentice, were you not?"

Madoc bowed his head. "I was. A poor one, I'm afraid."

"Are all the Dragons really gone?" Rose asked. "We have come back in time, after all."

Madoc rubbed his chin and thought a moment. "It seems I have seen some, now and again. But not for some time."

"They would have been captured and taken back through the same door we used," said Jack, "so if there was a Dragon here, it would have been taken by the Shadow King."

"How long have you been here?" Rose asked her father.

"Nearly two years," he answered, "although if you used the same door, you should have followed right on my heels."

"There is a discontinuity," said John. "A rift in time. That's why we've come here, Madoc."

The bookbinder sighed. "All right," he said, looking at Rose. "Tell me what's happened."

Between Rose's accounting of her visit from Mother Night, and the others' mishmash retelling of the events since the party at Tamerlane House, it was almost two hours before Madoc spoke again.

"I don't know enough about cartography to help you with mapping time," he said when they had finished. "That became my dear brother's specialty. But I know why you were told to seek out a Dragon to solve your riddle.

"Samaranth told me there were certain things that could only be known as a Dragon," he continued, "things that I could not know as a man. He promised me that if I ever chose to . . . If I ever became a Dragon, then I would understand.

"It was the Dragons, did you know?" he said to no one in particular. "The Dragons who made the doors for the Keep of Time. So I'd imagine that only a Dragon would be able to tell you how to harness those energies again. If," he added, "it can be done at all."

"If that's true, then why didn't Samaranth just tell us himself, or leave us instructions?" asked John. "Why force us to go searching for you?"

"Either his idea of a joke, or my final lesson as his apprentice," Madoc said darkly, "and as I told you, I was a very poor student."

"Or because he simply chose not to," Jack said, "given what the Watchmaker said."

Madoc shrugged. "He moves in mysterious ways. But you probably know that better than I."

"You said you had seen other Dragons," Doyle said hopefully. "Maybe it's one of them we're meant to find. What kind did you see?"

"Dragonships, mostly," said Madoc, "but none I knew too well. The last one I saw had the look of a sea serpent. A long neck, which rose high into the air. Sleek. It moved through the harbor and disappeared. But I have no doubt it was a Dragonship."

"Which one?" John asked. "What color was it?"

"Color?" said Madoc. "If I had to call it anything, I'd say it was green."

"The *Green Dragon* then?" asked Rose.

"No," John said, shaking his head. "The *Green Dragon* is

mostly blue. If the one Madoc saw was green, then it was quite possibly the *Violet Dragon*."

"Dragonships, maybe," said John, "but no other Dragons, then."

Madoc got up from his stool and moved to the window. He could see the Thames from there, and smell the tang of moisture in the air when the wind blew east.

"There were Dragons younger than Samaranth who had taken apprentices," he said at length, not turning from the window, "but they had taken no new apprentices in almost five thousand years. I think the last was during the Bronze Age, well before my time. Even so, I was not taken in as a student by Samaranth until I was quite old myself, chronologically speaking."

Archimedes nodded and squawked in agreement. "It was right around the time of the tournament, I believe."

"It was," Madoc acknowledged, returning the nod. "But you weren't there. How did you know?"

The bird shrugged. "I read things. I keep up."

"Hah!" Madoc laughed. "Of course you would. Anyway, it was after I left in a fury. I felt angry, betrayed. And Samaranth saw this, and decided to do something about it. So he approached me and made the proverbial offer you can't refuse."

"What does that mean?" asked Doyle.

"It's an old expression, coined by people conquered by Attila the Hun," explained Archimedes. "Basically, every time he approached a new country, he did it in the spirit of friendship, cooperation, and civilized, mutual progress."

"Really?" said Doyle. "How did that go over?"

"If his overtures were rejected, he'd basically order his armies to behead everyone until they changed their minds. It got a lot easier to offer his friendship to countries after he had a few of those under his belt."

"An offer they can't refuse," Doyle repeated. "So Samaranth threatened to behead you?"

"Not in so many words," Madoc replied, "but he made it clear that he thought I needed his guidance, and that were I to decline, the consequences would be drastic."

"We've had some experience with that ourselves," said Houdini.

"And the riddle?" asked Rose. "It doesn't mean anything to you?"

"It means one thing to a man," Madoc said, echoing his earlier remarks, "and another to a Dragon. To give you the answers you're seeking, I would have to . . ."

"Ascend?" said Jack.

"Call it what you like," said Madoc, "but I refuse to do it. Not for any reason. I am finally a whole man again—I will not give that up to become a Dragon."

"You were willing to sacrifice yourself once for a great cause," Rose said. "I know. I was there."

"I could never be that selfless," Madoc said, his voice subdued. "Not . . . again, at any rate.

"Once in my life, all that I sought was entry back into the Summer Country. But I chose poorly, in so many things, and eventually the reasons I wanted that so badly were forgotten. Only the idea of the prize remained. And then, when I lost it, and everything else, I started to remember. Then, miraculously, I was given a second chance—and I took it. And now, now that I truly understand what I have, I'm hard-pressed to ever give it up again."

Burton stepped forward. "I understand. Everything I have

done, everything I have sacrificed," he said, spreading his hands in supplication, "has been in your service, Lord Madoc."

Madoc looked at Burton, blinking impassively, then belched loudly enough to rattle the tools on the wall. "You chose your deity poorly then," he finally said, drawing out the words for emphasis. "I'm merely a bookbinder here, and a one-armed one at that. I'm no one to be worshipped."

"You were, once," Burton said, unwilling to drop his arguments, "and you could be again. I know. We are very much alike, you and I."

"We," said Madoc, "have very little in common."

"More than you think," Burton replied, as he pulled open the curtain. Through the rear window they could see into the courtyard, where Coal and Laura Glue were watching Edmund draw in the dirt with a stick. "That one, there," Burton said, indicating Coal. "That's our common link, Lor—Madoc. He is your nephew many generations removed, the heir to the Silver Throne, and my own descendant."

Madoc started, then peered more closely at the pastoral scene outside before turning around. He shook his head. "I've not had too much luck coming to the defense of my nephews," he said, holding up his hook. "I can count on one hand the number of times that choice turned out to be terribly wrong.

"Take it from one who knows," Madoc went on. "Your life will be what you make of it, and you draw to yourself that which you truly believe in. I've stopped searching for things that only cause me grief and pain. You ought to do the same."

"Twice I've been drawn to *you*," Rose said. "You helped us before. Will you please, please consider it again?"

He looked at his daughter's eyes—they were innocent, trust-ing. Hopeful. Then a movement at her feet distracted him. It was her shadow, shimmering, writhing, moving from darkness to darkness inside the shop. He could barely suppress the shudder that came over him, and the memories that came with it.

"It—It's too big, my dove," he said. Rose almost smiled—he'd never used an endearment with her before. "This is my final word. I have finally found a life that I . . . love. A work that gives me pleasure. And a peace I have never known. I have paid my debts, and more. So I want nothing more to do with the Archi-pelago, or the Caretakers, or any of it. I wash my hands of the whole thing."

With that, Madoc stood and walked out of the bindery. He did not look back.

Franklin's library was a treasure-house of knowledge, and even more crammed with books, maps, papers, and scrolls than his office downstairs had been. The windows were shuttered, so that the sunlight didn't fade the bindings on the books or the ink on the maps, and every other wall was covered with shelves that were full to spilling over with more books. The room had become much more organized since Myrret and the other animals had arrived—but the effect they had was to make the library more like the only other one they had ever known.

It was possibly the only place Coal could have been in all of London that felt like the Warren where he was raised back in the palace at Paralon. After the little escapade with the kite, John had given Myrret strict instructions to keep an eye on him—which, since the fox could not really leave Franklin's house, meant the little prince could not either. So to him, the jaunt to visit the mysterious bookbinder had been all too short.

"That was either a brilliant command performance," Houdini said as he slumped into a chaise in the library, "or we've just been dismissed as completely irrelevant."

"The latter, I'm afraid," said Doyle. "He's not going to be any help to us whatsoever."

Burton hadn't spoken for the entire walk back to Craven Street. Back at Franklin's house, he simply sat in a corner of the library, glowering.

"Would you like to read me a story now?" Coal asked, not really directing the question at anyone. "I've been very good, and I waited to ask."

"We've been giving you short shrift, haven't we, lad?" Houdini said as he knelt and tousled the boy's hair. "That's the way it is with grown-ups sometimes. We become too focused on the things that are urgent, so we forget the things that are truly important."

"We'll have time for that later, Coal," said Jack.

"I'm not surprised that he wouldn't help us," John said as he sat next to Burton. "All things considered, we're part of the reason he's had such a struggle all these years. We did play our part, however well-intentioned our motives were."

"He didn't seem too impressed by any of us, don't you agree, Burton?" asked Jack.

"He is," Burton said, then paused as his expression darkened, ". . . not the man I was expecting."

"This will sort itself out, Burton," John said as he laid a supportive hand on the other man's shoulder. "It will."

Burton glared at him and roughly pushed off John's hand.

"When I need comfort from the likes of you, little Caretaker," he growled, "I'll ask. But don't count on that ever happening."

"So," said Houdini, diplomatically trying to change the subject, "Hank Morgan really trained Edmund's great-grandfather in mapmaking?"

"Nice to see you've been paying attention," said Doyle.

"I've been paying attention!" Houdini snapped. "I'm a marvel at paying attention."

"Except," put in Doyle, "when you're preoccupied by a trick you can't figure out."

"I haven't been preoccupied!" the Magician retorted. "Not entirely, anyway. It is possible to think of two things at once, you know."

"So your pretending to pay attention is just an illusion."

"I'm a magician, not an illusionist," said Houdini. "There's a difference. But then, you knew that."

Coal looked bewildered. "What is the difference?"

"An illusionist shows people what they want to see," Houdini said, smiling down at the boy, "and convinces them it's real, even if they know how the trick is done. A magician does things that are real, and seem to be miraculous. The second is far far more work, by the way."

"I disagree with your assessment of illusionists," said Doyle.

"Was my life on Paralon an illusion, or magic?" asked Coal.

Houdini paused, not certain how to answer. Doyle stepped in and took the boy by the shoulder. "Let's just say that your life was an illusion until now, and everything that comes after will be magic, if you want it to be."

"That is such a load of horse manure," said Burton. "Why not tell the boy the truth? That everything worth having in life comes at a price. All that's left for you to decide is whether or not you're willing to pay it."

"It's always worth it," said Jack.

"Really?" asked Burton. "Do you think your friend Charles would agree?"

Jack didn't answer, but simply turned and strode from the room. After a silent moment, John followed him.

"I don't even know why the Caretakers Emeritis permitted him to come," Jack said in frustration as they climbed the stairs to the sleeping room and opened the door. "Houdini is not a bad sort—a bit irritating at times—and as far as I'm concerned, Doyle should have been a Caretaker all along. But I don't know why we need Burton at all."

"He is a Namer," said a voice from the corner of the room. In a smooth, fluid motion, Theo stood up from where he'd been reading and placed the book facedown on one of the beds.

"What were you doing on the floor?" John asked. "We've got plenty of beds."

"I find I am more comfortable on the floor," Theo replied. "It is how I have slept more nights than not."

"Look, Theo," Jack began.

"He is a Namer," Theo repeated. "Burton is fond of declaring himself to be a Barbarian, but he is a most educated man. His temper and impatience have caused him grief in his life, and closed doors that might otherwise have been opened. But he may yet become a champion of the Light, if we allow him to be."

"Allow?" said Jack. "I don't think anyone can stop him if he sets his mind to something."

"He can stop himself," said Theo. "The darker side of his own nature, which all of us share—as you know well, Jack."

"Yes," Jack harrumphed. "I do. But Burton's a different case."

"Not so different from you or me," Theo replied. "Not so different from Madoc."

"Are you saying that he is the way he is because someone wronged him?" asked John. "How do we fix that?"

"Do exactly as you are doing," said Theo. "Help him. Shape him. But do not disregard him. His choice is yet to be made, and you can still tip the balance."

The other men left the library soon after, arguing about magic boxes and reluctant Dragons, so none of them really noticed that they were leaving the little prince all alone. Again.

The door opened. And closed. Someone had entered the room.

Coal looked up, and his face broke into a wide grin when he saw the visitor. Someone familiar. Someone comfortable. Someone safe.

"It's a shame," the visitor said, "that you're left here alone while everyone else has all the fun."

"I don't mind," Coal answered. "I like to read. And they have many important things to do."

"I don't mind either," his visitor said. "It gives us more time together, and we've had some good fun, you and I, haven't we?"

The boy nodded, smiling happily. Then he stopped and frowned, curious.

"Why is it," he asked, "that you have no shadow?"

"Sometimes I do, and sometimes I don't," his visitor said. "I shall have one here if you like."

"No," the boy said, thinking of the dark thing on Paralon. He shivered. "I like you just as you are," he said, "and I'm glad we found this house."

Edmund had an errand to run for Doctor Franklin, and so he didn't go back with the Caretakers, but detoured to an outdoor market. Laura Glue, to everyone's surprise except for Rose, chose to go with him.

The men were mostly preoccupied with discussing the ramifications of Madoc's refusal, and so Rose and Archimedes continued down Craven Street past Franklin's house to the house of Ernest McGee.

"I'm sorry," Lauren said as she opened the door, "but Master McGee isn't in right now."

"I didn't come to see him," Rose answered. "I came to see you."

"Me?" the maid answered in surprise. "But why?"

"You love him, don't you?" Rose asked as the girl ushered her and Archie into the house. "Edmund."

Lauren snapped her head around, startled by the frankness of the question. At first she blushed furiously and twisted her apron in her hands, but then Rose's open and honest expression told her that there was no ulterior motive for the question. She really wanted to know.

"I—I do," Lauren answered, nodding. "I always have, I think. My mother and father served Master Elijah, and so as young children, it was natural that his grandson and I played together. But Master Ernest didn't approve. As he saw it, I was just being brought up as the next generation of Bonneville servants to the house of McGee."

"I see," said Rose. "And he wasn't happy about the prospect of his son courting a servant girl?"

Again, the blush rose in Lauren's cheeks. "Oh, no! Nothing like that!" she exclaimed. "I mean, we never courted. Edmund doesn't . . ." She paused and looked around for anyone who might be eavesdropping, but the only other one in the room was Archie, who was busy plucking at a pinfeather in the far corner. "He—he doesn't know, mistress. At least, I don't think he does. How I feel about him, I mean. There was never a courtship to it."

"That's really quite a shame," a pleasant, cultured voice said from behind them, "for I do so look forward to meeting new generations of McGees."

Rose turned around and gasped.

Daniel Defoe stood in the doorway of the mapmaker's house, eating an apple.

"Well met," he said with a practiced air of indifference. "I'm guessing you are from the Archipelago," he said to Rose, "as I haven't seen any other mechanical owls in this part of the world— or anywhere else, for that matter."

He dropped the half-eaten apple on the floor, then locked the door behind him. "Let's have a little talk, shall we, ladies?"

CHAPTER NINETEEN
The Maps of Elijah McGee

❖

"Actually, I'm from *this* world, you twit," Archie huffed. "You must be one of the stupider Caretakers."

"Archimedes!" Rose sputtered, grabbing at the bird. "Mind your tongue."

The bird looked at her strangely for a moment, then went silent when he realized what she was thinking. Defoe had been the great betrayer in the war against the Shadow King. He had not only turned his back on the Caretakers, but had tried to use the Spear of Destiny to become the King of the World himself. And while those events were yet to occur, this was still the same man. Still a traitor, who had murdered one of his best friends. And still someone who could be very dangerous, if they gave him any information he might use.

"You're wiser than the bird is," said Defoe, "although wisdom doesn't help much when you're caught in a mire."

"It does if you're wise enough to avoid it in the first place," said Rose.

Defoe smiled, and it seemed warm, but there was a calculating darkness behind it. "As I said, wise. But in the mire is in the mire . . . So what, pray tell, are denizens of the Archipelago

*. . . the Echthros . . . began to shimmer and change,
growing larger and darker . . .*

doing in London? Especially at the home of Ernest McGee?"

Rose held her tongue, as did Archie, and surprisingly, Lauren.

"I see," said Defoe. "I don't intend to cause you any harm, you know. I shan't bite."

"Maybe not now," Rose felt herself saying, "but someday you will."

"So," said Defoe, "you distrust me not for who I am, or what I've done, but because of what I have yet to do? That's a pretty judgmental attitude from a girl . . .

". . . without a *shadow*."

His voice dropped to a near whisper with the last words, but they all heard it clearly. He had seen, and he knew what it meant to be without a shadow.

For her part, Lauren reacted with mild surprise to this. She probably had noticed Rose's elusive shadow, but that was the sort of thing servants weren't supposed to notice—or if they did, they weren't supposed to mention it.

"It's not what you're thinking," Rose said, stumbling for the words. "I haven't given it up, I've just . . . misplaced it."

"I haven't made any judgment about you at all," Defoe said, "except maybe that you aren't where you're supposed to be—but now I think maybe you're exactly where you're supposed to be."

"What do you mean?" asked Rose, drawing back protectively in front of Lauren.

"Nothing happens by coincidence," Defoe said. "If you'll come upstairs with me, I think I can explain it to you more clearly. Of course," he added, gesturing at the door, "if you decide otherwise, you are of course free to leave."

"Great," said Archie. "We're leaving."

"No," said Rose. "I think I'd like to hear him out."

"You don't—," Archie began.

"Don't tell me I don't understand!" Rose said, her temper flaring. "This is my choice, Archimedes."

"All right, then," said Defoe. "Let's all go upstairs, if you please."

The door to the upper room swung open with a loud squeal as the two young women and the owl entered, followed by Defoe.

"It's about time someone came back up here," Captain Johnson said primly. "I've gotten very bored, you know."

"Well then," said Defoe, "we'll have to see if we can't liven things up a bit."

"Oh, shades," said Johnson.

"Remember what Captain Johnson warned," Archimedes whispered. "We can't trust him. We shouldn't trust him."

"Wait, Archie," Rose said. "I really do want to hear what he has to say. I don't think he intends to harm us."

"Clever girl," Defoe said, "and you're quite right. In fact, it's just the opposite. I want to ask for your help."

"He's lying," said the captain. "Don't listen to him!"

Before Rose could respond, a patch of darkness darted through the great round window at the end of the room and covered the portrait. The effect was the same as if a wool blanket had been cast over it—Captain Johnson's speech was almost completely muffled, and he could no longer see the others in the room.

"A good use of your shadow, my dear," said Defoe. "I wish I'd thought of that."

"But," Lauren said, feeling brave enough to venture an opinion, "you still have *your* shadow."

"Indeed I do," Defoe said, looking down. "That alone should tell you something about my intentions."

Rose looked questioningly at Archie. This was unexpected. If Defoe was truly the evil man they expected, then why would he still have his shadow?

"All right," Rose said tentatively, "we can talk to you, if you like. What is it you wanted me to help you with?"

Defoe smiled. "I was hoping you'd ask that."

"This is a mistake," said Archie. "We should leave, Rose."

"Lauren?" Rose asked. "What do you think?"

Lauren blinked. She'd very seldom been asked her opinion— and never as a peer. "I . . . I think I could stay, just for a little while."

"Excellent," Defoe said, rubbing his hands together. "So we've just the one dissenter—but we can find someplace to put you out of the way, I think. Come here, bird."

Archimedes snapped out his wings and flew into the Care-taker's face, then wheeled about and flew to the far side of the room. In an explosion of feathers and metal, the great owl burst through the round window at the end of the room and out into the street.

"Well played, bird," Defoe murmured. He turned to the young women. "He might have been useful, but it's you and your shadow that I think I needed," he said. "Now the clock is ticking. And our time . . .

". . . is quickly running out."

Benjamin Franklin sat watching in fascination as Fred simultaneously recited stanzas from the *Iliad* and ate Leprechaun crackers.

"What?" Fred asked, his mouth full of crackers. "Did I do something wrong?"

"Oh, no," Franklin said quickly. "I was just wondering how it's done. The talking, that is."

Fred frowned. "I'm not sure what you mean," he said warily. "This is because I'm a badger, isn't it?"

Franklin smiled disarmingly and held up his hands. "I mean you no disrespect, young Caretaker," he said jovially. "But you must understand, in my extensive experience, animals do not converse with humans. In any language. So having this particular group of houseguests has been quite an education."

"Maybe the animals you know didn't have much to say," said Fred. "Or they got a glimpse of your head wear and decided to keep their mouths closed." He tipped his head and indicated the raccoon fur cap hanging on the coatrack in the corner.

Franklin blew out a puff of air and chuckled. "I can't say I blame them. If it helps, that was a gift, not something I acquired myself."

"It really doesn't," said Fred, "but I appreciate the gesture."

"Who taught you how to speak, ah, English?"

Fred puffed out his chest slightly. "My father, Charles Mongolfier Hargreaves-Heald," he said proudly, "otherwise known as Uncas, squire to Don Quixote."

"You don't say?" Franklin replied. "Interesting. You know, I really hadn't expected to find you to be such a fascinating conversationalist. But it's the way you say things that's so intriguing."

"Well, there are some allowances made for the differences in our mouths," said Fred. "An animal's jaw is so much more adaptable to long vowel sounds, for example. But that's for spoken language. It's a lot easier than learning to read and write was, I can tell you that. So many of the words you use aren't spelled the way they ought to be."

"How do you mean?"

"For example," Fred started, warming up to his topic, "several letters in your alphabet are completely redundant. C, and q, and w, a, x, and y . . . a couple more, besides. You really don't need them, not if you want a word to look like it sounds."

"That's fascinating!" Franklin exclaimed. "To be frank, my friend Noah Webster and I have discussed something very similar."

"Then you get where I'm coming from," said Fred. "Also, if you made up a few combined consonants, like the 'ch' in 'chew,' you'd save a lot of time and trouble. It's not that the words are bad—just the rules about how they're spelled."

"Impressive," Franklin said in all seriousness. "Despite your short stature, may I compliment you on your thinking?"

"Thanks," answered Fred. "Despite your immense girth, may I compliment you on your civility?"

"Uh, ah," Franklin stammered. "Thank you."

Edmund and Laura Glue arrived with a box full of vegetables for the next evening's meal, and something else—Ernest McGee.

He stood hesitantly in the doorway, looking around at the interior of Franklin's house as if he was about to be pinched for some petty crime.

"It's all right, Father," Edmund said soothingly. "I'm his apprentice, remember? I'm allowed to have guests."

"I've never been here before," said Ernest. "I wanted to speak to the Doctor, and . . ." He paused. "Thank him."

Edmund beamed. "We can arrange that," he said. "Laura Glue? Would you see if the Doctor is about?"

While the Valkyrie went to look for Franklin, Edmund took

his father into the study, where a spirited discussion was taking place.

"I can't help thinking that the key we're missing is in Morgan's message," John was saying. "If only Captain Johnson hadn't lost his book . . ."

Edmund perked up at this. "Which book?"

Jack waved his hand dismissively. "It's not important now. He lost it decades before you were even born."

"You mean *The Maps of Elijah McGee*?" Edmund asked. "That book?"

John's jaw fell open. "How did you know?"

Edmund shrugged. "There were only ever three books that he worked on with my grandfather and Mr. Defoe," he replied. "The *History*, the *Pyratlas*, and the last one."

"Which does us no good if we don't know where it is."

"But we do," said Edmund. "*I* have it."

Every man in the room suddenly took on the same shocked expression. "You do?" exclaimed his father. "Since when?"

"Since I was a boy, and started making the maps," said Edmund. "When you made your, um, opinion clear, I started hiding them—and that book, the one Captain Johnson started compiling, was the best of our family's work. So I kept it, and have been adding to it ever since."

"Ah, me," his father said sadly. "I have done you a disservice, my boy. But we'll say our piece later—for now, let's see the book, hey?"

As Edmund went up to his attic workroom to fetch the book, Ernest took a seat among the Caretakers.

"He's a talented boy, you know," said John. "But then, it does run in the family."

"The talent, or curse, depending on which of us you ask and when, skipped a generation or two, I think," said Ernest. "Oh, I have the facility for it, as had my father. But neither of us has the innate skill that Elijah had. My son Edmund has it too. I'm more of a compiler, after the manner of my father," he continued. "We were always more interested in collecting them than we were in making them."

"It was good of you to let him apprentice to Franklin," said Jack.

"I didn't approve," said Ernest. "I'm still not sure I do. But I'm not a fool, either," he added as his son came downstairs to the study carrying a large book. "McGee maps are McGee maps, after all, and I'm loath to let the family legacy end just because I don't like it."

Edmund set *The Maps of Elijah McGee* in the center of the table and spread it open. It was not even a book yet, per se, but more a collection of notes written by Johnson, and maps, drawn on the same thick paper that Edmund had been carrying when they first met him.

"Do you know what these are?" Jack exclaimed excitedly. "These are maps to some of the places that Verne mentioned! To the places where imaginary lands never separated from the Summer Country!"

"You mean, like the Soft Places?" asked Fred. "Like the Inn of the Flying Dragon?"

"Not quite," Jack replied as he riffled through the pages. "More like places that found their own niches in our world and never pulled away when the Frontier was created."

"Pardon my asking, but did that badger just *speak?*" Ernest asked.

"Oh, that's just Fred," said Edmund. "Wait'll you go upstairs to meet the new librarians."

"Aha!" Jack exclaimed. "It's here!"

As Johnson had said, there was indeed a note from Morgan, tucked away in the pages of his book.

> To whoever finds this note:
>
> It was no accident. It was no malfunction. But for whatever reason, my watch will not work. I was kept here, in this time, through no will of my own. Someone is playing a deeper game and has learned how to manipulate time—someone better than the Messengers. Better than Verne. Possibly even better than Poe. Somehow I must reach you in the future—but the key to the past is hidden here, in the pages of this book. Find it. Use it. As for me, my friend Elijah and I are going to try to create a chronal map, which I hope to use to return to Tamerlane House. If it works, then we'll have a good laugh over this. If not, I hope you'll fare better than I. If Houdini is the one who finds this note, then I can only pray it remains intact.
>
> God be with you,
>
> Captain Henry Morgan, Lt. Governor, Jamaica

"Oh, now that's just a low blow," said Houdini.

"Intriguing," John said. "He believes that someone kept him here—someone better at time travel than he was."

"It's logical," said Doyle. "He was the one most likely to take the Cartographer's place, and according to the Watchmaker, that's what we needed."

"Whoever did this to him never expected that he might train someone else," said John, "or that he would stumble across a family like the McGees."

"I don't think it was accidental," said Houdini. "Not with what I've seen. Morgan chose Elijah McGee. Carefully, and with intent."

"I actually wish he were still here," said Jack. "I think it would be comforting, somehow, just to have him around."

"It's too bad he's dead, then," spat Burton. "The dead are useless, unless they're Caretakers, or we've run out of supplies."

"Do you remember reading anything about the McGees in the Histories?" John asked Jack. "Anything at all?"

"I can't recall," Jack said, thinking. "Those were more Charles's passion, not mine. Why do you ask?"

"I can't remember anything much about them either," said John, "nor can I remember any mention of them in anything having to do with the Cartographer. But just look at these, Jack! Can you imagine a family of this talent not coming to the attention of the Caretakers? Or the Cartographer?"

Burton clucked his tongue. "Maybe they just *did*."

"What's that supposed to mean?" asked John.

"I've had more experience in time than you have, young Caretaker. Just because something you think is important hasn't happened in the past doesn't mean it will not still happen in your own future. Even if that future takes you to the past."

"Every time he talks about this sort of thing, my head aches," said Jack.

"No, he's right," said John. "Time moves in both directions, isn't that what you said?"

"At the Eagle and Child, yes," Burton said with grudging admiration. "Maybe you aren't a waste of time, after all. And yes," he added, smirking at Jack, "the pun was intended."

"Oh, I got it," said Jack. "I just didn't think it was funny."

"What I'm thinking," John said, "is that the McGee family may in fact be Fictions, like Hank and Melville. That would explain why we haven't seen anything of them in the Histories before."

"When they met past the waterfall at the Edge of the World," he continued, "Captain Johnson told Rose that he and Defoe were training as possible apprentices to Cyrano de Bergerac, and that de Bergerac had his eye on Eliot as a possible apprentice to Merlin."

"The Caretakers don't document apprenticeships unless they become full Caretakers," said Jack, "no offense, Burton. And I don't think anyone but Verne knew of actual apprentices to the Cartographer."

"He never said that Eliot was a formal apprentice," said John, "just that de Bergerac thought he had a good hand for map-making."

"That's a good eye for talent," said Jack. "De Bergerac was one of the Cartographer's apprentices himself, remember?"

"There's another possibility," Doyle said. He paced the floor pensively, rubbing his chin in thought. "We've gone about this backward," he said slowly, "assuming that the McGees didn't come to the attention of the Caretakers, or were somehow overlooked. But what if they weren't?"

"What do you mean?" Jack asked.

"There are two possibilities," said Doyle. "One, that they were never meant to be mapmakers until Morgan came here to teach them, and so the Caretakers never knew about them in our time."

"Mmm, no," said Jack. "De Bergerac knew of them, remember? And he was also a skilled cartographer. He might have started training them even without Morgan."

"A possible paradox, then," said Doyle. "But it's the second possibility that's more troubling—that the current Caretaker *does* know about them and is trying to suppress them. Maybe even destroy them."

"Except there doesn't seem to be a Caretaker here now," said Jack. "There's a gap, unless it's Franklin—but surely he'd have mentioned it."

"There's no gap," Burton said with an almost regretful sigh. "Perhaps Verne wasn't brave enough to tell you the truth of it. Having three Caretakers at once was a safeguard, and kept the flames of prophecy fanned—but you three were the latecoming exception to the norm. There were not always three Caretakers available, not all at once. Sometimes there were two, and more rarely, one.

"There is a current Caretaker, but he's a tulpa, one of the first John Dee created after himself, and that fact extended his tenure for a very long time—well before making tulpas fell out of favor with the Caretakers Emeritis. It was before Blake began creating portraits, and well before Poe began traveling to the past, so the records of his tenure could be manipulated. So," he said again, "there's no gap. You just haven't figured it out yet, because the fact that he *was* a tulpa was kept a secret from all the rest later."

"He's correct," John said as he examined the list in the *Geographica*. "Swift was the last Caretaker in this era until he was replaced by Blake, and Goethe is the current living Caretaker—but he isn't one, not yet. That leaves only one name on our list."

"Oh, fewmets," Jack said under his breath. "Really?"

"I'm afraid so," said John. "The Caretaker can only be Daniel Defoe."

No one at the Doctor's house noticed when the End of Time slipped silently out the door, just as no one had noticed the Shadow leaving earlier.

The Shadow moved quickly and was difficult to track. But the End of Time had tracked beasts in impossible terrains, and London was no challenge. The End of Time leaped over the chimney tops of the houses that ran perpendicular to Craven Street as he followed it, until finally it was cornered and could flee no more.

"You are not meant to be here, in this time, and in this place," Theo said calmly.

"I'm impressed," the Echthros said just as calmly. "There are very few among your kind who are able to sense my presence, let alone track me—especially when I don't want to be tracked."

"But track you I have," Theo said quietly as he removed a small parchment from his pocket, "and now I will do what I must, and bind you, and cast you out."

The Echthros laughed, a chilling sound that reverberated off the walls in the narrow alley. "Go ahead and try," it said. "In fact, I insist that you do."

A flickering of fear danced across Theo's usually placid features, but he unfolded the paper and then began to read. His eyes grew milky and a faint shimmering appeared around him as he softly, carefully recited the ancient words of power. When he had finished, he looked up at his enemy.

"All done?" the Echthros responded, seemingly bored. "Is that all you've got? Or did you have something else you'd like to try?"

Theo's eyes grew wide with alarm. The creature should have been bound. This was one of the oldest of the Old Magics, and it had never, never failed.

"That's the thing about the Old Magic," the Echthros said as it moved closer to the End of Time. "It is reliable. It operates according to rules and laws, and those may be bent, but never broken. Especially when it comes to things like Bindings."

"I don't understand," Theo said, bewildered. "I spoke your name—your true name. You should be bound."

"I am bound," the Echthros replied, as it began to shimmer and change, growing larger and darker and less distinct. "I was already bound, and cannot be bound again by the same curse until the first is broken. So you see," it concluded, now huge and towering over the man, "I am bound, but you are not my master!"

With a shrieking sound that shattered windows and a rending of flesh with massive claws, the Echthros fell upon the End of Time. There was no screaming, just dying, which irritated the creature somewhat. But for the moment, its secret was safe.

Changing back to its original shape, the Echthros walked away from the still steaming body and made its way back into the crowd, where no one saw it pass, nor would have stopped it if they had.

Briefly Edmund explained about the book . . .

CHAPTER TWENTY
The False Caretaker

❖

It took a while for Laura Glue to track down Doctor Franklin, but the second time she looked there, she finally found him on the upper floor, discoursing with Myrret about Arthurian history. He was reluctant to leave, until she told him who his visitor was.

"The fox has some very unusual takes on history," Franklin said as they descended the stairs, "but I think he's got his dates confused. He seems to be off by a millennium or two."

"Foxes make great librarians," said Laura Glue, "but they're not so good at math."

"Mr. McGee," said Franklin, offering his hand.

"Doctor Franklin," said Ernest, taking it. "I'm pleased to finally meet you."

"What's all this?" Franklin asked as he looked over the spread of papers on the table.

Briefly Edmund explained about the book and what he'd been doing with it.

"How fascinating!" Franklin exclaimed. "You know, Edmund, I've got some similar writings and drawings in an old book of mine I keep in my desk. You might call it my own apprenticeship. I'll have to show it to you sometime. I think you'll find it very enlightening."

"I'd love to see it," Edmund said, as a look of interest flashed among the Caretakers. A book like this one? One that Franklin had not yet shown to Edmund? And more importantly, that he referred to as his own apprenticeship?

At that moment John noticed that a shadow had followed Laura Glue and the Doctor down from the rooms upstairs. The boy Coal was holding a kite. He suddenly had an idea.

"Doctor Franklin," John said amicably, "I'd promised Coal that we'd go out flying kites, but I forgot that we were meeting with Ernest. You wouldn't have some free time, would you?"

"Actually, I do," said Franklin. "I was thinking of going over to Trafalgar Square myself to try out a new kite design. I'm sure the young man wouldn't mind helping me, would you?" He looked down at the boy, who nodded enthusiastically.

Jack started to protest that it wouldn't be necessary, that they could look after the boy well enough, but John's tap on his hand stopped him. John nodded almost imperceptibly, then to Franklin he said, "That will be fine. Thank you, Doctor Franklin."

"What was that all about?" Jack asked as the Doctor left with the little prince, two kites in hand. "With all our suspicions, are you sure it's safe to leave the boy alone with him?"

"What's he going to do, really?" asked John. "Benjamin Franklin isn't exactly going to harm a child in broad daylight. Besides, it's to follow up on our suspicions that I agreed."

"I hadn't realized you expected me," Ernest said, confused. "We had a meeting?"

"We're having it now," John said as he headed up the stairs. "Harry can pick any lock, and we've got a good hour before they're back to look around unmolested. And I want to see that book."

The others laughed and trotted to catch up to the Principal Caretaker. "When you wrote about the little burglar in your book," Jack said, "I didn't realize you were writing from experience."

"Not experience," said John as they entered Franklin's private study. "Just unfulfilled ambitions."

"Do you like the kite, Coal?" Doctor Franklin asked as he led the boy into ever more crowded streets. "I made it just for you."

The boy nodded happily, clutching the brightly colored kite to his chest as the tail trailed along behind them. "It's very nice, thank you."

"What a polite young man," Franklin said, mussing the boy's hair. "I'm very glad we've gotten to be friends. We'll have some good fun, you and I, won't we? I was meaning to ask," he added, "where is it you come from, Coal?"

"I—I'm not supposed to speak of it," Coal stammered, looking suddenly very worried. Laura Glue and the Caretakers had given him very strict instructions not to talk about where he was from with strangers—but Doctor Franklin was not really a stranger, was he? After all, they had let him go to fly kites with the Doctor, and they had been staying at his house. If he could not be trusted, then who could?

"Perhaps you could tell me about it as a story," Franklin suggested. "You like stories, don't you, Coal? Like the ones in my library?"

"Oh, yes!" the boy responded. "I love to read."

"Well, then," Franklin said as they located a suitable place from which to launch the kite. "Why don't I tell you a story about myself, and then you can tell me stories about yourself. Is it a bargain?"

Coal murmured in agreement as he untangled the kite's tail from his legs. "It is. A bargain."

"Excellent!" said Franklin as they tossed the kite into the wind. "I'll start. I came here from a land far, far away, called America. Where did you come from?"

"Once upon a time," Coal began, oblivious to the intense scrutiny being fixed on him by the Doctor, "I came here from a land far, far away. It was called Paralon."

The Caretakers were so intent on getting a look at Franklin's mysterious book that they didn't notice Edmund and Laura Glue slip away and out the back door. They ran through a maze of alleys and ended up at an old barn that was mostly used to store grain. It was spacious, and best of all, private.

"They were going to go look at the Doctor's book," Laura Glue said as they climbed up to sit on a high crossbeam. "Didn't you want to see his secret maps?"

"I draw maps all the time," said Edmund, "and when I'm not drawing them, I'm reading about them. I spend most of my life buried in maps. And I do love them—but I want to do other things too, and spend time with . . ." He blushed. "Well, do other things. Otherwise, I'd be no better off than if I was an old hermit, stuck in a tower, doing nothing but drawing maps. And what kind of a way to live is that?"

Smoothly, he leaned in to kiss her, and she shied away. "You don't kiss boys where you come from?"

"It's never really come up," Laura Glue said matter-of-factly. "There were always kissing games when we were children— girls chasing the boys, and all that—but the point of it was that the girls chased the boys, who didn't want to be kissed."

"Didn't they?" asked Edmund with a lopsided grin. "Weren't the boys faster than you were?"

"Mostly," Laura Glue admitted, "except for maybe Abby Tornado. She could outrun everyone."

"Mmm-hmm. But somehow you always managed to catch them, didn't you?"

Laura Glue's brow furrowed, then her eyes widened. "I never really thought of that. I suppose they must have wanted to be caught."

"That's my point," Edmund said as he moved closer. "Boys liked kissing as much as the girls did. They were just too young to admit it."

Laura Glue sighed. "We shouldn't, you know. Not because I don't want to, but . . ." She hesitated. "I may be going away soon. To a place a long . . . a long ways away. A place it would be impossible to visit."

"All the more reason to spend as much time with you as I possibly can," said Edmund. "Besides, sometimes things don't go as we plan them to. I wouldn't mind if you had to stay here."

"I wouldn't either."

She unhooked the harness that held her wings and let them drop to the barn floor below, then moved closer to Edmund until their knees touched.

"Aren't you afraid you'll fall?" asked Edmund, peering down at the wings.

"I'm sure if I do, you'll do your best to hold on to me," Laura Glue said, her voice barely a whisper.

"And if I fall?"

"Then I'll catch you," she said, and then she leaned in and kissed him. Neither of them ran away.

It took Harry only a few seconds to open the lock on Franklin's desk, which was disappointing to Fred, who was ready to jimmy it with an awl.

"It doesn't hurt to have a backup plan," said the badger.

"He's quite a smart fellow for a badger, isn't he?" asked Ernest.

"You don't know the half of it," said Jack as Houdini handed him the book.

"That book," Fred said wonderingly. "It's almost like the Little Whatsit. Almost exactly like it, 'cept maybe a little older."

"Yes," said John. "Strange. It's very like the Little Whatsit."

"Not the Little Whatsit," said Jack. "One of the Histories. Just look at it!"

Jack held it up and pointed to the cover. He was right—it was identical to one of the Caretakers' Histories.

"I'm right, aren't I?" asked Jack.

"I'm afraid you are," John said, gritting his teeth in frustration. "It's the only explanation that fits. He *is* an apprentice of Daniel Defoe."

Just then there was a knock at the front door. Fred peered out the window. "It's that blind magistrate," he said.

"Uh-oh," said John. "I'd better go see what he wants."

If the body of the End of Time had lain in any other district in that part of London, it might have been discovered sooner. As it was, his body had already gone cold and rigid when the match girl found him. She told the potato vendor at the corner, who told one of the newly commissioned police force, who, in an effort to demonstrate his worth to his employer, told the magistrate. And it was he who realized who the victim was, and who needed to be told about the murder.

It was a good day for flying kites. Warm and overcast, the cloud-filtered sunlight cast no shadows. And so the boy was unafraid when he was led away from the park by his friend who had no shadow at all.

On days such as this, the trees ate many kites—and so no one questioned, or even noticed, when two kites were left unattended, to flutter in the breeze.

Under the circumstance, Jack felt compelled to tell his companions about the private discussions he had been having with Theo since the crossing of the Frontier.

"He wanted to wait to say anything," Jack explained, "until he'd gotten a better handle on what our enemy might be planning. I trusted him entirely."

"As you should have!" Burton roared. "I'll not have you talking about him like he was some laggardly half-wit. It would have taken someone—something—truly inhuman to have killed him like this."

Burton's words were brash and full of anger, but more than one of the companions noticed that as he paced back and forth his hands were trembling.

"You said Theo told you the Echthros had followed us through the door," said Doyle. "Do you think it's possible . . . I mean, the boy—"

"No!" Burton roared. He grabbed Doyle and threw him roughly to the floor.

"It's worth considering," said Houdini as he helped his companion back to his feet. "If you were not so upset, you'd see that, Richard. And the End of Time would say the same if he were here."

Burton stared at them, breathing hard, his eyes crazy with rage. But then the mood passed as he slowly realized the wisdom of Houdini's words. It was true—if it had been Theo speaking, he'd have at least considered the possibility. The boy, Coal, might be the very Echthros they were fighting against.

"Theo said that he had a way to control it," said Jack, "and I think I know what that way is." He reached into his pocket and pulled out a bloodstained piece of paper. "The magistrate said that Theo had this in his hand. They had to pry his fingers open to get it loose. It's a Binding. An Old Magic Binding."

Burton stared. "Why would the End of Time have such a thing?"

"Never mind why," said John. "How would he be able to speak it and make it work? I didn't think it was possible for just anyone to speak a Binding."

"It must have been possible," Jack replied, "or else he wouldn't have meant to try it. Poe did send him with us, after all. And as one of Verne's Messengers, he certainly would have known what it was."

"Not that it did him a lot of good," said Doyle. "Either it didn't work, or he didn't have time to speak it. Which means that the Echthros either caught him unawares . . ."

"Impossible," said Burton.

"Or," Doyle went on, "it appeared to him as someone he trusted and would not think to question."

"It may not be the boy," said John. "There's another possibility, remember?"

"That's almost as bad," said Burton. "If it is Defoe, then it's my fault the End of Time is dead, because I'm the one who recruited him to the Society."

"There's one way to find out," Doyle said, taking the paper from Jack. "We can bind him ourselves, and we'll ask."

"We can't," said John. "If we interfere with Defoe too much here, we'll risk derailing everything we've already accomplished back in 1945."

"And what do we do about Coal?" said John. "It's an unanswered question. What if he is our enemy?"

"Maybe *he's* the Fiction," Jack suggested. "He's certainly unique, given where he came from. He might not be an Echthros—he might just be a cypher. Something that shouldn't exist, but does."

None of them saw the shadowy figure that had been listening outside the cracked door, and none of them saw it leave. But it had heard everything it had to hear to know what it needed to do next.

PART SIX

"All of Eternity in a Speck of Dust"

Defoe had retrieved the portrait of Charles Johnson
and was holding it . . .

CHAPTER TWENTY-ONE
The Summer King

❖

The bookbinder sat in darkness, watching the dying light of the embers in his fireplace as he removed the hook from the stump of his arm. He rubbed at it gently, as if it was still raw, even though it had healed over long before.

Twice in his exceedingly long life he had been an apprentice—once to his brother, whom he had believed to be wiser than he, and once to a Dragon, who actually was. The first time, he was betrayed—and the second, he was the betrayer. Samaranth had never been anything but patient with him, showing faith and fortitude as he tried to teach the young man called Madoc how to make his way in the world.

But somehow he changed. The betrayals of his brother, and his nephew, Arthur, and especially the woman he loved, Gwynhfar, had taken their toll, and Madoc became Mordred, and all he knew was anger, and hatred.

But through all the years from that time to this, one thing still haunted him: Arthur's belief that Madoc was still Madoc, and that he was a good man.

The Dragon, Samaranth, had believed in him too. As had

Gwynhfar. And in the end, it was he who had walked away from them, determined never to look back.

It was he who had killed Arthur once, and then again, for the final time. And he who cast aside the mother of his child, and rejected all that Samaranth had offered to him.

You are strong enough to bear this, Arthur had said to him once. But that was before Mordred had become the Winter King— before he surrendered his Shadow, and made his choice about what kind of man he would be.

He never expected a second chance to live his life, free and unfettered by the choices of the past; but it seemed the past had come calling for him, and once more he had to make a choice. All that remained for him was to decide who would do the choosing. . . .

Madoc, or Mordred?

None of the humans in Doctor Franklin's house had ears sharp enough to hear it, especially while they were having a vigorous discussion. But the badger's ears were sharp, and he would have heard the sound right away, even if the mechanical owl hadn't been calling him by name.

At Fred's urging, the companions raced to the front door, where they found a bruised and battered Archimedes, dragging one wing behind him.

"I had to bust through a window to get here," the bird exclaimed, seeming nearly exhausted, "and methinks I have a screw loose. No jokes, please."

"What's happened, Archie?" John asked as he picked up the injured bird. "Fred, go find some tools."

"Trouble, right here on Craven Street," Archie replied as Fred ran to the shop. "Daniel Defoe—he's here, in London!"

"We know that, Archie," said Jack. "We just figured it out ourselves."

"No!" the bird exclaimed, growing more frantic by the second. "You don't understand! He's got Rose at the McGees' house!"

"Defoe is at my house?" Ernest said, frowning. "I have to get back there."

"We're all going," said John. "I think a lot of our questions are about to be answered."

His wing repaired, Archie flew ahead to keep an eye on the McGee house while the companions ran along below him. At the corner, they nearly collided with Edmund and Laura Glue.

"What's happened?" Laura Glue asked when she saw the alarm etched on all their faces.

"No time to explain," John said without slowing. "Come with us!"

Edmund and Laura Glue fell into step behind the Caretakers. "We've got to leave him be," John was saying in a tone that said he'd brook no resistance. "I'm pulling rank here, Jack. I mean it. Don't touch Defoe."

"I'll do my best," Jack replied, "but if he's hurt Rose, no promises."

"Are you up for a fight?" Doyle asked. "He was our ally once, you know."

"That was then, this is now," Houdini responded with a distracted expression. "We'll do what we have to do."

"Good enough," said Doyle, peering down the darkening

street. "And if we find that—" He stopped and looked at his companion, frowning. "I don't bloody believe it. You're thinking about that cursed box again, aren't you?"

Houdini started to protest, then sighed in resignation. "I can't help it, Arthur," he said, shrugging. "It eats at me. There was no displacement of air, and no evidence of kinetic energy expended. . . ."

Doyle closed his eyes and thumped his forehead with his fist. "The. Box. Is. GONE," he said through clenched teeth. "Will you just drop it already?"

"Shut up, you idiots," said Burton. "Look—there he is."

The companions turned the corner just as Defoe was exiting the house, carrying something with a sheet draped over it. He started when he saw them, then took a menacing stance. They stopped on the other side of the street, unsure of what to do, while Archimedes circled overhead. It was a standoff.

"You have your business and I have mine," Defoe said, just loud enough for them to hear. "I don't know what denizens of the Archipelago are doing in London, but this need not go in a bad direction for any of us."

"He thinks we're from the Archipelago," Jack whispered. "He doesn't have any idea who we are!"

"We're running around with a badger and a mechanical owl," said Houdini. "It's not a bad guess."

Burton took a step forward. "I know you, Caretaker," he called out. "We can discuss this amicably."

Defoe's eyes narrowed. "You know *nothing* about me."

"In point of fact," Burton said, eyes glittering, "I know you died in 1731, and I know that you're only here now through the good graces of John Dee."

That took the stuffing out of him. Defoe suddenly looked more confused than menacing.

"My name is Burton," he continued, "and I can give you access to the treasures you seek."

"Is he insane?" asked Jack. "We can't barter with Daniel Defoe!"

"All right. Perhaps we can do some business, Burton," Defoe said. "Let us talk of this further."

"Excellent," Burton replied. "But first, where is the girl?"

Defoe paused. "She's upstairs. She has her own role to play tonight—which is more than you ever allowed her to do."

"You dung heap!" Ernest shouted as he suddenly flew across the street. "You'll pay for what you've done to my family!"

"Drat!" John exclaimed. "Grab him! Quick!"

Before Ernest could reach Defoe, Doyle and Houdini caught him by the arms and held him fast. "You don't know!" Ernest bellowed. "You don't know what he's done!"

"I'm a Caretaker," Defoe exclaimed, his temper rising, "and I'll do as I please, boy!"

"You're evil, is what you are!" said Fred. "Even if you still have your shadow!"

"Hah!" Defoe said, smirking. "Maybe. But it isn't *my* shadow."

"Defoe, listen to me," John began, trying to contain the situation. "We've no wish to hurt you."

"I'm immortal!" Defoe proclaimed. "What can you possibly do that can hurt me?"

Fred's well-aimed muffin struck Defoe squarely between the eyes. He was unconscious before he hit the street. The parcel fell out of his hands, and the sheet dropped away from the portrait of Charles Johnson.

"Sorry," Fred said to John. "He was giving me a headache with all that hot air."

"Help me!" Johnson called out. "I'm being abducted! And oppressed!"

"And now the other shoe drops," said Burton, pointing away. "Look, John!"

Behind them, coming around the opposite corner past the park, Franklin and Coal were running toward Defoe. They hadn't yet seen the Caretakers, but Franklin had a firm grip on the boy, who was obviously terrified.

"Not on my watch," Jack murmured. "Doyle? Harry?" The men nodded, and as one they took off at a run, tackling Franklin as he rounded the corner. He fell roughly to the ground under the three men's assault, and the boy went sprawling into the grass.

By the time the others ran over, Jack had Franklin pinned to the ground.

"We know who you are, and we know what you are!" Jack said, his voice shrill with anger. "We're done being played by you!"

"Played?" Franklin exclaimed with genuine surprise. In an instant, his face turned stern. "You have completely misunderstood me, Jack," he said in a clear, direct tone they had never heard from him before. "Coal and I were flying kites in the square, and something led him away. I was more than an hour finding him again."

"What have we misunderstood?" said John. "We found the History, Doctor. We know you're an apprentice Caretaker to Daniel Defoe."

"Oh, do you now?" Franklin said, eyes flashing. "And what,

pray tell, is your proof of this? The fact that I knew about the Caretakers before you arrived? The fact that walking, talking beasts are no surprise to me? Or the fact that the heir to the Cartographer's mantle has been training as an apprentice in mine own house?"

Jack looked up in shock and surprise. Franklin had just named all the things they meant to accuse him of, and he really wasn't sure what to say next.

"Proclaim your own sins publicly," said Franklin, "and you take away the naming as a weapon in your foe's arsenal. Even if what you name aren't really sins."

"Something is amiss here," said John. "Pull him up."

Jack and Doyle pulled Franklin to his feet but kept a solid grip on him. "All right," John said. "We're listening."

"Not everyone who looks out for the welfare of this world has to travel to imaginary lands to do it," said Franklin, "or to the ends of time. Some of us like to remain involved in the affairs of this world, and help others where we can.

"I am not a Caretaker," the Doctor went on, his voice low, "I am a Mystorian, and I have only one other thing to say: Verne is with you."

"Verne!" John exclaimed. "What does he have to do with this?"

"When you're losing the game, sometimes you have to change the rules," said Franklin. "This is the Great Game, and there are new pieces on the board—Verne's Mystorians. The Caretakers cannot do all that is needed on their own, not even with the help of your enemies. So Verne has recruited more friends. It is the only way to defeat the Echthroi."

"I still cannot believe—," John began.

"John, the boy!" shouted Burton. "We've been focused on the wrong opponent!"

Defoe had retrieved the portrait of Charles Johnson and was holding it under one arm. The other was casually draped around the shoulders of the little prince.

"Don't hurt him, Defoe!" John shouted.

"Hurt him?" Defoe said mockingly. "I won't hurt him." He looked down at Coal. "We're friends, aren't we?'

The boy smiled hesitantly, then nodded.

"Coal," Jack said slowly, beckoning to the boy, "come here."

"You aren't my friends," the boy said softly. "You won't read to me, or play with me. But he gave me a present. No one's ever given me a present before."

"I don't think you'll be able to track him," said Defoe, "but you're more than welcome to try."

The Caretakers gasped as they realized what Coal was playing with, what gift Defoe had given him.

It was Defoe's watch. His Caretaker's watch.

An Anabasis Machine.

"They don't work, you know," John said, his voice steady. "There's something wrong with them."

"You mean they don't work properly," Defoe shot back. "That's why I've been stuck here in London for so long. But they're working now—at least as long as you don't care where—or when—you end up."

"Oh no," John breathed. "He wouldn't."

"You trust me, don't you?" asked Defoe.

The boy looked up at him, face open and hopeful, and nodded.

"Then," Defoe said, "turn the dial at the top of the watch just as I showed you . . .

". . . and make a *wish*."

"Coal, no!" Jack shouted. "Don't touch it!"

But it was already too late. The little prince spun the dial at the top of the watch . . .

. . . and *disappeared*.

"Defoe!" Burton roared. "I'll have your head on a stick for this!"

Suddenly an explosion rocked Craven Street, and all the companions were thrown to the ground. The force of the blast made their vision blur and their ears ring, and when they had regained their senses, Defoe and the portrait were gone. Worse, the house of Ernest McGee was in flames.

"Oh dear God," John exclaimed. "Rose is in there!"

"It's on fire!" Edmund yelled. "They've set my father's house on fire!"

"All our maps!" Ernest cried. "All of our family's work! It's burning!"

The companions had a choice: pursue Defoe and the portrait of Captain Johnson, or go rescue Rose and try to salvage what they could of the McGee legacy.

"The boy is already gone," John said to Burton. "There's no point in pursuing Defoe, not now. Rose comes first. It's not even a question."

Burton looked in one direction, then the other, wrestling with the choice before him, and finally, cursing, turned toward the fire. "Promise me, Caretaker," he hissed, "when this is all done, we'll have a reckoning with Defoe."

"I swear it," John said over his shoulder. "We will."

The flames had not yet reached the stairway, which was where John found Rose. She was already unconscious, but still breathing. Burton and Doyle ran past to look for the *Pyratlas* and the rest of the maps, but the heat was too intense. The fire had started in the library, and all the aged paper made for excellent tinder.

"Please!" Edmund pleaded. "Please, Jack! All the maps are there! Everything my family has created! We can't just let them burn!"

"There's nothing we can do, Edmund," said Jack as he held tightly to the panicked young mapmaker. "It's too late. I'm so sorry."

"Son, oh my son," Ernest gasped. "It's all right. They're only maps."

Edmund leaped up and embraced his father. "But it's your life's work!" he sobbed. "Yours, and Grandfather's, and Papa Elijah's!"

"Shh, now," Ernest said, stroking the boy's hair. "Never mind the maps. We'll make more. We are McGees, are we not?"

Suddenly a bolt of furry lightning zoomed past them and into the conflagration. "What was that?" Doyle shouted.

"That was the stupid badger!" replied Burton as they backed down the stairs, coughing. "Caretakers," he muttered. "They're all the same."

They got Rose to a clean spot on the grass where they could give her air, and she started to cough.

"She'll be all right!" said John, thrilled and relieved at once. "She's going to be all right."

"Hey—where did Franklin go?" Jack exclaimed, looking around for the Doctor. "John, he's disappeared."

"Curse it," John muttered under his breath. He hadn't been able to ask what the Doctor had meant by his cryptic remarks about Verne and being a Mystorian. And he was still not convinced that Franklin was not in league with Defoe, or worse, the Echthroi.

"Fred's in there!" Burton shouted. "He went in for the maps."

"I'll get him," said Laura Glue, her face set with determination. She pulled a cord on her blouse, and in an instant her wings popped out from the pack she wore on her back. In another moment she was airborne and winging her way toward the upper stories of the house.

"Good Lord!" John exclaimed. "When did she do that to her wings?"

"I did it," said Houdini, "when I was tinkering around in Franklin's workshop. It's nothing, really—just a simple matter of miniaturizing the mechanism."

"No doubt, you're a genius," John said. "I just hope the wings are flameproof."

Archimedes hovered at the edge of the flames and smoke and shouted instructions to Laura Glue as she darted close to the conflagration, searching for a way in.

At last she found her opening and dove inside. She emerged a minute later, wings trailing smoke, with the little badger draped over her slim arms. He was holding on to a stack of papers for dear life.

The flames took a terrible toll on her wings, nearly crippling their maneuvering ability, and she corkscrewed crazily against the firelight before plummeting toward the cobblestones below. But just before she hit them, a bulky figure threw itself across the street and under her and Fred, absorbing the brunt of the fall.

John, Houdini, and Burton rushed over to where Arthur Conan Doyle was staggering to his feet. "Never mind me," he wheezed, waving them off. "Just knocked the wind out of me. Look to the girl and the badger!"

Fred was in worse shape than the Valkyrie, but he was alive, and he had salvaged a large stack of maps.

"You were amazing, Fred!" said Jack. "I can't believe you got them all!"

"Not all," he said in a small voice. "I gots all I could, Scowler Jack." He was curled up in a ball, and the edges of his fur had been badly singed. His clothes and cap were blackened from the smoke and fire, but the maps were in near-perfect condition.

"I wouldn't have been burned at all," he whimpered, "'cept that my stupid scarf got caught on a windowpane when Laura Glue was helping me make my great escape."

"Any escape you walk away from is a good escape," Houdini said with real admiration, "but when it's by the skin of your teeth, it's truly a great escape—and everyone around you knows it."

Ernest and Edmund were examining the maps Fred had managed to salvage, and as they set aside each one the old mapmaker's eyes shone brighter and his smile grew wide.

"Bless your badger's heart," Ernest exclaimed as he laid down the last map. "You saved them all."

"All?" Fred said in surprise. "I only managed to get a dozen or so."

"Fourteen, to be exact," said Ernest, "but the *right* fourteen. The most important ones in the lot. The ones I could not have recreated, because all those who gave me their secrets are dead."

"The legacy of the McGee family will live on then," said Houdini.

"Of that," Ernest said as he hugged his son again, "I have no doubt."

Rose was sitting up now and seemed to be in shock. Her eyes were wide and her breath was coming in short gasps—and despite the bright light of the flames, her shadow was nowhere to be seen.

Suddenly a scream rent the night air, sounding clear and shrill even over the roaring of the flames.

"Dear God in heaven," Ernest wheezed. "Someone's still inside!"

"There! Look!" Laura Glue exclaimed. The others looked in the direction she was pointing and saw a face in the upper attic window. It was Lauren.

Edmund looked at Laura Glue and Rose with a mix of shame and fear; then his expression changed to one of resolve. He leaped to his feet and bolted for the building's facade—but the heat was too great to even approach.

Laura Glue jumped into the air, wings straining, but after a few staggered bursts upward, she fell back to the cobblestones. The effort to save Fred had taken its toll.

"Can you fix my wings?" she yelled at Houdini. "Make them work again?"

The magician shook his head and looked at the fire. "Not quickly enough!"

Lauren screamed again, then went silent as the flames and smoke covered the windows and rose past the rooftops.

"She's gone," Ernest said, sobbing into his son's shoulder. "Oh, Edmund, we've lost her!"

Suddenly a huge, muscular figure burst out of the adjacent alley, running full-out. Without a pause or look backward, he leaped over the threshold of the ground floor and disappeared into Ernest's house.

The companions looked at one another in amazement, as if they couldn't believe what they had just seen.

"Bloody hell," whispered Burton.

"That's the way to do it!" Archie exclaimed, whooping and screeching as he launched himself into the air. "Go, boy! Go!"

"Oh, father . . . ," Rose began.

Then, as quickly as he had entered the burning house, Madoc crashed through one of the upper windows carrying a limp figure wrapped in a sodden blanket. He plummeted to the earth with a sickening crunch, then rolled free of the unconscious girl. "Quickly!" he gasped, his face drawn tight with pain. "Get her to fresh air! Hurry! She may still live!"

Houdini, John, Jack, and Fred tended to Lauren, while the others moved Madoc to a cool spot on the grass. He was badly burned—all of his hair and beard were gone, and one eye was blistered shut. He was covered with burns—too many to survive for long.

"Why did you come?" Rose asked him, sobbing. "How did you know where we were?"

"He said . . . my daughter needed me." Madoc coughed. "How could I not come?"

"Who said that?" asked Jack. "Who told you, Madoc?"

In answer, Madoc lifted his hand and pointed . . .

. . . at Benjamin Franklin.

CHAPTER TWENTY-TWO
The Choice

You knew there was going to be a fire," John said, rising to his feet with fists clenched. "How?"

"I didn't know for certain," Franklin answered. "Let's just say it was a very strong might-have-been that ended up happening after all."

Burton growled and stood next to John. "All I want to know," he said, his voice low, "is whether you're in league with Defoe."

"Had I been formally apprenticed as a Caretaker, Defoe would have known about me, and I wouldn't have been able to help you," Franklin answered. "I was here in London for a different purpose. Hank Morgan started the process with Elijah, but someone had to be here a century later to build it up in young Edmund. That job fell to me. And I believe he's now ready for what you need him to become."

"The girl," Madoc rasped. "Is she all right?"

"Why did you go in there?" Rose asked him, sobbing.

"Thought . . . she was you," said Madoc. "Wasn't going to leave you in there alone."

"Rose is fine, Madoc," said John. "I got her out in time. But Lauren . . ." His voice trailed off.

... *a sleek, massive creature erupted out of the Thames and into the sky.*

"I didn't know she was still in there!" Rose exclaimed, her voice breaking. "Defoe told me she was leaving with him!"

"What?" John said. "Weren't you his prisoner, Rose?"

"That's not exactly what was happening," Archie said as he landed in the grass nearby. "It was more of a conversion than a kidnapping. He's a smooth talker, he is. And Rose is still very young."

"A conversion?" Fred asked, confused. "You shouldn't ought to have talked to him, Rose." He shook his head sadly. "He in't t' be trusted."

"Nor was I, once, too," Burton said quietly. "Yet here I am, your ally. Let her speak."

"I—I'm so sorry," Rose stammered. "I didn't understand. . . ."

"It's all right," said Madoc, taking his daughter's hand in his own. "I think I finally do."

Laura Glue reached out instinctively and took Edmund's hand in hers. They intertwined fingers and silently wept.

"John," Houdini said, his voice breaking with anguish, "I don't think the girl is going to make it. There's just too much damage."

"No!" roared Madoc as he lurched to his feet. He threw himself to the ground next to Lauren and clutched her hands. "No," he said again. "I won't allow it. Not while I can still prevent it."

"Madoc!" John exclaimed as he and the others tried to pull him back. "Don't make yourself worse. You've done all you can."

"Not yet," Madoc rasped. "Ask . . . my daughter. She knows. She knows there is still a way."

They looked at Rose, but she didn't answer. She was staring at her father.

"I don't think I can," she said finally, her voice dulled with remorse. "My shadow is gone, father. I've lost it. It isn't that I'm not willing—but I don't think I'm worthy. Not any longer. Not after this."

"Oh, my girl," Madoc said, touching her face. "I wasn't . . . wasn't suggesting that you offer yourself. You paid my price, a long time ago. Now . . ." He coughed, spitting smoke and blood. "It's my turn to pay yours."

With John's help, he sat up and moved close to Lauren. Madoc bent his head over the dying girl and whispered, so softly that it could barely be heard.

"Mine for hers," he said with faint breaths. "My life for hers . . . I offer this freely. . . . It is my will. . . . Mine for hers."

In that moment, a blinding light erupted from the injured girl. It enveloped all the companions, and when again they could see, the girl was gone. In her place, sitting on the grass, with Madoc's head on her lap, was a regal woman, dressed in a fine Elizabethan gown. Her skin was porcelain, and her eyes gentle. She could have been fifteen, or five hundred—either would have looked the same.

"Hello, Rose," she said with a voice of crystal. "I am Lady Twilight."

"The Starchild has been lost, but the Moonchild still remains," said Lady Twilight. "The new thread remains unbroken. And thus the tapestry may yet be woven once again."

"But I've failed!" said Rose. "All the choices I've made have been wrong."

"You have made the choices you made," came the reply, "and those choices have brought you here. Every choice, every decision, shapes you into who you will become."

"And my choices have ended an innocent life," said Rose bitterly, "and maybe my father's as well."

"The girl you called Lauren is a part of us now," Lady Twilight said. "It was her purpose to be here, now, so that you could be tested—but she lived a worthy life, and her heart was pure. And now she—I—am serving the Light as I was meant to, as the Three Who Are One."

"Like Gwynhfar," Jack murmured to John. "When she died, she became one of the Morgaine too."

"If I was being tested," said Rose, "then I failed."

"Perhaps not," said Lady Twilight, "but then, you were not the only one being tested.

"Now only one choice remains. Tell them."

This last she said to Madoc.

"Tell them," she repeated, her musical voice stern.

Madoc closed his eyes. "It was Rose. You started the fire, didn't you, daughter?"

Rose didn't answer, but simply closed her eyes.

"That's why Franklin went to find him," said Jack. "Somehow, he knew."

"This is exactly how it happened before!" Fred said bluntly. "She's being accused of something she didn't do, just as her father was! And all of history condemned him for it. This isn't right!"

"Hush, Fred," said John. "That isn't what's happening here, is it, Rose?"

"No," she answered, her voice shallow with anguish. "I didn't know Lauren was still—I—I only wanted to destroy the maps."

"Destroy them?" John said, incredulous. "But why, Rose?"

"Mother Night told me it was up to me to set things right, to find the Dragon's apprentice," said Rose, "but when I failed to convince Father to become a Dragon, everyone stopped paying any attention to me at all. Then another of the Morgaine reminded me that I still had Ariadne's Thread and told me I needed to act. And that was when I met Defoe."

"But Rose," Jack exclaimed, "you know what Defoe is! You know what he's done! How could you listen to him?"

"He hasn't done it yet," said Rose, "and the one I met here is still a Caretaker. He had to have been good, once."

"But he became evil," said Fred.

"So did my father, once," said Rose, "and then he changed again, when we gave him a second chance."

Jack sighed heavily and looked at John. They'd made a terrible choice themselves, and they were partly to blame for the events happening right now. They were both expecting Rose to act like an adult who had saved the world, while at the same time treating her like the child she still seemed to be. Defoe had taken advantage of that—and Rose was suffering for it.

"Everyone was sure that the McGees' maps were going to save us all," Rose went on, "and so when Defoe told me I needed to burn them, I thought you'd have no choice but to turn back to me to save us all. You'd have to listen to me again."

"Ah, me," said John. "I'm so sorry, Rose. We didn't see—didn't realize."

At this Madoc started weeping, and Lady Twilight pulled him closer.

"Now, Rose," she said. "Only you can make him believe. Only you can ask this last choice of him."

Madoc turned his head away. "No," he said. "I'm not worthy of it. Not any longer. And not for a long time."

"Not true," Lady Twilight said gently. "You earned your redemption when you chose to pay the price for your daughter's mistake with your own life. Your offer was true, and real, and you *are* worthy, Madoc."

Madoc turned his head to look at his daughter. "Rose," he said, his voice soft, "look at me."

Rose blinked and opened her eyes, looking at her father. She was afraid of what she would see there, in his eyes—but found nothing but love, and trust, and hope, and acceptance.

He believed in her, as she would always believe in him. And in that moment, she made her decision.

"If you can do it, I want you to become a Dragon, Father," she said, weeping again—but this time the tears were full of hope. "I believe in you—but I still feel as if I've cost you your life."

"You made the mistakes you needed to make to learn," said Madoc, "and growing up isn't just about making decisions—it's about taking responsibility for what happens after. I was just here to help you through it—because after all, isn't that what a father is for?"

Sobbing, Rose clutched her father and hugged him tightly.

"That's the most wonderful thing I've ever heard," said Fred, "considering th' source."

Madoc reached up and stroked his daughter's hair. "If," he said slowly, his voice strained and weak, "if I do this thing, will you make the badger stop talking?"

Fresh tears burst forth from Rose's eyes. She nodded. "I will, I promise."

"Wisdom runs in the blood," said Archimedes.

"Hey, now," said Fred.

"Rose," Jack said, touching her shoulder. "Look."

There, mingled with the shadows cast by the fire, was Rose's own elusive shadow. Still unattached, but not lost.

"You're still making choices, my daughter," said Madoc. "Make them good ones. Remember me. And do not despair—because this is why I was sent here through the door, to be here, for this moment, now." He looked his daughter in the eyes, strong and unafraid. "I can choose too. I can ascend. I can choose to become a Dragon."

The moment those words were spoken, there was a terrible shrieking sound that seemed to be everywhere and nowhere all at once. It pierced everyone who heard it to the core, as if it was trying to shatter their souls with its pain and anguish. As it sounded, a shadow passed across the setting sun, then vanished. The shrill cry faded into nothingness, and in seconds, it was as if it had never happened.

"The Echthroi," said Fred. "The enemy have lost one they hoped to make a Lloigor. For good this time."

Lady Twilight had gone. The choice had been made.

Rose pulled Madoc's head onto her lap and stroked his face as he closed his eyes. He was fading.

"What do you want us to do, Madoc?" John asked.

"Take me out of this place," said Madoc weakly. "Take me to the water."

Madoc was a large man, and his burns and fractures meant he was already in almost constant agony. It took all the companions to make a litter that would allow them to transport him down to one of the docks that jutted out into the Thames.

Within an hour, the torchlit processional had made its way to the water's edge, where John, Jack, and Burton gently lifted Madoc from the litter.

"Take me in, Caretakers," he said to John. "You, and Jack, and—and my daughter, if she will."

"Of course, Father," Rose said, weeping. "Of course I will."

"Don't cry, little dove," said Madoc, touching her face with his blackened hand. "I'm not going to die, after all."

"But you won't be with me anymore," Rose said, "and I feel like I only just got you."

"I wasn't with you for the whole of your life," Madoc said as they moved him farther out into the river, "but after this is done, I always shall be."

She leaned forward and kissed him on the forehead. "I love you, Father."

"And I you, little dove."

On his signal, Rose moved away, and the three men lowered him into the water. The swirling blackness closed over his face as he slowly became submerged.

"What now?" Jack asked the others. "I don't want him to drown."

"Wait for it," said John, watching anxiously. "Wait. We have to trust he knows what he's doing."

An explosion of light suddenly lit the bottom of the river and burst upward into the air, showering the companions with water and debris. John, Jack, and Burton were thrown off their feet and fell backward into the water as a sleek, massive creature erupted out of the Thames and into the sky.

Madoc had become a Dragon—the Black Dragon.

He wheeled around, wings outstretched, and landed skillfully on the dock, where he waited until the others had clambered out of the river.

Most of the companions had seen Dragons before, but this was a new experience for Franklin and the McGees. The Doctor seemed to switch back and forth between delight and terror, but the McGees were simply awestruck, looking at the Dragon with their mouths hanging open.

For John and Jack, it was still a thrill, as it had been the first time they met Samaranth—never mind the fact that he could have just as easily eaten them.

For Burton, Houdini, and Doyle, it was a bittersweet experience. They were realizing how the wheel of destiny turns—and finally understood that as with Rose, all their choices had also brought them to this place.

Rose walked across the dock to the Dragon and without a pause reached up and wrapped her arms around him. In response, he enfolded her with his wings.

"So," the Black Dragon rumbled in a voice not unlike Madoc's. "Speak. Ask of me what you will, and I shall do my best to answer."

"The riddle," Rose said. "The one given to me by Mother Night. I need to know what it means."

She repeated it in a clear, unhurried voice. There was no need to hurry now.

> *To turn, from time to time*
> *To things both real and not,*
> *Give hints of world within a world,*

And creatures long forgot.
With limelight turn to these, regard
In all thy wisdom stressed;
To save both time and space above—
Forever, ere moons crest.

The Dragon made a huffing noise, and the companions realized he was laughing. "She was not telling you what you needed to learn to fix the Archipelago," said the Dragon. "She was telling you what must happen in both worlds: no more secrets."

"That's it?" said Fred. "What a lousy riddle."

"Hardly, little Child of the Earth," the Dragon said. "It is a great truth, and one any honest creature should recognize."

"Mother Night said I needed to find you and say those words," said Rose. "Why was that so important?"

"Because," the Dragon replied, "only a Dragon could give you what you needed. Once, all the doors to the Keep of Time were locked, but the Dragons created the doors, and made them work by giving a piece of themselves to each one. They gave their hearts to the times they guarded. You came here through the last door, and I am the last Dragon. And I will give you what you need, Rose . . .

". . . I'll give you my heart."

The Black Dragon reached into his chest, which had begun to glow with an ethereal light, and removed a small stone circlet. "Take this with you," he said as he unfolded his wings. "When the time comes, use it wisely. Use it well. And never forget your father, my dove."

"Madoc," John began, realizing as he said it that it sounded rather stupid to call the Black Dragon by his human name, "what will you do now?"

"What I have already done," he said as he prepared to take flight. "I'm going to go where all Dragons go until I am summoned. And when that time comes, I will give myself to the making of a ship, so that the events that have played out will play out."

In a flash of imagery, John saw the future of this great beast—he would become the very vessel that the Winter King would use to sail into the Archipelago. "But why?" he called out as the Dragon lifted itself into the air. "Why, when you can still choose and change everything?"

"Because," the Dragon replied, "every choice I've made, good or ill, has made me what I am now. And what I am is a father who has given his heart to his daughter, and who I think has finally earned hers. What more would I wish?"

And with that, he wheeled away and disappeared into the night sky.

"Well, that's going to change one thing in the future," said Fred.

Jack frowned. "What's that?'

"We're going to have to stop referring to the Black Dragon as a 'she.'"

As one, all the watches belonging to the Caretakers Emeritis began to hum, then just as quickly, fell silent.

By reflex, all of them checked the watches, and one by one expressed relief, or joy, or both.

"A new zero point," Verne murmured, waving Bert to his side so they could compare readings. "It's a new zero point at last."

Several other Caretakers were shaking hands and nodding, while voicing various platitudes of congratulation.

"It isn't over yet!" Bert barked at them. "We know when they are now, but they still have to find a way to come home."

"Can't they just use the watches?" asked Shakespeare. "It should be simple now, shouldn't it?"

"In the past, the zero points were located behind the doors of the keep, and the tower itself connected them," said Bert. "The zero points exist, but nothing has connected them yet. And until they find a way to connect those points, the only way to return is the way Hank Morgan did."

He looked at his watch and frowned. "This isn't over."

Burton stood . . . watching the small craft
as it became consumed by the flames.

Chapter Twenty-three
The Revolution

✧

It took the better part of the night for the fire to burn itself out. When the companions returned to Craven Street, there was little left of Ernest's house except for a stone and brick skeleton and ashes.

"I'm so sorry, Father," said Edmund. "We can rebuild it, if you want."

"No," Ernest said, shaking his head. "I think I'm done here. I have you, and I have the maps. That's all that matters."

They walked the short distance to Franklin's house, arriving there just as the sun was rising. Myrret met them at the door.

"The magistrate was here looking for you," Myrret said. "He'd like to ask if you know anything about the fire down the street."

"What did you tell him?" asked Franklin.

"I said you'd be back soon, and I'd have you contact him," the fox said. "And then he told me I'm very articulate for my species."

"Oh dear," said Jack.

The companions all went to their separate corners of Franklin's house to better come to grips with the events of the night. The Doctor graciously opened another spare room for Ernest to use, with the promise that breakfast would soon be ready.

When Doyle had dressed in clean clothes, he found Houdini in the kitchen with Franklin.

"You're obviously a man of learning," the Magician was saying, "so let me ask you. His voice dropped to a whisper. "If you were to have a box about yea big, and say, for the sake of argument, it was a magic box—"

"Harry!" Doyle said sharply. "Nix, brother."

Houdini scowled at Doyle, then switched to a charming smile for Franklin. "Another time, perhaps."

A few moments later John and Jack came in. They had questions for Doctor Franklin—which he'd already anticipated.

"Here," said the doctor, handing a cream-colored multipage letter to John. "That should answer many of your questions."

"It's a letter from Jules," John said to Jack. "This is why Franklin helped us."

"I'd have helped you anyway," said Franklin. "As much as I could have. But this letter made it easy. Verne delivered it to me himself years ago and told me who he was, and why he needed my help. I thought it was some sort of prank—but when you showed up at my door, I knew it was all real."

"So the Mystorians . . . ," John began.

"All I know is what he told me, and what's in that letter," Franklin said with a shrug. "I knew enough to anticipate certain events, and to assist you as best I could. And that's all I was asked to do. And he gave me this," he added, holding up the watch, "so that you would trust me. And it seems you did. Although mine doesn't allow me to travel in time."

"That's all right," said Jack. "Neither do ours at the moment."

"The watch would have been more help," said John, "if you'd shown it—and the letter—to us when we got here. We trusted you when we had to, but we wasted a lot of time thinking you might be . . ."

"Echthroi?" Franklin finished, nodding. "That's the very reason I could not confirm who I was, nor whom I worked for. I knew I could trust you Caretakers, as Verne told me I could. But you came with an entourage—including an Echthros. I couldn't reveal more until events had played themselves out. Other than mentoring the boy, assisting you was all that Verne asked of me."

"So a Mystorian is sort of a single-mission Caretaker," said John, "at least in your case, Doctor. I don't know whether to be grateful to Verne or if I want to beat him within an inch of his life."

"Let's get you home first," said Franklin with a wink, "and then I'm sure you'll be able to decide."

After breakfast, the companions reconvened in the study. "There's something that needs doing," Burton announced somberly, "and I'd rather do it quickly."

The companions all nodded in understanding, especially John and Jack. To them, it was not so long ago that they had lain their friend to rest. Now Burton wanted to do the same for his.

Theo's funeral was a small, private affair—only Burton, Houdini, and Doyle, and John, Jack, Fred, and Franklin attended. The body had been wrapped in the style of Theo's culture and placed in a shallow boat on the river.

With no platitudes, and little ceremony, Burton and John set the boat aflame and pushed it out onto the water.

"In broad daylight?" Franklin whispered to Jack. "Isn't this quite risky?"

"Not really," Doyle whispered back, pointing.

There on the dock behind them, Houdini stood with his back to them, hands outstretched. His fingers made delicate tracings in the air, but the muscles on his neck and the beads of sweat soaking his shirt showed the obvious strain he was under. They could hear him whispering arcane words of magic under his breath as he worked the illusion.

"No one will see us, or the funeral barge," Doyle explained. "Burton considered the End of Time to be his friend—perhaps his only friend. And he deserves the chance to do this in peace."

Burton stood on the dock, watching the small craft as it was consumed by the flames. Finally it drifted too far to see clearly. He spun about and cleared his throat.

"All right," Burton said gruffly. "Let's get back to work."

Back at Franklin's house, they found Rose already poring over the maps in Johnson's book.

"What are you looking for?" Ernest offered helpfully. "Perhaps I could give you a hand?"

Rose looked up at him as a flash of fear and worry crossed her features. She'd basically confessed to trying to destroy the work of his entire family—that would not be easily forgiven. But there was no guile or malice in the man's face—the offer was sincere.

"Hank Morgan traveled back to our time with a map your grandfather made him," Rose replied. "I was hoping to find something similar that we might use to duplicate his efforts."

"What are you thinking, Rose?" Jack asked as he and the others came into the room.

"Mother Night told me that I had all the things I needed to connect the threads of time," Rose replied, "and the Watchmaker told us we needed someone who was able to map time. Doctor Franklin told us that he was instructed by Verne to help Edmund become a mapmaker. I think," she finished, "that together, Edmund and I may be able to get us home."

"When we first met," Ernest said to John, "I told you that I did not have the skills of my father and grandfather. That is still true. But," he added with no small pride, "there is a member of the family McGee who does. My son Edmund can make the kind of map you need."

"I have the extra pages," Jack said as he removed a large folder from Fred's pack. "The ones Bert and the Cartographer took out of the *Geographica* for safekeeping."

He spread out the large sheets of parchment and selected one, handing it to Edmund. "Here," Jack said. "Let's try your skills out on one of these."

"All right," said Edmund. "What do you want me to map?"

"About twenty years shy of two centuries," said Jack.

"Hmm," said Edmund. "I'm going to need more ink."

As the young mapmaker worked, John moved over alongside Burton, who was compulsively checking his watch and looking out the window. "You're thinking about the boy, aren't you?" John asked.

Burton responded with a short, sharp nod.

"We'll find him, Burton. We will," said John, gripping the man's shoulder. "I swear it."

And this time, Sir Richard Burton didn't knock aside John's hand, but allowed it to remain on his shoulder, steadying him. John wondered if that was deliberate, or if Burton, for the first time since he'd known the man, was simply weary. It didn't really matter, he supposed. Or maybe, it just shouldn't.

"What I'm concerned about," Doyle was saying, "is whether the conflict with Defoe will have any ill effect on the future. After all, he sells the portrait of Captain Johnson to, well, *us*, in around a decade or so."

"They mean me," said Burton, turning from the window. "I came here in the *Indigo Dragon*, specifically searching for Defoe to strengthen his ties to the Society. Our pact was sealed with the purchase of the portrait."

"I don't think the future will be affected," said Jack. "That Burton isn't you, Richard—he won't have had this experience and will have no reason to distrust Defoe. And for all we know, Defoe will end up trusting you *more* then because of your having met *now*."

"He didn't mention it," said Burton. "Why?"

"I don't think he would," said Jack, "just as he won't care about having seen us here. All he'll recall is that he got the best of us."

"That's not really a consolation," said Houdini.

"I'm actually more worried about what happens when we get back than I am that we'll get back at all," said Jack.

"Why is that?" asked John.

"Aven," Jack replied simply. "How are we going to tell Bert? He's already lost his wife in Deep Time—and now we're going to have to tell him that he's lost his daughter as well."

"Time enough for that later," said Burton, sitting. "No pun intended. But we have more pressing matters to attend to, do we not? First we need to make sure we can get back at all. Then we'll deal with grief and the grieving."

"Of course you wouldn't feel that was important," Jack said, frowning. "You took the news of your own daughter's loss with barely a blink."

Burton leaned back in his chair and observed Jack with a wry expression on his face. "And you have determined from that reaction that I don't care for Tiger Lily, or mourn her death?" he said evenly. "You would be wrong, little Caretaker. I will mourn her, in my own fashion, when I have time to do so. But now is not that time.

"She lived her life as I raised her to," he continued, "rich and full and honorably. She married well, and gave me an heir. I mourn that I was not there to share in more of her years, but that does not weaken the pride I feel as her father, nor does it make me love her less."

With that he spun around and strode from the room.

John clapped Jack on the back. "I can't say he's wrong, old fellow."

"You know," said Houdini, "if Theo were here, he'd have something profound to say."

Doyle looked on impassively. "It is from the dust that we came, and it is to the dust we must all return."

"Oh, shut up," said Jack.

"And what about Coal?" Rose asked. "What can we do about him?"

"We can't stay here," John stressed, "even to try to find Coal.

Wherever Defoe sent him can't be helped now. And if we are to have any hope of finding him in the future, the only way to do it is to keep our eyes on our larger goal. We have to fix the Archipelago. And then we'll have a chance of finding Coal."

"In Morgan's note, he said he and Elijah were trying to create a 'chronal map,'" Rose said. "We know they did, eventually. That's how he attuned his watch to get back."

"Shouldn't we be able to do the same?" asked Fred. "The zero point he mapped to Tamerlane House is still there."

"Except," said Jack, "he didn't start from a mapped zero point, so even when he had the map, he spent two centuries trying to leap forward in time."

"Which," Burton noted, "is exactly how long it would have taken him doing it the ordinary way."

"Do you remember when we moved through time using the trump?" John asked. "They tried it again and it never worked—and it didn't really work for Hank, either."

"That may not have been Morgan's fault," said Rose. "Basically, he was trying to mix two incompatible means of travel. The trumps were meant to be used in space, and the watches in time."

"That's what worries me," said Jack. "His map worked in exactly a way it wasn't supposed to. It effectively functioned as a 'chronal trump,' moving him in time *and* space. I'm worried that we'll just be duplicating Hank's efforts, and with just as little success."

"Fruitless?" said Fred. "He *did* make it back."

"Just in time to die," said Burton. "I'd rather stay here, if that's the choice."

"No, I think it may be just the direction we need to be looking," said Jack. "Think about it—the Keep of Time functioned in the same way. Stepping through the doors moved you in time and space—and they were changeable. Basically, the keep itself intuited where and when we needed to go. If we can find a way to recreate that . . ."

"I'll settle for getting to Tamerlane House in 1945," said John. "If we can."

"We're about to find out," said Edmund. "I think I'm done."

Edmund had followed the notes in Elijah's maps, as well as the calculations that accompanied them. As well as he could determine, the map he'd made was identical to the one his great-grandfather had made for Hank Morgan.

"All we have to do now," said Burton, "is figure out how to use it without spending two centuries lost in history."

"He stepped through in space, but it didn't let him step through in time," said John. "It was the same problem he had with the projected message he left at Magdalen Tower."

"I think I understand what to do," said Rose. "I think I know the reason I needed to be here." She reached into her pocket, and just as she had before, she found the glowing ball of Ariadne's Thread.

She looked at the ball, then at the others. "Reweave the threads of history, that's what Mother Night told me," she said. "Somehow I have to use this thread to get us home."

"You're forgetting the original purpose of the thread from mythology," John said. "With it, you can always find your way back."

Experimentally, Rose unwound one end of the thread and let it dangle on the table.

"Now that's very interesting," said Edmund. "How do you get it to extend into the map that way?"

"What are you talking about?" asked Rose.

"The glowing thread," Edmund said, pointing from the ball in her hand to the parchment on the table. "It's connected directly to my drawing, see?" He grabbed the edge of the sheet and slid it back and forth. "It follows the map. How are you doing that?"

"Edmund," said Jack. "We can't see anything."

The young mapmaker never heard the comment. He'd already become too absorbed in the strange light, and something deeper it seemed to mean to him.

Dipping a quill in his ink, he started adding some new notations to the map, pausing every few seconds to observe his handiwork. He added another sketch to the center, and several symbols to the edges. Finally he put down the quill. "There," he said, breathing rapidly from the anxious effort. "Now it's done. The thread just showed me a few things I hadn't understood before."

"All right," Jack said. "Let's give it a try. Everyone, please focus on the map."

Half in fear that it might work, but more out of fear that it wouldn't, the companions gathered closely about the table and stared at the map.

The parchment trembled; once, then again. And again. And then suddenly it started to expand.

"Here!" Jack exclaimed. "Hold up the other side, John!"

Together the Caretakers held up the sheet as it continued to grow. In minutes it filled the whole width of the room, and as they watched, a picture began to form amid the symbols and equations.

"What do you think?" Jack asked. "Should one of us go through first, to test it?"

John shook his head. "It's either going to work, or it isn't," he said, his voice full of resolve. "We all go together."

"What about Edmund?" Laura Glue asked. "Don't we have to take him?"

"She's right," said John. "If this works, and we want to do it again, we're going to need him, just as the Watchmaker said."

"I agree," said Ernest. "This is your destiny, my boy. You must go."

Edmund hugged his father. "What of Elijah's maps? And all of his notes?"

"You saved them from obscurity," Ernest said to his son with honest pride. "They should stay with you."

"What of the rest of these?" said Houdini, eyeing the treasure maps. "These could be very . . . ah, useful."

"Not in our purview," John said. "We aren't treasure seekers, Harry."

"It was worth a shot," said Houdini.

"I'll take the treasure maps with me," Ernest said. "My time here in London is done, I think. The fire decided that, if for no other reason. I'm now officially retired from this whole business of maps, and I think maybe I'll spend some time on a plantation in the Caribbee Sea."

"As a gentleman farmer?" asked Jack.

"Or as a pirate," Ernest replied, "but then again, these days, who can tell the difference?"

"Doctor Franklin?" John said. "I'd like to invite you along, but I don't think I can."

"Not a problem," said Franklin, holding up his hands. "My place is here, in this time, and I'm content to leave it that way. Give my best regards to Verne—whenever he is."

"All right," John said. "Bring down the animals from Paralon. I think we're ready to go."

Good-byes were said, farewells given. And then the companions stepped through the map and into the future. It did not take long to discover if it worked. One moment they were in Franklin's study in London, and the next they were elsewhere.

They were in Rose's attic room at Tamerlane House.

"It worked!" Jack exclaimed. "Well done, Rose!"

"Wait," Burton said, holding up a hand. "We've moved in space, but we don't yet know if we moved in time."

Together, he, Houdini, and Doyle all checked their watches, then nodded in agreement. "It's all right," Burton proclaimed with uncharacteristic relief in his voice. "They all say we're back in 1945. Right when we're meant to be."

CHAPTER TWENTY-FOUR
The Third Alternative

The companions' successful return was met with great rejoicing at Tamerlane House. Not only were they home, safe and sound, but the journey had given them the seeds of hope that time might be fixed, and the Archipelago restored. But none of the good news made relaying the bad news any easier. During the celebration, Jack took Bert aside and told him privately about Aven's last moments.

"I can still hope," Bert said somberly. "The Archipelago runs according to Kairos time, and that is not absolute. If it were here, in the Summer Country, I would be more fearful. But I'm glad you were able to speak to her, Jack. Very glad."

"You won't be able to interact with her as we did," Jack said as he pulled the reel from Paralon out of his pack, "but you'd still be able to see her, if you like."

Bert began to reach for the reel, then hesitated. He seemed to be debating the matter in his mind; then finally he decided.

"Thank you, Jack, truly," he said, curling up his fingers and folding his hands together. "Perhaps later."

The Far Traveler quickly moved on to give more instructions to the Caretakers Emeritis, and Burton moved over to a slightly

. . . a tall, lanky man was just stepping through.

puzzled Jack. "He's putting up a brave front," he whispered. "Give him time."

Jack tilted his head and replaced the reel in his pack. "I guess I was expecting him to respond more as you did."

"Maybe," Burton said as he moved past Jack to grab a bottle of wine, "I was just putting on a brave front too."

Deftly Burton maneuvered himself alongside Bert, and then drew them both to a balcony where they could speak privately.

"So, Far Traveler," Burton began.

"So, Barbarian," Bert answered. "What did you want to speak to me about that was not for the ears of our colleagues?"

Burton looked at him oddly for a moment, then poured wine into a glass that he handed to Bert before taking a swig from the bottle. "It seems we have something in common, you and I," he said at length. "The lost boy, my heir . . . he's your descendant too."

Bert nodded thoughtfully and sipped at the wine. "I've considered that. It certainly gives him a colorful heritage."

"That's an understatement. He has the potential to conquer the world, if he wished it."

"Lineage isn't everything," Bert countered. "Environment and upbringing have a lot to do with one's potential. And all this boy knew was a legacy he couldn't touch, a sheltered Aladdin's cave of fairy tales read to him by hedgehogs, and several well-meaning adults who didn't pay attention to him until someone else did. Yes, what he'll grow up to become is exactly what troubles me about him, never mind his lineage."

"Do you think it's possible?" asked Burton. "Will we be able to discover what's happened to him?'

Bert didn't reply. After a minute, Burton returned to the party.

Edmund McGee was already settling nicely into a suite of rooms Poe had offered him at the opposite end of the corridor from Basil Hallward's studio. In a matter of hours, Edmund and Laura Glue had set up drafting tables, shelving, and enough reference material that the main room had already begun to resemble the old Cartographer's room near the top of the Keep of Time.

The main differences, Jack noticed, were that this Cartographer's room had windows that opened, and a door that would never be locked.

He even noted, with some amusement and a little mild understanding, that Archimedes had all but nested in one of the alcoves, which pained Rose ever so slightly. He had been her most constant companion and teacher during those years when she was maturing from a child into a young woman, and he was her closest friend.

Still, he was also what he was—and his memories of the early days with Rose's father and uncle still resonated strongly. Rose had a passing interest in her uncle's handiwork, and she certainly had the facility for mapmaking—but it was not her passion. For young Edmund, it was. Not only did he have three generations of mapmakers behind him, but they had developed the family trade during one of the most exciting, thrilling, and unpredictable periods in human history.

If anything, Jack concluded, Edmund was better primed and prepared to become a Cartographer of imaginary lands than Merlin was.

♦   ♦   ♦

"Hank knew exactly what he was doing," said Twain. "He didn't choose Elijah McGee at random, and the skills of the family McGee are not mere coincidence."

He flipped open one of the Histories that Hank Morgan had been annotating through his jaunts in time and indicated a series of notes along one margin. "It's here, you see—in the genealogy."

"This says that Elijah McGee was descended from François Le Clerc," John said. "He was a pirate, wasn't he?'

"Among the first who were called so," Edmund Spenser said as he entered the room and the conversation. "In some quarters, he was even called the Pirate King. Quite a scoundrel—which, I suppose, is not a bad quality to possess if you're going to be a pirate. He was a contemporary of mine, and we met on two occasions before his presumed death."

"Presumed?" said Jack. "There was a question?"

Spenser nodded. "Eminently so. He supposedly perished after trying to commandeer a Spanish galleon and sail it, unassisted, through the Frontier."

John's mouth gaped. "He knew about the Archipelago?"

"Of course he did," Spenser replied. "He was *from* the Archipelago. Sinbad wasn't the only seafarer who made a practice of crossing from world to world when the occasion presented itself. He was just better at it than Le Clerc."

"Spenser never confirmed that the pirate was dead," Twain said, "but Verne's Mystorians have a working theory that he and his subsequent ships became the original source of the Flying Dutchman legends. Edmund did, however, manage to save Le Clerc's ship."

"What did you do with it?" asked John.

Spenser smiled, a broad, warm expression. "You know as well as anyone," he said impishly. "It's sitting in the south boathouse."

"The *Indigo Dragon*," Jack exclaimed. "Brilliant!"

"So you see," Twain finished as he added a new notation to the book, "that boy was not selected at random. He has a fine lineage from the Archipelago itself—all Hank did was to bring the family trade full circle."

Eventually, as the companions knew it must, talk turned to the topic of Hank's note, and the mysterious others who were able to manipulate time.

"They must have discovered some way to combine the attributes of the trumps with the mechanism of the watches," Verne said, looking askance at Bert, "and there are very few among us who could even conceive such a thing."

"Do you think the Watchmaker may have had a hand in it?" asked John. "Could Dee have coerced him, or somehow bribed him to modify them?"

"I doubt it," said Verne. "He may be above our petty little alliances with their shifting lines, but he's also a good judge of character. And he can tell a Namer from an Un-Namer."

"At least we're in the Summer Country now," said Bert. "Our experiments would not have worked if we were still in the Archipelago."

"Why not?" asked Jack.

"We have never been able to traverse time inside the Archipelago," Verne explained, "only in the Summer Country. It's the nature of Kairos time, you see. It's more pure, more fluid—almost imaginary. Events there are given meaning only because of the connection to Chronos time, here in the Summer Country. That's why residents there age slowly, or not at all, and why without the keep, time travel was impossible. There are exceptions to this, of course, but we have come to realize that this should be treated more as a rule than a guideline."

"We'll have plenty of opportunities to practice," said Rose, "but even with all of our successes, I can't help feeling sad for all that we've lost. It seems too high a price to have paid."

"Maybe not so high as you think, dear child," said Verne. He was smiling broadly. "We have a surprise for you—for all of you, in fact." He pointed to the door of the banquet hall, where a tall, lanky man was just stepping through.

"Hello, Rose," he said warmly.

Rose looked up, and her gasp of surprise turned into a squeal of glee as Charles walked toward her.

Rose's delighted reaction was echoed by John and Jack, both of whom were moved to hug their colleague several times while tears filled all their eyes.

"Well done!" John kept exclaiming as he clapped his friend on the back, as if Charles not being dead was some sort of carnival award. "Well done, my man!"

"Thank you, John, Jack," Charles said amiably. "I'm only disappointed that when you needed me, I wasn't ready to accompany you. So sorry about that."

"It's fine, it's fine," Jack exclaimed. "We managed somehow, and your stand-in comported himself very well, very well indeed."

"Stand-in?" said Charles.

"We recruited Hugo," said Jack.

Charles's face froze in a mix of amusement and horror. "You're joking! Ah, no offense, Rose."

"They are joking, and none taken," Rose said as she chucked Jack on the shoulder. "It was Fred, of course."

"Right," said Charles. "Where is the young fellow, anyway? I should quite like to see him."

"He'll be down in a bit," John assured him. "He's upstairs assembling a lamp for our new Cartographer."

It was Charles's turn to be surprised. "New Cartographer?" he sputtered. "I die and everyone starts rearranging things on me."

"You don't know the half of it," said Jack. "But there'll be time for that later. Tell us how . . ." He stopped. The initial excitement now past, they could finally take a good look at their old friend—who was no longer quite so old.

"I say," Jack murmured as he squinted at Charles. "Did you do something to your hair?"

"Got it back," Charles said jovially. "That's one of the positive things about becoming a tulpa—the body you create is exactly the one that you think of when you think of 'yourself.' It's the ideal you, so to speak—and mine happens to be around thirty."

"That's about how old you were when we first met, back in 1917," said Jack. "Remember, Bert?"

Bert nodded. "I do very well," he said, clearing his throat. "It was a good age for a Caretaker."

"The third alternative, they call it," Charles said when they'd settled back in their seats. "Everyone dies eventually. And there's also the course that almost all the Caretakers have chosen for ethical and moral reasons, which is to become portraits in the gallery and reside at Tamerlane House. But there's also the third way, becoming a tulpa, which Jules and Bert both advocated to me after that meeting at the Inn of the Flying Dragon."

"*Bert* advocated?" John said, surprised. "I didn't expect that."

"My personal feelings about it haven't changed," Bert offered, "and it remains a sore point between Jules and me. But something very significant happened that we've never had to deal with before. And that changed everything."

"What was that?" asked John.

"Stellan," said Bert. "We've always known the risks of leaving Tamerlane House, but never in our history had we lost a Caretaker in that way."

"We defeated the Shadow King only by the slimmest of margins," said Verne, "and Stellan was key to that victory. But had the journey taken just a little longer, or had they been delayed . . ."

"We'd never have reached the wall, or my father," said Rose, "and we'd have lost everything."

Bert nodded. "None of which would have been an issue if Stellan had been a tulpa," he said, not really enjoying the admission. "Charles is still vitally important to the work we're doing now, and we didn't want to risk the same thing happening to him. So we offered him the choice, and he accepted."

"Also," added Charles, "I'm getting on amazingly well with Rudyard Kipling."

"It doesn't make you immortal, you know," Jack cautioned. "As we saw with Defoe, a tulpa body can still be destroyed."

"Oh, I'm completely aware of that possibility," said Charles, "and if we see that coming, I can still have my portrait done by

Basil, and join the others in the gallery. And if that happens, then I'll have something really interesting to explore. I'm not terribly worried about it."

"After our discussion about his impending, uh, discontinuity," said Bert, "progress on Charles's portrait was halted while Jules and Rudy began to prepare him to create a tulpa."

"What did you do with the uncompleted portrait?"

"We found another use for it, which didn't require as much alteration as you'd think," said Verne.

"And I'm very glad you did," said a familiar voice, "or else I'd have missed out on too much fun."

Jack pulled out a chair next to himself and waved Ransom over. He paused to shake hands with Charles, who, Jack noted, looked less like his other-dimensional counterpart now that he was younger. Ransom sat next to Jack and winked at Rose.

"My days as a Messenger may be a lot more restricted now," he said with undisguised melancholy, "but that's better than not having any days at all."

"Doesn't it take a long while to create a tulpa, though?" asked Jack. "When did you do it?"

"It does take some considerable time, yes," said Verne, "and more so in Charles's case, because we weren't there when he actually died. If he hadn't begun the process in 1943, then there might have been no way to save him—except with a portrait."

"It's an act of visualization, as much as anything," said Charles. "The Buddhists were particularly adept. You simply create a spirit form in your mind, and then, at the time of your death, it takes on solid flesh as your, ah . . ." He scratched his head and looked at Verne. "Spirit? Soul? Aiua? Well, whatever it is that makes you 'you' moves into the new body."

"Even if I don't fully comprehend it, I'm impressed," said Jack. "Especially since you could do it so well on the first try."

Verne and Bert both reddened and pulled at their collars at the same time, in a gesture the companions had come to realize meant they were slightly embarrassed about something.

"There was a practice run, so to speak," Charles offered, glancing a bit nervously around the room as he tried not to tug at his collar, "sort of like a final exam before graduation."

"What was that?" Jack asked with a wry grin on his face. "Making a tulpa of the Queen?"

"I, ah," Charles stammered, "I made a tulpa of *you*, Jack."

"Me?" Jack exclaimed. "You practiced by making another *me*?"

"Really, you ought to take it as a compliment," said Verne. "If he didn't respect you greatly, and have a good understanding of what makes you tick, he wouldn't have been able to do it at all."

Jack was still frowning, and he looked distinctly uncomfortable. He glanced around the room. "So is he—ah, I mean, am I around here somewhere?"

"No," Verne said firmly. "As I said, it was only a dry run, to see if Charles could do it. One doesn't have to make a tulpa out of himself—traditionally, it was done to create workers, or guardians of some sort. But those would fade after the death of their maker. It was Dee, and then Blake, who realized that by making a tulpa of oneself, the consciousness, the soul, if you will—"

"Or intelligence, which I prefer," said Charles.

"Or intelligence," Verne added, "could be transferred after death to the tulpa, and thus could live on indefinitely. But a tulpa of anyone else, be it a manservant or a colleague, would simply have to be ignored to make it fade back into the ether. A tulpa can only be maintained by a deliberate act of will—and when he was certain it could be done, Charles switched his attention to his own."

John ran his hand through his thinning hair and smiled crookedly at his now more youthful friend. "I can't say I'm not slightly jealous," he said, "but you do realize that in some respects you're now more like Burton than us?"

"I'll learn to cope," said Charles.

"You don't miss your old body?" asked Jack. "The, ah, deceased one?"

"This is where I reside now," Charles said with a touch of somberness. "Here in this body, and at Tamerlane House, and wherever else I might traipse around to with Verne and Kipling. I don't miss what I was, because I'm still me. Still your Charles."

"So," said Twain to the Magician and the Detective, "did you fellows learn anything on this trip, or were you just window dressing?"

"Yes," Houdini said with a hint of gloomy self-realization. "I found out that I don't need to find everything out."

"Really?" exclaimed Twain. "I'm actually rather impressed, if that's truthful."

"Oh, it is," Houdini complained. "I'm not very happy about it, but it's true. As a magician, I should have realized it all along—some secrets are better off remaining mysteries."

In that instant, the Serendipity Box suddenly reappeared on the tabletop in front of Houdini.

"Oh, good Lord," said Doyle. "Quick, someone take this thing away before he changes his mind."

There was still one reunion to be had, which Charles was a little less prepared for. Fred stopped in the doorway with crackers falling out of his mouth.

"Hey ho, Fred!" Charles said, arms outstretched. "Aren't you happy to see me?"

Unexpectedly, the little mammal took a step backward, then another. "You in't Scowler Charles," Fred whispered, his whiskers trembling. "You in't. You just in't."

"Of course he is," John offered, stepping forward. "He's just been, ah, youthened, is all."

But the badger wasn't having it. As far as he was concerned, this personage might be Charles in appearance, and in voice and mannerisms, but in one way he was sorely lacking—a way that was a crucial part of identity to the Children of the Earth.

"He din't smell right," said Fred. "He din't smell like Scowler Charles. I—I mean he does in some ways. But he in't quite right."

Charles was utterly crestfallen. This was one reaction he had not anticipated in any way.

"My memories are the same," he said gently. "I remember finding Perseus's shield with your grandfather. I remember meeting you for the first time, and how we could not have rescued Hugo without you. And I remember when I chose you to be my apprentice."

"If you're back," Fred said hesitantly, "and you're the third Caretaker again, then what happens to me?"

"You've read the story of the Three Musketeers, haven't you?"

Fred nodded.

including the most profound secret of all, which I think will be the key to saving the Archipelago and our future."

"What is that?" asked John.

Verne smiled and arched an eyebrow. "Rose knows. Don't you, my dear child?"

Rose nodded. "Who built the Keep of Time?"

The entire room went silent as they realized that she was right. Of all the mysteries, all the secrets, that was the one question that had eluded them all. No one had questioned it, not even the Dragons, because the keep had always been. Its origins were lost so deeply in time that no one believed it had an answer at all. But if it was indeed a secret, and not a mystery . . .

"And if, by some miracle, we do answer that question," said Jack, "what then? How will knowing help our terrible situation?"

"Because," Rose answered, "if we can find out who built it, we might be able to find out how. We can't keep jumping through time and space trying to bandage the symptoms—not when what we really need is the cure. We need to repair what was broken. To mend what was torn. And to finally weave all the threads back together the way they were meant to be."

"What are you proposing, Rose?" John asked, although he already knew what her answer would be, and he could feel the electric crackle of the hair rising on the back of his neck.

Rose stood, folded her arms, closed her eyes, and smiled. "We must seek out the Architect," she said, simply and openly, "and rebuild the Keep of Time."

Epilogue

Eventually the last embers from the fire at the mapmaker's house on Craven Street were extinguished, and nothing remained but ash and memory. Scavengers, the kind that walked upright, picked through the charred remains seeking something to steal, or barter with, or sell, but found that nothing of value remained. All that had been worthwhile had been carried away on the winds of time.

From the narrow townhouse across the street, the Chronographer of Lost Times watched impassively as a blind magistrate chased away the low-born rabble, who abandoned their scanty finds as they ran.

"When Sir John appears, order cannot be far behind," a voice said from the rear doorway. The Chronographer turned.

"Good afternoon, Mr. Defoe."

"Good afternoon, Dr. Dee," Defoe replied as he entered the room and sat heavily in a chair.

"It went as you expected?" Defoe asked.

"Well enough," said Dee. "You'll be paid, as agreed. Now if you'll excuse me, I am expecting visitors."

Defoe scowled but rose to his feet; then, with a bow, he walked out the door. In his place a Shadow arose, and soon formed into something solid. Something alive.

"He suspects something. He knows you keep secrets from him," the Shadow said.

"All the more reason to have kept our distance," said Dee. "We knew Burton would eventually defect to join the Caretakers, and the others were weak-willed to begin with. Defoe will be much the same—and only by remaining strong in our convictions will we prevail."

"The girl is learning too much," said the Shadow.

"Is she what they think?" Dee asked. "Is she the Imago?"

The Shadow shook his head. "It's possible. The Mystorians have yet to confirm it. She may not be the person she—and the Caretakers—believe her to be. Her lineage is false."

"If hers is, then isn't the boy's also?" said another voice.

"Ah, Tesla," Dee said primly. "So glad you could join us."

"I was only late because I was fetching Crowley, as you asked."

Dee turned to the Shadow, which now looked more like a cat. "You may go," he said.

"Remember our deal," Grimalkin answered, as he began to disappear. "When this is done, you will remove the Binding, once and for all."

"Of course," answered Dee. "That's the promise I made when I bound you to begin with. And so many centuries of service deserve a just reward."

Satisfied with the answer, the Cheshire cat smiled its cheshire smile and vanished.

"And what of the boy?" asked Tesla. "What's to be done with him?"

"I'm taking a page from Verne's own book," answered Dee. "I'm going to hide the boy when no one else will be able to find him."

"Where is that?" Tesla inquired. "Between the Caretakers, the

Mystorians, and the Imperial Cartological Society, all of history is open to them."

"I'm going to put him where he truly belongs," Dee replied. "In the future."

"Elegant, elegant," said Crowley. "Well done, Dee. So, do you think she noticed? That the shadow she returned with isn't her own?"

"Unlikely," said Dee as he peered at a small vial. Inside, a shadow writhed about, seeking a way to escape—but the glass vessel was too securely stoppered. "But even if she does, it's already too late. The Caretakers' secrets are an open book to us now."

"So the plan moves forward?" asked Crowley.

Dee nodded. "Yes. The daughter of the House of Madoc," he said, "will be the downfall of them all."

With that pronouncement, Dr. Dee removed the silver watch device from his pocket, spun the dials, and, as one, the Cabal disappeared.

Author's Note

If it's possible to both broaden and narrow the scope of an extended storyline simultaneously, then the closest I have come to doing so is in writing *The Dragon's Apprentice*. I had to mix together time travel (in several directions at once), the destruction of imaginary worlds, the introduction of new enemies (the Echthroi) and new allies (the Mystorians), and the death (so to speak) of a major character, and begin the introduction of a new pantheon of Caretakers—while at the same time telling the next more personal chapter in the story of the unlikeliest of heroes: Madoc.

Because of his real-world prominence, many readers have assumed John is the central protagonist of the Chronicles of the *Imaginarium Geographica*, but in my heart of hearts, I've always believed it to be Jack (and remember, there are more books to come, so I'm by no means done with his story arc). He was my youngest Caretaker, and so almost by necessity will undergo the most changes. Similarly, Madoc has evolved from our original villain (who never quite went away) into a conflicted character whose story is closer to the heart of the series than any of the others. He has swung through what are probably the most dramatic transformations of any of the characters, and yet, he remains somewhat of an enigma. Asking if he is good or evil may be too simple a way to pose the question, and the answer would not be a very interesting one, because it wouldn't be true—not as long as Madoc is still actively playing a role in my story. In fact, I don't really believe it would be true of almost anyone, fictional or otherwise. As long as there is an opportunity for choice, there is an opportunity to change direction.

Dag Hammarskjöld said, "In any crucial decision, every side of our character plays an important part, the base as well as the noble. Which side cheats the other when they stand united behind us in an action? When, later, Mephisto appears and smilingly declares himself the winner, he can still be defeated by the manner in which we accept the consequences of our action."

I believe this to be a Thing That Is True. And it is why I wanted to write this story.

The evolution of Rose as the possible Imago was necessary to the plot, as was the chaos in the Archipelago, and the looming menace of the Dark Caretakers. The inclusion of Franklin was great fun, as was the full-circle introduction of Edmund McGee as a possible new Cartographer, fulfilling the early promise of his mapmaking family from the book I created with my brother, *Lost Treasures of the Pirates of the Caribbean*. The deepening mystery of Tamerlane House is a thrill to write, and the story of the vanished young Prince has, in part, already been told elsewhere, in another series of books I wrote for publication in a faraway land. But all of that is plot and story. To me, the heart of this book, and perhaps, when I'm done, of the series as a whole, is character and theme.

A writing acquaintance recently asked the open question as

to whether the theme of a writer's work could be summed up in a single word. I replied that it could, and wrote, simply, "Redemption."

There is always a chance to choose. And, as in Hammarskjöld's example, even when you believe you have chosen the wrong path, how you accept the consequences of that choice, and then choose anew, can be redeeming in and of itself. This is true in all the best stories, all the ones we hope are real, and want to believe in. And in this story, it was true for Madoc. Just as it would be true, I hope, for me. Just as it would also be true . . .

. . . For *you*.

James A. Owen
Silvertown, USA